THE
CALLIGRAPHER'S
SECRET

رفيق شامي

THE CALLIGRAPHER'S SECRET

Rafik Schami

Translated from German by Anthea Bell

ARABIA BOOKS
LONDON

The translation of this work was supported by a grant from the Goethe-Institut
which is funded by the German Ministry of Foreign Affairs

All calligraphy courtesy of and © Ismat Amiralai
www.salem-verlag.de

First published in English in 2010 by

ARABIA BOOKS Ltd
70 Cadogan Place, London SW1X 9AH
www.arabia-books.com

This paperback edition published in 2011

First published in German as
Das Geheimnis des Kalligraphen by Rafik Schami
© 2008 Carl Hanser Verlag München

Translation copyright © Anthea Bell 2010

Typeset in Minion by MacGuru Ltd
info@macguru.org.uk

ISBN 978 1 906697 28 0

Printed in Great Britain by
CPI Cox & Wyman, Reading, RG1 8EX

Cover images courtesy of Alamy

CONDITIONS OF SALE

Dedicated to
Ibn Muqla
(886–940)
the greatest architect of
Arabic characters, and his misfortune

الإشاعة
أو كيف تبدأ
القصص في دمشق

The Rumour
or
How Stories Begin in Damascus

The Old Town of Damascus still lay under the grey cloak of twilight before dawn when an incredible rumour began making its way to the tables of the little snack bars, and circulating among the first customers at the bakeries. It seemed that Noura, the beautiful wife of that highly regarded and prosperous calligrapher Hamid Farsi, had run away.

April of the year 1957 brought summer heat to Damascus. At this early hour the streets were still full of night air, and the Old Town smelled of the jasmine flowering in the courtyards, of spices, of damp wood. Straight Street lay in darkness. Only bakeries and snack bars showed any light.

Soon the call of the muezzins made its way down streets and into bedrooms. Muezzin started after muezzin, setting up a multiple echo.

When the sun rose behind the eastern gate leading into Straight Street, and the last grey was swept from the blue sky, the butchers, vegetable sellers, and the vendors at food stalls already knew about Noura's flight. There was a smell of oil, charred wood, and horse dung around the place.

As eight o'clock approached, the smell of washing powder, cumin, and – here and there – falafel began spreading through Straight Street. Barbers, confectioners, and joiners had opened now, and had sprayed the pavement outside their shops with water. By this time news had leaked out that Noura was the daughter of the famous scholar Rami Arabi.

When the pharmacists, watchmakers, and antiques dealers were opening at their leisure, not expecting much business yet, the rumour had reached the east gate, and because by now it had assumed considerable dimensions it would not fit through the gateway. It rebounded from the stone arch and broke into a thousand and one pieces that scuttled away like rats, as if fearing the light, down the alleyways and into houses.

Malicious tongues said that Noura had run away because her

3

husband had been sending her letters speaking ardently of love, and the experienced Damascene rumour-mongers stopped at that point, well aware that they had lured their audience's curiosity into the trap.

"What?" asked their hearers indignantly. "A woman leaves her husband because he writes to tell her of the ardour of his love?"

"Not his, not his," the scandalmongers replied with the calm assurance of victors, "he was commissioned to write to her by that skirt-chaser Nasri Abbani, who wanted to seduce the beauty with letters, but though he struts like a rooster the fool can't write anything much himself, apart from his own name."

Nasri Abbani was a philanderer known all over the city. He had inherited more than ten houses and large orchards near the city from his father. Unlike his two brothers, Salah and Muhammad, who were devout, worked hard to increase their wealth, and were good husbands, Nasri slept around wherever he could. He had four wives in four houses, sired four children a year, and in addition he kept three of the city's whores.

When midday came and the scorching heat had driven all the smells out of Straight Street and the shadows of the few passersby were only a foot long, the inhabitants of the Christian, Jewish, and Muslim quarters alike knew that Noura had run away. The calligrapher's fine house was near the Roman arch and the Orthodox church of St Mary, just where the different quarters came together.

"Many men fall sick from arak or hashish, others die of an insatiable appetite. Nasri is sick with the love of women. It's like catching a cold or tuberculosis, either you get it or you don't," said the midwife Huda, who had helped all his children into the world and knew the secrets of his four wives. She placed the delicate cup containing her coffee on the table deliberately slowly, as if she herself suffered from this severe diagnosis. Her five women neighbours nodded, holding their breath.

"And is the disease infectious?" asked a plump woman with pretended gravity. The midwife shook her head, and the others laughed, but with restraint, as if they thought the question embarrassing.

Driven by his addiction, Nasri paid court to all women. He did not distinguish between society ladies and peasant girls, old whores and adolescents. It was claimed that his youngest wife, sixteen-year-old

Almaz, had once said, "Nasri can't see a hole without sticking his thing into it. I wouldn't be surprised if he came home one day carrying a swarm of bees on his prick."

And as usual with such men, Nasri's heart really burned only when a woman turned him down. Noura did not want to know anything about him, and so he was almost crazy for love of her. People said he hadn't touched a whore for months. "He was obsessed with her," his young wife Almaz confided to the midwife Huda. "He hardly ever slept with me, and if he did lie beside me I knew his mind was on the other woman. But I didn't know who she was until she ran away."

Then the calligrapher had written love letters that could have melted a heart of stone for him, but to the proud Noura that was the height of impertinence. She gave the letters to her father. The Sufi scholar, a man of exemplary calm, wouldn't believe it at first. He suspected that some wicked person was trying to destroy the calligrapher's marriage. However the evidence was overwhelming. "It wasn't just the calligrapher's unmistakable writing," said the midwife, and added that Noura's beauty was praised in the letters so precisely that apart from herself and her mother, only her husband and no one else could have known all the details. And now the midwife's voice sank so low that the other women were hardly breathing. "Only they could say what Noura's breasts and belly and legs looked like, and where she had a little birthmark," she added, as if she had read the letters herself. "And all the calligrapher could say," added another of the neighbours, "was that he hadn't known who that goat Nasri wanted the letters for, and when poets sing the praises of a strange beauty with whom they aren't personally acquainted, they describe only what they know."

"What spinelessness!" This sigh went from mouth to mouth over the next few days, as if all Damascus could talk of nothing else. Many would add, if there were no children within hearing distance, "He'll just have to live with the shame of it while his wife lies underneath that bed-hopping Nasri."

"She isn't lying underneath him. She ran away and left them both. That's the strange part of it," malicious tongues would say mysteriously, putting the record straight.

Rumours with a known beginning and end do not live long in Damascus, but the tale of the beautiful Noura's flight had a strange beginning and no end. It circulated among the men from café to café, and from group to group of women in their inner courtyards, and whenever it passed from one tongue to the next, it changed.

Tales were told of the dissipated excesses into which Nasri Abbani had tempted the calligrapher in order to get access to his wife. Of the sums of money that he had paid the calligrapher for the letters, Nasri was said to have given him their weight in gold. "That's why the grasping calligrapher wrote the love letters in large characters and with a wide margin. He could make a single page into five," said the scandalmongers.

All that may have helped make the young woman's decision easier for her. But one kernel of the truth remained hidden from everyone. The name of that kernel was love.

A year before, in April 1956, a tempestuous love story had begun. Noura had reached the end of a blind alley at the time, and then love suddenly broke through the walls towering up before her and showed her a crossroads of opportunity. And Noura had to act.

But as the truth is not as simple as an apricot, it has a second kernel, and not even Noura knew anything about that one. The second kernel of this story was the calligrapher's secret.

النَّوَاةُ الأُولَى لِلحَقِيقَة

The First Kernel of the Truth

I follow love
wherever its caravan goes,
love is my religion
and my faith.

Ibn Arabi (1165–1240)
Sufi scholar

1

A shopkeeper staggered out of his grain store to the sound of young men shouting. He was desperately trying to hold on to the door, but the noisy mob struck his fingers and arms, tugged at him and hit him, although not with any particular violence. As if the whole thing were a game, the young men were laughing and singing a ridiculous song, in which they gave thanks to God and at the same time made indecent remarks about their victim. It was in the rhymed obscenities of the illiterate.

"Help!" shouted the man, but no one came to his aid. Fear made his voice hoarse.

Like wasps, small children in shabby clothes swarmed about the group of young people surrounding the man, hermetically sealing him off. The children kept whining and begging as they too tried to lay hands on the man. They fell to the ground, got up again, spat noisily over a long distance like adults, and followed the pack.

After a drought that had lasted for two years, it was raining on this March day in 1942 as it had rained without interruption for over a week. Relieved, the inhabitants of the city could sleep soundly again. Serious trouble had weighed down on Damascus like a nightmare. A flock of Pallas's sandgrouse, the harbingers of disaster, had arrived as early as September in the first year of the drought, in search of food and water in the gardens of the green oasis of Damascus. From time immemorial it had been known that when these pigeon-sized birds of the steppes with their dappled, sand-coloured plumage appeared there was a drought coming. It came in that autumn of 1942. It always did. Farmers hated those birds.

As soon as the first sandgrouse was seen, wholesalers raised their prices for wheat, lentils, chick peas, sugar, and beans.

Imams had been praying in the mosques since December, along with hundreds of children and young people who, accompanied by teachers and those in charge of their education, were descending on the prayer houses in hordes.

The sky seemed to have swallowed up all the clouds. It was a dusty blue. Seed corn waited in the dry soil, yearning for water, and any seeds that did briefly germinate – putting out green shoots as thin as a child's hair – died in the summer heat that went on until the end of October. Farmers from the surrounding villages would take any job that was going in Damascus for the sake of a bit of bread, and were grateful for it, because they knew that soon the even hungrier farmers from the dry south would come and would accept even lower pay.

Sheikh Rami Arabi, Noura's father, had been utterly exhausted since October, for as well as saying the official five prayers a day in his little mosque, he had to lead the groups of men who sang religious songs all night until dawn, hoping to induce God to look kindly on them, begging for rain. He had no rest by day either, because in between official prayer times, students and schoolchildren arrived en masse, and he had to join them in singing sad songs intended to soften God's heart. They were lachrymose ditties, and Sheikh Rami Arabi disliked them because they positively oozed superstition. Superstition dominated the people like a magic spell. These were not uneducated but well-respected men, yet they believed that the stone columns in the nearby mosque were already weeping in sympathy with the prayers of Sheikh Hussein Kiftaros. Sheikh Hussein was semi-literate, and sported a large turban and a long beard.

Rami Arabi knew that stone columns never weep, but in cold air vapour from the breath of those praying aloud will condense on them. However, he couldn't say so. He had to put up with superstition so that the illiterate in his congregation would not lose their faith, as he told his wife.

On the first of March, the first drop of water fell. A boy came running into the mosque, while hundreds of children were singing. His shrill cry rose to such a high pitch that they all stopped. The boy took fright when silence fell, but then he timidly and quietly said, "It's raining." A wave of relief ran through the mosque, and prayers thanking God could be heard from every corner of it. *Allahu Akbar.* And as if their own eyes had been touched by the blessing of God, many of the grown men present wept with emotion.

It was indeed raining outside, first hesitantly, then in torrents. The dusty earth leaped for joy and then soaked up the water, turning calm and dark. Within a few days the paving of the Damascus streets was free of dust, and the yellow fields outside the city were covered with a tender layer of pale green.

The poor breathed again in relief, and the farmers set off back to their home villages and their fields.

But Sheikh Rami was displeased. It was as if his mosque had been swept empty. Apart from a few old men, no one came there to pray anymore. "They treat God like a waiter in a restaurant," he said. "They order rain, and as soon as he brings them their order, they turn their backs on him."

The rain slackened, and a warm wind swept its fine droplets into the faces of the young people dancing around the man in the middle of the road. They linked arms to encircle him, and turned him round and round. Then his shirt flew overhead, and as if it were a snake or a spider the smaller dancers on the outskirts of the crowd stamped on it, then reduced it to rags, tearing and biting it.

The man stopped resisting, because all the blows he was receiving confused him. His lips moved, but he did not utter a sound. After a while his thick-lensed glasses flew through the air and landed in a puddle on the pavement.

One of the young men was already hoarse with agitation. He was not singing the rhymes any longer, but shouting a tirade of abuse. The others, as if intoxicated, raised their hands to the heavens and chanted, "God has heard us."

The man seemed not to notice anyone as his eyes wandered, trying to fix upon something. For a moment he stared into Noura's face. She was only six or seven at the time, and she was standing out of the rain under the big, colourful awning of the candy store at the entrance to her street. She was about to begin enjoying the red lollipop she had bought from Elias the confectioner for a piastre. But the scene before her held her spellbound. Now the young people were tearing at their victim's trousers, and still none of the passersby went to his aid. He fell to the ground. His face was pale and rigid, as if he already had some idea of what was coming next. He seemed not to feel it when the young men kicked him. He did not scream or plead with them, but groped about on the ground among the thin legs of the dancers as if in search of his glasses.

"In the puddle," said Noura helpfully.

When an older man in a shop assistant's grey coat tried approaching him, he was roughly held back by a man in elegant traditional clothes: backless shoes, baggy black trousers, a white shirt, a coloured waistcoat, and a red silk scarf around his waist. Over his shoulders lay the black and white folded *keffiyeh*, the headcloth worn by Arab men. He carried an ornate bamboo cane. A muscular man of about thirty, he was clean-shaven except for a big black moustache waxed at the ends. He was a well-known type of thug. The Damascenes called such men *kabadai*, a Turkish word for a ruffian. They were powerful and fearless, they often invited trouble, and they lived by doing such dirty work as blackmailing or humiliating someone on behalf of prosperous folk who wanted to keep their hands clean. This *kabadai* seemed to approve of what the young men were doing. "Let the children have their fun with that unbeliever, the robber who steals the bread from their mouths," he cried in admonitory tones, grabbing the man in the grey coat by the neck with his left hand, bringing the cane down on his buttocks, and laughing as he propelled him back into the shop. The onlookers, both men and women, laughed at the shop assistant, who began pleading for mercy like a schoolboy.

Now the alleged robber was crouching naked in the street, weeping. The young people moved away, still singing and dancing in the rain. A pale little boy with a thin, scarred face ran back to give the prostrate victim one last kick in the back. Shouting with delight, arms outspread and imitating a plane, he ran back to his comrades.

"Go home, Noura. This is no sight for little girls," she heard Elias say in his gentle voice. He had been watching the whole scene from the window of his shop.

Noura jumped slightly, but she did not go away. She watched the naked man slowly sit up, look around, and retrieve a fragment of his dark trousers to cover his genitals. A beggar picked up the glasses, which were still intact although they had been thrown a long way, and took them to the naked man. He got to his feet and, paying the beggar no more attention, went into his shop.

At home over coffee in the living room, when Noura breathlessly described the incident, her mother was unmoved. Their fat neighbour Badia, who came to visit every day, put her cup of coffee down on the little table and laughed aloud.

"It serves that heartless cross-worshipper right. That's what comes of raising his prices," hissed Noura's mother. Noura was shocked.

And Badia, amused, told them how her husband had said that near the Umayyad Mosque a Jewish tradesman had been dragged naked to Straight Street by a crowd of young people, and was abused and beaten there to the sound of howling voices.

Noura's father was late home, and when he arrived his face was drained of all colour. He looked grey, and she heard him arguing for a long time with her mother about the young people. Godless, he called them. He did not calm down until supper time.

Years later, Noura thought that if there had been anything like a crossroads on the way to her parents, then on that night she would have decided to go the way leading to her father. Her relationship with her mother always remained cool.

The day after the incident, Noura was curious to find out how the man with the glasses could live without a heart. The sky was clear now for hours on end, with just a fleet of little clouds sailing over the ocean of the heavens. Noura slipped through the open front door of their house and went along the alley to the main road. She turned left, and passed the big grain store, which had an office with big windows on the side facing the street. Next to it was the big warehouse into which workmen carried jute sacks full of grain, and then weighed them and stamped them.

As if nothing had happened, the man was sitting at a desk covered with papers, well dressed in dark clothes again, writing something in a big book. He raised his head for a moment and looked out of the window. Noura immediately turned her face away and hurried on to the ice-cream parlour. There she took a deep breath and turned round. This time she avoided looking into the office as she passed it, so that the man couldn't recognize her.

Years later, the picture of the man lying naked in the street still followed her into her dreams, and then Noura always woke with a sudden start.

"Yousef Aflak, Grain, Seed-Corn" she read some time later, when she could decipher the words above the entrance to the store, and soon after she found out that the man was a Christian. It was not that her mother hated him in particular, but as she saw it anyone who was not a Muslim was an unbeliever.

The sweetmeat seller Elias with the funny red hair was a Christian as well. He was always laughing and joking with Noura, and he was the only person in her life who called her "Princess." She once asked him why he never came to visit her, hoping that he would call one day with a big bag of brightly coloured sweets, but Elias just laughed.

There was another Christian working at the ice-cream parlour, Rimon. He was odd. When he had no customers, he would take his *oud* down from the wall, play it and sing until the parlour was full, and then he would call out, "Who wants an ice?"

So Noura worked it out that her mother didn't like Christians because they were odd and they always sold truly delicious things to eat. Her mother was thin as a rail, seldom laughed, and ate only when she couldn't avoid it.

Noura's father often told her mother, in tones of reproof, that she soon wouldn't even cast a shadow. In old photographs she had attractive curves and looked beautiful. But even Badia, their stout neighbour, was soon saying she was afraid that the next breath of wind would blow Noura's mother away.

When Noura had nearly come to the end of Class Nine at school, she heard from her father that Yousef the grain merchant had died. The story went that before his death he had spoken of losing consciousness for a moment at the time when the young men were tormenting him, and at that moment, as if in a film, he had seen that his daughter Marie and his son Michel would both convert to Islam.

No one took him seriously, because just before his death the old man was in a delirium. He had never been able to accept his daughter

Marie's decision to marry a Muslim after a stormy love affair. The marriage ended unhappily later.

And he had been angry with his only son Michel for a long time before his death, because Michel did not want to take over the running of his grain business, but planned to be a politician instead. However, Yousef's dream came true, for fifty years later, just before his own death, Michel, now an embittered old politician in exile in Baghdad, said he was converting to Islam, and he was eventually buried in that city under the name of Ahmad Aflak. But that's another story.

Ayyubi Alley was in the old Midan quarter to the southwest of the Old Town, but outside the city walls. It smelled of aniseed, but Noura thought it was boring. It was short, with only four buildings in it. Noura's parents' house was at the very end of the street, which was a blind alley. The windowless wall of the aniseed store dominated the right-hand side of the street.

Badia lived in the first house on the left-hand side of the street with her husband. He was tall and shapeless, and looked like a worn-out old wardrobe. Badia was Noura's mother's only woman friend. Noura knew Badia's nine sons and daughters only as grown-ups who always said a friendly hello to her, but hurried past like shadows, leaving no trace. Only Badia's daughter Bushra lingered in Noura's childhood memories. She liked Noura, kissed her whenever she saw her, and called her "darling." Bushra smelled of exotic flowers, so Noura liked it when she gave her a hug.

A rich, childless, and very old married couple lived in the second house, and had hardly any contact with the rest of the street.

A large family of Christians lived in the house next door to Noura's. Her mother would never say a word to them. Her father, on the other hand, exchanged friendly greetings with the men of the family when he met them in the street, while her mother muttered something that sounded like a magic charm to protect her in case these enemies cast one of their own spells on her.

Noura counted seven or eight boys in the Christians' house, and not a single girl. They played with balls, marbles, and pebbles. Sometimes they romped happily around all day like exuberant puppies.

Noura often watched them from the door of her house, always ready to slam it the moment one of them came close to her. As soon as two of the boys, rather older and taller than the others, set eyes on her they used to make gestures suggesting that they would like to hug and kiss her. At that point Noura hurried indoors and watched, through the big keyhole, as the boys fell about laughing. Her heart raced, and she dared not go out again all day.

Sometimes they behaved really badly. When Noura was on her way back from the ice-cream parlour or the confectioner's, the boys would suddenly appear and bar her way like a wall, demanding a taste of her ice or her lollipop, and threatening not to let her pass until she gave them some of it. Only when Noura started to cry did they disappear.

One day Elias saw this scene as he happened to be sweeping the street outside his shop and glanced down the alley. He came to Noura's aid with his big broom, scolding the boys. "If one of them ever dares to stand in your way again, just come to me," shouted Elias, loud enough for the boys to hear. "My broom is just itching to get at their backsides." It worked. From then on, the boys stood aside whenever they happened to meet.

Only one of them didn't give up. He often whispered to her, "You're so beautiful. I want to marry you right away."

He was fat, with white skin and red cheeks, and he was younger than Noura. The other, bigger boys, the ones who made eyes at her, laughed at him.

"Idiot, she's a Muslim."

"Then I'll be a Muslim too," said the boy desperately, earning himself a resounding slap from one of his brothers. The fat boy's name was Maurice, and another of them was called Jirjis. Funny names, thought Noura, and she felt sorry for the fat boy, who was howling out loud now.

"Why not? I'll be a Muslim if I want to, and I like Muhammad better than I like you," he shouted defiantly, and the other boy gave him a second slap and a hefty kick in the shins. Maurice sniffled, and kept looking at Noura's house as if he could expect rescue from that quarter.

Soon a woman called to him from indoors, and he went in slowly, with his head bent. It wasn't long before Noura heard his mother shouting at him while he pleaded with her.

After that day Maurice said no more about getting married. He avoided meeting Noura's eye, as if that might make him fall sick. Once he was sitting at the entrance to his house, sobbing, and when he saw Noura he turned to the wall, crying quietly. Noura stopped. She saw his big, dark red ears, and realized that someone had been hitting him. She felt sorry for him. She went closer and very gently touched his shoulder. Maurice abruptly stopped crying. He turned to her, smiling from a face covered with tears and snot, which he had spread over both cheeks with his sleeve.

"Noura," he whispered, astonished.

She blushed and ran home. Her heart was thudding. She gave her mother the bag of onions that she had bought from Omar the vegetable seller.

"Did the vegetable seller say anything?" asked her mother.

"No," said Noura, turning to the front door to see what Maurice was doing.

"You look so upset. Have you been up to mischief?" asked her mother.

"No," replied Noura.

"Come here," said her mother. "I can read it all over your face." Noura was badly frightened, and her mother scrutinized her face as if reading it and then said, "You can go. You haven't done anything bad."

For years Noura believed that her mother really could read any wrongdoing in her face, so every time she had met the fat boy she looked in the mirror to see if it showed. To be on the safe side she scrubbed her face with olive soap, and then rinsed it off thoroughly.

Her mother was a strange woman anyway. She seemed to feel responsible for the whole world. Once Noura's father took her and her mother to a party where dervishes were dancing, and Noura had seldom felt as lighthearted as she did that evening. Her father too seemed to be floating above the ground with delight. One of the dervishes danced with his eyes closed, and the others circled around him like planets circling the sun. But all her mother saw was that his robe had several dirty marks on it.

On religious festival days her parents and the other Muslims in the street decorated their houses and shops with coloured cloth. Rugs hung out of windows and over balconies, flower pots stood outside the entrances to the houses. Processions went through the streets, singing and dancing. There was fencing and fighting with bamboo canes in some of the processions, others staged a fireworks show, and rosewater rained down from the windows on passersby.

The Christians celebrated their own festivals quietly, without coloured cloths or processions. Noura had noticed that difference very early. The church bells rang a little louder on such days, that was all. You saw the Christians in their best clothes, but they had no fair or giant wheel or coloured banners.

Christian holidays also came at the same time every year. Christmas at the end of December, Easter in spring, Whitsun in early summer. Ramadan, however, wandered all through the year. And if it was in high summer there was no bearing it. Noura had to go without even a bit of bread or a sip of water from morning to evening, even when the temperature was forty degrees in the shade. Maurice was sorry for her. He whispered to her that he too was fasting, so that he would feel just as wretched as she did.

She never forgot the day when Maurice caused a certain amount of confusion for love of her. She was fourteen then, and Ramadan was in August that year. She was fasting, and it was hard. Suddenly the neighbours heard the call of the muezzin and fell on their food. Only Noura's mother said, "That can't be right! Your father isn't home yet, and the cannon hasn't been fired."

Half an hour later, they did hear the muezzin calling over the rooftops, and a cannon shot rang through the air. Her father, who soon came home, said people had broken their fast too soon because of a fake muezzin call. Noura knew at once who was behind it. An hour later two police officers knocked on the Christian family's door, and there was shouting and tears.

Of all the feast days and holidays, Noura liked the twenty-seventh day of Ramadan best. On that day heaven opened, said her father, and for a little while God heard the wishes of mankind. Ever since she could remember, she had been restless for days before it every year, wondering what to ask God for.

He had never, in fact, granted a single one of her wishes.

God didn't seem to like her. However, fat Maurice told her God was sure to like beautiful girls, but he couldn't hear their voices. And Maurice knew why: "The grown-ups pray in such loud voices that night that it gives God a headache, and heaven closes before he's heard even a single child's wish."

Sure enough, her father gathered his friends and relations together in the courtyard that night, and together they asked God out loud to forgive their sins and grant their wishes for health and happiness. Noura looked at the assembled company, and knew that Maurice was right. She suddenly called out loud, right in the middle of the prayer, "And dear God, please send me a bucket of vanilla ice cream with pistachios." The praying people laughed, and in spite of repeated attempts they couldn't say any more prayers, because one or another of them kept interrupting their devotions by bursting into laughter.

Only Noura's mother feared divine retribution, and she was the only one to come down with diarrhoea next day. Why, she wailed, did God have to punish her of all people, although she had hardly laughed at all? Noura's mother was very superstitious. She never cut her fingernails at night, to keep bad spirits from punishing her with nightmares. She never ran hot water into the washbasin without calling the name of God out loud first, to make sure that the spirits who like to live in the dark water pipes didn't scald themselves and punish her for it.

From then on Noura wasn't allowed to pray with the grown-ups on the twenty-seventh night of Ramadan. She had to stay in her room and make her wishes quietly. Often she just lay on her bed, looking out through the window at the dark and starry sky.

She noticed, when she was quite young, that on those festival days her father seemed to be haunted by a strange grief. He, whose word gave fresh heart to hundreds of men in the mosque, and whom all the shopkeepers in the main street greeted respectfully when he passed

– sometimes even interrupting their conversations to ask him for his advice – he, her powerful father, was unhappy after the festive prayer every year. He stooped his shoulders as he went to the sofa, hunched down on it and sobbed like a child. Noura never found out why.

2

After Salman's difficult birth on a cold February night in the year 1937, misfortune dogged his footsteps more faithfully than his shadow for years. The midwife Halimeh had been in a hurry when he was born. Faizeh, the traffic cop Kamil's lively wife, had woken her in the night to come to her friend Mariam, and so the midwife arrived at the little apartment in a bad temper, and instead of encouraging Mariam, a thin young woman of twenty, as she lay on the dirty mattress in labour with her first baby, she snapped at her not to make such a fuss. And then, as if the Devil were bent on displaying his entire spectrum of malice, along came Olga, the rich Farah family's old maidservant. Faizeh, a strong little woman, crossed herself, because she had always been afraid that Olga had the evil eye.

The Farahs' handsome property lay right behind the high wall of the dusty courtyard full of miserable hovels known as Grace and Favour Yard.

It was a place where people who had come from all points of the compass and were stranded in Damascus could live. The yard had once belonged to a large property with a magnificent house and big garden, as well as a spacious tract of land with workshops, stables, granaries, and dwellings for over thirty servants who worked for their master in the fields, the stables, and the house. After the death of the Farahs, who had no children, their nephew Mansour Farah, a rich spice merchant, inherited the house and garden, while the many fields and the pure-bred horses went to other relations. The yard with its many dwellings was left to the Catholic church on condition that indigent Christians were taken in there, so that, as the will touchingly phrased it, "no Christian need ever sleep without a roof over his head in Damascus." And before a year was up the rich spice merchant had built a wall too high to be climbed, cutting off his house and garden from the rest of the property, which now offered refuge to a set of destitute persons the mere sight of whom made that fine gentleman feel sick to his stomach.

The Catholic church was happy to have this large yard in the middle of the Christian quarter, but was not prepared to spend so much as a piastre on repairs. So the hovels became more and more dilapidated, and the people who lived there patched them up as best they could with sheet metal and mud bricks, cardboard and wood.

They went to a great deal of trouble to gloss over their poverty a little with pots of brightly coloured flowers, but the ugly face of want peered out of every corner.

Although the large yard was in Abbara Alley, near the east gate of the Old Town, all those years it was isolated like an island of the damned. As the wooden gate was burnt as fuel by the indigent inhabitants, bit by bit, until only the open stone archway was left, no one else living in the street outside willingly went in to visit the poor there. Over the years, they remained strangers to each other. Grace and Favour Yard was like a little village that had been uprooted by a stormy wind from its old place on the outskirts of the desert, and blown into the city complete with its inhabitants, its dust, and its skinny dogs.

A distant cousin helped Salman's father get a large room here when he came to Damascus from Khabab, a Christian village in the south, in search of work. His father acquired the second, smaller room after a fistfight with his competitors, who were trying to move in even before the corpse of the old lady who used to live there was taken to the graveyard. Each of those competitors told his story, which was clumsily designed to show that the old woman's one dying wish had been to leave him, the teller of whichever tale it was, the room, so that her soul would rest in piece. Many of them made out that the dead woman was a distant relation, others claimed that she owed them money, but a glance at the hands of those liars showed that they had never in their lives had any money to lend. When the audience had seen through all the stories as lies, and hoarse voices were rising higher and higher, the question was decided by sheer force, and here Salman's father was unbeatable. He flattened all his rivals and sent them home to their wives empty-handed.

"And then your father put a door into the wall between the two rooms, and so you had a two-room apartment," Sarah told Salman, years later. Faizeh's daughter knew everything. "Sarah Know-It-All," everyone called her. She was three years older than Salman and a head taller.

She was extremely clever, and she could dance more beautifully than any of the other children. Salman had found that out by chance. He was eight or nine, and wanted her to come out and play when he saw her dancing in her own home. He stood motionless in the open doorway, watching. She was deep in thought as she danced.

When she saw him, she smiled shyly. Later she would dance for him when he was sad.

One day Salman and Sarah walked to the long road called Straight Street, where Sarah spent her five piastres on a popsicle. She let Salman lick it now and then, on condition that he didn't bite any right off.

They were standing at the entrance to their alley, licking the popsicle and watching the carts, bearers, horses, donkeys, beggars, and itinerant traders who populated Straight Street at this time of day. When there was nothing left of the ice but the coloured wooden stick and the red tongues in their cool mouths, they decided to go home. Then a big boy barred their way. "I'm having a kiss from you!" he told Sarah. He ignored Salman.

"Yuk!" said Sarah, disgusted.

"You're not having any such thing," cried Salman, getting between Sarah and the colossus.

"Out of my way, midget, or I'll squash you flat," said the boy, pushing Salman aside and grabbing Sarah's arm, but Salman jumped up on his back and bit his right shoulder. The boy screeched and flung Salman against the wall, and Sarah too screamed until the passersby took notice and the big boy had to vanish into the crowd.

The back of Salman's head was bleeding. He was taken off quickly to the pharmacist Yousef at the Kishleh Road junction. Yousef rolled his eyes and bandaged Salman's head without asking to be paid for it.

It was only a small lacerated wound, and when Salman came out of the pharmacist's Sarah looked affectionately at him. She took his hand, and they walked home together.

"You can bite a piece off my popsicle tomorrow," she said as they parted. What he really would have liked better was for Sarah to dance just for him some time, but he was much too shy to come out with that request.

So now back to Salman's difficult birth and the old maidservant Olga, who had appeared as if at the Devil's summons. She had come hurrying up in her dressing gown and slippers, begging the midwife to come to her mistress, whose waters had just broken. The midwife, a pretty woman, on whose fresh, bright appearance her forty years of life had left no trace, had been tending the spice merchant's sensitive, always slightly ailing wife for months, and she was paid more for each visit than ten poor families could have offered between them. Olga didn't want to let her mistress down at the moment of greatest danger, she proclaimed in a shamelessly loud voice, and she turned and shuffled away making remarks about riffraff and ingratitude. Faizeh sent two magic spells after the old woman to wipe away the trail of bad luck that certain people leave behind them.

As if the old maidservant's words had more effect than any prayers, the midwife now lost her temper. Her interrupted slumbers, and the beginning of two labours at the same time, soured her mood. She hated working in Grace and Favour Yard anyway.

However, Olga's husband Victor, the Farah family's gardener, gave the midwife a bag full of fruit and vegetables whenever she visited the house. Everything grew well in the rich Farahs' big garden, but the Farahs themselves loved to eat meat, and served sweetmeats, vegetables, and fruit only out of politeness to their guests.

It was rumoured that the suntanned, wiry gardener was having an affair with the midwife, who had been widowed early. He didn't look as old as his sixty years, while his wife Olga had been aged by exhaustion. All she wanted to do in bed at night was sleep. There was a small pavilion for exotic plants in the garden, with a door leading straight out into the street, and that was where the gardener saw his many lovers. He was said to give them the fruit of a Brazilian plant that sent them wild with desire. But the midwife loved the gardener because he was the only man who could make her laugh.

On that cold morning, when she saw that the young woman was going to be in labour for some time yet, she left the little apartment to go over to the Farahs' house. Faizeh tried to stop her in the gateway of Grace and Favour Yard. "Mariam has nine lives, like a cat, she won't die that easily," said the midwife, as if to salve her own conscience, because the woman lying on the mattress looked terrible, like everything around her.

Faizeh let the midwife go, tied back her long black hair in a ponytail, and followed her with her eyes until she turned in the direction of the chapel of St Paul. The Farahs lived in the first house on the right.

Day was already dawning, but the dusty street lights in Abbara Alley were still on. Faizeh breathed in the fresh breeze and went back to her friend Mariam.

It was a difficult birth.

When the midwife looked in at around eight, Salman was already wrapped in old towels. The midwife was babbling, and she smelled strongly of spirits. She cheerfully described the Farahs' pretty newborn baby, a little girl, glanced at Salman and his mother, and croaked into Faizeh's ear, "Cats don't die that easily, right?" Then she staggered away.

Next day the inhabitants of Abbara Alley all received a little porcelain dish of pink sugared almonds. Brief prayers and congratulations to the Farah family on their newborn daughter Victoria passed from mouth to mouth. The name was said to have been suggested by the midwife after the parents were unable to agree. And the girl was still known as "Victoria Sugared-Almonds" years later. Her father didn't give away any sugared almonds on the birth of her brothers George and Edward. Apparently that was because there had been gossip in the alley about a relationship between his wife and his youngest brother. Since from the moment of their birth the two boys looked very much like their uncle, a rakish goldsmith, and squinted just as he did, there was some reason for the ill-natured to gossip.

But all that happened later.

When Salman came into the world his mother did not die, but she was very sick, and when, weeks later, she recovered from the fever, it was feared that she had lost her mind. She howled like a dog, and wept without stopping. Only when her baby was near her did she calm down and stop whimpering. "Salman, Salman, he is Salman," she cried, meaning that the boy was safe and healthy – so soon everyone was calling the baby Salman.

His father, a poor locksmith's assistant, hated Salman and blamed him for driving his wife Mariam to madness through his ill-fated birth. After a while he began to drink heavily. The cheap arak made him bad-tempered, unlike Faizeh's husband Kamil the traffic cop, who sang tunelessly but happily every night when he got drunk. He claimed that he lost a kilo of inhibition with every glass of arak, so that after several glasses he felt as light and carefree as a nightingale.

His wife Faizeh was glad to hear him singing – out of tune, to be sure, but with fiery passion – and sometimes she even sang with him. Salman always thought it strange to hear the two of them singing. It was as if angels were herding swine and singing along with them.

The Jewish vegetable seller Shimon also drank a great deal. He said he wasn't really a drinker, just a descendant of Sisyphus. He couldn't bear the sight of a full glass of wine. So he drank and drank, and when the glass was empty the sight of its emptiness made him melancholy. Shimon lived in the first house to the right of Grace and Favour Yard, where Abbara Alley led into Jews' Street. He could see right into Salman's apartment from his first-floor terrace.

Shimon drank himself unconscious every night, laughing the whole time as he got drunk and telling dirty jokes, although when sober he was grouchy and monosyllabic. People said that Shimon prayed all day because his conscience pricked him over his nocturnal escapades.

The arak turned Salman's father into an animal who never stopped cursing and beating him and his mother until one of the neighbours came along and talked the furious man into a calmer state, when his raging would suddenly break off and he could be guided to his bed.

Salman learned while he was still very small to pray to the Virgin Mary, so that one of the neighbours might hear what was going on and come quickly. None of the other saints were the faintest use when you needed them, said Sarah.

Like Salman himself, she was thin as a rake, but she had inherited her father's beautiful face and her mother's vigour and sharp tongue.

For as long as Salman could remember Sarah had worn her hair in a ponytail – she still wore it that way later, when she was a grown woman – leaving her beautiful little ears free. Salman envied her those ears. Above all, however, Sarah read books whenever she could find the time, and Salman soon came to respect her knowledge.

Once he had laughed at her and the Virgin Mary, and immediately the May bug he was flying in the air on a thread broke loose. The thread, with a small lifeless leg attached to it, fell to the ground. Sarah's May bug, however, flew cheerfully as long and as far as it liked at the end of its thin thread, and the bony girl whispered to the Virgin to watch over its legs. She brought the May bug down from the sky as often as she liked, fed it with fresh mulberry leaves, and put it in matchbox, then, head held high, she marched into her apartment, which was divided from Salman's only by a wooden shed.

It was Sarah, too, who first told him about the men who visited Samira when her husband the fuel pump attendant Yousef was not at home. She lived at the other end of the pensioners' yard, between the baker's journeyman Barakat and the henhouse.

When he asked Sarah why the men went to see Samira and not her husband, she laughed. "Stupid!" she said. "Because she has a slit in her down below, and the men have a needle to sew up the hole, but then the slit opens again and the next man comes along."

"But why doesn't her husband Yousef sew up the slit himself?"

"He doesn't have enough yarn," said Sarah.

She also explained to Salman why his father got so angry when he was drinking. It was a Sunday, and when his father had ranted and raged enough, and Shimon and the other men had finally put him to bed, Sarah sat down with Salman. She stroked his hand until he stopped crying, and then wiped his nose for him.

"Your father," she said quietly, "has a bear in his heart. It lives in there," she added, tapping his chest, "and when he drinks it maddens the animal. Your father is only its outer covering."

"Outer covering?"

"Yes, like when you throw a sheet over yourself and dance about singing. People see the sheet, but that's just your outer covering, and you're the one in there dancing and singing."

"And what does your father have in *his* heart?"

"He has a raven there, but a raven that thinks it's a nightingale, that's why he sings so badly out of tune. And Shimon has a monkey in his heart. That's why he doesn't tell jokes until he's drunk enough."

"What about me? What do I have in my heart?"

Sarah put her ear to his chest. "I can hear a sparrow. It's pecking around cautiously, and it's always scared."

"What's in your own heart?"

"A guardian angel for a little boy. You can have three guesses which little boy he is," she said, running off because her mother was calling for her.

In the evening, when he lay down beside his mother, he told her about the bear. His mother was surprised. She nodded. "A dangerous bear at that. You must keep out of his way, my child," she said, falling asleep.

Salman's mother did not recover from her sickness until two years after Salman's birth, but her husband kept on drinking all the same. The neighbourhood women dared not come close to him. Because his father was as strong as a bull, only men could calm him down. Meanwhile Salman tried to protect his mother's head with his own body, but in vain. When his father was in a rage he would fling Salman into a corner and beat his mother as if he were out of his mind.

Since Salman had begun praying to the Virgin Mary, someone always did come along quite quickly. But that was because Salman screeched at the top of his voice as soon as his father so much as raised an arm. Sarah said that his screeching was so loud it had short-circuited the electricity in their home next door.

Salman's mother was grateful to him for making such a noise, and as soon as her inebriated husband came staggering through the doorway she whispered, "Sing, little bird, sing," until Salman started screeching so loud that sometimes his father didn't even dare to come in. Even years later, Salman still remembered how glad his mother was to spend a day without being beaten for once. When that happened she would look happily at Salman with a smile in her round eyes, she would kiss him and stroke his face, and then she lay down in their corner to sleep on the shabby mattress.

Sometimes Salman heard his father come in during the night, pick up his mother as if she were a small child and carry her into the other room, and then he heard his father apologizing to his mother for being so stupid, and laughing awkwardly. And then his mother would utter quiet, happy little squeals, like a contented bitch.

Ever since Salman could remember, he and his mother had lived with his father's alternating hot and cold moods until one spring Sunday when, after church, his father got drunk in the wine bar on the nearest corner and was already beating his mother in the early afternoon. Their neighbour Shimon came to her aid, calmed Salman's father down, and finally put him to bed.

Then Shimon quietly entered the smaller room and leaned against the wall, exhausted. "Did you know that the dead weaver's house near the Chapel of St Paul has been standing empty for the last six months?" he asked.

Like all her women neighbours, Salman's mother did know. "Of course," she faltered.

"Then what are you waiting for?" asked the vegetable seller, and he left before he had to listen to all the questions on Salman's mother's mind.

"Let's go before he wakes up again," Salman urged her, without knowing just where they could go.

His mother looked around, rose to her feet and paced up and down the room. She looked at Salman with concern and then, with tears in her eyes, said, "Yes, come on, we're going."

Outside, an icy wind was blowing over Grace and Favour Yard, and dark grey clouds hung low above the city. Salman's mother put two sweaters on him, one on top of the other, and threw an old coat around her own shoulders. Their neighbours Maroun and Barakat were repairing a gutter. They gave the two of them a brief look, never guessing what they were doing, but Samira, who lived at the other end of the yard and was busy today with cooking, laundry, and listening to the radio, suspected something.

"My school exercise books!" cried Salman, worried, as they reached the gate. His mother didn't seem to hear. Silently, she led him away with her, hand in hand.

The alley was almost empty this cold afternoon, and they soon reached the little house. Salman's mother opened the door, which was not locked, and darkness and musty, damp air came out to meet them.

He sensed his mother's fear, because her firm grip was hurting his hand. It was an odd house. The door led to a long, dark corridor, and so to a tiny inner courtyard in the open air. The ground-floor rooms were wrecked, with windows and doors torn out.

A dark staircase led to the first floor, where the weaver had lived and worked until his death.

Cautiously, Salman followed his mother.

The room was large but shabby, with rubbish lying everywhere, along with broken furniture, newspapers, and the remains of food.

Salman's mother sat down on the floor and leaned against the wall under the window, which was dim with all the soot, dust, and cobwebs over it and let in only a faint grey light. She began shedding tears. She wept and wept so that the room seemed damper than ever.

"When I was a girl, I always dreamed…" she began, but then she stopped, as if life's disappointments had drowned even those last words in her mouth, and went on weeping silently.

"Where have I ended up? I wanted…" she said, trying again, but this thought died on her lips as well. In the distance, thunder was rumbling, like heavy stones rolling over a corrugated iron roof. Just before sunset, a fleeting ray of sunlight made its way through a narrow gap between the buildings. But as if wretchedness would not make way for it, it disappeared again at once.

Salman's mother clasped her knees, laid her head on them, and smiled at him. "I'm stupid, aren't I? I ought to laugh with you, cheer you up… but all I do is cry."

Outside the wind blew hard, sending a loose gutter banging against the wall. And then it began raining again.

He wanted to ask if he could do anything to help her, but she was crying again, after briefly putting out her hand to stroke his hair.

He soon went to sleep on a mattress smelling of rancid oil. When he woke up, it was pitch dark and raining heavily outside. "Mama," he whispered anxiously, thinking she was sitting far away from him.

"I'm here, don't worry," she whispered through her tears.

He sat up, laid his head on her lap, and in a soft voice he sang her the songs he had learnt from her.

He was hungry but didn't like to say so, because he was afraid that might cast her into utter despair. All his life Salman never forgot that hunger, and whenever he wanted to say something had taken a very long time, he said it was "longer than a day spent starving."

"I'll clean the window tomorrow," said his mother, suddenly laughing. He didn't understand.

"Isn't there a candle here?" he asked.

"Yes, we must think of that too," she said, as if something had suddenly occurred to her. "Do you have a good memory?"

He nodded in the dark, and as if she had seen him she went on, "Then let's play. Tomorrow we'll bring old rags."

He got the idea. "We'll bring old rags and two candles."

"We'll bring rags, candles, and a box of matches," she added. And late that night, when he was lying in her arms, so tired that he couldn't keep his eyes open anymore, she smiled and cried, "Why, if we were really going to bring all those things tomorrow we'd need a truck."

The rain pattered regularly on the window panes, and Salman pressed close to his mother. She smelled of onions. She had been making his father onion soup that day.

It was a long time since he had slept so soundly.

3

Noura's mother, who could sometimes treat her husband like an insecure, clumsy boy, trembled before him where Noura was concerned. She seemed more afraid of him then than her little daughter was. She decided nothing without adding, "if your father agrees."

It was like that on the day when Noura went out with her uncle Farid, her mother's half-brother, for the last time. He was a handsome man. Only years later was Noura to discover that Uncle Farid had already been penniless in those days, although you couldn't tell by looking at him. The three textiles businesses his father had handed over to him had gone broke within a very short time. Farid blamed his father, who was always interfering, and whose old-fashioned ideas got in the way of any success.

Thereupon his father, the great Mahaini, had disinherited him. But not even that could spoil the playboy Farid's sunny disposition.

As he had been educated in the best schools, had a gift for language and beautiful handwriting, he practised the unusual profession of an *ardhalgi*, a scribe who wrote out applications. In the Damascus of the 1950s, more than half the adult population could neither read nor write. However, the modern state insisted on doing everything in form, and its bureaucrats wanted to have every question, however slight, presented in writing. They could then go through the written application in the approved manner, and return it to the citizen who had sent it in with a number of rubber stamps and other marks pertaining to the state on it. By doing that, the state hoped to win something approaching esteem among the population, whose Bedouin roots always inclined them toward anarchy and lack of respect for any laws.

These applications, petitions and requests proliferated to such an extent that they were the subject of much local wit in Damascus. "If your neighbour's a civil servant, you're not supposed to say good morning to him, you have to submit a stamped application to wish him good morning. And then maybe you'll get an answer back."

But it was also said that bureaucracy was necessary so that the civil servants of the state could work in a more productive, modern way. If you let the loquacious Syrians make requests and petitions by word of mouth, every application would grow into a never-ending story of arabesques and continuations, all jumbled up. The civil servants could never have got any sensible work done. Furthermore, it was hard to mark the spoken word with a rubber stamp.

So the scribes sat at tiny desks by the entrances to civil service offices under their faded sun umbrellas, and wrote out requests, appeals, applications, petitions, and other paperwork. As the police would allow only one chair and one desk per scribe, their customers had to stand. They told the scribe more or less what it was all about, and he would start at once. At the time it was all handwritten, and the *ardhalgi* wrote with lavish gestures of his hand, to make it clear how much trouble this particular application was costing him.

The better a scribe's memory, the more flexible he was, for applications to a court of law were not the same as applications to the Finance Ministry, and those again were different from applications to the Residence Registration Office. Many a scribe had over fifty versions ready, and could move with his chair and folding desk from the entrance of one of those official bodies to another depending on the day and the season.

Uncle Farid always sat outside the Family Court, under a fine red sun umbrella. He was more elegant than any of his colleagues, and so he always had plenty of customers. People believed he would go down better with the judges and lawyers, and Uncle Farid did nothing to shake their belief.

The *ardhalgis* did not just write applications, they also advised their customers on the best place to make an application, and how much it ought to cost to get the state to stamp and mark it. They comforted the desperate and strengthened the resolve of protesters, encouraged the faint-hearted, and advised optimists to moderate the exaggerated ideas they usually entertained of the effect their applications would have.

If he hadn't been too lazy, Uncle Farid could have filled a big book with the stories, tragedies and comedies alike, that he had heard from his customers while he wrote, but that never found a way into any application.

Uncle Farid wrote not just applications but letters of all kinds. Most often of all, however, he wrote to emigrants. You had only to tell him the name of the emigrant and the country where he was working, and he would already have a long letter composed in his head. As Noura found out later, they were letters saying nothing, for their message could usually be summed up in a single line. In the case of letters to emigrants, it usually amounted to: Please send us money. But that single line was hidden in voluble paeans of praise, exaggerated expressions of longing to see the recipient again, promises of loyal affection, and protestations sworn by the Fatherland and the sender's mother's milk. Anything that stimulated the tear glands was grist to his mill. The few letters of his that Noura was allowed to read later, however, struck her as simply ridiculous. Uncle Farid never talked about these letters during his lifetime; they were his secret.

Those who had a little more money would make an appointment for Uncle Farid to visit them at home, and dictate what he was to write or apply for at their leisure. Of course that cost more, but those letters were very well composed.

Damascenes who were even richer did not go to an *ardhalgi* but to one of the calligraphers who wrote beautiful letters, adorned with calligraphic ornaments around the edges, and usually had their own libraries from which to draw words of wisdom and appropriate quotations to offer their clients. Unlike the mass-produced letters written by scribes in the street, these missives were unique.

The calligraphers made the simple act of letter-writing into a cult full of secrets. They wrote letters to husbands or wives with a copper pen, letters to friends and lovers with a silver pen, letters to particularly important persons with a golden pen, letters to a promised bride with the beak of a stork, and to enemies and adversaries with a pen carved from a pomegranate twig.

Uncle Farid loved Noura's mother, his half-sister, and visited her as often as he could until his death in a car accident two years after

Noura's wedding. Only later was Noura to discover that dislike of their own father, old Mahaini, was the link between her mother and her uncle.

Noura liked her uncle because he laughed a lot and was very generous, but she couldn't tell her father that. He called her uncle a "painted drum." His letters and application forms, said her father, were just like him: colourful, loud, and empty.

One day Uncle Farid came visiting in the morning. Not only was he always elegantly dressed, he also wore shoes of fine, thin red leather that made noisy music as he walked. That was a sign of distinction at the time, for only good shoes squeaked. And when Noura opened the door, she saw a large, white donkey. Her uncle had tied it up to a ring near the front door.

"Well, little one, would you like a ride on this fine donkey with me?" Noura was so surprised she could hardly close her mouth again. Uncle Farid told her mother that he had to visit a rich client nearby to write some important applications for him. The man would pay generously, he said. So he had thought he'd take Noura with him to give her mother a little rest. Her mother liked the idea. "Then she'll stop ruining her eyes with reading books. But she must be back just before the midday call of the muezzin, because His Excellency is coming to lunch," she said with a knowing smile.

Noura's uncle took both her hands and swung her up on the donkey's back. She felt her heart slip right down to her knees, and clung anxiously to the pommel emerging in front of her from the saddle, which was covered by a rug.

You often saw donkeys like this one hired out in the city streets, and one of the many donkey-stands where you could get one was in the main street, not far from Noura's house. Only a few rich families had cars, and apart from the trams there were only two or three buses and a few horse-drawn carriages to transport passengers into and around Damascus, not nearly enough.

The tail of a hired donkey was coloured bright red, so that you could see it a long way off. As a rule customers returned their donkeys when they had done whatever they set out for, and if the customer didn't want to ride a donkey back himself the man who hired the donkeys out would send a little boy to run along beside the rider until he was home, then take the animal over and bring it back to the stand.

So now Uncle Farid rode along the streets with her. They followed the main street for a while and then turned into an alley. A labyrinth of simple, low mud-brick houses swallowed them up. At the end of one alley Uncle Farid stopped outside a fine stone house. He tied the donkey up to the lamppost near the entrance and knocked. A friendly man opened the door, talked to Uncle Farid for a while, and then he invited them both into his fine inner courtyard, and made haste to bring the donkey in too. Uncle Farid was about to say that didn't matter, but the man insisted. He tied the donkey up to a mulberry tree and put some melon rinds and fresh maize leaves down in front of it.

Noura was given a lemonade, and soon she was standing around the donkey with the man's children, patting and feeding it. They were the most unusual children she had ever seen. They shared their biscuits and apricots with her without asking for anything in return, or pestering her for even a moment. She would have liked to stay with them.

Sitting on the shady terrace, Uncle Farid wrote what the man dictated to him. Sometimes they stopped for a little while so that Uncle Farid could think, and then they went on until the call of the muezzin rang out, whereupon they hastily started for home.

As soon as Noura was back her father started scolding her and her mother. Her uncle had prudently made his excuses at the door and gone off in a hurry.

Why did her father always have to be so cross? Noura closed her ears so as not to hear him.

As she didn't want anything to eat either, she went to her room and lay down on the sofa. "Did you notice how happy that family is?" her uncle had asked on the way back, and Noura had nodded.

"The man is a stonemason. He doesn't go hungry, but he can't save anything. Yet he lives like a king. And why?"

She didn't know.

"Neither my father's money nor your father's books make people happy," he told her. "It's all in the heart."

"All in the heart," she repeated.

Her uncle went on visiting her mother, but Noura was never allowed to go for a ride with him to see a customer again.

4

In the autumn of 1945, when Salman was eight years and seven months old, he went through the low gateway of the St Nicholas School for poor Christian children for the first time. He didn't want to go to school, but even the fact that he could already read and write was not enough to get him out of it. Sarah had taught him reading and writing, and practised with him again and again. She made him call her Miss Teacher while she introduced him to the mysteries of letters and numbers. When he worked hard and gave clever answers she kissed him on both cheeks, on his eyes or on his forehead, and when he was particularly brilliant, on the lips. When he made mistakes she shook her head and wagged her forefinger back and forth in front of his nose. Only when he was cheeky or grumpy did she affectionately pull his earlobes or tap him on the head with her knuckles, saying, "This is a butterfly calling to warn you not to go too far."

He didn't want to go to school, but Yacoub the priest had convinced his father that education would make him a good Catholic child. "Otherwise his first communion will be in danger," he pointed out, and Salman's father understood that the apartment where he lived solely by the grace of the Catholic Church would be in danger too.

Those were months of hell. In lessons the teachers mercilessly knocked Salman about, and in the schoolyard he was teased because of his thin frame and large jug ears. "Skinny Elephant," he was called. Not even the teachers thought there was anything wrong in laughing at him.

One day the children were to learn the verbs used for movement. "Human beings?" asked the teacher, and the pupils answered out loud, "Walk." Fish swim, birds fly, everyone knew that. When it came to snakes, the children were all talking at once to start with, until they agreed that "Snakes wriggle." All that most of them knew about scorpions was that they sting. "Scorpions scrabble," said the teacher.

"So what about Salman?" he asked. The pupils smiled awkwardly and tried all the verbs of movement they could think of, but the teacher wasn't satisfied. Salman lowered his gaze and his ears went dark red.

"He sails through the air with his big jug ears," said the teacher, roaring with laughter, and the whole class laughed with him. Except for one of them, Benjamin who sat next to Salman. "Old Baldy!" he whispered to his downcast friend, and Salman had to laugh, because that teacher did have a particularly large bald patch.

Salman hated school and felt he was going to stifle to death there, but then Benjamin showed him the gateway to freedom. Benjamin had already had to go through Class One twice. He was a tall boy with the biggest nose Salman had ever seen in his life. Even though he was twelve he still hadn't taken first communion. His father, who kept the little stall on the junction near the Catholic church, fried huge quantities of falafel balls every day, so a powerful odour of rancid oil often clung to Benjamin. His father, like Salman's, didn't really want to send his son to school. And he wouldn't have sent him, either, if Father Yacoub, the fanatical new priest at the Catholic church, hadn't stirred up opinion in the neighbourhood against him, quietly expressing some doubt of his Christian faith and the cleanliness of his hands. So quietly, indeed, that it was a month before Benjamin's father heard about it, and then he stopped wondering why many of his regular customers had started going to buy falafel from that terrible hypocrite George, whose wares tasted of old socks but whose stall was crammed as full of crucifixes and pictures of the saints as if it were a place of pilgrimage.

One day, after Salman had been given a thrashing in the schoolyard by the supervisor, Benjamin told him a great secret. "The teachers in this God-forsaken school don't notice who's present and who isn't," Benjamin told him quietly. "It's only on Sundays they check the kids before they go to church. Otherwise that bunch often don't even notice what class they're in, and they don't find out they've been taking Class Two for Class Four until the end of the lesson."

Salman was terrified of skipping school. Gabriel the dressmaker's son had told him truants were shut up for a whole day in the cellar, where the hungry rats nibbled their ears, which had been rubbed with rancid fat first. "Those rats would make a good meal of you," Gabriel had said, with a nasty laugh.

"Gabriel is a scaredy-cat," Benjamin explained. Just before Christmas, Benjamin told him how he could skip school for four days, and no one would notice. Now Salman felt brave enough to do it, and on a cold but sunny January day the two of them spent several entertaining hours walking around the markets, amusing themselves by nibbling sweet things when the stallholders weren't looking.

No one had noticed anything at home, so Salman skipped school more and more frequently. Only on Sundays did he stand in line, well washed, his hair combed, holding out his hands with their clipped fingernails for inspection. He seldom got hit with the broad wooden paddle that came down on grubby hands.

"I'll have to leave school after my first communion anyway," Benjamin explained. "Otherwise Father says I'd only get more scars on my behind, and my head would still be just as empty. I'm supposed to earn money to help keep my nine brothers and sisters."

"And I want to go to Sarah's school," said Salman. Benjamin thought that must be some high-class establishment, and asked no questions.

The only pupil whom Salman and Benjamin envied was Jirji, the mason Ibrahim's son. His father was an imposing figure, two metres tall and one metre broad.

One day the teacher Koudsi hit Jirji for slinking into the staffroom and eating the teacher's two sandwiches, while Mr Koudsi himself was "engaged in single combat with the powers of darkness in the hearts of his pupils." He used to deliver this remark to every class, so that even the other teachers called him, derisively, "Sir Powers of Darkness."

Jirji's father, Ibrahim, was just repairing the outer wall of the house where the rich Sihnawi family lived. This handsome property lay diagonally opposite the alley leading to school. Today Ibrahim was in a particularly bad temper, because the air stank. Two young workmen were slowly opening up a blocked sewage pipe. And like all employees of the city, they had the gift of spinning out their work. They brought a black, foul-smelling mass into the light of day, piled it up by the roadside, and then went off for coffee in the nearby café.

Suddenly two girls ran up to the mason and told him, breathlessly, how they had seen a teacher armed with a bamboo cane laying mercilessly into his son Jirji, while shouting insults to the boy's father and mother, saying they were not Christians but idol-worshippers. The teacher had told Ibrahim's son to repeat that, and Jirji, in tears, had repeated his teacher's words after him.

The mason marvelled at the way the girls spoke in turn, telling him all about it in convincing detail in spite of being so upset. His son Jirji could never have done it so well.

He closed his eyes for a second, and saw a fine rain of burning needles against a dark sky. Then he strode ahead of the girls to the school, which was a hundred metres away, and by the time he reached the low wooden gate with the famous picture of St Nicholas – the saint was just taking the children out of the pickling tub – he was accompanied not just by the two girls but also by the barber, who had nothing to do at this time of day but shoo flies away and twirl the ends of his already perfectly waxed moustache for the umpteenth time, as well as the rug-mender, who worked outdoors on a day like this, the two city workmen, the vegetable seller, and two passersby who were perfect strangers and had no idea what was going on, but were sure they should soon find out. Their expectations were to be fulfilled.

Giving the wooden gate a kick, and bellowing like Tarzan, the infuriated Ibrahim arrived in the middle of the small schoolyard.

"Where's that son of a whore? We're not idol-worshippers, we're good Catholics," he shouted. The school principal, a stocky little man with glasses and a ridiculously camouflaged bald patch, came out of his office, and even before he could express his indignation at Ibrahim's coarse expressions a resounding slap in the face took him by surprise. It sent him staggering several metres back and falling to the ground. His toupée flew after him, alarming the mason, who thought for a moment that he had scalped the principal, as if he were in some kind of Western.

The principal began wailing, but Ibrahim kicked him in the belly, and at the same time grabbed the man's right foot, as if he were kicking cotton wool into a sack.

The principal begged him to let go of his foot. He had never doubted, he cried, that Ibrahim was a good Christian, and he had toothache.

"Where's that bastard who's mistreating my Jirji?"

School students came streaming out of the classrooms where their lessons had been interrupted by all this noise.

"Koudsi's in the toilets. He's hiding there," one excited schoolboy told the mason, just as Ibrahim saw his son, who was pale and smiling awkwardly at him. Ibrahim stormed off to the toilets, followed by a crowd of children. The sound of several blows was the first thing to be heard in the schoolyard, followed by the voice of Koudsi the teacher begging for mercy and repeating the remarks: "You're a good Christian… yes, you're a good, devout Catholic… no, Jirji is a good boy, and I…" Then there was silence.

Ibrahim came back to the yard, sweating, and called out, "And it'll be the same for anyone else who dares touch Jirji or say we're not good Catholics."

From that day on Jirji was left alone. But that was only one of the reasons why Salman envied Jirji: the other reason was that the pale boy, whose father was very poor, like his own, always had money in his pocket. He bought something delicious from the school kiosk at break every day, and licked, nibbled, sucked, and thoroughly enjoyed all kinds of brightly coloured sweets. He never gave anyone else a taste.

Salman's father had never once given him any money, even when he was drunk.

The neighbours were short of money too. If Salman lent them a hand, at best they rewarded him with fresh or dried fruit. Only Shimon the vegetable seller paid cash for everything Salman did for him. But Salman was needed only when he had too many orders to deliver himself. The pay was small enough, but there were plenty of tips, so Salman was glad to help out when the vegetable seller wanted his services.

At weddings and other festive occasions Salman could spend a whole day earning a few piastres by delivering baskets of fruit and vegetables. And when he stopped for a rest in the shop he could sit on a vegetable crate and watch Shimon selling his goods and throwing in good advice for free.

Shimon himself was an excellent cook, unlike his wife. She was a small, pale little woman who later died of a gastric haemorrhage. She ate little, and wandered about their apartment all day in a bad temper. Shimon, who loved her, once said his wife was looking for something she had lost, but he never told anyone what it was. However, since her mother's death she had been looking for it all day, going to bed in the evening determined to go on searching the next day.

The women who bought vegetables from Shimon often asked his advice. He knew exactly which vegetables, spices and herbs would stimulate their husbands and which would soothe them at any given season of the year. He recommended tomatoes, carrots, figs and bananas, dill, peppermint, and sage for soothing men's passions, and advised ginger, coriander, pepper, artichokes, pomegranates, and apricots as stimulants. And he always recommended the women to perfume themselves with neroli oil, which they could distil them-selves from bitter orange blossom.

As a rule they were grateful to him, because the effects were soon felt. But it could happen that a man showed no erotic interest at all in his wife anymore. Once Salman heard a disappointed woman saying her husband's prick was even limper now. Shimon listened intently. "Then your husband's liver has gone into reverse," he explained, and recommended a vegetable normally used for people whose livers had not "gone into reverse." He often gave women "the remedy" for free.

Salman had no idea exactly what a liver in reverse would be like, but many of the neighbouring women were enthusiastic about the cure for it.

Sometimes, when there was nothing to do in the shop and Shimon had a little spare time, he would pick up a vegetable, maybe an auber-gine or artichoke or celeriac, stroke it and lean over confidentially to Salman. "Do you know all the dishes that can be made from this one vegetable?" And as he didn't expect any answer, he would go on, "We counted twenty-two different dishes the other day, old Sofia and I. Twenty-two absolutely different dishes. Think of that – a huge table covered with a snow-white cloth, serving dishes both long and wide, shallow and deep, rectangular and round standing on it, all full of delicious aubergine or artichoke or potato recipes, and red and yellow rose petals scattered among the serving dishes, the platters and bowls. And in front of my plate a glass full of Lebanese dry red wine. What more can God himself offer me in Paradise, eh?"

All Salman could say to that was, "A water pipe and a coffee with cardamom," and Shimon laughed, stroked his head and affectionately tugged his earlobe.

"My boy, my boy, you're all right. If your father doesn't beat you to death when he's drunk, you'll amount to something, mark my words."

Working for Shimon wasn't difficult, but he insisted on Salman always arriving washed, with tidy hair, and in clean clothes. "Vegetables and fruit delight the eyes and the nose even before the mouth tastes them with pleasure." He himself was always clean and well dressed, even better dressed than Yousef the pharmacist.

Once he sent Salman away because he turned up straight from football, all sweaty. "You're my ambassador to my customers, and if you're grubby and unwashed, what are the customers going to think of me?"

In fact Salman entered houses with inner courtyards rather more beautiful than Paradise itself as the priest described it in religious instruction lessons. So he liked delivering orders better than working in the shop.

The customers were generous, all except for one, who was a miser. He was a professor at the university. He lived alone in a little house and never paid his bill until the end of the month. "Customers like that," Shimon told Salman, "are decoration for my shop rather than coins clinking in my pocket."

"Why aren't you married?" Salman asked the professor one day. The miser laughed. "I'm such a nasty piece of work," he said, "that I'd get divorced from myself if only I could."

Three or four of Shimon's women customers used to give Salman either a piece of chocolate, or a sweet, or sometimes a kiss. But best of all he liked delivering orders to the widow Maria. She was rich and had a house all to herself. The inner courtyard was like a jungle, and even had brightly coloured parrots in it.

The widow Maria ordered in lavish quantities and paid at once. However, she often just picked out one small item from the full basket, and asked Salman to give the rest away to the house next door. "The widow Maria sends the children some vegetables to make their cheeks red!" he would tell the poor people who lived there.

But the main reason why he liked going to see the rich widow was that she would put a chair under the old orange tree for him, and feed him all kinds of exotic jams that he had never tasted before. She made bitter oranges, quinces, blue plums, rose petals, and other fruits and herbs into preserves, jellies, and jams. She worked for hours on new recipes, although as she was diabetic she could never eat a spoonful of them herself. But she liked to see people enjoying all these delicacies. She told Salman, who had gobbled his first roll and jam, to eat more slowly and tell her exactly what it tasted like, and then he would get another one.

So Salman was sorry he had been greedy. He would have loved to take some of these delicious confections back to his mother or Sarah, but he dared not ask the widow to let him do that.

When he had eaten enough she would tell him about her life, but like many other widows she never said a word about her dead husband. And there was always a sense of sadness about her.

When Salman asked the vegetable seller why, he only sighed. Maria's husband had wounded her deeply, and that was why she never talked about him. It was not a story fit for children anyway, he said, spraying radishes with water and arranging apples in a crate.

Only years later did Salman learn that Maria came from a well-known and very rich family. She was one of the first girls ever to gain a higher school certificate in Damascus in the 1920s. Her husband was unfaithful to her with the cook on the second day after their marriage. But he always pretended to be madly in love with her, so she would forgive him, and by way of thanks he was unfaithful again. Even at the age of sixty he was still chasing every woman he saw, drooling, until syphilis carried him off.

After that she lived very quietly. She wasn't even in her mid-sixties yet, but she looked like an old lady of eighty.

When Salman, talking to Sarah, went into ecstasies about the widow Maria's delicious jams and jellies, Sarah started wondering how she could get rolls spread with those exotic confections for herself.

"Maybe I'll just knock on her door," said Sarah, "and tell her I'm very poor, and I dreamed she has a warm heart and lots of different kinds of preserves, and I'm soon going to die, so I'd really, really love to eat ten rolls spread with different preserves, just for once."

Salman laughed. Faizeh, Sarah's mother, had heard what they were saying through the open window. She came out and gave Sarah a loving hug. "You don't have to do that," she said. "I'll make you rose-petal jelly tomorrow."

Sarah smiled happily. "And quince jelly the day after tomorrow," she said, just as a police officer rode into Grace and Favour Yard on his bike. He spotted Sarah and Salman, smiled briefly, and asked where a certain Adnan lived. Adnan was going to be arrested for breaking into several expensive limousines, stealing car seats, radios, and in one case even the steering wheel, and selling them on.

"Aha," said Sarah, and she pointed to the apartment where Samira, Adnan's mother, lived at the other end of Grace and Favour Yard.

"With all his wonderful talents, that Adnan could be a famous car mechanic or a racing driver," said Sarah.

"You're crazy," Salman protested. All Adnan's ideas were unpleasant. He would grab cats, small dogs, rats and mice by their tails, whirl them round and round in the air, and then put them down again. The poor creatures staggered away as if they were drunk, tottering back and forth, and sometimes throwing up. The people who lived in Grace and Favour Yard laughed themselves silly and encouraged him to think up other brutal tricks. Salman just thought he was horrible.

And it was Adnan who finally forced Salman to get fit. It was on a Sunday, and Sarah was going to let him have a lick of her ice again. They strolled off to the ice-cream vendor on the Kishleh Road junction, and Sarah decided to have a lemon popsicle. They turned, and were on their way home again. Not far from their alley, the unpleasant Adnan was standing with three other lads, grinning all over his face.

"If you're scared, just run off fast. I'll be all right," Sarah whispered. But Salman saw how she was trembling.

"Don't you worry, I'll deal with them. Eat your ice and don't let them bother you," he said, feeling his chest swelling with the pride of showing off.

"Jug-Ears, Elephant-Ears!" Adnan struck up this chant, and the other boys fell about laughing. Adnan grabbed Sarah's shoulder and held her. She licked her ice at amazing speed, breathing fast and audibly like someone with asthma.

"Take your filthy fingers off my girlfriend," cried Salman angrily, and before Adnan knew it, Salman had kicked him in the balls. He bent double. Sarah ran away, but the other boys stopped Salman from following her. The ice-cream vendor saw the scuffle, and shouted to the boys to stop. When they didn't react but went on laying into Salman the man made for them with a broom, bringing it down with all his might on their backs and buttocks. They let go of Salman and ran away, screeching.

That day Salman decided to make his muscles stronger. He dreamed at night that Adnan barred Sarah's way again, but he, Salman, flung him right through the vegetable seller's first-floor window and up into the sky.

As if heaven were ready to oblige him, soon after that he found an iron bar over a metre long by the roadside. He took it home. He knew how to make any metal bar into dumbbells. You poured concrete into a bucket, put the metal bar into the mixture of cement, sand and water, and let it dry. Then you put the other end of your bar into the same mixture. Mikhail the mason gave him the concrete. For the first end of the dumbbells, Salman used the rusty bucket he found behind the henhouse. Unfortunately he couldn't find a similar bucket for the other end, but after searching for a long time he decided to use an old and battered cylindrical tin can.

When the whole thing had dried, the dumbbells looked rather funny, with a cylindrical lump of concrete hanging from one end, and a peculiar shape like a squashed sausage from the other. That didn't bother Salman. He was impressed by the idea of raising the dumb-bells, which weighed almost ten kilos. It was difficult, because the cylindrical end was more than a kilo lighter than the sausage-shaped end. So Salman could raise the whole thing in the air only for a few seconds before he fell over sideways and the device crashed to the ground. Sarah, much amused, was watching the whole performance.

Salman went on training, but always with the same result. Once Sarah found him lying on the floor and staring at the ceiling. The weight lay askew behind his head.

"That thing's never going to give you more muscle power," she said. "It'll only leave you walking sideways like a crab and falling over like my father when he's drunk and sees his bed."

So Salman broke off the two ends with a hammer, and took the iron bar to the any-old-iron man, who weighed it and gave him a whole thirty piastres for it.

"Six ices," whispered Salman, whistling with delight at his new wealth. He bought Sarah three ice-cream cones, and her loving look made his chest muscles expand. He could feel them growing.

5

The Midan quarter lies southwest of the Old Town of Damascus. The caravans of pilgrims bound for Mecca used to set out from that place, and they were welcomed back to it on their return. So there are many mosques, shops selling the things that pilgrims need, hammams and wholesale dealers in wheat and other grains along the broad main street that bears the name of the quarter: Midan Street. A branching network of many small alleys lay around this long street. Ayyubi Alley turned off the busy main street, and had only four houses, and a large aniseed warehouse in it. The entrance to the warehouse was in the parallel street.

Noura loved the smell of aniseed. It reminded her of sweets.

Ayyubi Alley was called after the great clan that had once lived in those four houses. The head of the clan, Sami Ayyubi, had been wanted by the police after the 1925 uprising against the French occupying forces. He and his family fled to Jordan, where he was protected by the British. Later, after the founding of the kingdom of Jordan, he became the king's private secretary and spied for the British in the royal palace. He took Jordanian citizenship, and never went back to Damascus.

Soon after Ayyubi's flight a rich merchant called Abdullah Mahaini bought the four houses cheaply. Mahaini, a rich man whose ancestors had come from central Syria in the seventeenth century to settle here in the Midan quarter, dealt in textiles, fine timbers, leather, weapons, and building materials through the several branches of his company all over the country. He also represented a Dutch electrical firm, a German sewing machine manufacturer, and a French car constructor.

The small house at the end of the blind alley was an architectural and artistic gem of old Damascus. Mahaini gave it to his daughter Sahar, Noura's mother, as her dowry when she married. He sold the other three houses at a large profit. Unlike Mahaini's first wife, who bore him four sons, his second, Sahar's mother, seemed to have only girls in her womb. She gave birth to eight healthy girl babies, and the merchant had no intention of feeding a single one of them longer than necessary. He wanted each girl to have a husband to look after her from her fifteenth year of life onward. A number of his neighbours said, maliciously, that only the age difference between his daughters and the seven wives he had married in the course of his life embarrassed him. The older the rich merchant Mahaini grew, the younger his wives became.

Until his death, he lived in a palace close to the Umayyad Mosque. Suitors for his daughters came and went the whole time, because marrying one of Mahaini's daughters was like winning the lottery.

That was the case with Sahar who, like most of his daughters, couldn't read but was very pretty. Many men wanted to marry her, but Mahaini sent all the merchants and tailors, pharmacists and teachers away. He just smiled sympathetically at Sahar's mother when she said she was sorry about his rejection of them.

"I have already found an outstanding husband for Sahar," he said, sounding like a man who knew his own mind. "You'll be proud to call yourself his mother-in-law."

Abdullah Mahaini was a well-read and humorous man. "I'm occupied all day," he said, "keeping the peace among my nine warring wives, my forty-eight children, ten servants, and two hundred and fifty employees. Napoleon had a much easier time."

He liked the traditional ways, but was open to innovations. He married nine wives but would not allow any of his wives or daughters to wear the veil. When a strictly observant Muslim asked for his reasons, he would repeat the words of a young Sufi scholar whom he respected highly. "God created faces for us to see and recognize. It is the heart and not the veil that makes a woman devout."

He told his wives and daughters that the veil was not an Islamic introduction, but dated from ancient Syria a thousand years before the coming of Islam. At that time only women of noble birth were allowed to be veiled in public. It was a symbol of luxury. If a slave-girl or a peasant woman wore a veil, she was punished.

Mahaini liked a convivial life, and happily surrounded himself with clever men whom he invited to his house and with whom he went to the baths and did business. His closest friends included two Jews and three Christians.

He greatly admired the highly regarded but impoverished Sufi scholar Rami Arabi, whose sermons he followed with much interest Friday after Friday in the little Salah Mosque in the Midan quarter. He preferred them to the pompous prayers recited under the direction of the Grand Mufti of Damascus in the nearby Umayyad Mosque.

And so the thin little sheikh became the great Mahaini's son-in-law, and later Noura's father.

Of Noura's paternal grandparents, her grandmother did not get on with Noura's mother, while her grandfather adored his daughter-in-law. He was a shy man, lived a secluded life, and avoided paying visits unless they were absolutely necessary. Noura's mother always made much of him when he did call. His wife, on the other hand, Noura's grandmother, was an energetic old lady who often looked in to see the young couple. "I've only dropped by to see our clever, dear little Noura," she would cry. "The servants can get lost! And the sooner I have a good cup of coffee the sooner I'll be gone again."

Noura's mother never made coffee so quickly for anyone else.

Grandfather Mahaini came to lunch every Friday after prayers. Friday was the only day of the week he could sleep in peace, he used to say, because then he had no questions left.

As if a fairy had told the young scholar what questions were chasing around in the old merchant Mahaini's head during the week, he would answer exactly those questions from the pulpit. Sahar, Noura's mother, is said to have told a woman neighbour once, "My husband ought to have married my father, not me. They'd have suited each other very well."

That was not entirely true, for the two of them, friends though they were, often argued when they were on their own. Mahaini would tell the young sheikh that he should be only months ahead of his congregation, not decades. He went so fast that no one could keep up with him, said Mahaini. That way he made things easy for his enemies, and instead of rising to be mufti of Syria he would be stuck in this dilapidated little mosque preaching to the illiterate and the hard of hearing.

"Oh, come along. Are you, for instance, illiterate?"

"What, me?" cried the rich merchant, laughing.

"The Damascenes," said Noura's father, "lie snoring as the train of civilization rushes past. Do what you like, a man asleep and snoring will always get a shock when you wake him," he added, dismissing the matter with a helpless gesture.

And whenever they met the great Mahaini would blame himself afterwards for having criticized his upright and learned son-in-law so harshly. Sheikh Rami Arabi, on the other hand, often went to bed resolving to take wise Mahaini's advice and administer bitter medicine to his flock by the spoonful rather than in buckets.

Years later, Noura remembered an incident that, in its simplicity, seemed to her to symbolize the deep friendship between her father and her grandfather Mahaini. One day her father was repairing a little box to hold Noura's toys. Then her grandfather came to call, and as usual seemed to have many burning questions on his mind. But Noura's father went on screwing and hammering without paying any attention to the old man, who was shifting restlessly back and forth in his chair.

When he began making sharp remarks about wasting time over children's stuff, her father rose to his feet, disappeared into his study, and came back with a pair of scissors and two sheets of paper. "Can you fold a paper swallow that will fly?" he asked his father-in-law in a kindly tone.

"Am I a child?" growled the old man.

"I could wish for both our sakes that you were," said Noura's father, turning his attention back to the hinges of the box. Her mother, who was just bringing the coffee she had made for her father, stopped in the doorway, rooted to the spot. She was not a little surprised when the old man smiled, knelt down on the floor and began folding the paper.

It was Noura's first paper swallow, and it flew slowly, sometimes getting stuck in a tree or falling head first to the ground when she launched it into the air from the first floor of the house.

Noura's parental home was very peaceful, despite being so close to the main street. All sounds died away in the long, dark corridor down which you went, after coming in from the alleyway, to reach the inner courtyard and be in the open air again.

It was a small, shady courtyard, its paving adorned with coloured marble ornamentation that continued on the floors of the rooms surrounding it. There was a little fountain in the middle of the courtyard, and its water played in arabesques that were music to the ears of the Damascenes. There was nothing they would rather hear in the hot months of the year.

Her father sometimes sat beside the fountain for a long time, with his eyes closed. At first Noura thought he was asleep, but she was wrong. "Water is a part of Paradise, and that is why no mosque is without it. When I sit here listening to the music of the fountain I am going back to my origin in my mother's womb. Or even farther back, to the sea, and I hear its waves breaking on the coast, like the sound of my mother's heartbeat," he told her once when she had been sitting close to him watching him for a long time.

A staircase led up to the first floor. The flat roof over it was surrounded by a beautiful wrought-iron balustrade. Most of the rooftop was used for drying the laundry, and fruits, vegetables, and many kinds of preserved foodstuffs were laid out here to dry in the hot sun. About a quarter of the space had been extended into a large, light attic room which Noura's father used as the study where he wrote.

The lavatory was a tiny closet under the stairs. As in many Arab houses, there was no bathroom. You washed at the well or in the kitchen, and went to the baths in the nearby hammam every week.

Noura liked her parents' house best in summer, for as soon as shade fell across the courtyard in the afternoon, and her mother came home from drinking midday coffee with their neighbour Badia, she would sprinkle the tiles and the plants with water, and wipe down the marble paving until it gleamed and all its bright colours shone.

"Now the carpet of coolness is spread and the evening can begin," her mother would say every day, contentedly. It was a ritual. She put on a clean, simple house dress and turned the tap to start the fountain playing. The water sprayed up from the little holes and fell musically into the basin, where Noura's mother would place a large watermelon in summer. Then she would fetch a platter of salty titbits to nibble and sit by the fountain. By the time Noura's father came back from the mosque, the watermelon was cool and tasted refreshing. Noura's mother's good temper lasted until then. But as soon as her husband was home she became stiff and cold. There was an icy chill between her parents in general. Noura often saw other couples embrace, crack jokes, or even kiss each other, for instance Badia next door and her husband. And she was amazed to hear how freely women spoke at coffee parties about their most intimate moments in bed, giving each other tips and talking about the tricks they used to seduce their husbands and make sure that they too had physical pleasure. They discussed lingerie, drinks and perfumes, and revelled in descriptions of all kinds of kissing. These were the same women who sometimes scurried or shuffled along the street with scarves over their heads, eyes cast down, as if they had never felt any pleasure in their lives.

Noura's parents never kissed. An invisible wall separated them. Noura never once saw them embrace. One day, when the door of the room was open just a crack and Noura was on the sofa, she could see her parents in the courtyard. They were sitting by the fountain drinking coffee. They couldn't see Noura, because her room was in the dark. Both were in a good mood, and laughing a lot about some male relation who had behaved very stupidly at a wedding. Suddenly her father put out his hand to touch her mother's bare shoulders; it was a very hot day, and her mother was wearing only a thin nightdress. When he touched her, she leapt up. "Don't do that, you have to go to the mosque," she said, and sat down on another chair.

As well as her parents' cold relationship, another thing that ran like a thread through Noura's childhood was the books.

"Books, stinking books everywhere," her mother would often complain. The books did not stink, but they were certainly everywhere. They filled the shelves of both rooms on the ground floor, as well as the shelves in the attic, where they also lay stacked in piles or open on the floor. The only space clear of them was a chair at the desk and a sofa. Later, Noura would often sit there for hours on end, reading.

No books were allowed in her parents' bedroom or the kitchen. That was by her mother's wish, and her father, although he regretted it, went along with what she wanted, for after all the house belonged to her, even after their wedding. "Your father had nothing when we married but thirty lice and three thousand books stinking of mould," said her mother to Noura, laughing. She was not exaggerating. Rami Arabi was a learned Sufi who thought little of worldly goods, and preferred the pleasures of Arabic script to all others.

Unlike his first wife, Noura's mother Sahar could not read. She was seventeen years younger than her husband, and had been just seventeen when he married her. Rami Arabi had three sons by his first marriage. They were almost his second wife's age, and now had families of their own. They seldom visited their father's house, for Noura's mother did not like them, and she disliked talking about them and their dead mother. She despised her stepsons because they were not only poor, like their father, but also stupid. Noura's father knew that himself, and it was a grief to him that none of his sons was clever. He loved Noura, and used to tell her she had the brains he could have wished for in a son. "If you were a man you would turn people's heads in the mosque."

He himself lacked the fine voice and appearance that matter a great deal to Arabs. Although his sons were a disappointment to him, he always spoke well of his first wife, which was particularly annoying to Noura's mother. Sometime she would hiss, "Graveyards are supposed to smell of incense, but this one just stinks of decomposition."

On the other hand, Noura's mother looked after her husband loyally and with respect. She cooked for him, washed and ironed his robes, and consoled him when he suffered one of his many setbacks. But she never for an instant loved him.

The house belonged to Noura's mother, but he had the last word. Sahar would have liked to wear the veil, to show a clear distinction between her own sphere and the world outside it, but he hated veils, just as her own father had done. "God has graced you with a beautiful face because he wanted people to like looking at it," one of them used to tell her before her marriage and the other after it.

When a distant aunt, fascinated by Noura's lovely face, suggested that it might be better for her to wear a veil so as not to lead men astray, Noura's father laughed. "If all were just and right, as God and his Prophet say, then men ought to wear veils too, for many men also lead women astray with their handsome looks, or am I wrong?"

The aunt leaped to her feet as if a snake had bitten her and left the house, because she understood what he meant. She was having an affair with a handsome young man in her neighbourhood. Everyone knew about it except her husband. Noura's mother had been cross for two days, because she did not think her husband's allusions were the right thing to say to a guest. She was oddly prudish anyway. When she hung out the washing she always took care that her own underclothes were on the line in the middle, where they would be shielded from prying eyes on both sides of the rooftop. She felt curiously ashamed, as if her underwear were not made of cotton but was her own skin.

Their neighbour Badia was not allowed to wear the veil either. Her husband even wanted her to receive his guests. He was a rich textiles merchant in the Souk al-Hamidiyyeh, and often had visitors – even Europeans and Chinese. Badia welcomed them, but with reserve, because she was convinced that infidels were unclean.

Unlike Badia, however, who did not particularly respect her husband, Sahar was afraid of her own husband Rami, just as she was afraid of all men, ever since her father had once thrashed her as a little girl when she unthinkingly called him "a strutting rooster with a lot of hens" in front of his guests, embarrassing him. At the time he waited patiently until the guests had left the house, and then told one of the servants to give him a cane and hold Sahar down by both hands. Then he beat her, and neither her mother's tears nor the servant's pleas were any use. "My husband will be the crown on my head," she had to repeat in a clear voice. But her voice was stifled by her tears many times, and her father seemed to be hard of hearing that day.

Her own husband could also lose his temper within seconds. He never struck her, but he lashed her with his tongue and it went to her heart more sharply than a knife made of Damascene steel. Whenever his lips quivered and the colour of his face changed, she was afraid.

She longed for a son, but after Noura all her children died just before or just after they were born.

Years later, Noura remembered her mother taking her to the cemetery near Bab al-Sagheer. This old graveyard contained not only plain graves but also cupolas containing the tombs of particularly distinguished men and women of the early history of Islam, members of the Prophet's family and his travelling companions. Her mother always sought out the grave of Umm Habiba, one of the Prophet's wives, and the grave of his granddaughter Sakina. There were always many Shiite women standing there, wrapped in black garments, especially Iranian women on pilgrimage. They walked along the rows of shrines with ribbons and scarves, as if by merely touching a relic they could take it home with them. And although her mother was one of the Sunni majority, and hated Shiites worse than Jews and Christians, she prayed for a son there. She passed her hand over a shrine and then stroked her belly. She dared not bring a scarf, because her husband laughed at such superstition, and she was afraid that the angry dead would punish her with a deformed baby.

Indeed, as Noura remembered it, her mother spent more time in graveyards than among the living. With hundreds of other believers, she visited the tombs of famous scholars of Islam and companions of the Prophet, climbed Mount Qasioun with them and laid flowers and green branches of myrtle on the graves. Noura did not enjoy this exhausting procession, which began early in the morning and went on until the muezzin called the faithful to prayer at midday. It was held on certain days in the holy months of Rajab, Shaban, and Ramadan, whether it was bitterly cold or blazing hot outside. Noura always had to go too, but her father wriggled out of it. He thought all such rituals were superstition, and despised them.

And every time the procession ended at the doors of a mosque at the foot of Mount Qasioun. Hundred if not thousands stood there and called out loud, sending their prayers and wishes up into the sky. It was all done in great haste, the visit, the laying of the flowers and green myrtle boughs, the prayers. For prophets, like angels, listened to prayers only until noon, said Noura's mother. And sure enough, when the muezzin called them to midday prayers, they all instantly fell silent. For years it was also the custom for believers to activate the many bronze knockers and metal rings adorning the doors to that mosque, making a terrible racket, until the sheikh of the mosque, annoyed, had them removed and told the disappointed crowd, "If God and his Prophets don't hear your cries and prayers, then they won't listen to that raucous noise either."

Noura's mother loved the procession, and took part in it as if she were in a hypnotic trance. So she also knew, much better than Noura's father, when you should visit which graves and at what time of day.

Sometimes he would sigh despairingly, "Am I the sheikh around here or are you?"

Noura's father had forbidden her mother to visit quacks, saying she would do better to consult a proper doctor. Nor did he want to know about his wife's attempts to petition saints dead or alive. So Noura never said anything about any of her mother's visits to sacred graves or holy men. She was sorry for her. Things reached the point where Noura herself began begging God to send her mother a son.

Eight times her mother's belly grew, swelled to a great size above her legs, and then, when her mother was thin again, there was still no child. Noura soon learnt the word *miscarriage*. But not all her mother's torments could sap the strength of her dream. The eighth miscarriage was particularly hard, and the doctors were only able to save her mother's life by luck, although at the price that she would never be pregnant again. Her husband told her she had brought her infertility on herself by taking the diabolical stuff that the quacks prescribed for her.

Noura remembered this eighth and last miscarriage particularly well. Her mother came home from hospital looking years older. At the time, when they were bathing in the hammam together, her mother found the first little swellings of her daughter's breasts. Noura was eleven or twelve at the time. "You're a woman now," she cried in surprise. And there was a touch of reproof in her voice.

From that moment on her mother stopped treating her as the girl she still was, but as a grown woman surrounded by slavering, greedy men.

When Noura told her father about her mother's exaggerated fears, he just laughed, but later he realized that he ought to have felt more respect for his daughter's premonitions. Her mother regarded every young man with suspicion, as if fearing that he would instantly attack Noura.

"I have a rope ready down in the cellar. If anything happens to you I shall hang myself," she said one morning. Noura searched the cellar. All she could find was a thin washing line, but she still feared for her mother, and began keeping quiet about everything that happened to her.

Her father was always ready to listen to questions, and was sought out at home as well as in the mosque by people who wanted his advice. He was famous for his patience and frankness, and he seldom got annoyed, even when he was asked such questions as why God created flies, and why human beings have to sleep. He replied patiently and in friendly tones. But he would answer no questions, none whatsoever, about women. He quite often interrupted a man seeking his advice on the subject abruptly. "That's women's business. You'd better ask a midwife or your mother." He was afraid of women. Quite often, he used to say that the Prophet himself had warned his companions against women's wiles. But even more often he told the story of the fairy who promised to grant a man one wish. The man wished for a bridge from Damascus to Honolulu. The fairy rolled her eyes and complained that his wish was just too difficult for her. Didn't he have one that she could grant more easily? Yes, he said, he'd like to understand his wife. At that the fairy asked if he wanted the bridge to Honolulu to be a single or a dual carriage-way.

How was Noura to tell her father or her mother about the young smith who was always lying in wait in the main street, quietly asking if she wouldn't like him to sew up the crack between her legs? He had just the right needle for the job, he said. At home, she looked at herself in the mirror. Yes, the place between her legs did look a bit like a crack. But sewing it up?

Of course she saw boys naked in the hammam, for on the day when women went they could take their small sons with them until the boys first showed signs of being aroused. After that they had to go to the baths with their fathers instead. But all these years she had believed what a woman neighbour told her in the hammam: boys were handicapped from birth and weren't very good at peeing, so God had given them a little tube to keep them from wetting themselves all the time.

She learned a lot in the hammam. It was not just a place for body care and cleanliness, but for rest and laughter. She was always hearing stories there, and older women told her things that you wouldn't find in any book. The women seemed to shed all their inhibitions and shame along with their clothes, and talked frankly about all kinds of subjects. The warm, steamy room smelled of lavender, ambergris, and musk.

Noura enjoyed exotic drinks and dishes here, things she never tasted at home. Every woman was anxious to improve her cookery skills and would bring the delicious results of her efforts with her. Then they all sat in a circle tasting over twenty different dishes and drinking sweet tea. Every time Noura went home feeling her heart was richer.

When she told her school friend Samia about the smith pestering her, Samia said, "Oh, he's deceiving you. Men don't carry needles, they have a chisel and they just make the hole bigger with it." And she advised Noura to tell the young man bothering her to go home and sew up his sisters' cracks, and if he had enough yarn left after that to try it with his mother some time.

Noura would also have liked to ask her father or her mother why she kept thinking up a thousand reasons to see the pale boy with the big eyes who began his apprenticeship to an upholsterer in the autumn of 1947, when she was in the fifth class at school.

The upholsterer's shop was quite close. The boy saw her strolling past on his first day, and gave her a shy smile. When she went the same way next day, to see the boy again, he was kneeling on a small mat in the corner praying. He was praying on the next day too, and on the day after that. Noura wondered why, and asked her mother and father about it, but they had no idea why either. "It may be just coincidence that he's praying when you happen to pass," said her father.

"Or he's broken something," said her mother, before pouring soup into their bowls.

When she saw the boy praying again next time she asked his master, an old man with a short, snow-white beard, whether the boy had done something wrong.

"Dear me, no, he's a good lad," said the master upholsterer, with a kindly smile. "But before he learns how to handle cotton, wool, textiles, and leather, he must learn how to handle customers. We do our work in the inner courtyards of people's homes, and often there's only the mistress of the house or an old granny there. Sometimes our customers even let us come into their houses when there's no one there at all, so that we can mend beds, mattresses, and sofas while they're out shopping or at work, or visiting neighbours. And if an upholsterer isn't one-hundred percent trustworthy he harms the reputation of the guild. That's why we're told to train apprentices to be devout before they first go into a customer's house."

At these words the boy rolled his eyes, and Noura smiled at this brief but unmistakable message.

When the boy went to bring water from the public well to the shop at midday, she was planning to wait for him. Many shops had no water supply of their own, so the boy had to make several trips to fetch buckets.

One day Noura was waiting at the well. The boy smiled at her. "I can help you if you like," said Noura, showing him her little metal watering can. The boy smiled. "You'd be welcome, but I mustn't accept or I'll have to pray for half an hour longer. But I can stay here with you for a moment if you like," he added, putting a big can under the tap.

Not many people came to the well, and they didn't linger for long.

Noura often thought of that boy when she heard poems and songs about beautiful angels. She didn't know why a creature like an angel with huge wings should be beautiful, but Tamim was more beautiful than any other boy in the whole quarter, and when he spoke her heart beat time to every one of his words.

Tamim had spent only two years learning to read and write from a sheikh. After that he had to work, because his parents were poor. He really wanted to be a ship's captain instead of upholstering mattresses and chairs, beds and sofas. "And praying in every free moment. My knees hurt," he told her.

Once, when Tamim had told her that he had to go to the Souk al-Hamidiyyeh the next day to get his master a great deal of sewing yarn and coloured thread from a wholesaler, she decided to meet him there. She would wait for him near the Bakdash ice-cream parlour.

In the morning she announced that she had her period. As usual, her mother advised her to stay away from school. She herself hated the school, but didn't dare to say so, since her father wanted her to take her middle school certificate.

He too thought she looked pale. If she began feeling worse, he said, she could take the tram home. So Noura went to school. An hour later, with her pale face and shaky voice, she convinced the headmistress that she wasn't well. But ten paces from school her face regained its colour and her steps were firm and steady again. The school wasn't far from the Souk al-Hamidiyyeh. She saved her ten piastres for the tram and went on foot.

Tamim arrived at ten. He was carrying a large empty basket for his purchases. He looked even more handsome here in the market than at his master's shop.

"If anyone asks, we're brother and sister, so we ought to walk holding hands," she suggested. She had spent all night thinking that up. He gave her his hand, and she felt she would die of happiness. They walked through the lively souk in silence.

"Say something," she asked him.

"I like your hand," he said, "it's warm and dry like my mother's, but much smaller."

"I have ten piastres," she said. "I won't need them for the tram, I'll go home on foot. What flavour of ice cream do you like best?"

"Lemon," he said.

"And I like Damascus Berry best," she said. "It leaves your tongue all blue."

"And I get gooseflesh from the lemon ice." He licked his lips in anticipation.

They bought popsicles and strolled through the market. Spring was filling the streets with the scent of flowers. Noura wanted to whistle her favourite tune, as boys did, but girls weren't allowed to whistle.

They were walking separately now, because Tamim needed one hand for his basket and the other for his ice. Noura had to laugh at the noisy way he was licking it. But soon the souk was so full that she had to wind her way through the crowd ahead of him. A blind beggar fascinated her with his singing. Why, she wondered, did blind people have that special kind of voice? At that moment she felt Tamim's hand. She was only halfway through her ice, and he had finished his already! She turned to him, and he smiled. "Don't worry, it's only your brother," he said softly.

When they had to part again, outside the way into the market, Tamim held both her hands in his for a long time. He looked into her eyes, and for the first time in her life Noura felt breathless with joy. He drew her close. "Brothers and sisters say goodbye with a kiss," he said, kissing her cheek. "And as soon as I'm a captain I'll come back for you with my ship," he added, and disappeared quickly into the crowd as if ashamed of the tears that were running down his face.

A month later another boy was kneeling on the little prayer mat.

"But where is…" she asked the master upholsterer, and bit her tongue so as not to say his name. She had been whispering it into her pillow all these nights.

"Oh, him!" said the master upholsterer, amused. "He ran away, sent a message to his parents a few days ago that he'd signed on board a Greek freighter ship. Crazy boy!"

That night her father had to send for the doctor. She had a fever for a whole week.

Two years after Noura's flight, a strong man in naval uniform knocked at the door of her parents' house. He was a sea captain, he told her father. Her mother was in the hospital at the time for an appendicitis operation.

When he heard how Noura had run away, it is said that he smiled and shook her father's hand in a friendly way. "Noura always did go in search of the wide waters of the sea," he is reported to have said. Her father was so impressed by those words that – to his wife's annoyance – he often spoke of that meeting, even on his deathbed.

But that was not until decades later.

6

No one asked Salman where he'd been when he failed to turn up at school several days running. And of all the hundred children and five teachers, only one person smiled at him. That was Benjamin who sat next to him on the same bench.

When he came home at midday, his mother was still busy cleaning their hiding place. She worked hard to put the rooms in order. She cleaned and washed, threw the rubbish into the inner courtyard and then swept it into the rooms of the former weaver's workshop.

She worked until early in the afternoon at home in their apartment to get everything ready for her husband, and then fled back to her hiding place with the boy. Shimon told her there was no need to worry. She could stay there for a few years, because the old weaver's heirs were going to court against each other. Apparently the tiny house was likely to bring in good money because it was so close to the historic chapel of St Boulos.

After a short time his mother stopped crying, and their hiding place didn't smell of mould anymore but of onions and thyme. There was no electricity in the house, but candlelight banished the darkness and cold. And the lavatory and bath were in working order, because in their quarrel about the inheritance the weaver's heirs had forgotten to turn off the water.

Soon mother and son were beginning to laugh like two conspirators as they imagined the stupid expression on Salman's father's face when he came home in the evening dead drunk, and found no one there for him to beat.

But the happiness of the poor is short-lived.

One night Salman's father was suddenly there in the room with them. His shadow danced frantically over the walls. The two candles seemed to tremble before him. His voice and his odour, an unpleasant mixture of arak and decay, filled all the space that his body left available. Salman hardly dared to breathe.

Only later did he learn from Sarah that their neighbour Samira, wife of the fuel station attendant Yousef, who lived at the other end of the yard between the chicken run and the baker's journeyman Barakat's apartment, had given the secret away in return for a lira. Nothing escaped Samira. From her own apartment, she watched all that went on in Grace and Favour Yard: the eight apartments in all, two lavatories, two woodsheds, and the chicken run. Salman could never forgive her for that act of treachery. He would not speak her name, but called her only "the telltale woman."

That night Salman's father dragged his mother downstairs by her hair and out into the street, and if Shimon and Kamil, who came hurrying up, hadn't barred the way he would have hauled the poor woman all the way back to the yard. They freed Mariam from his grasp, and while Shimon helped her to her feet, Sarah's father the police officer pushed the furious man ahead of him back into Grace and Favour Yard. "Now then, calm down and don't make me put my uniform on, or you know where I'll be taking you," he growled, to bring the furious man to his senses.

Salman stood at the window and looked at his tear-stained face in it. He was afraid his father would come back and haul him out of the house by the hair as well. But when all was still, there was only one thing he wanted, and that was to go to his mother. At that moment he heard loud barking from the ground floor. It changed to a whine, as if a dog down there was afraid or hungry.

Salman held the candle above his head and tried to look down at the inner courtyard from the window, but deep darkness swallowed up the candlelight before it reached the ground.

Curious and frightened at the same time, he slowly went downstairs. Even before he reached the last step a tangled mass of black hair collided with his legs, and a pair of bright eyes stared at him.

The dog was large, but his clumsiness and playfulness showed that he was young. He had a fine head and a large muzzle. Only the encrusted blood on the hair of his chest showed Salman that the animal's throat was wounded. It looked as if someone had injured the dog severely and left him in these ruins.

"Wait here," Salman said, and went back upstairs. He found a clean piece of an old dress among the rags that his mother kept in a drawer. He wrapped it carefully around the neck of the injured dog, which had followed him and stood surprisingly still.

"You're not going to die," said Salman, patting his head. "Like my Mama," he added, and he hugged the dog. The dog was whining hungrily. Salman remembered the mutton bone that the butcher Mahmoud had given them. His mother had used it to make their last bowl of soup, and she had kept the bone so that Salman could nibble the scraps of meat off it next time he was hungry. Salman gave it to the dog, who devoured everything on it happily, wagging his tail constantly. Only when Salman stroked his head for a long time did the dog calm down. They looked at each other like two outcasts, and Salman was never to forget the expression in the dog's eyes.

He slipped away, but not without closing the door to the courtyard carefully, as if he were afraid the dog would disappear.

Day was already dawning when he slipped into his parents' apartment. His mother was still crouching on the mattress, while his father snored loudly in the second room

"He won't be scaring you much longer," he whispered into his mother's ear. "I've got a big dog, and he'll soon grow even bigger and eat up anyone who touches you, Mama," said Salman, and his mother smiled, took him in her arms, and fell into a deep sleep at once. But Salman stayed awake and didn't move until his father shouted "Coffee!" and his mother woke up. When she went into the kitchen Salman nodded off. He saw the dog, huge and powerful as a stallion with snow-white wings. He, his mother, and Sarah were on his back, flying over the Christian quarter. His mother clung to him anxiously, and Salman heard Sarah reassuring her, saying that the dog was an enchanted swallow who knew its way around very well and would never throw them off.

Above his mother's head, Sarah called out to him, "Salman, Salman, you must give the dog a name or he'll get lost."

"What shall I call him?" he shouted into the wind.

"Pilot," he heard his mother and Sarah say in chorus.

The dog flew round the Church of St Mary. It was the first time Salman had seen it from above. Then they flew down Abbara Alley to

Grace and Favour Yard. Salman saw the neighbours come out of their homes. They pointed up and called out, "Pilot!"

He woke with a start. His father was just lighting his second cigarette and setting out on his way to work. "My dog's name is Pilot," murmured Salman, jumping up.

7

At Easter of the year 1948, Salman took first communion. However, now that he had enjoyed the liberty of days off, St Nicholas's School seemed to him even more intolerable in his second year. He avoided the place. Only in winter, when it was icy cold outside, did he go to school, convincing himself yet again that this damp building, where everyone knocked the weaker children about, was no place for him.

When inviting spring weather came, Salman went out and about with Benjamin in the fields beyond the city walls. He smelled life there, the air was fragrant with apricot blossoms, and they ate young, bitter almonds still green and straight from the trees.

They laughed a lot and played with the dog. Pilot soon made friends with big, strong Benjamin, and would let him drape him over his shoulders like a fur collar. Within six months Pilot grew into a handsome, powerful animal. After a while Benjamin couldn't lift him off the ground anymore. "This is a donkey in disguise," he said, groaning under the dog's weight and falling on his behind. He let Pilot go and laughed.

"You're the donkey," said Salman. "My Pilot is a tiger in camouflage."

Early in the summer, Father Yacoub had made himself so unpopular in Damascus with his fanaticism that the bishop moved him to a mountain village on the coast. Soon after that, and before the end of his second year, Benjamin finally left school. He went to work with his father, a nice little man with a face with scars and wrinkles all over it. He marvelled at the strength of his young son, who towered a head above him, and sometimes, when there were no customers around, would pick him up with one hand.

Two days after Benjamin had left, Salman too said goodbye to St Nicholas's forever. He never set foot in the school again.

None of the neighbours asked why he wasn't at school like other children. School didn't count for much in Grace and Favour Yard, where they struggled merely to survive. To Salman, it seemed natural to stay at home and look after his sick mother, who stopped shedding tears and whimpering as soon as he was near her.

"Why aren't you going to school anymore?" asked Sarah one day.

"My mother…" he began, about to invent something, but when Sarah looked at him the lie died away on his tongue. "I hate school. It's horrible… I don't want to learn anymore," he stammered angrily.

"Would you like me to read aloud to you the way I used to? Read you good stories?" asked Sarah, trying to find out the real reason for his dislike of school.

"I don't like books now. Tell me something else," he said.

"Don't be stupid, books are wonderful. No one can tell stories as well as the books I've read," she said.

And so she read aloud to him, and with every new book what she read grew more interesting and exciting. One day Sarah brought along a book with peculiar arithmetical problems and ingenious number puzzles. From then on Salman took special pleasure in solving complicated calculations. Sarah was amazed at the speed with which he could do mental arithmetic, and as a reward she gave him three kisses on his forehead and one on his lips that day.

Salman was especially fascinated by a book about the earth, and he patiently practised tracing the course of the great rivers of the world, and could soon place many countries precisely where they should be on the map. It was only reading aloud that gave him trouble. He went too fast, overlooking letters and sometimes whole words. Sarah stroked his head and whispered, "Slowly, take it slowly. We're not on the run."

It was a whole year before he could read aloud without making mistakes, putting the right emphasis on the words. Sarah was delighted with her own success as a teacher, and sat with him almost every day.

They made a remarkable couple, an image of calm and beauty.

Sometimes the neighbours made fun of them, and Samira in particular said she could just see them as a bridal couple. That annoyed Sarah's mother, who told her off in no uncertain terms. "And don't forget, my husband's in the police!" Faizeh finally warned her, marching off to her apartment in front of all the neighbours who were sitting outside that day, her head held high. After that they were left alone.

Sarah went on leading Salman into distant lands and introducing him to foreign people. She taught him for years on end without any breaks for a holiday, sometimes mercilessly. She gave him the last lesson just before her wedding. They laughed a lot that day. When she had discussed the closing pages of Guy de Maupassant's novel *Strong as Death* with Salman, she said, "I've been expecting to bore you rigid all these years." Salman said nothing. He had no words to express his gratitude.

Sarah had everything ready. She gave Salman a certificate that she had designed for him. "Salman is my star pupil," it said in Arabic and French. It was dated and signed, and the three red, green, and blue marks stamped on it made the document look official. But Salman recognized the police station stamp that Sarah's father had brought home. "They make it look like something to do with prison," he said, laughing.

However, that was not until nine years later. Let us go back to the summer of the year 1948, when Salman had just left school.

When the weather grew warmer, Salman often took the dog for long walks in the fields in the afternoons by himself, because Benjamin usually worked at the falafel stall at that time of day. The dog loved jumping in the little river and running after sticks.

Pilot ate everything that Salman put in front of him, and understood every word he said. He would stay in the yard even without a chain when his master said goodbye to him. He whined quietly, a heartrending sound, but he did not move from the spot if Salman told him to stay.

One August day the dog chased two big farmer's boys away when they attacked Salman on his walk. They were strong lads, and thought they would have a bit of fun with this weedy city boy. They didn't see the dog until he jumped out of the water, anxious about his screaming master. Salman's cheeks glowed with pride. That day he gave his protector a big bowl full of bits of meat, let him eat it at his leisure, and then went home to Grace and Favour Yard.

"We can sleep peacefully in our hiding place tonight," he said.

"But there's no point in it. He'll come to fetch me in the night," replied his mother.

"No one will fetch you. Pilot can deal with two men like Father at once," said Salman, and he would not give up until his mother agreed to go back to their hiding place with him. She was amazed to see how handsome and powerful the black dog had grown. And when Salman told her about the two farmer's boys, running away with the seats of their trousers torn and shouting out magic charms which they hoped might protect them from the dog, she even laughed.

"The dog doesn't understand Arabic," said his mother.

They ate bread and olives and drank tea, and then they lay down to sleep. Years later, Salman still used to say that no olives had ever again tasted as good as those.

He woke up when he heard his father's first desperate cries from down below. Salman went downstairs with a candle. His father was lying face down in the corridor, whimpering with fear, and the dog was standing over him in the attitude of a victor.

"Don't you ever come here again," shouted Salman, calling the dog off. He had never before seen his father stagger away at such speed. Only his curses still hung in the air behind him.

But before a year was up the weaver's heirs had come to an agreement, and they sold the house to the Church for a good sum of money. A modern Catholic old people's home was soon to be built on the site, very close to the chapel of St Boulos.

However, the dog couldn't go to live in Grace and Favour Yard. Not only was his father against it, so were most of the neighbours, saying that they'd be scared for their children. It was no good for Sarah and Salman to show them all how fond of children Pilot was. Samira, who never stopped talking, led the campaign against the dog. "Samira's afraid he'll tear all the men who visit her by night to pieces," said Sarah.

"What men?" asked Salman.

"It's not a suitable subject for little boys," replied Sarah, looking into the distance with a meaning expression.

Sarah found a place to hide Pilot in the ruins of a former paper factory near the East Gate. It was a deserted watchman's hut over-grown with ivy, and had stayed in good condition. The dog lived there until his mysterious disappearance seven years later. But many important things happened in Salman's life before that, and the story should turn to them first.

When Sarah wasn't reading to him, his mother didn't need him, he wasn't out with his dog and there were no odd jobs for him to do, Salman played in the alley. Over ten boys used to meet there every day. He joined them, but never pushed his way into the middle of the group, and never really became one of them.

Five of them also lived in Grace and Favour Yard, and were just as poor as he was, but as soon as they were playing in the alley with their friends, who always looked cleaner and better-fed, they acted as if he, Salman, was the only one from Grace and Favour Yard. His jug ears were the particular target of their witticisms. Adnan, Samira's son, told a nasty story of how he came to have them. "The midwife was in a hurry, but Salman refused to come into the world. He was shit-scared of life. So the midwife just grabbed his ears and pulled until he popped out." He laughed unpleasantly, infecting the others.

Later, Adnan took to calling him "the madwoman's son." Salman was deeply horrified. His mother wasn't mad, she was sick. Very sick. But how could he explain that to this rough boy?

The word "bastard" was on the tip of his tongue, but his fear sent it back into his mouth, and he swallowed hard. Adnan was big and strong.

Later, he couldn't remember how old he was when he first began cooking, but it must have been in the year when he and his mother finally moved out of the weaver's house. Faizeh realized that Mariam was too confused to be allowed into the kitchen on her own safely. So now Faizeh cooked both for her own family and her friend's. Sarah helped, and one day Salman joined in.

"Teach me to cook," he asked Faizeh, but she laughed and sent him out to the others in the alley. "You should be playing with the boys. The kitchen is no place for men," she said. There was nothing to be done about that, so he began surreptitiously watching her, noticing how she washed rice, cooked noodles, peeled onions, crushed garlic, and broke up mutton bones to extract the delicious marrow. Before a year was up he could prepare several simple dishes. Faizeh and Sarah enjoyed them. As for his father, after five years he still didn't notice that his wife wasn't cooking for him. But when her health went from bad to worse he stopped shouting at her and beating her. Once, when Salman was pretending to be asleep, he saw his father caress his mother's head and sing something to her quietly.

"Your family is all topsy-turvy, the woman lies in bed and the man does the cleaning," said their neighbour Maroun, who lived with his wife and ten children in two tiny rooms opposite, when he saw Salman cleaning the windows of the apartment.

"Maroun's eyes are asleep," Sarah whispered to Salman as their neighbour walked on, "but his ass makes music all night long. I can hear it all the way to my own mattress," she added in a low and conspiratorial tone. Maroun was a pathetic failure who took the tickets in the Aida Cinema, a place that had once seen better days, but was now dilapidated and showed nothing but old movies. It cost only twenty piastres to get in, and you could have guessed it from the auditorium and the screen. Salman had heard quite enough about this insalubrious place to know that he never wanted to set foot in it. The cinema was full of men trying to grab boys' behinds, and a bunch of hungry, quarrelsome characters who were often drunk. Maroun sometimes came home with a black eye or a torn jacket. His wife Madiha was an intelligent and beautiful little woman. She used to tell him, every day, about the men she could have married if she hadn't made the mistake of her life by listening to him in the first place.

"Not that she seems to have learnt anything from her mistake," said Sarah dryly. Madiha had a baby every year around Easter. But none of the children had so much as a glimmer of their mother's beauty and brains. They all looked at you with copies of their father's stupid face when he stood abstractedly taking tickets at the entrance to the cinema, tearing off one part and handing the rest of the ticket back to the cinema-goer without even looking at him. The children were famished. "They aren't just starving, they're starvation itself," said Faizeh, Sarah's mother.

Salman was desperately looking for work. He had a long day, because Sarah didn't come home from her own full-time school until the afternoon. And his ever-empty pockets troubled him more than boredom. His father gave their neighbour Faizeh only exactly as much money as she needed to buy the food.

And Salman was also looking for a job because he wanted to get away from his father, who was treating his mother rather better now but treated him worse. He never wanted to set eyes again on that large, dirty man with his dark and usually unshaven face. Or hear him shouting, "Get up, you lazy omen of bad luck!" Or feel the kicks he got if he was so sleepy that he didn't understand how serious the situation was at once.

Salman envied the neighbours' children who were seen off to school every morning by their parents and other relations with a singsong in all musical registers, and in his heart he responded to every greeting that he heard in the Yard. But he was also sorry for them, because they still had to go to St Nicholas's. Only one of them didn't, and Salman admired him because he already had a job, and everyone treated him respectfully, like an adult. That was Said.

Said was an orphan. Since his parents' death in a bus accident, he had been living with the old widow Lucia. She had a small apartment right opposite the gateway between the baker's journeyman Barakat and the big communal kitchen. The widow took in Said because she was childless, and the Catholic church would pay for him. His father had been caretaker in the top Catholic school for decades. It was close to St Nicholas's, and was reserved for the sons of rich Christians.

Said was the same age as Salman, as pretty as Barakat's daughters, and slightly simple like Maroun's children. After his parents' death when he was in the fourth class, he didn't want to spend another day at school. He worked as an attendant in a hammam near Bab Tuma. He had no pay, but he passed on to his foster mother the few piastres he got as tips because the men were pleased with him, and she too was pleased with him.

When Salman asked Said to ask his boss whether they could do with another boy in the hammam, Said seemed as surprised as if this was the first time he had heard that question. It was a year before

Said told him that the boss would see him. That day Salman rubbed his pale cheeks with pumice until they were almost bleeding. Sarah watched him washing and combing his hair in the kitchen.

"Getting married today?" she asked.

"No, the manager of the baths wants to look at me. I don't want him thinking I'm sick," he laughed.

"Are you scared?" she asked. Salman nodded.

In fact the hammam manager, in his undershirt and with a towel around his waist, did look as fearsome as a samurai warrior. He examined Salman, and then shook his head. "You said you had a good strong friend," he told Said. "This one's a toothpick. If my customers see him they'll think we're a hospital for hopeless cases."

8

"Arabi," Noura's grandmother told her, "is my husband's surname, and therefore your father's too, but my first name is Karima, so if you mean me just say Granny Karima, not Granny Arabi. And do you know what my name means, little one?" Noura shook her head.

"Karima means noble, valuable, generous. And a woman should be generous above all. Men like that, because they're rather anxious and are always expecting famine. I learned to be generous very early, so you can ask me for anything you like and I'll give it to you – even if you want sparrow's milk," she said, and she went on making a brightly coloured paper kite.

When Noura asked her father what sparrow's milk tasted like, he laughed and said that was one of his mother's many inventions, and she should try it some time.

Noura's mother, on the other hand, was furious. "What's all this nonsense your mother talks? Sparrows lay eggs, they don't give milk. Putting such notions in the girl's head will ruin her," she said, rolling her eyes.

So next time she visited, Noura asked for sparrow's milk. Her grandmother disappeared into the kitchen and came back with a glass of milk the colour of lilac. "That sparrow ate a lot of berries today," she said.

The alley where Granny Karima lived had an especially nice smell. The fragrance of newly baked bread kept streaming out of the bakery not far from her house. It was a small bakery, and it specialized in a particularly thin flatbread half a metre in diameter. The bread was cheap. Farmers and labourers bought it in large quantities. Noura's parents didn't like it. They said it tasted burnt and too salty.

But whenever Noura went to see her grandmother, Granny Karima went to fetch a large, fresh flatbread, and they ate it without putting anything on it as they sat together at the big table. Grandfather, watching, laughed at the two of them.

"As if we didn't have anything to eat," he protested, "you sit there like fakirs eating plain bread."

"A girl," said Noura's grandmother, "must learn to enjoy small pleasures at an early age. Men don't know how."

Noura wanted to visit Granny Karima as often as possible, but while she was still little she had to wait for her father to take her. Her mother seldom went to see her parents-in-law. Whenever Noura wanted to go, her mother had a migraine and asked her father to take Noura on his own.

Years later, Noura still remembered her grandmother in her little house. The inner courtyard was a rampant jungle of plants. The chairs and corner benches were positively hidden behind curtains of climbing jasmine and dwarf orange trees, oleanders, roses, hibiscus, and other flowers growing in pots on green-painted wooden stands. As soon as Noura arrived at her grandmother's, the old lady hurried to make her a wreath of flowering jasmine and put it on her head.

Her grandfather was a small, silent man, very old, who used to sit somewhere in this jungle, reading or saying his prayers. His face, with its big ears, was like her father's, and his voice was even thinner and pitched even higher.

Once she surprised her grandfather by reading the newspaper headlines aloud. "So you can read!" he said in amazement.

When exactly she had learnt to read she couldn't remember, but she could already read fluently when she went to first class in school at the age of seven.

Her grandmother made Noura a coloured paper kite every time she visited. Her kites were much prettier than the ones you could buy from Abdo the shopkeeper. She flew a kite every time she went out on an excursion, and was always surrounded by a cluster of boys begging her to let them hold the string and make the kite loop the loop in the air.

Her mother was horrified and upset, because kite-flying was a game for boys, not girls. Her father just laughed at that, but when she was ten he told her she must stop.

"You're a young lady now, and a lady doesn't need paper kites," he said.

But what Granny Karima loved even more passionately than growing flowers or constructing kites was making preserves. She didn't just make the apricot, plum, and quince preserves usual in Damascus, she made everything she could lay hands on into a purée: rose petals, sweet oranges, bitter oranges, herbs, grapes, figs, dates, apples, mirabelles, and cactus figs. "Preserves sweeten the tongue of friend and foe alike, so that they won't say so many sour things about you," she claimed.

One day Noura went looking for her grandfather to show him her new dress, but she couldn't find him anywhere. She suddenly remembered a remark made by her mother, who never touched any of Granny Karima's preserves, and had told their neighbour Badia that Granny was a witch, she even suspected her of making frogs, snakes, and spiders into preserves.

"Where's Grandfather?" asked Noura suspiciously. "You haven't made him into a preserve, have you?"

Her grandmother smiled. "No, he's gone on a long journey," she replied, hurrying into the kitchen. When Noura followed her, she saw that Granny was crying her eyes out. Even later she couldn't understand how Death had taken her grandfather away so quietly that she never noticed.

By the time Noura was ten at the latest, she had given up any hope of playing with the neighbouring children. They were all so innocent! But she couldn't have played with them anyway, because her mother was always calling to her to come in.

So she began taking an interest in books. And when her father came home from the mosque he read anything she liked aloud to her. Then, one day, he showed her how to write Arabic letters. He was amazed to find how quickly she learned to read and write. She devoured everything, and looked at all the pictures to be found in the books in her father's large library. One day she surprised him by reciting a poem in praise of the Creation that she had learnt by heart. He was so overwhelmed that he began to weep. "I always dreamed of having a child like you. God is gracious to me," he said, kissing her, and scratching her cheek with the stubble of his beard.

Until now, whenever Noura climbed up to the top of the house her mother had wailed, "What does a girl want with all these dusty books?" But when her husband called Noura's love of books "the grace of God," she didn't dare to make fun of it anymore.

Noura read aloud slowly and with expression. She relished the taste of the words on her tongue, hearing how every word she read had its own melody. As the years went by, she developed a sense of the way to speak each word to make it sound good, and if her father were to be believed, she could recite quotations from the Quran and poems better than a Class Five child even before she went to school.

Noura counted the summer days that still separated her from school, like a prisoner counting the last days before he gets the freedom he has longed for.

There were only a few girls' schools in Damascus at the time. The best were the Christian schools, and there was a very good one, run by nuns, not far from Noura's home. But her mother threatened to leave the house or kill herself if her daughter was sent to school with unbelievers. Her father lost his temper, there were tears and a good deal of noise, and in the end it was agreed that Noura would go to the best of the Muslim schools, a long way off in the Souk Saruya quarter.

The decision to send her to this school was made in August, and then came the greatest surprise of all. One day her father announced happily that his good and very devout friend Mahmoud Homsi had told him at the mosque that his own daughter Nadia was about to go to the good school in the Souk Saruya quarter, travelling there by tram.

Noura's mother almost fainted away. She shed tears and accused her husband of thoughtlessly risking his daughter's life, entrusting a delicate girl to that moving iron monster. Suppose someone abducted her because she was so beautiful?

"No one can abduct a tram, it always goes along the same tram-lines," said her father, "and the Number 72 has a stop in the main street only twenty-five paces from our door, and exactly the same distance from my friend Homsi's house."

Noura felt so lighthearted and happy that she could have flown through the air. That evening they went to the circumcision party being held by the rich Homsi family, where Noura was to meet her future schoolmate Nadia.

The house was full of guests, and Noura clung to her mother's hand. People she didn't know kept patting her head and cheeks. The only guests she did know were their plump neighbour Badia and her husband.

Nadia looked like a princess in her red velvet dress. She took Noura's hand and led her through the crowd to a corner where sweet cakes were piled up in great pyramids. "Help yourself, or the grown-ups will eat it all and leave only crumbs," she said, and took a dough-nut stuffed with pistachios off one of the pyramids.

Noura felt excited. She had never seen so many people and such a big house before. They were all cheerful, the mood was festive. That day was the first time that Noura had heard of the *tuhour* ritual cir-cumcision ceremony. Nadia explained that it would make her brother into a real, pure Muslim.

The tables groaned under the weight of all the delicious things to eat, as if the hosts were afraid their guests might die of starvation. The sight of those pyramids of sweet puff pastries filled with nuts and sprinkled with sugar soon made Noura feel hungry, but she was shy and didn't like to take anything, while Nadia stuffed herself with pastry after pastry.

Suddenly there was a sense of anticipation in the room, and several women whispered, "Here he comes, here he comes!" And Noura saw Salih the barber, who had his salon on the main street not far from Elias the confectioner's shop. He was a tall, thin man, always well shaved, with his hair oiled and combed back. He always wore a white coat, and had five canaries who chirruped in unison like a choir. Sometimes, when he had no customers, Noura saw him miming as if he were conducting them.

Mr Salih responded to the men's greeting with a dignified nod. Carrying a case in his right hand, he went to the far end of the inner courtyard, which had been decorated for the occasion. At that moment Noura saw the pale boy in brightly coloured clothes. Many of the children at the party were making their way over to him. He wasn't much older than her.

"You stay here," Noura heard her mother call as she and Nadia slipped through the crowd of grown-ups, who were keeping a respectful distance from each other, but she had already reached the front row.

A man, probably an uncle, told the circle of children to move further out so as not to disturb the barber at his work.

"Don't be afraid," said the barber. "I only want to see how big you are so that I can make you a shirt and trousers."

"Why would a barber make a shirt and trousers? Why not go to Dalia the seamstress?" Noura asked Nadia, who didn't hear her question. All her attention was on the man asked by the barber to measure the boy for his shoes. It was the man who had told the children to widen the circle around the boy and the barber. He came up behind the boy and took hold of his arms and legs, so that the child – who now began crying – couldn't move. The grown-ups started to sing, as if a choirmaster had given them a signal, clapping their hands at the same time. No one could hear the boy's cries for help. Only Noura heard him calling to his Mama.

The barber took a sharp knife out of his case. A boy standing next to Noura groaned and put his hands in front of his legs as if something there hurt, and he retreated to the back rows. Noura couldn't see what exactly was being cut, but Nadia's brother was crying pitifully. When she looked around, only she and another pale boy were still in the front row. Nadia too had retreated to the back of the crowd.

Now two women put a wreath of flowers on the boy's head and gave him some money, but he looked miserable all the same. Everyone applauded him. Noura stroked his hand as he was carried past her and up to a quieter room on the first floor. The boy looked at her with tired eyes, and a faint smile touched his mouth.

Noura's mother accompanied the two girls to school only on their first day. After that they went by tram on their own. Nadia always sat still, staring at the streets down which the tram took them without much interest, but to Noura it was like an almost daily adventure.

Nadia was a quiet, red-haired, rather plump girl. She didn't like either school or books. Even at the age of seven, what she wanted was to get married and have thirty children. She never wanted to play either. She thought all the games played by the girls in their neighbourhood and at school were childish. Noura, however, played whenever and wherever she could.

Besides skipping, there were other games that Noura particularly liked. One was hide and seek. It was her father's opinion that the first ever to play hide and seek had been Adam and Eve, when they hid from God after eating the forbidden fruit. When it was Noura's turn to hide, she imagined she was Eve, and whoever was looking for her was none other than God.

The other game that she liked had been invented by Hanan, a very clever girl in their class. Two schoolgirls stood facing each other, one defending women, the other defending men.

The first listed all that was bad, nasty, and masculine, and the second responded to everything she said with the feminine equivalent. They had to get the grammatical gender in Arabic of everything they said right.

"The Devil is male, and a coffin is masculine too," said the first.

"And sin is feminine, and so is the plague," replied the second.

"The ass is masculine, and so is a fart," said the first quietly, and the schoolgirls standing around giggled.

"And Hell is feminine, and so is a rat," replied the other. This went on until one of them made a mistake of gender or didn't reply fast enough. A third girl, acting as referee, had to decide on that. If the game went on for a long time, and neither was the winner, the referee would raise her hand palm upward to signal a change. This time the competitors had to concentrate on what was best, finest, and most noble about the two sexes.

"Heaven is masculine, and so is a star," said one girl.

"And virtue is feminine, and so is the sun," said the other, and so on, until one of them won or the referee raised her hand and turned it again to make them describe the two sexes in gloomier terms.

Nadia didn't think that was any fun. With difficulty, she made it to the end of the fifth year and then left school. She got fatter and fatter, and at the age of fifteen married her cousin, a lawyer, who was able to set up in a modern office with the dowry his rich father-in-law gave them. Nadia, so Noura heard from neighbours later, had no children, but that didn't make her husband divorce her, as was usual in such cases at the time. He loved her.

From the sixth class on, Noura went to school alone, and soon noticed that she wasn't even missing Nadia.

She liked the tram conductor in his fine grey uniform with his box of tickets. The inspector, who came once a week and asked to see the passengers' tickets, wore a dark blue uniform. He looked like a king, wearing gold rings on both hands, and for a long time Noura thought he was the owner of the tramline.

Two stops further on, an old gentleman in a black suit boarded the tram every day. He was over seventy and still a fine figure, tall and lean, always neatly and elegantly dressed, and he carried a handsome cane with a silver knob. Noura soon found out why neither the conductor nor the inspector ever made Baron Gregor buy a ticket. He was crazy. He firmly believed that he was going to find out one of Solomon's secrets, and when he knew that secret he would be king of the world. Until then, everyone had to call him Baron. He was an Armenian and had a wife, and a son who was already a famous goldsmith and watchmaker in Damascus.

The Baron walked around the city all day, handing out grand positions in the world he would rule one day, with his blessing, to the passersby and passengers he met. If someone pretending to respect him deeply bowed and called him "Your Excellency," the Baron smiled. "I'll make you governor of Egypt, and Libya into the bargain," he would say, patting the joker kindly on the shoulder. He could eat and drink for free in all the restaurants and cafés, and the tobacconists gave him the most expensive cigarettes. "For you, Baron, no need to pay, just remember my humble self when you crack that secret."

"I certainly will, my dear fellow. You can print the banknotes, and after work in the evening you can get a few more printed just for yourself."

Week after week, so Noura's father told her, the Baron's son would pay all his father's expenses, and he was so grateful and polite that many of the people who gave the old man their wares even asked for less than they were worth.

"He's mad, but he lives the kind of life others can only dream of, even if they toiled for it all their days," the conductor told a tram passenger one day when he was making fun of the Baron.

The Baron got out of the tram one stop away from Noura's school, after saying a majestic goodbye to everyone. The tram driver rang the bell twice in his honour, and the Baron would turn and wave. The pallor of his hand and the slow gesture made him look extremely dignified.

Sometimes Noura would ride all the way to the tram terminus and then back again to school just out of interest. The conductor turned a blind eye. "Oh, we forgot to ring for your stop," he would say, and she smiled, with her heart thumping. She explored parts of the city that her mother didn't know at all, but she couldn't tell her about them, because her mother always expected the worst, so she was waiting anxiously to collect her from the tram stop every day when she came home.

That went on from Noura's first day at school to her last.

As an example of Arabic architecture, Noura's school in the elegant Souk Saruya quarter was a true work of art, a fantastic structure with an inner courtyard and a magnificent fountain in the middle of it. The windows had stained glass borders, and arcades gave the pupils shelter from the blazing sun during breaks as well as from rain. About two hundred schoolgirls were educated here from Class One to Class Nine.

Soon after Noura had passed her middle school certificate exam, the building was torn down and a tasteless modern one put up instead, with premises for several shops and a large warehouse for domestic electrical items.

There were eighteen schoolgirls in Noura's class. Each girl was a world in herself, but they stuck together like sisters. At school, Noura discovered that she had a beautiful singing voice. She liked singing, and sang a great deal, and even her mother enjoyed listening to her.

Her father admired her voice, and spent years training her to breathe properly. He himself couldn't sing at all, but he was a master of the art of breath control.

Noura's favourite lesson, however, was religious instruction.

Not just because the teacher was a young sheikh, a student of her father's, and one of those who revered him most, but also because he was a very handsome man. He admired Noura's voice, so he was always asking her to recite texts from the Quran. She put her whole heart into it when she sang the verses, making many of the girls shed tears. He would stroke her head gratefully, and his touch went through her like lightning. She was all aflame. Soon she realized that she wasn't the only one; all the girls in her class were in love with the young sheikh.

Years later, Noura still had happy memories of her schooldays, apart from one bitter experience. She was the best in all subjects in Class Seven, except for mathematics, where she had problems. She did not like the new math teacher Sadati at all, and geometry was in the nature of a medium-sized disaster to her. The simplest calculations of the angles and sides of triangles turned into a maze through which she could never find her way. The whole class was bad at math, but to Noura the subject was like sweating in a hot bathhouse with her heart thudding.

So what was bound to happen did: one day the teacher was in a bad temper for some reason, and called her up to the board to give clear examples of all the rules of geometry that they had learnt so far. Noura fervently wished he would catch the plague while she herself died on the spot.

She didn't say a word until the bamboo cane went whistling through the air and the first blow struck her hand. Her heart stood still. More blows followed, on her legs and her back, until she realized that she was supposed to keep her hand held out, palm upward. She didn't feel the blows of the cane raining down on her. Through her blur of tears, she saw the whole class sitting there as if turned to stone. Some of the girls were crying and asking the teacher to stop, but he didn't until he was out of breath.

At home Noura's mother scolded her, but her father stood up for her. Sadati was a donkey, he said, not a teacher. He knew him, his father, and his uncle, and they were a whole herd of donkeys. Noura heaved a sigh of relief.

"I hate him," she told her father. "I hate him…"

"No, my child," said her father calmly. "God does not like those who hate, he protects only the loving with his boundless grace. You should feel sorry for Sadati and his underdeveloped brain. He chose the wrong profession, and that's bad enough for him."

A year later the teacher suddenly disappeared. He had lost his temper with a girl in Class Six, never guessing that her father was an officer high up in the Secret Service. The Ministry of Culture moved the teacher to the south. It was a catastrophe for Sadati, because he hated the rural people of the south like poison.

Noura was only able to go to school until she had her middle school certificate; to take her higher school certificate she would have had to attend another school, and here her mother rebelled. Using tears and illness as her weapons, she forced Noura's father to submit, threatening to kill herself if she had to suffer the torments of anxiety for her daughter any longer.

What a woman needed in life was not book learning, she said, but a husband to give her children, and if Noura could sew and cook and bring up his children to be good Muslims, that was more than might be expected of her.

Her father gave in. That was the first time Noura's confidence in him faltered, and its foundations were shaken more and more until the day of her flight. Confidence is fragile as glass, and like glass it cannot be repaired.

Her mother liked the idea that Noura could be a dressmaker, so when she was fifteen she sent her to train with the dressmaker Dalia whose house was in Rose Alley, in the same quarter.

At almost the same time, a new family moved into the next house but one. The old owner had died two years earlier, and his widow sold the house and moved away to live with a niece in the north. The new owner was employed by the electricity works. He had a small, very friendly wife, and four sons who brought a great deal of laughter to the alley, because they often used to stand outside their front door cracking jokes. They were Muslims, but they were happy to play with the Christians, and got on well with them. They were very polite to Noura from the first, and she felt that she liked them. She laughed with them, and liked to listen to their adventurous stories about Africa. They had lived in Uganda for years, and when their mother's health suffered there her husband had given notice, left his lucrative job, and moved to Damascus. Since the day their mother set foot on Damascene soil she hadn't had a day's illness.

Noura particularly liked Mourad, the second eldest son. He always smelled very good, and when he laughed Noura longed for him to embrace her.

Six months later, he confessed that he had fallen in love with her on the very first day they met. Mourad was four or five years older than Noura. He was almost as handsome as Tamim, and for the first time in a long while she felt her heart dancing at the sight of a young man again.

Once, when her parents were out, she ventured to meet him inside her door. Noura put two onions in a paper bag so that if her parents unexpectedly came home early, Mourad could take the onions, saying he had come to borrow them, thank her politely and leave. They could hear every sound out in the street from the dark corridor. They were both trembling with excitement when Noura felt a long kiss on her lips for the first time. Mourad was experienced. He touched her breasts, too, and assured her at the same time that he wasn't going to do anything immoral with her.

"A woman may not do that before her wedding," he said. She thought that was absurd, and laughed.

Next time they met, he undid her housedress and sucked her nipples. She felt gooseflesh, and could hardly keep on her feet. He kept whispering, "Don't be afraid, it's perfectly innocent."

Once he asked if she loved him and would wait for him until he had finished his training as a barber. Then he would marry her and open a barber's salon here in this part of the city. "A super-modern salon," he emphasized.

The question horrified her. She was not just ready to wait, she assured him, she would die for him. He laughed, and said that sounded like an Egyptian film, one of those tearjerkers. She'd do better to stay alive and turn down the next proposal of marriage. She was so beautiful, he said, and beauty like hers lasted a long time.

How, she wondered, could she convince him of her boundless love? She would come to him at night, she told him, she was ready to run any risk.

He didn't believe her. She mustn't show off, he said in paternal tones.

That hurt Noura's feelings. "Tonight, when the church clock strikes one, I'll be on the roof of your house," she said.

He told her she was a crazy girl, but if she did come, he would make love to her up there on the flat roof.

"I'm not crazy," she said. "I love you."

It wasn't difficult; there was only a narrow gap to cross. The air was cold, but she felt an inner warmth, and longed to press close to him.

He wasn't there. She couldn't understand it. After all, he had only to come upstairs from the first floor, where his bedroom was, to reach his own rooftop. She waited beside the dark-painted containers in which water warmed up in the blazing sun by day. She huddled by the warm containers and waited.

Mourad didn't come. Time crept by. And every quarter of an hour that passed, with the bell striking once in farewell to it, seemed to her like an eternity.

Only when the church clock struck two did she get to her feet. Her knees hurt and her hands were freezing. There was a strong, icy cold wind that March night. She saw Mourad's outline at the window of his bedroom. He waved, and she thought he was waving to her, her heart longed to go to him, but then she realized that his wave merely meant she should go away. Oppressive darkness suddenly fell on her. Her bare feet felt heavier than lead. She went slowly back over the roof, and was suddenly facing the huge abyss separating her from the flat roof of her own house. She looked down. Somewhere in the far depths of the courtyard the faint light of a lamp flickered.

She began crying, and wanted to jump, but she was paralysed with fear.

She was found next morning, a picture of misery, and taken home. Her mother began wailing out loud. "What will people think of us, child? What will people think of us?"

She wept and wailed until Noura's father growled at her, "Oh, stop that whining! What are people supposed to think if a girl has a fever and goes walking in her sleep?"

"Whatever the reason was, your daughter ought to have a good strong husband to take care of her as soon as possible," said her mother. Her father pointed out that Noura was too young, but when her mother said that he hadn't thought she was too young to marry him at the age of seventeen, he agreed.

Two weeks later, Noura saw Mourad again. He was pale, and smiled at her. But when he asked if he could come round and borrow a couple of onions for his mother, she simply spat at him contemptuously. "You're crazy," he said, startled. "Crazy, that's what you are."

9

Years later, Salman could still remember every detail of that morning. It was just before Easter. Benjamin brought them two falafel rolls that morning, as usual, and for the first time he also brought cigarettes with him. They walked Pilot to the river, where Benjamin lit the first cigarette, drew deeply on it a couple of times, coughed and spat, and passed the cigarette to Salman. Salman too drew in the smoke and coughed until his eyes were popping out of his head. He felt as if his insides were trying to come up. Pilot looked at him distrustfully and whined.

"No, I don't like this. It smells like my father," he said, giving the cigarette back to his friend.

"How will you ever get to be a man, then?" asked Benjamin.

"I don't know, but I don't want to smoke anyway," replied Salman, and he went on coughing. He picked up a small branch lying on the ground and threw it into the river, to give Pilot something else to think about.

Benjamin was in a particularly bad temper that day, because he had discovered in the morning that his childhood was over. He was soon to marry his cousin. Benjamin hated that cousin, but she had inherited a lot of money and his father wanted to pay off his debts at long last.

Salman didn't know anything about that, though. All he knew was that Benjamin was in a prickly mood and kept urging him to smoke. When he said no, Benjamin raised his voice, and said in venomous tones, "I can't stand boys who won't join in. They tell tales. You wouldn't join in the wanking competition last week, and now you won't smoke. You're a coward, a stinky little fart." Salman was near tears, for he felt that he was losing his only friend.

At that moment he heard Pilot barking frantically.

The river was running high that spring, its small channel had changed into a racing torrent overflowing its banks and sweeping away countless trees and huts, and it had destroyed a bridge near the Abbani family's big apricot orchards.

Salman jumped up anxiously, and saw Pilot desperately trying to reach the bank. He was holding the arm of a drowning man in his jaws, swimming sideways to avoid the strong current. But doing that took him further and further away. Salman shouted to Benjamin and ran. Beyond the broken bridge, Pilot was just dragging a small, unconscious figure up on land. When Salman arrived, the dog was standing in shallow water wagging his tail. The man lay on his back. He seemed to have injured his head.

"Come on, help me," Salman shouted to Benjamin, who had stopped some way off and was watching the scene.

"Let's get out of here. The man's dead, and that'll mean trouble for us," Benjamin shouted back.

Salman felt rage rising in him. "Help me, you idiot. He's still alive!" he desperately shouted. Pilot was leaping around him and barking, as if he too were calling Benjamin to help, but by now Benjamin had disappeared without a trace among the dense foliage of the weeping willows whose branches hung down to the water like a green curtain.

Those were the last words that Salman exchanged with Benjamin. Later, bitterly disappointed, he avoided meeting him, and all he knew was that Benjamin had married his cousin and moved to Baghdad with her. But that was two or three years later.

So Salman got the man onto dry land on his own and tried to revive him. He thumped him on the chest and slapped his cheeks. Suddenly the man opened his eyes and coughed. He looked at Salman and Pilot, bewildered. "Where am I? Who are you?"

"You were in the river and the dog rescued you. He's a wonderful swimmer," said Salman with enthusiasm. "You almost drowned."

"Just my luck. They caught me and were going to kill me."

Years later Karam – that was the name of the man they had saved – was still telling guests in his café that he had lived two lives: he owed the first to his mother and the second to Salman and Pilot.

From that day on Salman worked seven days a week for Karam,

who owned a beautiful little café in the elegant Souk Saruya quarter.

Karam never said why he had been knocked unconscious and thrown into the river. It was from one of the waiters in the café that Salman heard it had had to do with an affair.

"That means," said Sarah, who seemed to know everything, "that there was a woman involved, and several men who didn't like it that the man you saved got into bed with her."

"Why would they get into bed?" asked Salman.

"Oh no, don't say you have no idea what men and women do together in the dark," said Sarah, exasperated.

"You mean they made love, and that's why Karam was thrown into the water?"

Sarah nodded.

Salman couldn't sleep all night. Why would a man risk his life to make love to a woman?

He couldn't imagine.

When, worried that his good luck might not hold, he asked Karam whether he was going to meet the woman again, Karam looked at him blankly.

"Woman? What woman?"

"The one they threw you into the water about," said Salman, suddenly fearing that Sarah might have been wrong.

Karam gave an odd laugh. "Oh, her. No, I'll never see her again," he said, but Salman could tell from his voice that he was just covering up for a lie.

Only a year later was he to know the real circumstances, and with them the certainty that this time Sarah really had been wrong.

The café had become his second home. He was paid no wages, but there were plenty of tips, and at the end of the day they came to more than the wages that his father earned as a master locksmith. He often got a tip when he was delivering orders to the grand houses in the neighbourhood: refreshing drinks, small dishes, everything you could need to fill a small gap or serve to guests who had arrived unannounced – and in Damascus guests seldom said they were coming in advance.

The café's other two errand boys didn't like Salman. The elder of them was called Samih, and he was an embittered, wrinkled little midget. Darwish, the younger, was elegant, always clean-shaven and with his hair well combed. He had a placid nature, a smooth way of walking, and a woman's soft voice. It was some time before Salman realized that Darwish seemed friendly as a nun but was really as venomous as a cobra. Samih used to say that if you gave Darwish your hand, you'd better check that you still had all your fingers afterward.

His two colleagues now had to share delivering orders in the neighbourhood and waiting at tables in the café with Salman. But they couldn't do anything about it, because they knew how fond their employer was of this bony young man with the big ears. They had their own ideas about why their boss treated the boy so kindly, but kept them to themselves, because they knew how merciless Karam could be.

But neither of them stopped pestering Salman and setting traps for him, so that he wouldn't be the one serving the better sort of customers, the ones who gave good tips – not until Salman left the café in the autumn of 1955.

That didn't matter to Salman himself, because since he was courtesy itself and very friendly, all the guests liked him well enough for even the stingiest of misers to soften and give him a tip.

What particularly annoyed his two colleagues, however, was the privilege given to Salman, after only a week, of going to Karam's home. Once or twice a week, his boss would tell him to go shopping for him and take what he had bought to his house.

Karam lived in a green district near Mount Qasioun, which rose above Damascus to the northwest of the city. Well-tended gardens full of fruit, myrtle bushes, and cactus figs surrounded the few houses. Karam's house was not far from Khorshid Square, also known as Terminus Square because the tramline stopped there.

Apple, apricot, and myrtle trees filled half of Karam's garden; cactus figs and roses formed a dense screen along the fence; and even in the house you could hear the splashing of the river Yassid, from which Karam could draw all the water he wanted with a large hand pump. He had inherited the house with its luxuriant garden from his childless aunt, and he lived there alone.

From the garden gate, you went down a narrow path bordered by oleander bushes and then up three steps to reach the entrance to the house. Its wooden front door was a masterpiece of Damascene craftsmanship.

A dark corridor divided the house in two, leading to the bedroom at the far end. A large kitchen and a tiny bathroom lay on the right-hand side. On the left-hand side were the spacious living room, and a bright room with a window looking out into the garden.

The bedroom at the end of the corridor had no windows. It always smelled a little musty in there, and Karam's attempts to cover up the smell with assorted *eaux de toilette* only made it worse. But anyway Karam didn't like anyone to enter that room.

This was strange to Salman. In his parents' apartment you washed, cooked, lived and slept in either of the two rooms.

"My bedroom is my temple," Karam had once said. And it did sometimes smell of incense. The older waiter in the café, Samih, said it wasn't incense, it was hashish, and Karam smoked large quantities of it at night.

One day, when Salman had been shopping for Karam, took his purchases home, and found himself there on his own, curiosity drove him to the bedroom. A large dark wood double bedstead occupied the centre of the otherwise very ordinary room. But above the bed Karam had put up a little altar with photographs. When Salman switched the light on, he saw that the photos all showed the same person: Badri, the barber and body-builder, who often came to the café and needed a whole table to himself just to accommodate his muscles.

Badri appeared in all imaginable poses in the photos, grinning and exaggeratedly grave, fully dressed or in nothing but bathing trunks, with and without a silver cup in his hand. The muscleman trained hard every day at a body-building club, and was always showing off his figure. His chest, arms and legs were shaved as smooth as a woman's. His skin was tanned, and he had a stupid expression on his face.

Salman had lessons from Sarah every day. After that he took Pilot the scraps of meat he bought cheap at the butcher's, and played with him in the deserted paper factory until they were both exhausted.

Salman always gave Faizeh money to cook his mother something really good to eat, because what his father paid was only just enough to keep her from starving. Sarah kept any money Salman had left over in a safe hiding place for him. He could depend on her, but she wanted a large pistachio ice once a month for looking after his money. She called it her interest. It was years before Salman was able to make sense of that and convert the deal into bank charges. But he was happy to buy her the pistachio ice, not just because he loved Sarah and her mother but also because he had no safe hiding place at home.

After almost two years Salman had saved enough money to give his mother a surprise. Ever since his early childhood she had been in the silly habit of telling him, just before Easter, "Come along, Salman, we're going to buy new clothes for Easter like the high society people do."

When he was still little he fell for it. He thought his father must have given her some money. He washed his face, combed his hair, and went off with her to the Souk al-Hamidiyyeh, which was full of shops displaying fine clothes in their windows.

Salman was glad, because he had worn his shoes all winter, their soles were giving way and had holes in them, and the uppers were hard as bone. Poor people's shoes, said Mahmoud, the errand boy from the nearby bakery, were designed to be instruments of torture so that the poor would do penance for their sins and go straight to heaven when they died. And he tapped his own shoes, which left bleeding blisters on his feet. The leather sounded like wood.

Year after year, Salman's longing for a better pair of shoes made him hopeful. He walked through the souk with his mother, who would stop in front of the colourful display windows, seemed to forget herself entirely at the sight of a dress, made little noises of delight, and when she saw a boy's suit or a pair of shoes she would look Salman up and down as if taking his measurements, or wondering whether the colour would be right for him, only to move on again. After an hour Salman was tired of this.

"Mother, when are we going in?"

"Going in? What for?"

"To buy shoes for me and a dress for you."

"Oh, child, where would I get the money?"

He looked at her, horrified. "Don't look so silly," she said with an innocent expression, "just look at the clothes and shoes and imagine how you'd feel walking around in those wonderful things." And then she would walk quickly on through the market.

A week before Easter this year, Salman invited his mother to go to the Souk al-Hamidiyyeh, and she laughed a lot on the way here. Then she saw a beautiful dress in a shop window, and Salman asked her casually whether she liked it. She looked at him, her gaze transfigured, and said, "Do I like it? I'd be a princess in that dress," she said.

"Then it's yours. You must try it on and haggle with the shopkeeper first. I have the money," said Salman boldly, although his voice almost failed him.

"Aren't you joking?" asked his mother, uncertainly.

Salman took his hand out of his trouser pocket. His mother was amazed when she saw two blue hundred lira banknotes and several ten lira notes. "I've been saving up so that you can be a princess at last," he said. "And you must buy yourself shoes today, and I want a new pair of trousers, a shirt and a pair of patent leather shoes. I've worked it all out. If we drive a good bargain it will come to between a hundred and ninety and two hundred lira," he added.

In spite of her frailty, his mother was an excellent haggler. That evening they went home heavily laden, and Salman still had thirty lira in his pocket. He had brought back a pair of white socks for Sarah as well. Sarah laughed herself silly, because the socks were three sizes too big. She gave them to her mother.

Salman took time off at Easter and went to early Mass with his mother. She walked proudly up the nave of the church, and sat down in the front pew, just like a princess. She really did look enchanting. When she went up to take communion and the priest recognized her, his mouth dropped open. He forgot to say "This is the body of Christ" to Salman, who was following his mother, and stared in astonishment at the elegant apparition as she walked on.

At this hour Salman's father was sleeping off his hangover from the day before.

His mother's happiness lasted exactly three weeks, and then she caught a cold. As she did not take things easy, the cold turned into pneumonia. And when no herbal teas did any good, nor did compresses on her legs or to cool her forehead, Faizeh fetched the doctor. He was nice, but he wanted five lira in advance. Salman paid, but the medicine that the doctor prescribed was very expensive.

The neighbours, including Faizeh, recommended Salman not to listen to the doctor, saying that a few herbs would be enough. Salman was sure that only that medicine would save his mother. But now his savings with Sarah didn't cover the expense.

It was Monday, the quietest day at the coffeehouse, so his boss Karam didn't come to work that day. Samih, the older of his two colleagues, was at the cash desk, and when Salman asked him for an advance of twenty lira, Samih roared with laughter. "You can think yourself lucky if I give you twenty piastres. Do you know how much twenty lira come to? Two hundred cups of tea, or a hundred cups of coffee, or seventy-five hookah pipe smokes – you think I'll just hand you that much money? The boss would hang me and stick a notice on my chest saying 'Strung Up For Stupidity.'"

Darwish and Samih laughed so much that Salman left the café in annoyance. He knew where his boss lived, so he set off straight away.

The garden gate was ajar. Salman went through the garden, and as he reached the front door of the house he heard indistinct laughter in the distance. The door wasn't locked either, so he quietly went in. The sounds came from the bedroom.

Years later, Salman still remembered how he had felt his pulse thudding beneath his skull. He had often been to Karam's house, and he could come and go whenever he liked. So the place was not strange to him. He had also met Badri the barber there many times.

Now, as he stood in the corridor, he looked through the open bedroom door and saw the barber lying underneath his boss. In everyday life, Badri spoke broad Damascene dialect in a deep voice. But now he was pleading ecstatically, in the high tones of a film diva, for more of whatever Karam was doing to him. At that time Salman was nearly fourteen, but he didn't understand what was going on. His parched throat felt rough and dry as sandpaper. He slowly walked backwards to the door and left the house. Not until he was outside did he take a deep breath. It was beginning to dawn on him that the barber was playing the part of a woman in this game of love. Of course Salman had heard the word "gay" used in the street, but only as a term of abuse. He would never have thought there were men who made love to each other so tenderly.

Although he couldn't see himself, he knew he looked paler than usual. His cheeks were cold as ice. He crouched there outside the door until he heard the two men laughing and playing around in the bathroom. Only then did he stand up, bringing the knocker down on the door three times.

It was quite a while before Karam looked out through the spy hole in the door at Salman, inspecting him in alarm. "Is something wrong?" he asked, worried.

"No, no, but my mother is very sick. I need twenty lira urgently. She... she has dangerous pneumonia. I'll pay you back in instalments," said Salman, near tears.

"Wait here," replied Karam, and he disappeared into the house. Soon he came back, now wearing his new blue pyjamas, and gave Salman a twenty-lira banknote as well as five lira in coins. "Buy your mother some fruit with the five lira. That's a present from me, you only have to pay me back the twenty."

Salman could have kissed his hand, but Karam patted him briefly on the head. "Close the garden gate behind you," he said, disappearing into the house. Salman heard him double-locking the door on the inside.

After his mother had taken the medicine, she slept peacefully that night for the first time in a long while. But Salman tossed and turned in bed, unable to sleep. Why did his boss, who had money and a house, love a man instead of a woman? And a man who seemed to consist entirely of muscles at that, and thought of nothing but his oiled hair and his figure? Badri couldn't even move gracefully. When he picked up his coffee cup he did it as stiffly as if the cup weighed ten kilos.

When Salman described the love scene in the bedroom to his friend Sarah, she said, "Life's nothing but a carnival. In his heart the muscleman is a woman, but God was in such a hurry that he gave him a man's body." And when Salman stared at her, bewildered, she tried to explain it more precisely. "It's like in the hammam when the bath attendant hands you someone else's clothes." Sarah stopped for a minute. "Said is a woman in his heart as well," she added. "That's why all the men love him." She pointed to the handsome orphan Said, who had just come home from his work in the hammam.

"God got a few details mixed up," Sarah continued. "That's not surprising, when you think of all the billions of things he has to organize."

Sarah listed a dozen divine mistakes. Beside her, Salman felt very small, and he admired her. She was amazing. She went to the school run by nuns of the order based in Besançon, and she was top of her class. Salman often imagined her as a doctor in Africa in the future, or helping the American Indians. When he told her so, she laughed. "You're an idiot. The Africans and the American Indians can get on fine without me. I want to be a teacher, and get married and have twelve children, and I'll make sure that they grow up to be a butcher, a baker, a joiner, a locksmith, a barber, a cobbler, a tailor, a teacher, a policeman, a flower-seller, a doctor, and a pharmacist, and then I know I'll be looked after to the end of my days."

Sure enough, Sarah did become a teacher, one of the best in the country, and after a stormy love affair she married a bus driver who loved her to the last day of his life. As well as going on with her own career she brought up twelve children to be excellent craftsmen, teachers, and tradesmen. One of the girls among them became a doctor, another girl a lawyer, but none of the twelve wanted to be a butcher.

At that time Salman also found out that on the day when Pilot saved him from the river, half-drowned, his boss had been beaten up over a young man and not a woman. He had been going to meet the young man, but the boy's two brothers were there instead, lying in wait to murder him.

Darwish had had a long affair with his boss, but then Karam had broken it off, although he let him go on working in the café. However, Darwish still loved Karam, and suffered from their parting. He was married, and didn't like his wife, but all the same he had seven children with her.

Around this time Salman began to feel a little sympathy for Badri the muscleman, and he sometimes felt sorry for the woman inside him who had to carry so much muscle around.

Badri could not only pick Salman up with one hand, he could do it with his teeth. Salman had to lie on the floor and go rigid. Then Badri would get Salman's belt between his teeth and lift him. His neck swelled in the process to a mighty pyramid of muscles, with finger-thick veins standing out.

Badri often came into the café, but Karam acted as if he knew him only slightly. He had drinks served to him, and joked with him, but he always kept his distance. However, if you looked closely you could see that the two of them loved each other. Darwish saw that clearly, but it intrigued him that the man didn't come every day, and he always paid. So he suspected that Karam had fallen for the confectioner's assistant who came to the café daily to deliver the little delicacies offered by Karam along with other small dishes. Karam often cracked vulgar jokes with the plump assistant, who seemed to like the game, but it never went beyond cheerful teasing, tickling, hugging, and pinching.

Badri was rather stupid and fanatically religious. His was a danger-ous mixture of ignorance and certainty. It was only because Karam liked Salman that the muscleman would shake hands with him. "I've never given my hand to a Christian before," he boasted. "If a Chris-tian happens to stray into my salon, my assistant has to deal with him. And afterwards all the scissors and razors have to be boiled to get the smell of the unclean Christian off them."

"Take my word for it, that man lives in fear," said Sarah. "If the fanatics catch him they'll make mincemeat of him."

"Then they'll have rather a lot of mincemeat that day," said Salman. It just slipped out as he imagined the muscleman disappearing into a mincer, surrounded by a crowd of the bearded fanatics who went around Damascus denouncing immorality at this time.

"And you're getting sillier every day, working in that café," said Sarah, revolted. All her life she never ate meat.

Years later, Salman had to admit that Sarah was the first to realize, long before his boss, that although it brought him money, working in the café was getting him nowhere.

Sarah told Salman so in the summer of 1952, but he didn't leave the café until the autumn of 1953.

Later, when he looked back, his memory of those years in the café was vague. Only events involving one person stuck in his mind, and that person was Sarah. She went on teaching him almost every day. He had to write summaries of the novels he had read, and she commented critically on them later. She taught him algebra, geometry, biology, geography, physics, and a little French, a language that she herself could speak without a trace of accent.

Sarah had passed her higher school certificate with brilliant results, and she was now teaching small children while she studied for two years at teacher training college. After that she taught mathematics and French in an elite school. She was also in great demand as a private tutor for the children of rich Christians, but she accepted only the daughter of the Brazilian consul for a good sum of money per hour. She didn't want more private pupils; she wanted time to read a great many books and go on teaching her favourite student Salman.

Then she married the bus driver, a rather stout man with a bald patch who loved her more than anything in the world. And when her cousin Leila made snide remarks, saying she herself dreamed of an actor who lived nearby, and she wasn't going to marry anyway until love took her heart by storm and set it ablaze, Sarah who knew so much was exactly the person to give her a lecture for free. "Then you'll have to marry a fireman. Actors are knights and heartbreakers on screen, but in real life they fart and snore, they have pimples on their behinds and bad breath. I think stout men are very attractive, and best of all they have a good sense of humour. They laugh forty percent more than thin men. And if a stout man has a good heart he makes me feel like a queen."

Sarah's wedding was a great event. She had luck even with the weather. That February was dry, and as warm as if it had changed places with May. Sarah's bridegroom came from Homs. He was an orphan, so it made no difference to him where the wedding was held. Sarah's father, who knew how to organize a good celebration, wanted his daughter to be married in Damascus. Ten of his colleagues from the police force formed a guard of honour for his daughter at the church door, and Sarah walked past the men in their best uniforms like a princess as she entered the church.

Grace and Favour Yard celebrated the wedding for seven days as if all the people who lived there were Sarah's family. Salman was particularly surprised by the part Samira and her son Adnan played on this occasion. Adnan was now married, lived in Jews' Alley, and drove a taxi. They paid Sarah as much attention as if they had always loved her. Samira cooked for the guests, and Adnan acted as errand boy. Salman's mother Mariam also helped as far as she could. And everyone decorated the yard and bought drinks for the others. Shimon too was generous, providing crates full of vegetables and fruit.

The bridegroom was overjoyed. He had never before known anything like this wedding, and he marvelled at it for all seven days.

And if Salman's dog had not disappeared a week before the wedding, Salman too would have been happy. A nearby restaurant had given him some bones and meat for his dog, but when he went off to take them to Pilot all he found was some drops of blood and a tuft of his dog's black hair. What had happened? He hadn't said a word to Sarah about Pilot's disappearance so as not to spoil her pleasure in anticipating the wedding.

After the festivities, Sarah went with her husband to Homs, the beautiful city on the river Orontes. That was in March 1955. Sarah hugged Salman when they said goodbye, and whispered in his ear, "1955 is a lucky year for you and for me. I've married the man I love, and you will take your first step through the gateway of your own happiness this year too."

Grief for his sick mother and his lost dog stifled his voice. He just nodded, hugged Sarah tight, and thought of Pilot who, if he wasn't dead, must be even lonelier than he was himself.

It was to be years before Salman saw Pilot again, but that autumn he was to find out that Sarah really did know everything, even about the future.

10

"Aren't you rather overdoing things," the pharmacist asked his friend, "having your three wives living in streets so far away from each other?" Why, he wondered aloud, couldn't he accommodate them in separate parts of a large harem, as his grandfather and father had done before him?

"My wives can't be far enough away from each other. Otherwise they'd scratch each other's eyes out within an hour. Three oceans keeping them apart would be even better. Then I'd live on an island in the middle of the oceans. My compass," said the elegant guest, "would lead me unerringly to one of them every night."

"I'd be happy with three deserts between me and my wife," replied the pharmacist, "but we Christians can have only one wife until death parts us. Your Prophet was a playboy. Our Lord Jesus Christ was a revolutionary, and he had no idea about women."

"Are you sure? Maybe that's why he never married, even with women throwing themselves at his feet," replied the man in the white suit.

They were drinking coffee served to them by the pharmacist's plump assistant in her white coat. The pharmacist had a laboratory behind the shop, with a cooking niche and a refrigerator filled with ice cubes in it. He always kept a bottle of the best arak there. Now he stood up. "Drops for an inflammation of the eyes, was it? Who for?"

"I don't know," said Nasri Abbani, surprised.

"I have to know if they're for a child or an adult," said the pharmacist, dismissing his friend with a noncommittal handshake.

"I'll ask my wife. Do you have a telephone?"

"How would a poor pharmacist afford a telephone? My name's Elias Ashkar, not Nasri Bey Abbani."

"Very well, I'll find out today and let you know tomorrow," replied the elegant gentleman, leaving the pharmacy.

That's what comes of talk, he thought as he walked out. Lamia talks too much, and in the end no one knows what she really wants.

If only his father had married her, instead of urging him to do it. He, Nasri, had still been young and inexperienced at the time. It would be a good idea to put the brakes on his desire for women, as his father had expressed it. Lamia seemed just right; she was the daughter of a famous judge and smelled of books and ink more than sensuality.

She turned out to be opinionated to the nth degree. She could not refrain from commenting on anything he said, and never dreamt of agreeing with it. There had always been some Greek, Chinese, or Arab idiot who lived centuries ago and had proved the opposite of what he said. And if Lamia couldn't cite anyone else she presented her father as evidence for the truth of her own opinions.

He had never felt at home with Lamia as he did with his other wives, because the big house with the magnificent garden near the Italian hospital was a wedding present from her father. She always, without a second thought, called it "my house" and not "our house."

She was a killjoy who began yawning the moment he even touched her. "Your body's not covered with skin, it's all over light switches," he once told her angrily in bed. "As soon as I touch you the light goes out."

"That's a contrived metaphor without any wit or *esprit* in it," she said, yawning with tedium. She was terribly thin, she was flat-chested, and she was mad about reading. Nasri himself could make nothing of books. The newspaper was enough to show him that the world sickened him.

"A son with your good looks and her clever brain would be a godsend to the clan. He could be called after me," said Nasri's father as he left on the wedding night.

It didn't turn out that way. They had six children – but all girls, and all six girls took after their mother. That marriage had been his father's worst mistake. Nasri went to sleep with that thought in his mind every third evening at Lamia's house, after doing his duty. He was only ever happy there in the last months of her pregnancies, because then he wasn't allowed to touch her. He found it easy to go along with that ban.

It was Nasri Abbani's custom, after eating a light breakfast, to go first to a café, where he drank a cup of sweet coffee and read the newspaper, and then stroll through the souk. In passing, he left his orders with shopkeepers, giving the address of one his three wives, depending on which house he would be spending the coming night in. The vegetable sellers, fishmongers, spice dealers and confectioners, bakers and butchers conscientiously supplied what he wanted, and always delivered the best of everything, for Mr Abbani was well known for his generosity. He didn't haggle, he didn't sample the goods. He paid. And he never forgot to tip the errand boys generously.

Nasri Abbani always wore fine European suits, and as the weather was often hot in Damascus he owned more pale suits tailored from fine linen and Damascene silk than suits in dark English wool. He wore silk shirts and Italian shoes, and put a fresh carnation or rose in his buttonhole every day. Only the arabesque patterns on his ties gave an Oriental touch to his appearance. He also owned a large collection of walking sticks with silver or gold knobs.

He was always addressed as Nasri Bey. Bey and Pasha were Ottoman honorifics that had no real value in Damascus, being a relic of the past, but they gave the bearer an aura of noble descent, for the Ottoman Sultan had honoured only the noblemen close to him with that invisible but audible distinction.

Nasri Abbani was very proud, and despite the friendship all and sundry felt for him he hardly talked to anyone except the pharmacist Elias Ashkar, whose medical knowledge was far greater than any doctor's. Ashkar's modern pharmacy lay in the new Salihiyyeh quarter of Damascus, close to Nasri's office and not far from the house of his second wife Saideh, right next to the fashion house of the famous Albert Abirashed in busy King Fouad Street, a name which had been changed to Port Said Street after the Suez war of 1956. The change of name was intended to honour the resistance of the people of the Egyptian harbour town of Port Said to the English, French, and Israeli invasion. Nasri Abbani thought this reasoning ridiculous, and spoke of King Fouad Street to the end of his life.

Nasri Abbani visited the pharmacist almost every morning, and soon rumours spread that he was buying secret potions there to keep his boundless lust for women physically unimpaired.

Around ten in the morning – sometimes later but never earlier – Nasri Abbani arrived at his large office on the first floor of the magnificent modern building that was his own property. The ground floor was let to a large electrical items store and Air France. The second floor was the central office of the Persian carpet trade in Syria. These firms and businesses paid high rents, for King Fouad Street was the main artery of the modern city, with the best hotels and restaurants, bookshops, press agencies, import-export firms, cinemas, and expensive fashion stores that boasted of getting in *haute couture* from Paris for their shows. Nasri's first-floor office had two rooms, as well as a kitchen, a modern washroom, and a storeroom for the archives and stock. One of the rooms was large and light, with a window looking out on the street, and it was furnished like a sitting room. Two dark wood sofas upholstered in red velvet, a low coffee table, and several grand armchairs dominated the room, leaving only a small corner for a delicate table on which lay a desk pad and a telephone.

Going down a narrow corridor, you reached the second room, which was also large but had no windows, and seemed to consist only of desks and shelves full of files. This was where Nasri's colleague of many years' standing, Tawfiq, sat with two older clerks and three young assistants.

Tawfiq was no older than Nasri, but his thin form, stooped shoulders, and prematurely grey hair made him look as if he belonged to a different generation. Dark rings under his eyes showed exhaustion.

Nasri had inherited Tawfiq from his father, who was said to have told him, on his deathbed, "Your two brothers have good brains and you have Tawfiq. Pay attention to him, because if he leaves you'll go under."

Old Abbani, whose wealth was proverbial, retained his sharp eye for a man's qualities to the end. He was a manufacturer, real estate broker, and large landowner. It was said that every other apricot eaten by a Damascene came from his fields, and that all the products in the capital derived from apricots were made in his factories. He was also the largest dealer in apricot kernels, which were in great demand for making peach marzipan, oils, and aromatic substances.

At the age of fifteen, Tawfiq had gone to Abbani as an errand boy.

He was small and half-starved at the time, so he was teased by the warehouse workers who filled jute sacks with apricot kernels and sewed them up. But the experienced Abbani recognized Tawfiq as not just a mathematical genius but a young man with a razor-sharp mind and courage. Tawfiq had given evidence of that when he once contradicted Abbani, which no one else dared to do.

At the time old Abbani had been furious, in fact furious with himself, because without the objection raised by the pale young man he would have ruined himself over a stupid calculation. When he felt calmer, he went down to the warehouse to give the boy a lira as a reward. But Tawfiq was nowhere to be seen. When he asked about him, he found out that Mustafa, head of the warehouse, had beaten the boy to a jelly with a stick for being impertinent enough to correct the boss. All the rest of them, although of course they too had spotted the mistake, had kept their mouths shut out of respect. When Tawfiq was finally found and taken to the boss, Abbani said, "From now on we work together, my boy. And everyone here must show you respect, because you are now my first secretary." He added, to the rest of them, "Anyone who so much as gives him a nasty look is fired."

A few months later, Tawfiq had mastered all kinds of arithmetical calculations, including working out percentages and drawing up tables. He knew all the clever tricks to use in applying for exemption from duty, an art that old Abbani hadn't even tried to teach his two accountants in ten years.

From now on Tawfiq was treated like a son of the Abbani family. When he was eighteen, his patron arranged a good marriage for him with a well-to-do young widow from the village of Garamana south of Damascus. She was a good wife, and from that day on Tawfiq lived happily. Old Abbani had been a dispensation of Providence for him.

With time he became prosperous, and his wife bore him three children. He was as unassuming as ever, and spoke quietly and respectfully to everyone, even the errand boys. Out of gratitude to his patron, he stayed loyal to Abbani's spoilt son, who was more interested in women's underclothes than interest rates and property prices. Soon he became sole ruler of a small financial empire. As the years went by he also became fond of Nasri, who had absolute confidence in him and never accused him of making a mistake. Unlike his two close-fisted brothers, Nasri was generous. True, he knew little about business, but he did know a great deal about life, and like his father felt not the slightest respect for the powerful men whom he enjoyed wrapping around his little finger.

"God made everyone what he is," he said to himself and to others. You can't expect a champion boxer to be good at ballet.

Tawfiq stuck to his method of getting Abbani's agreement before doing any business deal. And Abbani always did agree, for he understood nothing about all the business done with apricots and the countless products derived from them. Nor did he take any interest in selling plots of land in order to buy others because, it was said, the most expensive quarter in Damascus was soon to be built where pomegranates, oleander bushes, and sugar cane now grew, the reason being that an embassy was giving up its magnificent residence in the Old Town and planned to move here.

"Do what you think right," said Nasri Abbani half-heartedly. And within two years the value of the land had multiplied by five.

But when Abbani, delighted by such profits, wanted to sell, Tawfiq dismissed the idea. "This is our moment to buy really large tracts of land. In another five years' time you'll get five hundred times the money."

"If you say so," said Nasri, although he was not really convinced. Five years later the plots in the new Abu Roummaneh district were indeed the most expensive in the city. Tawfiq worked out that they had made a profit of six hundred and fifty percent.

When Nasri arrived at the office in the morning, he would ask Tawfiq in friendly tones, "Any news?" And every morning Tawfiq replied, "I'll be coming in to see you right away, Nasri Bey." Then he would send an errand boy to fetch two coffees from the nearby café, one very sweet for his boss, one without sugar but with plenty of cardamom for himself.

Over their coffee, Tawfiq gave a brief and precise account of all developments in the business, well knowing that his boss soon got bored. In just seven minutes he could outline all the financial dealings of the firm, including exports, rents and repairs to the many buildings it owned, and all the new plots of land they had bought.

"Then that's all right," Abbani would say abstractedly, even if there had been a negative figure in this account for once.

After that he would talk to his friends on the telephone for an hour, and hardly a week went by when he didn't arrange to have lunch with one of the powerful men of Damascus in his favourite restaurant Al Malik, near the parliament building.

"I can smooth the way for us over lunch," he told his business manager, and he was not exaggerating. Nasri had charm, he knew the world and his fellow men, and he knew all the latest gossip. His guests were impressed. Of course they were never allowed to pay, only to enjoy themselves. The chef came from Aleppo, and if any cuisine could boast of aromas and delicious concoctions that outdid even the cookery of Damascus, then it was the cuisine of the largest city in northern Syria.

If there was no one for him to invite, he went out to lunch on his own. And only on such days did the restaurant proprietor venture to exchange a few words with his distinguished customer. Nasri Abbani did not like to eat lunch with any of his wives and their children; he ate with them in the evening.

After lunch Nasri would set out to visit his favourite whore Asmahan. She lived in a little house less than a hundred paces from the restaurant. Asmahan was glad to see him because he always came in the middle of the day, when none of her distinguished clients had time for her. Nasri joked with her, and she genuinely enjoyed his sense of humour and laughed until she cried. Then he made love to her, had half an hour's siesta, made love to her again, showered, paid, and left.

Sometimes, as he walked away, he thought that the young whore let him do as he liked too willingly, too mechanically, and he could have wished for a little more passion. Only years later was he to find out, by chance, what Asmahan's heart was capable of. But apart from that, she had everything he loved: a beautiful face with blue eyes and blonde hair, a bewitching body that could have been carved from marble, and a tongue that spoke only honeyed words.

The same could not have been said of any of his three wives.

11

One rainy January day in the year 1952, Nasri Abbani entered Hamid Farsi the calligrapher's studio. He was pleasantly surprised to find the place so neat and clean. He had never been to a calligrapher before, and had imagined he would meet an old man with a beard and dirty fingers. But here sat a slender young man, elegantly dressed, behind a small walnut desk. Nasri smiled, said good day, shook the water off his umbrella and put it in a corner beside the display window.

Suddenly it occurred to him that he should have come to the shop better prepared, for he had never ordered any calligraphy before. He looked around him. Beautiful examples of script hung everywhere, poems, maxims, verses from the Quran. But he did not see what he wanted.

"Do you take commissions to provide for special wishes?" asked Nasri.

"Of course, sir," replied the calligrapher quietly.

"And discreetly? This is about a present for a distinguished person."

"Yes, anything that is to be written in fine calligraphic script, as long as the wording does not offend God and his Prophet," said the calligrapher, giving a routine reply. At this point he already knew that he could ask whatever price he liked of this prosperous man who smelled so fragrant.

"It's a maxim for the president of our state," said Nasri, fishing out of his pocket a note on which Tawfiq had written: "For His Excellency Adib Shishakli! Lead our nation on to victory."

The calligrapher read these lines. He obviously did not like them. He moved his head back and forth. Nasri sensed the man's discomfort. "That's only an indication of the kind of thing it should say. You can make your own judgment and work out how and what you write for such a great man."

Hamid Farsi breathed a sigh of relief. This is a man of quality, he thought, and his suggestions came promptly. "I'd put the names of God and his Prophet in gold at the top, and underneath, in red, the name of our President. Under that I would put, in bright green: You are chosen by God and his Prophet to lead our nation." The calligrapher paused. "I have heard that he's very devout, so putting it like that would be in line with his own ideas and wouldn't read like an order. You are courteously expressing an assumption, a wish, that God has chosen him to reign over us. All rulers like that sort of thing."

"And suppose it wasn't God who chose him to lead that coup?" asked Nasri, making a joke of it to dispel the chill that he felt.

"Then the CIA or the KGB had a hand in it, but we can't write that, can we?" said the calligrapher, never turning a hair. Nasri laughed out loud, but he felt lonely.

Hamid Farsi showed him the fine paper and the gilded picture frame he would choose for this saying. Nasri was enthusiastic.

The calligrapher agreed to drop everything else and complete his commission within the week. He named the price, which he had set very high, but Nasri smiled. "Let's leave it like this. I won't ask your price, and you will do your very best for me. Agreed?" he asked, offering his hand, because he never expected anyone to turn down his generous offers.

"Agreed," said Hamid quietly. Nasri was surprised to see that the man didn't even smile or thank him for the commission. A strange fellow. Tawfiq had advised him to make the president a present with a view to getting the large number of machines he was importing past customs. That would raise their profits by three hundred percent.

"Nothing can be done without the president, not since the coup," Tawfiq had said, "and the president loves fine calligraphy, drinks himself silly every day, watches Hitler films for hours on end and puts on a show of devout belief for the faithful." Nasri marvelled at Tawfiq's cunning. He knew as much as if he had his own secret service.

In Tawfiq's opinion, Farsi was the best calligrapher in Damascus. He knew that Farsi was expensive, unapproachable, and arrogant, but what he wrote in his beautiful calligraphy was always a unique work of art. Above all, he was reliable. The present had to be given at exactly the right moment. In two weeks' time the ship carrying the machines would put in at the northern port of Latakia, and by then he needed the consent of the president. "One phone call from him, and the minister of trade will hurry on ahead of me to keep those idiotic customs officers quiet until our trucks have driven the machinery out of town."

Tawfiq was a devil, and the most diabolical thing about him was his weary but angelic face.

Nasri looked out of the window. It had stopped raining, and he suddenly remembered the additional request that was to accompany the present.

"And something else," he said, already at the door. "Could you also write me a letter to go with it in your beautiful script? In my name? It would be bad taste for me to write it myself in my terrible scrawl…"

"Of course I can, but I shall need your full name and address so that I can provide the letter with an elegant letterhead that no secretary or receptionist will keep from him," said Hamid, pushing a blank sheet of paper toward Nasri. When the latter had written down his name and address, Hamid Farsi knew that this elegant gentleman had been speaking no more than the truth.

The sun was shining outside and Nasri heaved a sigh of relief. The calligrapher was a capable and intelligent craftsman, but his mouth odour was intolerable. It reminded Nasri of the smell of the beasts of prey in a circus he had once gone to with his father. As the manager of the circus revered his father, Nasri had been allowed to get quite close to the animal cages, accompanied by one of the keepers. The cages stank of urine, which was bad enough, but when a tiger or lion roared or a hyena howled, the stench of their breath almost stifled Nasri.

A week later Tawfiq surprised him early in the morning by giving him the calligraphy, which he had personally collected and paid for. It was even more beautiful than Nasri had pictured it. A magnificent frame of ornamentation surrounded the script giving it an almost sacred look.

"I think there's nothing in our way now," said Tawfiq, and Nasri saw the devilish gleam in his eye.

A week later Nasri received a personal invitation to dinner with the president. A chauffeur collected him and took him to the presidential palace. The president enjoyed the evening so much that from then on he dined once a week with Nasri and a few carefully selected businessmen of the city.

Friendships in such circles were as good as impossible, but through his wit and fearlessness Nasri was soon particularly close to the president. Behind the stiff uniform he discovered a lonely man who hadn't had a happy day in his life since he was young, but had spent his time miserably occupied with conspiracies and counter-conspiracies.

Nasri regarded the other businessmen as hypocrites. They watched the same film with the dictator every week, only to laugh at him in private afterward. President Shishakli worshipped Hitler and wanted to imitate him. He was impressed by Leni Riefenstahl's film *Triumph of the Will*, and watched it once a week in the private cinema of the presidential palace.

Nasri disliked both the Germans and the war, and he always made an excuse to leave the palace. Shishakli, son of a peasant, respected him for that, recognizing Nasri as a cultivated man and a free spirit who listened carefully and gave his own opinion with perfect civility.

Three weeks later, the consignment of machinery, three full truckloads, had already arrived duty-free. It included machines for kneading dough and dividing portions destined for bakeries, as well as drills and lathes for metal-working and car repair shops, the first imports from Hungary. To give the firm a second secure footing, Tawfiq explained, he had acquired the sole agency for engineering works in Syria.

"Second, did you say? I get the impression you've made our company into a millipede," Nasri replied, and both men laughed.

That day Nasri took some expensive perfume with him when he visited the whore Asmahan. When he entered her apartment he saw that she was busy cutting a beautifully written maxim out of a magazine at her living-room table. Asmahan thanked him for the perfume, and while she went on cutting out the maxim and framing it very carefully, she told him that she had always had a liking for calligraphy. Calligraphy was the photography of words, she said, and she loved words more than any man in the world.

Only now did Nasri notice that all the walls in her bedroom and living room, kitchen and bathroom were covered with framed sayings. He felt ashamed of his blindness, but now he knew how he could please Asmahan.

When she went away to make herself beautiful for him, he wrote down the maxim she had just been cutting out. It said, "The Wisdom of Love is its Madness."

That day he thought, yet again, that he should have married the whore, and to hell with his clan and his reputation. She was as clever as his wife Lamia, she was witty and could laugh enchantingly like his wife Nasimeh, and in addition she had the bewitching body of his wife Saideh. And, unlike any of his wives, she was grateful. Of course she wanted money for her prowess in bed, but his wives charged him double what he paid her, only in other ways – he had worked it out. None of them, however, was as grateful when he took her a present. Asmahan was sometimes happy for days on end over a bottle of perfume or an expensive French fashion magazine from the Librairie Universelle bookshop.

But as he was about to immerse himself wistfully in these thoughts, an inner voice woke him from them, as always. It sounded like his father's. "Do you really think you'll be enough for her, you fool? A woman like that is sexy enough for seven men, and what's she going to do with the rest of her sexiness when you're lying beside her exhausted and snoring? She'll soon find another man, and then a third and a fourth. You'll be wearing seven pairs of horns, and you won't fit through doorways."

Nasri was shaking his head, downcast, when Asmahan came back into the room wearing a thin silk wrap. She had piled her blonde hair up in a pyramid and adorned it with paste gems and feathers. She was the most beautiful whore in Damascus, and only her high price kept men from queuing up outside her door. She charged a hundred lira every time she slept with someone – it was as much as Tawfiq's weekly salary.

Only parliamentarians, ministers, large landowners, generals, and rich businessmen could afford the pleasure she gave them.

Today, after a little love play, Nasri asked out of frustration and a little shame how many men she had had today.

"You're the third," she said, putting on her underclothes.

"And now you've had enough?" he asked, hoping that after sleeping with him she would say, "Oh yes!" Asmahan just laughed her clear laugh and did not reply.

"Hurry up, the parliamentary speaker will soon be here! He wants me to play the innocent student and he'll seduce me. He's a professor, you know."

"And after that?"

"Oh, do hurry up. After that another three or four, maybe five, it all depends how jealous their wives are," she said, and laughing but forcefully she propelled him toward the door.

She was a strange woman, with no sense of shame – as if she weren't an Arab woman at all – but a sober and accurate idea of what she did. "Whoring is a profession as old as the hills," she told him one day. "Some sell their strength and the work of their hands, their eyes and their backs, and I sell the work of my cunt." You could look at it like that, of course. Nasri didn't like to. She added, "Suppose a beautiful and clever woman is ripe for marriage, what husband will her parents choose out of a hundred suitors? They won't pick the most sensitive or the cleverest or the one who has the best way with words, let alone the most honourable, they'll pick the richest and most powerful. It's just a case of buying and selling. Beautiful, healthy women are sold in exchange for power and security for the woman and her family. But I see you don't understand what I'm saying."

Nasri was bewildered. She was speaking Arabic, yes, but this was not the kind of language he was used to.

This time Nasri waited until afternoon before going to the calligrapher, hoping that by then the man's bad breath might have worn off, and sure enough, today his breath smelled of orange and coriander.

"Did the president like the last calligraphic work?" he asked, after returning Nasri's greeting.

"Yes, very much. How could he fail to when it came from your pen?" said Nasri, looking at the keen blade of the knife the calligrapher was using to sharpen the point of the reed.

"I'll be through with this in a minute, do sit down," he said, pointing to an elegant chair. One of his assistants came in and asked quietly for some gold leaf. The calligrapher stood up and took a thick book out of a cupboard. "There are still seventy leaves – when you've finished, enter the number you took out and the date in the list you'll find at the end, and take care of the tiniest pieces left over. It's gold, understand?" he said in a soft but stern voice to the assistant, quite an old man who found this admonition in front of a customer embarrassing.

"Yes, I always do take care," he said.

"Send me Yousef," added Hamid Farsi. "I want him to fetch us two coffees."

A small boy came out of the workshop and asked Nasri politely how he liked his coffee.

"With plenty of sugar and a little cardamom."

The boy, who had a bad squint, set off for Karam's café at the end of the street.

Nasri, watching him go, wondered about his clean clothes. Everyone in this place seemed a little more elegant than the people working in the other nearby shops, as if by order.

"Slovenliness and calligraphy don't go together," Hamid Farsi replied briefly to his customer's compliment.

"I have an unusual request today." After drinking his coffee, Nasri moved his chair closer to the master calligrapher's desk. "It's very intimate. For a woman, you understand," he whispered. "Of course, not one of my wives. Who writes love letters to his own wife?"

The calligrapher gave a wintry smile.

"No, it's a saying about love. Here," said Nasri, taking the small piece of paper out of his wallet and unfolding it on the table. Hamid Farsi read the saying and liked it.

"How large is it to be?"

"The size of the palm of my hand, but very fine, please. Perhaps in gold," Nasri added.

"Is it wanted in a hurry?"

"Yes, as usual. And this time, please, another suitable accompanying letter in your wonderful script, but no letterhead and address. The lady might show it to other people, you see. It's enough to end the letter with my first name, Nasri."

"But you must tell me what the letter is to say. Then I will work out the right form of words."

Nasri was in difficulty. He had thought out everything in advance, but not the answer to a question like this.

"Oh, something or other… you know the kind of thing. About love and so forth," stammered Nasri, and suddenly he seemed to himself ridiculous. The calligrapher was privately amused by this rich man, who wanted to show that he was a person of great stature, but couldn't put together a couple of sentences about his own feelings.

"Very well," he said, in the superior tones of one reaching out his hand to a drowning man, "then tell me what the lady likes, what's most beautiful about her, and I'll see what can be made of it."

Nasri hadn't been so embarrassed since his childhood, but then he began talking about Asmahan's blue eyes, her body, and her beguiling charm. And finally he mentioned the remark that had shaken him so much, that she loved words in fine script better than she loved men.

The calligrapher wrote it all down. He envied this rich man for loving a woman who herself loved calligraphy.

When Nasri left the calligrapher's workshop and stepped out into the street, he realized that he was sweating profusely.

12

Even years later, Noura thought nostalgically of her time with the dressmaker Dalia. She spent three years with her, and she had learned so much there! She always used to say that her father had taught her how to read, her mother had taught her how to cook, and Dalia had taught her how to live.

Noura also enjoyed working with Dalia because it meant she could get away from her mother. She didn't have to do any cooking or cleaning at home, because she had a profession, and her mother was very respectful of a profession.

The dressmaker's house stood where the ends of two alleys met, and was triangular, an unusual shape in the city. It looked like the bows of a mighty steamship and had two front doors, one on each alley. There was no inner courtyard, but a narrow garden behind the living quarters where tall plants screened the house from the neighbouring buildings in the two alleys. A gnarled old bitter orange tree, a tall palm, and two lemon trees were the columns framing a jungle. Among them oleander and rose bushes grew to a great height. Jasmine made a dense curtain of white flowers and dark green leaves in front of the neighbouring houses.

A tiny fountain adorned the terrace, which was paved with red and white tiles like a chessboard. The dressmaker and her assistants relaxed here. They drank their tea and coffee on the terrace for ten months of the year, and they could also smoke here, which was strictly forbidden in the workshop.

The dressmaking premises were on the ground floor, and consisted of a beautiful reception room, two well-lit workshops, a large kitchen, and a small storeroom for sewing materials. The washroom was a little shed hidden behind the bitter orange tree in the garden.

Dalia lived upstairs. She did not like to be visited there, not even by Noura. A stairway behind the façade of the house led up to the attic on the next floor. Beside the attic room there was a wide space to hang out washing. But the flat roof was not surrounded by railings, like the roof of Noura's house at home. She did not like going up there to hang out washing. She felt dizzy on the stairs, which always swayed slightly.

Dalia loved her house. She had bought it and renovated it herself. Her four brothers had divided her father's inheritance between them, cunningly tricking Dalia out of her share after their parents' death, when she was already burdened more than enough by personal disasters. By the time she found out that she had been cheated, it was too late. She never said another word to her brothers all her life, or with their sons and daughters who kept trying to make peace with the famous dressmaker whose work was in such demand.

"Give me back what your fathers stole from me first," she would say, brusquely dismissing her relations. "Otherwise you and your slimy ways can go to the devil."

Dalia the dressmaker's house was only a stone's throw from Noura's home. At first that was the one disadvantage, for over the first few weeks Noura's mother would drop in several times a day for a word with her daughter. Noura was cross, because her mother spoke to her as if she were a little girl. Dalia was quick to notice that this got on her young assistant's nerves, and one fine morning she put an end to Noura's embarrassment. "You listen to me," she snapped at Noura's mother. "Bring your daughter up as you like at home. Here she has to learn from me, and I and no one else am in charge here. Do we understand each other?"

Noura's mother did understand, and she never dropped in again. But oddly enough she bore the dressmaker no grudge for her reproof. "She's a strong woman. She has buried three husbands, and she knows what she's doing," said Noura's mother.

Noura lay awake for a long time that night, wondering how her parents could bear to live together. Her father was an incorrigible philanthropist who saw even a criminal as a man in need of love. Her mother, on the other hand, distrusted everyone. She saw every passerby as a wolf in human form, waiting under cover of a friendly smile to devour Noura alive. "Mama, men don't smile at me, and if one does I'll soon send him on his way," she said untruthfully, to soothe her mother's fears. She didn't mention her fears of the barber, whose looks burnt her skin, or her liking for Ismail who sold beans in his shop not far from her alley. He was always friendly, well dressed, and neatly shaven, but he was also uglier than any other of the men in this quarter. He had a face like a vulture and a body like a hippopotamus, but he was always good-tempered and full of praise for his baked beans, fried falafel, and the other little vegetarian dishes that he sold over the counter. His shop was so small that there was only room in it for Ismail himself, his pans and his deep-fat fryer. Noura's father used to say that if Ismail put on any more weight there'd be nowhere left for the salt sprinkler. Yet like all the neighbours he appreciated Ismail's dishes, the secret of which he had inherited from his forebears. For twenty-two generations, said a notice above the little door, the family had been cooking and frying vegetables in that shop. And it was said that the Ottoman Sultan Selim had stopped here on his way to Palestine and Egypt because the delicious aromas coming from the shop gave him an appetite. The sultan had written a letter of thanks to the shopkeeper of the time. It had hung in the shop for four hundred years, and to the end of the Ottoman Empire it forbade any official to harm the shopkeeper.

When Ismail saw Noura, he would purse his lips into the shape of a kiss, and sometimes he even did give his mighty ladle a hearty kiss, making his eyebrows dance a suggestive jig at the same time.

"Rose of Damascus, marry me," he called to her one morning as she was walking past his shop, lost in thought. For a moment she took fright, but then she laughed at him. And from that day on she felt something like warmth when she set eyes on him, and walked past his shop slowly with her head held high, enjoying the flow of his poetic remarks.

What danger could this corpulent man represent? She twice saw him in her dreams as a little falafel ball swimming in oil, blowing bubbles, and calling out "Eat me, eat me," in a singsong chant. She woke up laughing.

No. Noura hadn't confided in her mother since she was ten or eleven. That spared both of them trouble. All the same, there were constant arguments when her mother found out something that stoked her fears for Noura.

At that time all young women idolized the singer and actor Farid al-Atrash, who sang popular, melancholy love songs. He had the saddest voice in the Arab world, and it moved all women to tears. Week after week the newspapers were full of him. Farid al-Atrash was a bachelor all his life; it was said that he loved horses and boys more than women, but the women didn't believe that.

The singer left Noura's father cold, and her mother hated him because he seduced women with his songs. "He's a Druze, and what would you expect a man whose mother played the lute for money to be? Did you hear how his sister ended up? Drowned in the Nile. She was the most beautiful woman in the Arab world, but instead of marrying a king she sang in night clubs, and her lover, a jealous Englishmen, strangled her and threw her body into the river."

Dalia the dressmaker was one of those who idolized Farid al-Atrash. She didn't just like singing his songs, she went to see all his films at the Roxy Cinema. In fact she had seen some of those films, like *Ahlam al Shabab* (Dreams of Youth) and *Shahr al Asal* (Honeymoon), over ten times. The wall above her workshop was adorned with a large poster for the film *Makdarshi* (I Can't Do It). Farid al-Atrash seemed to be saying just that to whoever looked at the poster while his screen partner, the famous dancing girl Tahiya Karioka, watched him jealously. And whenever her customers urged Dalia to hurry with their dresses, she just pointed to the poster in silence and went on working.

One day, when Noura had been learning dressmaking from Dalia for over a year, the assistants were all talking excitedly about the singer's latest film, *Akhir Kizbeh* (Last Lie), which was coming to the Roxy in a couple of weeks' time, and saying that Farid al-Atrash, who had been living in Cairo since he was a child, would be here for the première.

Dalia never told anyone where she got the five complimentary tickets, but in any case she and all her assistants went to the cinema.

Ninety percent of the audience were women who, as Dalia had prophesied they would, had come in the most expensive and fashionable dresses to please the singer, that confirmed bachelor. When he appeared a soulful murmur ran through the auditorium.

The singer was not as tall as you might have expected from the poster. His face was pale and smooth, and he did not sport the moustache usual at the time. Noura blushed and felt her heart sinking to the depths as the singer's large, sad eyes rested on her for a moment. She instantly fell madly in love with him. She didn't take in much of the plot of the film, but when Farid sang she felt as if he were singing not for Samia Gamal, the girl he loved in the film, but for her alone. She wept, and laughed, and then there was the brief encounter that was to rob her of sleep that night.

As the audience left, the singer stood at the entrance flanked by the important personalities of the city, who liked to have themselves photographed with him, handing out copies of his signed portrait. And the women of Damascus, who never usually formed a queue and would scratch each other's eyes out at the vegetable sellers' shops when they were in a hurry, lined up meekly like good girls in a convent school because they wanted the singer to think well of them. They accepted the picture and walked demurely out. Dalia, who was standing behind Noura, whispered to her, "Now or never." But Noura was feeling far too excited in the expensive dress she had borrowed, which really belonged to a bride.

When it was her turn the singer gave her his portrait, smiled at her briefly, and touched her fingers. She was almost fainting.

Not so Dalia. Plucking up her courage and seizing her opportunity, she gave the startled singer a resounding kiss on the cheek.

"I, Dalia – Dalia the little dressmaker, a widow three times over – I've kissed Farid al-Atrash. Now I can die and God can send me to Hell for all I care," she said triumphantly on the way home. Her assistants giggled.

When Noura went home at noon next day, she found that the picture under her pillow had been torn into a thousand pieces.

She froze. And then she felt rage that almost took her breath away. More and more often these days she felt a desire to get away from her parental home. She wanted to get married soon just to be rid of her mother.

Nothing escaped Dalia's notice. "Oh, child, dry those tears, here, you can have another photo," she said, giving Noura her own picture. "I've finished with it. Isn't he cute? And such a lovely smell!"

Noura hid the photo under a loose board at the bottom of her wardrobe at home, but she soon forgot it.

Only after she ran away did she remember it again, and wonder whether someone, in some century to come, would discover the picture at the bottom of the wardrobe and guess at the story behind it. She shook her head and smiled.

Dalia was a true mistress of her craft. She hated sloppiness, and was sure all her life that everything only half done would be avenged. She herself had great patience, but it was often her bad luck that her assistants didn't put the necessary enthusiasm into their work. Many of them thought themselves dressmakers already just because they had once made an apron or an oven cloth at home. "Girl, girl, you're not attending to what you're doing," was Dalia's most often repeated remark, because most of her trainees only wanted to learn to sew a little so that they would be considered a good catch for a man. After cooking, sewing was the ability most prized by a Damascene in his future wife.

"Scissors and needles, thread and a sewing machine are only an aid," she told Noura in her very first week. "You can cut out a dress properly after two years at the latest, but you can't call yourself a dressmaker until you know, the moment you set eyes on a fabric, what dress it would be best to make of it. And you can't find that out from any book. You have to get a feel for the craft before you can pick the raisins out of the porridge of possibilities."

Noura watched closely to see how Dalia unrolled the material her customers brought her, touched it, held it to her cheek, thought, picked it up again and held it up to the light. Then a shy smile would appear on her mouth, a sure sign that Dalia had an idea now. She would take a sheet of paper, draw the cut of the dress on it, and then hold her drawing against the fabric to check. Once Dalia was happy, Noura saw how the idea went from her head to her wrist, moving from her fingers to the fabric. After that there was no more hesitation, and soon the dress was held together with pins and tacking stitches.

None of the assistants was allowed to cut fabric except for Fatima, who was already experienced. But Dalia encouraged them to practise on the pieces that were left over. "With cotton first, cotton is kind to you, and then onward and upward till you reach the majestic heights of velvet and silk."

In her first year of training, Noura often marvelled at the long discussions Dalia had with her customers. As a rule they came with very definite ideas of what kind of dress they wanted. But Dalia often thought that a dress like that wouldn't suit her customer.

"No, madame, orange and red don't suit your eyes, your hair colour, and particularly not the curvaceous figure you're blessed with."

"But my husband loves red," wailed the wife of al-Salem the bank manager.

"Then either he should wear it himself, or you should lose ten to fifteen kilos," said Dalia, showing her how well blue would suit her and how slimming it would be.

"How do you manage to see all this?" Noura asked one day, when the wife of a famous surgeon was quite beside herself with delight and gratitude over her new dress.

"I've learnt to know what it should be like before I make the first cut. Try to understand the rippling of the waves, the enchanting green of orange leaves, the white of jasmine flowers, the slender palm trees, and you'll find that they have all mastered the art of elegance."

Dalia was never satisfied, and not infrequently she was unjust. Even Fatima was not spared. "Look at Fatima," she often said in mock despair of her oldest and best assistant. "She's been with me for ten years, and to this day she can't make a proper buttonhole."

Fatima hated buttonholes, but otherwise she was an excellent dressmaker. She was the only assistant who had been in the workshop before Noura, and who was still there after Noura had left. She didn't just work hard enough for three, she was the heart of the workshop, offering comfort, helping the younger women, and even contradicting the boss out loud if Dalia went too far.

There was a rapid turnover among the other assistants. They did not love the work. They came with the idea that after a year they would have mastered the craft, and only then did they realize how complicated it was.

Sometimes the girls left of their own accord, sometimes Dalia sent them away. "You know enough now to make underwear for your husband," she said.

She paid a minimum wage, just enough to cover the monthly expense of a tram or bus ticket. But every assistant got a hot meal once a day and unlimited coffee. No one but the boss was allowed to drink alcohol.

In retrospect, Noura found the first year the most difficult one. From the second year on she was full of enthusiasm for the work, and she could soon make dresses entirely by herself. When she began dreaming of her work, Dalia laughed and patted her on the shoulder. "You're making progress, even in your sleep," she said. But the dream was far from enjoyable. Noura dreamed of a customer visiting the dressmaker to try on her wedding dress. The dress was almost ready, in real life as well as in the dream. The customer was not satisfied, although it was a wonderful dress and hid her pregnancy very well. Noura thought she had better make coffee to calm the customer, who was standing in front of the mirror in her new dress, close to tears. On the way to the kitchen Noura asked her boss to speak to the customer, who felt great respect for Dalia. But at that moment she heard relieved laughter. "It's all right now," cried the woman happily. She had cut the dress off a hand's breadth above her knees with a big pair of scissors, leaving it pitifully short with a zigzag hem.

Noura had woken up, gasping for air.

"Now the profession's in your body and your blood, and soon it will set up house in your brain," said Dalia, laughing, when Noura had finished her story. The dress had been the first one that Noura made by herself.

She worked hard, and went to her room every day after the evening meal to learn the difficult names of all the different colours and dress materials, practising many different cuts and many different seams on the scraps of fabric she was allowed to bring home from the workshop. Dalia could recite the eleven shades of the colour blue in her sleep, from marine to plum blue, a colour also called prune. There were even sixteen shades of red, from cardinal red to pink, and she never got any of them mixed up.

Dalia was very direct in her manner, even to her customers. Once one of them put on weight at alarming speed between the various fittings of her wedding dress, because of all the invitations out that came during the preparations for the ceremony. She was fatter from fitting to fitting in the workshop, and Dalia had marked it all out and pinned it in place again three times already. But at the next fitting, when she saw that the customer wasn't going to be able to fit into the dress at all, she waved a dismissive hand. "I make dresses for fashionable ladies, not for lumps of dough. So make up your mind, my girl: do you want a wedding dress or would you rather have pistachio nuts and cakes?" The young woman went red in the face and hurried away. Ten days later she came back looking very pale, but slim.

"Beautiful people don't need dresses. God has made the loveliest of clothes for them himself. But those people are few and far between, and for all the others our art is to emphasize their good points and conceal the bad ones," was the way Dalia summed up her profession.

She sat working for hours at her Singer pedal sewing machine, which she was very proud of. There were three older machines worked by handles for her assistants to use.

Even years after her flight, Noura often thought of Dalia, and of all she had learnt from that mysterious woman.

13

"Of course I married my first husband partly because of my parents," the dressmaker told Noura one day. "They lived here in the Midan quarter, they were well respected and kept an open house. My father liked to drink arak and my mother liked it even more, just as if they were Christians. Yet they were both devout Muslims. However, they considered the commandments and prohibitions to be only rules necessary for regulating primitive societies. I never saw them the worse for drink.

"Our Midan quarter had been known as a trouble spot ever since the days of Ottoman rule, and it stayed that way under the French. Sometimes the whole quarter was barricaded off with tangles of barbed wire, and everyone going in or out was checked. And when not even that did any good, the French bombed the district.

"In a way my father was the leader. We all lived very close together and knew each other well. My parents were famous for their hospitality, and so any stranger was taken, either politely or by force, to my father. If the newcomer was all right he was welcomed as a guest, and all the neighbours held a festive meal for him. But if he had bad intentions he was shown the way out, or treated even more harshly. During those years of unrest two spies were unmasked, executed, and their bodies left beside the barbed wire with a piece of paper on their chests saying, 'Best Wishes to Sarai.' General Sarai was the leader of the French forces in Syria.

"One cold day in the year 1926 – the country had been in turmoil since the great uprising against the French in 1925 – a young man from Aleppo arrived. He wanted to learn how the people of the Midan quarter organized their resistance to the French. His name was Salah, and he could recite poetry beautifully.

"When he saw me he wanted to marry me on the spot, and my father agreed at once. The man came from a well-respected family, and was quite prosperous. From my father's point of view, it made sense to give a man who revered the Midan quarter a daughter of the Midan as his wife. No one asked my opinion. I was a young thing of sixteen, and the way the man looked at me made me feel weak. He had beautiful eyes and long, curly hair."

Dalia poured some arak into her glass, added water, and took a good gulp. "Salah was charming to me all through the wedding evening. And while the guests danced and sang, he recited love poem after love poem to me. I was in love with him. After the celebrations, we went into the big bedroom. He closed the door behind him and smiled at me. I felt breathless, as if he had tied a sack around my head when he closed the door.

"I tried to remember my mother's advice. Put up a little resistance, she had said. I was shaking all over with uncertainty. How did you pretend to put up a little resistance? He unbuttoned my dress. I was almost fainting. 'Would you like a sip of arak?' he asked. The bottle had been placed discreetly in the room, in a bucket full of crushed ice. I nodded. Alcohol gives you courage, I thought. And my mother had told me it would also awaken a woman's own desires, so that she'd get some pleasure out of the first night herself. Salah took a small sip. I tipped a whole glassful down my throat, and felt the liquor hissing as it met the heat inside me. His hands were busy trying to get at me, and unbuttoning his fly at the same time.

"When he touched my breasts, so my mother had said, giving me a good tip for the wedding night, I ought to groan to make him go on, and if he touched me anywhere I didn't like I was to go as rigid as a piece of wood.

"But the moment Salah put his hand between my legs I went rigid from head to foot, like a raft trying to break free but stuck in a log-jam somewhere. Everything in me was numb. He undressed me entirely, and then I saw his prick. It was small and crooked. I couldn't keep from laughing. He gave me a slap because his prick wasn't reacting. He pushed my legs further apart as if he were an elephant. I looked at him, naked between my legs. How ugly he is, I thought. Any desire of mine had flown away through the open window. He was sweating, and he had an odd smell, not strong but strange, almost like freshly sliced cucumbers.

"Over the next few hours, he kept trying, quite considerately, to push his semi-limp prick into me. In the end he got proof of my virginity with his finger, making my parents and relations rejoice volubly and with relief outside the room.

"Three weeks later Salah was stopped at a checkpoint. He was carrying weapons, so he tried to run for it, and he was shot. The whole quarter followed his coffin, with everyone swearing to take revenge on Sarai and the French. Grown men cried like orphaned children. I'd be lying if I were to tell you I mourned Salah myself. He had seemed a stranger to me all those three weeks. Onions helped me out at the time. I think God made the onion to help widows save face. It worked with me. My relations soothed me, and worried about my health. I felt like a monster, but my heart was mute."

Noura had always been slightly long-sighted, and soon she was finding it difficult to get her thread through the eye of the needle. So she got a pair of glasses. They were the cheapest, ugliest glasses shown to her, but that was what her mother wanted. So that Noura wouldn't go tempting anyone in a prettier pair, was her explanation. Noura was ashamed to wear those glasses in the street or at home, and kept them in her drawer at the dressmaker's. Her mother advised her not to tell anyone about them, because no one wanted a daughter-in-law who wore glasses, let alone a long-sighted one.

Dalia, on the other hand, always wore glasses with thick lenses, and Noura was surprised when she once took them off. Suddenly she had big, beautiful eyes, and not, as usual, little buttons under the discs of glass.

Noura liked the peace and calm of doing light mechanical work for hours on end, because then she had time to think of all sorts of things. Oddly enough, unlike the other women in Dalia's workshop, she never thought about marriage. She very much wanted to love someone passionately, someone who would captivate her heart and her mind, but she never met him. Often, in her imagination, she put together the man of her dreams out of separate parts: he would have the eyes of a beggar, the mind and brain of her father, the wit of the ice-seller, the passion of the bean-seller, the voice of the singer Farid al-Atrash and the elegant bearing of Tyrone Power, whom she had admired onscreen at the cinema.

Sometimes she had to laugh when it occurred to her that some mistake might put the wrong parts together, and the man of her dreams would turn out to be as small as her father, with a belly and a bald patch like the bean-seller, the singer's expressionless face, and Tyrone Power's bad character.

One day one of the assistants came to work in floods of tears, and said, sobbing, that she had failed the test. "What test?" asked Dalia.

"The bride test," said the young woman, weeping. Relieved, Dalia went back to her sewing machine. The assistant had to clear up the kitchen and make coffee that day, and at midday Dalia sent her home to get over it, so that none of the customers would see her tear-stained face.

What had happened? The parents of a young butcher had their eye on the girl as a bride for their son. They examined her, tugged her this way and that, and were not pleased with her because she had bad teeth and was sweating with anxiety. The bridal inspection ended in the hammam with a defeat: two large, ugly scars on her stomach were discovered. The dream was over!

While the young woman was despairingly lamenting her fate in the kitchen, Noura remembered a book of pictures of French paintings, one of them showing a beautiful naked woman with a delicate body and pale skin in a slave market, being felt all over by a heavily built man wrapped in robes. He was looking at her teeth, like a farmer when he is thinking of buying a donkey.

Noura's mother was delighted by her daughter's dressmaking skills. All her life, she was proud of the housedress that Noura had given her for the Eid festival. It was dark red, with a pattern of pale arabesques. The cut was simple, and Noura hadn't even gone to any particular trouble with it.

But never before or afterward did she see her mother as moved as she was that day. "All my life I wanted to be a dressmaker and make people look beautiful in the fabrics they wore," she sighed. "But my father thought it was shameful for a woman to earn her living by working."

Curiously enough, her mother had complete confidence in Dalia, although she could be so ungraciously outspoken. When Noura once told her that she had been invited along with Dalia to the house of a rich man for whose wife Dalia made clothes, her mother had no objection. "Dalia is a lioness, she'll look after you," she said confidently, "but don't let your father know. He doesn't like the rich, he'd spoil your fun with a sermon."

"Let's stop work for today," said Dalia one late afternoon, finishing the last seam of a dress for a good friend of hers.

She examined the dress one last time, and handed it to Noura, who put it on a hanger and smoothed it down. "Sofia will look at least ten years younger in this," she said.

Dalia took the arak bottle, her cigarettes, and a glass and went out to the terrace, where she turned the fountain on. Water splashed softly into the little basin. Noura followed her. Her curiosity finally brought the conversation around to Dalia's life after the death of her first husband.

"My second husband Kadir," Dalia said, "was a motor mechanic. He was my cousin, and he worked in a big car repair shop on the outskirts of Damascus. I knew him as a silent boy who was as hairy as an ape. Family members joked and said his mother must have had an affair with a gorilla. But it wasn't as bad as all that.

"Kadir turned up when my first husband died. He was opening his own workshop. I still wasn't even seventeen, and I didn't live in the streets of Damascus at the time, I lived in the films I went to see.

"He was a good motor mechanic, and customers came flooding in. When he came to visit he always smelled of petrol. Most of the time he either kept quiet or talked to my father about cars. My father was one of the first at that time in Damascus to drive a Ford.

"I didn't like my cousin Kadir, but my mother did, and my father liked him even better. From then on he got his car repaired for free.

"'Kadir has lucky hands,' he said. 'Since he first touched that car, the old tin can hasn't given me any more problems.'

"My fiancé was the exact opposite of the lover I had imagined in my dreams. The dream lover was good with words, a slender Arab with large eyes, a small moustache, and neatly trimmed side-whiskers. He came to visit whenever I liked, with his face smoothly shaved. His hair was wavy and glossy, and he always had a newspaper or a magazine under his arm. And this lover was more interested in my lips and eyes than my behind. He thought my words were exciting, and he drowned in my eyes.

"However, that lover fell dead when faced by my bridegroom on our wedding night. Kadir didn't think much of elegant hairstyles, or magazines, and films, as he saw it, were mere pretence. Anything not made of flesh or metal didn't interest him. He ate no vegetables, he never sang, and he never went to see a single film in his life. He didn't even notice that I had a mouth and eyes. He was looking at my bottom and nothing else.

"On the first night, I lay underneath him without getting a single kiss, and he whinnied like a powerful stallion and sweated. His sweat smelled of fuel oil. I could only just manage to keep down the lavish wedding feast in my stomach.

"I didn't just have to be his lover in bed, I also had to be a mother looking after him, and a businesswoman, and a household servant. His work clothes alone would have kept a washerwoman busy full-time. He wanted clean clothes every day. I'd have rather had one of the old school of Arab men! They kept everything neatly apart, a mother, a wife to run the household, a slave girl to do the housework, a cook, a beautiful mistress as playmate, a governess for the children, and heaven knows what else. These days men want to have all that in a single woman. At as cheap a price as possible, too.

"For a year he climbed on top of me twice a day, so that soon I could hardly walk in comfort. And then, one night, came release. Right in the middle of his orgasm he let out a shriek and fell sideways on the bed. He was dead – dead as a doornail. I cried for three days with the shock of it. People thought I was crying for grief."

Noura heard some amazing things. She would have liked to ask some questions, to get to know more about the details, but she didn't dare to interrupt Dalia's stories.

This time the dressmaker had been clever, and she moved rather faster than her husband's family. She sold the workshop to his oldest journeyman, and she sold the big 16-cylinder Cadillac to a rich Saudi for a large sum of money, and she laughed herself silly when her husband's brothers and sisters were left empty-handed.

Dalia never talked about her third husband. Even when Noura asked about him, just before she left after nearly three years training with Dalia, the dressmaker dismissed the subject. It seemed as if she had suffered a deep wound. The wound was indeed deep, as Noura learned later from a woman neighbour.

Dalia had met her third husband when she was visiting a sick girl-friend in hospital. He was young, but he was sick with cancer, and it was incurable. The wife of the head doctor at the hospital was an enthusiastic customer of Dalia's, so she could get permission to see the man she loved whenever she liked. She decided to marry the sick man, whose name she never mentioned. All her friends and family warned her against it, but Dalia had always had a will of her own, and it would have stood comparison with iron. She married the man, took him home with her, and nursed him lovingly until he could stand on his feet again, the pallor of death left his face, and some colour came back to it. Dalia was in Paradise, with a witty, handsome man beside her. It never troubled her than he was an idler, she was happy for him to do nothing, and replied to everyone who criticized him, "You just let him enjoy life, you envious misers! He's suffered for so many years." She spent money lavishly on him and worked like a woman possessed to make sure she ran up no debts. Her husband was very charming, and at first he was very loving to her, but then he began to be unfaithful. Everyone knew except Dalia, who refused to look facts in the face.

One beautiful summer evening Dalia was waiting for him to come home for the evening meal, because it was the third anniversary of their wedding, and she hoped that three was a lucky number. Then the telephone rang, and a woman's voice said in curt, cold tones that she'd better come and collect her husband's body, he'd had a heart attack and was lying on the stairs.

The caller was a well-known madam in the new part of town. Sure enough, Dalia found him lying on the stairs of the brothel. His face was distorted into an ugly grimace. Dalia called the police, and it turned out that same evening that the dead man had been a regular visitor to the place, and the women and servants in the house knew him as a rich, extravagant man who only wanted very young whores. The heart attack had carried him off.

After that shock Dalia loved other men, but she never wanted to live with one again. Noura was sure that Dalia had a lover, for she sometimes saw a bluish love-bite on her throat. But Noura never managed to find out who the lover was.

As an experienced woman, Dalia advised her assistants and her customers when they complained of their husbands to her. Noura often had the impression that some of these women didn't need dresses, they just wanted the dressmaker's good advice.

From where Noura sat working, she could hear every word spoken on the terrace as long as she wasn't using her sewing machine. So she heard all about the troubles of elegant Mrs Abbani, a rich young woman who was not exactly blessed with beauty, but had an enchanting voice. Noura noticed a wonderful change coming over Mrs Abbani; as long as she kept quiet, you felt quite sorry for her, but once she began talking she was transformed into a very attractive woman. She was very well educated, and knew a great deal about astrology, poetry, and above all architecture. But she had no idea about men, and she was desperately unhappy with her husband.

Mrs Abbani ordered twelve dresses a year from Dalia, so that she could drop in once a week and pour her heart out over a coffee. The boss was allowed to call her Nasimeh; all the assistants addressed her as Madame Abbani and showed her the utmost respect.

Nasimeh Abbani had been the best student in her class at school, and had never wanted anything to do with men. She dreamed of a career as an architect, and in her girlhood she drew ambitious designs for houses of the future that made the most of the hot climate and could almost entirely manage without heating in winter. The secret of these houses was a sophisticated ventilation system that Nasimeh had seen on holiday in Yemen.

Her mother had been widowed very young, but she was extremely rich. Her great ambition was to make sure that her late husband's property didn't go to a fortune hunter. So she decided to consider only good matches for her two sons and her daughter, and she achieved that ambition. All three married into even richer families.

In Nasimeh's case, her husband was the son of a friend of her mother's. Obviously the fact that she was this man's third wife troubled no one but Nasimeh herself. Dalia knew Nasimeh's husband. He owned many buildings and landed properties, and he was a powerful man in Damascus.

Nasimeh's great problem was having to act the part of a wife yearning for her husband every third day. Afterward she hated herself for the next two days. She could never say an honest word to her husband, she could only ever agree to what he said. It made her feel exhausted, because telling lies is tiring work if your heart isn't in them, and Nasimeh's heart was as pure as a five-year-old girl's. She always had to act cheerfully and massage, kiss and arouse him until he got going properly. But she didn't like his body. It was snow-white and doughy, and as he sweated profusely he was as slippery as a frog. He always drank arak before making love, so that soon she couldn't stand the smell of aniseed. In addition he had a prick that was unequalled in Damascus, and the more she asked him to spare her the more arousal he felt. It was torture having to lie under him. By now she had three children whom she loved, and she enjoyed life with them as a means of recovering from her husband's visits.

One day Dalia advised the woman to smoke three hashish cigarettes before having sex with him. Some of her customers did that, and it helped them to put up with their husbands' attentions. However, Nasimeh decided that she wouldn't tolerate the effects of the hashish because the sight of her husband nauseated her.

Dalia tried to console her customer by saying that her husband obviously produced too much semen, and had to get rid of it whether he wanted to or not. Nasimeh laughed bitterly. "If you ask me," she said, "my husband has semen on the brain and his is made of nothing else."

Both women laughed, and for the first time it struck Noura what a delightful, gurgling laugh Madame Abbani had. If she were a man, thought Noura, she herself would fall in love with her instantly. She had no idea how close to the facts she had come. Nasri Abbani too had decided to marry the young woman when he heard the sound of her laughter in her parental home. He wasn't allowed to see her at the time, but he had taken his mother's advice and married her.

And at some point, just before the end of her training, Noura heard the dressmaker giving her friend Nasimeh Abbani another piece of advice. "All you can do is get divorced! And after that you can look around for a man you can love."

Toward the end of Noura's third year she was also allowed to work by herself on the most expensive materials, like velvet and silk. And then, if she carried out an order entirely on her own, Dalia showed her clearly how much she thought of her, which in turn aroused the jealousy of her long-standing assistant Fatima.

She could have come to the end of her three years' training with pleasure and satisfaction if the aunt of a famous calligrapher had not turned up one day.

On the morning she was to meet this woman, Noura saw two policemen shooting a dog on her way to the dressmaker's. There had been local rumours for weeks of a gang catching dogs, writing the name of President Shishakli on their backs in hydrogen peroxide, and then letting them loose in the city. The dog that had been shot before Noura's eyes had a light brown coat, and the bleached letters shone white as snow on it.

That morning, when Noura told Dalia how miserably she had seen the dog die because the shot didn't kill it outright, Dalia froze. "This means bad luck," she said. "God preserve us from what's about to come." In the course of the day, however, Dalia and Noura forgot the dog and the president.

Colonel Shishakli, who had come to power in a coup, was overthrown by an uprising in the spring of 1954. But it was to be years before Noura understood that on that morning Dalia had not fallen victim to mere superstition. She had uttered a true prophecy.

14

It took Noura years to piece together the image of her marriage from the separate scraps of her memory. And as she did she often thought of her grandmother, who used to sew whole landscapes of brightly coloured scraps of fabric into patchwork.

As she discovered shortly before she ran away, it had been her school friend Nabiha al-Azm who inadvertently led Hamid Farsi to her. Nabiha's rich family lived in a beautiful house less than fifty paces from Hamid's studio. Her brother, who had known Noura since she was a girl, was crazy about calligraphy, and a good customer of Hamid Farsi. One day he was telling Nabiha about the lonely life led by the calligrapher, and a name instantly sprang to her mind: Noura!

Later, Noura recollected a chance meeting with Nabiha in the Souk al-Hamidiyyeh, where she was buying special buttons for Dalia. She had plenty of time to spare, so she accepted her former classmate's invitation to eat an ice together. Nabiha, who was already engaged and very soon to be married, said she was surprised to find Noura still single.

"I always thought that, with your beautiful face, you'd snap up a rich husband the moment you were fifteen. I'm a bedraggled chicken compared to you!"

Two weeks later, Noura's father said some rich man or other, the descendant of a noble tribe, wanted her as his fourth wife. He had, of course, said no, he added, because his daughter deserved a husband who loved her alone.

A month later their neighbour Badia invited Noura and her mother to coffee. Noura did not want to accept, but she went with her mother out of politeness.

If she thought back carefully she always came to the conclusion that her mother already knew, that day, what it was all about, and that was why she had urged Noura several times to make herself look pretty. That was unusual, because neighbours usually visited each other in everyday clothes, and often in their slippers.

A distinguished-looking lady of a certain age was sitting in Badia's living room. She was introduced as Mayyada, and she was the daughter of the well-known merchant Hamid Farsi, said Badia, and was a friend of hers. Her husband was working in Saudi Arabia, so she didn't often come to Damascus. The lady told them, several times, how highly the Saudis thought of her husband, and said they lived in a positive palace, but she thought the country itself very tedious, so she liked to go to her little house in the Salihiyyeh quarter of Damascus for a visit in summer.

As she talked she fixed her small but sharp eyes on Noura, and Noura felt the woman's glance going right through her clothes. It made her uneasy.

All this was nothing but a farce, only she hadn't seen through it. On that first visit Badia asked Noura to make the coffee, saying that she particularly liked the way she brewed it. Noura had never in fact made especially good coffee; she made it as well or badly as any other girl of seventeen in Damascus. But as she knew her way around her neighbour's house, she got up and went into the kitchen. She had no idea that the stranger was checking the way she moved with a practised eye. When Noura served the coffee, she cried enthusiastically, "So graceful!"

The women discussed all sorts of subjects very frankly, and Noura thought the conversation was a little too intimate for a first exchange with a stranger. Suddenly Badia began praising the woman's nephew, a rich calligrapher who had been left a widower prematurely, and she evidently knew a great deal about him. Noura's mother assured the others that the prospect of a widower made no difference to her or to any other sensible woman, not if the widower in question was childless.

"Yes, he's childless, thank God, but if he takes a young gazelle as his second wife, he'd like to have a few nice children with her," replied the stranger, examining Noura and making her eyebrows dance in a meaningful way. By now Noura realized that she herself was being discussed, and felt greatly embarrassed.

A little later she and her mother said goodbye, and left. Once outside the door her mother stopped, and indicated to Noura that she should listen to what the other two women had to say about her. They didn't have to wait long before the talk inside the house turned to her again. The stranger said to her hostess, loud and clear, "A gazelle. God protect her from envious eyes. She's still rather thin, but with a little feeding up she'll be a beauty. Her build is beautiful, she moves in a very feminine way, her hands are warm and dry and her gaze is proud. Perhaps just a little too proud."

"To be sure, to be sure. All women who read books are proud, but if your nephew is a real man he'll break her pride on the first night and show her that he is master of his house, and if he doesn't, well, never mind. Then her husband will live as ours do with you and me, which is not too bad either."

Both women laughed.

Noura's mother seemed fascinated by this intimate conversation, but she herself thought it embarrassing, and longed to get away.

Months later, Noura discovered that her mother had gone to her future bridegroom's studio the very next day and had taken a good look. It was a fine, light studio, with a marble and glass reception area like a modern museum. The Souk Saruya quarter was considered a very good address. All the same, Noura's mother couldn't imagine how anyone could make a living by writing – after all, her husband had written several books and was still poor. When she confided her doubts to Badia, their neighbour reassured her: Hamid Farsi was one of the best calligraphers in Damascus, she said, and he owned a wonderful house. He was not to be compared with Noura's father. She even got hold of the key to the house. But Noura's mother didn't like the idea of intruding on the future bridegroom's premises without his aunt. So they met at the spice market, Souk al-Busuriyyeh, and walked to the house together.

"It's not so much a house as a piece of Paradise," whispered Noura's mother, and all her reservations were swept away. The house did indeed have the features of Paradise as the Damascenes imagine it. Once you entered through the front door on the east side of the house, you were in a dark corridor that reduced the noise, dust, and heat of the street to a minimum. About halfway down the corridor a door opened into a very large kitchen, the kind that Noura's mother had always dreamed of. Opposite, besides a modern toilet, there was a storeroom for old furniture, empty jars, large preserving pans, domestic still and other household equipment needed at most only once a year. The corridor then led to an inner courtyard which was everything you could wish for, with coloured marble, fountains, lemon, orange, and apricot trees, as well as several rose bushes and a climbing jasmine. Niches protected from the elements and spacious living rooms, guest rooms and bedrooms surrounded the courtyard. Noura's mother didn't need to see the first floor. All she had seen on the ground floor was enough for her.

She did not tell either her husband or Noura, then or later, about this secret visit.

But from then on she was convinced that Hamid Farsi would be a great catch for her daughter. So she began cautiously preparing the ground by talking to her husband. Later, however, after Noura's flight, she claimed that she had had her doubts about the man from the first. Noura's father seldom fell into a rage, but when his wife misrepresented this phase of the negotiations as she remembered them, he reproved her.

A week after that expedition to see the house, Badia and Mayyada came to coffee with them. They sat beside the fountain and talked about the dreams of women, which all seemed to agree on one point: they dreamed of making their husbands happy.

At the time Noura thought this kind of talk was hypocrisy, for neither her mother nor Badia lived by that precept. Even as a child, she had been sure that her father would have been happier with any other woman.

Mayyada talked to her for a long time, uttering civil nothings to which Noura must and indeed did respond, like any Damascene girl. On leaving, Mayyada surprised her by giving her a hearty and powerful hug. She said Noura could call her just by her first name of Mayyada. But then Noura took fright when the woman kissed her right on the mouth. It was not unpleasant, for the woman smelled fragrant and had an attractive mouth, but it embarrassed Noura.

"Why did she do that?" she asked, irritated, when she and her mother were alone again.

"Mayyada wanted to find out what you smell like at close quarters and whether you have an appetising mouth."

"But why?" asked Noura in surprise.

"Because Mayyada's nephew the famous calligrapher, is looking for a wife," replied her mother, "and you can count yourself lucky if this comes off."

Noura felt oddly happy to think of a famous man wanting to marry her. A week later she and her mother were to go to the hammam, and meet Mayyada and their neighbour Badia there.

Only later did she realize that Hamid Farsi's aunt wanted to inspect her naked body before making her final assessment.

But now came the next surprise. Her mother, who was ashamed even to show herself to a sparrow in the courtyard, allowed the stranger to feel her own daughter and inspect her in detail. Noura felt dazed. She let the woman do as she wanted, checking up on her vagina, her breasts, her armpits, nose and ears.

Noura was spared another embarrassment, one that was usually part of the process. The high reputation of the Arabi family was known far and wide, and made it unnecessary to ask their neighbours questions.

Then followed weeks of uncertainty.

After that visit to the hammam, nothing was heard from the woman for a long time. Noura's mother could hardly sleep, as if she herself were about to get married.

But then she did come to visit, and reassured Noura's mother with the glad tidings that Hamid Farsi would very much like to marry her daughter. Noura's mother wept for joy. Aunt Mayyada and she fixed all the details, from the dowry to be paid to the date when the men would discuss everything that the women had been negotiating over for weeks.

Hamid's uncle, Aunt Mayyada's husband, travelled from Saudi Arabia specially. He came to visit accompanied by three very rich merchants from the Souk al-Hamidiyyeh, as if to demonstrate the kind of men who were behind the bridegroom.

Noura's father, Sheikh Arabi, impressed the visitors with his knowledge. They competed in asking him tricky questions to do with morality and religious faith and, at their leisure, ate fruit, smoked, and drank sweet black tea. Only then did they come to speaking of the purpose of their visit, and soon both parties had agreed. When the conversation got around to the bride price, Noura's father, contrary to what his wife wanted, assured them that it was a matter of complete indifference to him. The main thing was, he added, that he could be sure his daughter was in good hands. Money is transitory, he said, but not the respect and love of a woman's partner, and that was what he wanted for his daughter. His wife, eavesdropping in the kitchen, later told him accusingly that with a little skill he could have bargained for a considerably higher bride price, the sum on which she and the bridegroom's aunt had already agreed. He was giving his daughter away cheaply, she said, as if Noura were an old maid. Hamid's uncle shared that opinion, but he kept his mouth shut and privately laughed at Noura's father, who confirmed his view that a man interested in books had no idea of business or real life. He himself, he thought, would have made sure he got three times that bride price for such a pretty, clever daughter.

When they had also agreed on the date of the wedding, they all rose to their feet and shook hands, and Noura's father recited a sura of the Quran to seal the alliance.

A few days later a messenger came from the bridegroom bringing part of the bride price, and then everything happened very quickly. Dalia the dressmaker got her biggest order of the year; she was to provide the most beautiful dresses possible for the wedding. In retrospect, Noura felt that had been a time of frenzy. Never before had she visited so many shops and spent so much money, and she never did again. Her mother couldn't buy her enough china, clothes, and jewellery, although Noura was moving to a house already furnished, a house that her future husband had bought years ago, and where he had lived with his first wife. Noura's mother, however, insisted on new china and new bed linen. The bridegroom tried at least to save his own expensive china, but Noura's mother said it was unlucky to eat from plates that a dead woman had once used. Reluctantly, the bridegroom surrendered, gave his future mother-in-law a second key to the house, and took no more notice of what was being removed from it. And he closed both eyes to the changes that his future mother-in-law made to it. As Noura's mother saw it, he was showing generosity and a noble attitude, and from that moment on she took him to her heart.

Only the heavy furniture, however, was delivered straight to Hamid's house. Everything else was stored in Noura's parental home until the wedding day. Room after room filled up with new purchases, and her father longed for the day when all this stuff was taken to the bridegroom's house. However, he still had to wait for some time.

Dalia was working solely for Noura's wedding. She often groaned and complained that she wouldn't get it done in time, she drank a lot of arak and hardly snatched any sleep.

"By the time I spend the wedding night with my husband, you'll be in the cemetery," joked Noura, trying to placate her own guilty conscience.

Years later, she remembered those last weeks at the dressmaker's. Dalia was very sad. "The people I love always leave me," she said suddenly one evening when she and Noura were working on their own. She was sorry that Noura's bridegroom was very rich, she said, for Noura was her best assistant, and would make a good dressmaker. And as they said goodbye to each other, tears ran down Noura's cheeks. Dalia gave her a silk shirt as a present. "Here – I made you this in secret," said the dressmaker, much moved herself. "The silk was a remnant, and I pinched the expensive buttons from a rich customer. So you don't have to give it another thought. Stolen goods taste better and look better than if you'd bought them."

Dalia was dead drunk.

Later, Noura remembered that goodbye with particular clarity, because she went to the hammam that evening and had an unpleasant experience. There was not long to go now before the wedding. A few minutes after she arrived a midwife well known in the quarter approached her mother, and a little later Noura was told to follow her. The women in the big room were making a lot of noise, playing with water like young girls. They were sitting in groups, soaping themselves and scrubbing one another, or singing songs.

Noura followed the plump woman to a distant niche that looked like a cubicle without a door. The midwife glanced inside and said, "We can do it in here."

Noura knew from her mother that all her body hair was to be removed for the wedding day. The midwife went about the process as if it were routine, and without any consideration for Noura as she removed the hair with a special sugary dough, strip by strip. It hurt like being struck with a nail-studded board or stung by a wasp. The pain got worse, and when her pubic hair was removed it was unbearable. Noura felt as if the midwife were tearing the skin off her body. She wept, but instead of comforting her the midwife slapped her face. "Quiet, girl!" she growled. "If you can't bear a ridiculous little bit of pain like this, how are you going to bear your husband's prick? This is child's play." She washed Noura roughly and hurried out. A few minutes later the hairdresser came along. She soothed Noura, telling her the midwife was always rather harsh. She cut Noura's toenails and fingernails, washed and arranged her hair, and told her tricks to use if she didn't like what her husband was doing and wanted to bring him to a climax quickly when he slept with her.

In retrospect, Noura thought she had been like a lamb being seasoned and prepared for cooking in the days leading up to the wedding. The hairdresser powdered and perfumed her. Her throat felt terribly thirsty, but she dared not say so. Her body was burning, and the air in the hammam grew hotter and hotter. When she tried to stand up the walls were going round before her eyes. The hairdresser immediately took her under the armpits. Noura felt the woman's breath on the back of her neck. The hairdresser kissed her throat. "What's the matter, my child?" she whispered tenderly.

"I'm thirsty," said Noura. The hairdresser let her slowly sink to the floor and hurried out. She soon came back with a brass bowl of cool water, and when Noura gulped it, her dry throat hurt. As if dazed, she watched the hairdresser's hand stroking her breasts. She had no will of her own, and saw her nipples swelling as if they belonged to another woman.

"You can always visit me if you like. I'll spoil you the way no man ever can," whispered the hairdresser, and kissed her on the lips.

After the bath Noura and her mother went home in silence. Noura was sad because all her pleasure in anticipating the wedding was gone.

The official betrothal party was held in her parents' house, which was just able to take the crowd of guests. The place smelled of incense, heavy perfume and wax. Her mother had ordered hundreds of big candles of the best quality from Aleppo, to supplement the electric light. Her mother didn't trust electricity. It had always worked while the French were still in the country, but since independence there were power cuts twice a week in the Old Town. Darkness on the night of the betrothal or the wedding seemed to Noura's mother the worst misfortune on earth, a bad omen for married life.

When her niece Barakeh was married, her mother was always saying, no one would listen to her. Noura remembered that there had been a power failure then. No one else minded, only her mother panicked. Oil lamps were lit, but her mother said the smell of the oil was stifling her.

Three years later, after her third miscarriage, the young woman poisoned herself. Noura's mother accounted for it by the power cut on the wedding night.

Long after her betrothal party, Noura remembered the incense. Her father hoped to turn the house into a temple by burning it. She thought the smell was very sensual. A young niece, on her mother's instructions, added little pieces of the desirable incense resin to several copper bowls where it was burning.

When Noura's father got up on a table with a book in his hand, the guests fell silent. He read a couple of stories from the life of the Prophet aloud, now and then looking sternly at several women who kept stuffing sweets and candied fruits into their mouths.

The official religious ceremony of betrothal, at the wish of the bridegroom, was conducted by Mahmoud Nadir, the well-known sheikh of the great Umayyad Mosque. The bridegroom himself was not present. Custom forbade him to see his bride before the religious act of betrothal had been concluded.

Noura did not take in much of the long betrothal ceremony. As her bridegroom's father was dead, Hamid's uncle appeared as the representative of the Farsi family. He and his wife had flown in again from Saudi Arabia the day before, and it was whispered that he had been allowed to use the royal plane for this family occasion, since he was a close friend of the Saudi king. The man gave his hand to Noura's father before the sheikh, confirmed that it was his nephew's wish to marry, and handed over the remaining part of the agreed bride price. The men prayed briefly together, and then Sheikh Nadir made some instructive remarks about the sanctity of marriage.

Noura had to sit some way from everyone else on a high chair like a throne, surrounded by roses, basil, and lilies. She must not smile, for that would be taken as sarcasm and mockery of her own family. "You should cry if you can manage it," her mother had recommended. Noura tried to think of sad scenes in her own life or out of films, but the only films about weddings that occurred to her were comedies. Several times she had to work hard not to laugh when she saw a guest behaving as comically as someone in a cheap Egyptian movie.

To make matters worse, Uncle Farid also kept making her want to laugh. He was standing very close to her with a group of guests. He had now been divorced for the sixth time, and he was as round as a watermelon. He kept telling jokes and making his audience laugh out loud and infectiously. Finally Noura's mother asked Uncle Farid to go somewhere else and leave Noura in peace.

Noura was grateful, but only when she closed her eyes and thought of the helpless boy being circumcised and crying so miserably did she begin to cry herself. She listened, unmoved, to the consoling words of her mother and the other women.

Her father's voice came to her from some way off. Now he was reciting out loud, with the other men, the chosen quotations from the Quran to bless the marriage.

"My little princess," said her mother, her face tearstained with her sympathy when Noura opened her eyes, "it's our fate. Women always have to leave their parents' homes."

Then came the henna day, a few days before the wedding. A large quantity of henna was bought, and the house was full of women from the family and the neighbourhood. They were all celebrating, dancing, and singing. They coloured their hands and feet with the reddish mineral. Some had geometric patterns painted on them, others just dabbed colour on the palms of their hands, their fingers and their feet.

And then at last the wedding day itself came. The newly bought stuff was carried to the bridegroom's house in a long procession. Noura's father breathed a sigh of relief.

More than ten respected men of the Midan quarter walked slowly at the head of the procession. They were followed by a tall man in an Arab robe. He was holding a large, open Quran up in the air. After him came a little boy, beautifully dressed, carrying the bridegroom's pillow on his head, followed by another with the bride's pillow. After them came four strong young fellows carrying the new mattresses and bedsteads. After that was a column of six men walking in pairs, each pair with a rolled-up rug over their shoulders. Next came four men pushing a cart with two small cupboards and two bedside tables fastened to it. A man of athletic build was carrying a large framed mirror in which the houses did a little dance as it passed them. Ten more men were laden with china, six with kitchen equipment large and small, others followed with chairs and stools, pillows, folded curtains and bed linen. Noura's clothes alone, packed in large, brightly coloured bundles, needed six young men to carry them.

In the bridegroom's house the procession was received by friends and relations with rejoicing, singing, and refreshing drinks.

The bearers were well paid for their help by Noura's father. They kissed his hand and went away singing happily.

Noura had another visit from the hairdresser, who examined her body and plucked out little hairs here and there that had escaped the first depilation, and then she massaged Noura's body with jasmine oil. It had a powerful fragrance. And then Noura slipped into the heavy wedding dress, ten gold bangles were pushed up her left arm, a broad gold necklace went around her neck, and two earrings, also gold, were placed in her ears. Then came the powdering of her face and the rest of the make-up. When the women had finished, Noura didn't recognize herself in the mirror. She was much more beautiful than before, and much more feminine.

Now Noura was led by her mother on her right and Mayyada on her left out of her parents' house to a decorated carriage. Noura thought this must certainly be copied from some Egyptian tearjerker. Behind them, friends and relations got into twenty more carriages, and the column started moving through the quarter in the direction of Straight Street. Many passersby, beggars and street sellers looked wide-eyed at the procession of horse-drawn carriages. And many of them called, "May the Prophet bless you and give you the gift of children."

"A niece of mine," said Mayyada, "had a disaster instead of a wedding last week. Her bridegroom's parents are rather old-fashioned, and two hours before the wedding her new mother-in-law asked a midwife who was a friend of hers to check my niece's virginity. My niece, who loved her future bridegroom dearly and felt she was approaching Paradise, had no objection, because she was indeed *virgo intacta*. But her parents rejected the idea. They felt it was a deliberate insult on the part of the mother-in-law, who had been against this marriage from the start. There was a great to-do, and in the course of it the two families came to blows. Only an hour later was the alarm raised, and the police managed to separate the two sides. The inner courtyard was a heartbreaking sight. Nothing but a heap of rubble, and my niece's happiness lay broken to pieces among it."

Noura's stomach turned. Why is she telling me this, she asked herself, is it meant as a helpful hint to me?

At the door of her future home she got out of the carriage and went toward the assembled guests, and as soon as she had taken a few steps they began to rejoice and welcome her in chorus. There were more than a hundred of them expressing their delight. Dalia gave her a quick hug. "You're more beautiful than any princess in the movies," she whispered, and then melted into the background. A man from the bridegroom's family placed a chair in front of the entrance to the house for her, and a woman handed her a lump of dough the size of her fist. Noura knew what she had to do. She took the lump of dough, climbed up on the chair, and slapped the dough down hard on the stone arch that framed the doorway. The dough stayed in place. The guests rejoiced. "Like the dough, you two will increase and multiply," they called.

Noura entered the house, and was fascinated by the inner court-yard, where her mother had placed a large number of candles and incense burners, as she had in her own house for the betrothal.

Noura looked for her father among the rippling sea of men and women. She felt strangely lonely, and hoped for an encouraging word from him, but he was nowhere to be seen.

Without a word, her mother drew her into a room where a pack of old women grinned at her. And now she had to put up with half an hour of the cheap spectacle that her girlfriends had already told her about. The women spoke to her both separately and sometimes in unison. She stood by herself in the middle of the room, while her mother leaned against the wall watching the whole scene with as much detachment as if Noura were not her own daughter. The women were reciting precepts learnt by heart to her.

"Whatever he says to you, don't contradict him. Men don't like that."

"Whatever he asks you, you don't know the answer even if you know it perfectly well. Men like women to be ignorant, and our knowledge is none of their business."

"Never give in to him, resist him so that he has to conquer you. Men like that. If you give yourself readily – even if it's out of love – he will think you're a girl of easy virtue."

"And when he takes you don't be afraid. You just have to clench your teeth for a second and then he's inside you, and before you can take ten breaths he's letting the juices of his desire flow into you. Start counting, and before you reach one hundred you'll hear him snoring. If he's very potent he'll do it three times, but by then at the latest he'll be nothing but a limp, sweaty rag."

"You must make sure to pump him empty on the wedding night, because it's not the first ejaculation but the last that puts his heart in your hands. From then on he'll be your slave. If he's not satisfied on the wedding night he'll be your master, and he'll go to visit whores."

They went on at Noura like this as if she were on her way to face an enemy. Why should she treat him like that, so that he would seem to be what he wasn't because she was not what she was pretending to be?

Noura stopped listening. She felt the women and the room beginning to go round and round as if she were standing on a turntable. Her knees gave way beneath her, but the women held her arms, made her sit on a bench, and went on talking to her. But Noura tried to dig herself a tunnel through the noise they were making, so that she could hear what the people out in the courtyard were doing. Suddenly she heard her father call to her.

After a while there was a knock at the door, and there he was. Noura pushed the women aside and made her way out into the fresh air. Her father smiled at her. "Where were you? I've been looking for you."

"And I was looking for you," whispered Noura, shedding tears into his shoulder. She was safe with him. But she felt a surge of hatred for her mother, who had left her to the mercy of those old women. The nonsense they talked stuck in her memory, word for word, for many long years.

Out in the courtyard, women were dancing with coloured candles. Her mother was busy giving orders, and Noura stood there for a while as if lost. Then she heard noise out in the street. A distant cousin of the bridegroom took her hand. "Come with me," she said, and before Noura knew it she was in a dark room. "We're not allowed to do this," she whispered, "so take care." She went to the window and lifted the heavy curtain. Then Noura saw Hamid for the first time. He was a handsome sight in his white European suit, striding toward the house in a group of torchbearers and sword-players.

Noura had wanted to get a sight of him ever since her betrothal. Her mother had told her where his studio was, but she avoided going near it for fear he might recognize her. "Men don't like inquisitive women at all," her mother had said. "It makes them feel insecure." The photograph that her mother had obtained in secret, by devious means, didn't say much about him. It was a group photo taken at a picnic, and Hamid was visible only as a vague outline in the back row.

The solemn procession stopped, and at that moment he was so close to the window that if she'd opened it she could have touched his face. He was not tall, but his bearing was proud and athletic, and he looked much more handsome and virile than all the descriptions she had heard of him. "The torches make all men better-looking," she heard the woman beside her say, but at that moment Hamid seemed like a prince to her.

It was all so unreal in the torchlight.

"Now you must go out and sit on the throne," said the woman as the procession reached the door of the house, to be welcomed with rejoicing and trilling song. Noura slipped out of the room and ran straight into her mother's arms. "Where've you been all this time?" her mother said crossly.

At that moment Hamid entered the house, and his keen eyes fixed on her at once. She blushed. He strode firmly toward her, and she looked down. Then he took her hand and went into the bedroom with her.

Hamid spoke reassuringly to her. He had known what she was like only by hearsay before, he said, and now she was much more beautiful than he had ever expected. He would make her happy, he told her, she should obey him but not fear him.

He took her face in his hands and moved so close to her that she had to look into his eyes. Then he kissed her, first on the right cheek and then on her lips. She kept still, but her heart was racing. He smelled of lavender and lemon blossom. His mouth tasted slightly bitter, but the kiss was pleasant. Then he left her alone and went into the bathroom.

At that moment her mother and their neighbour Badia came into the bedroom as if they had been waiting outside the door. They took off her heavy wedding dress and the jewellery, gave her a beautiful silk nightdress, straightened the bed, and disappeared. "Remember, we've all gone through this and we're still alive," said Badia ironically, with a dirty laugh.

"Don't disappoint me, child," whispered her mother in tears. "He will be captivated by your beauty, and you'll rule him by submitting to him." She kissed Noura, who was sitting on the edge of the bed, looking lost, and hurried out. Noura felt sure that both women were lurking outside the door.

Hamid came out of the bathroom in red pyjamas, and spread out his arms. He looked even more handsome, she thought, than in his suit.

The women in the courtyard were singing love-songs about the longings of women waiting for their husbands who had emigrated, about their sleepless nights and unquenchable thirst for tenderness, and at the third verse Hamid was already inside her. He had treated her very carefully and with great consideration, and she moaned and praised his virility, as her girlfriends and her mother had said she should. He did in fact seem to like that very much.

The pain was not as bad as she had feared, but she didn't really get any pleasure from the whole performance. For him, it was far from over yet. As she went into the bathroom to wash herself, he took the sheet off the bed and handed it to the women waiting outside the door, who hailed it with rejoicing and more trilling.

When Noura came out of the bathroom, Hamid had already put a clean sheet over the mattress. "I gave the other one to the women waiting outside – they'll leave us in peace now," he said, laughing a little. And he was right; after that no one took any more notice of them.

Hamid was much impressed by Noura. "You are the most beautiful woman I have ever seen in my life," he said in amorous tones. "My grandfather was wrong about Aunt Mayyada," he added, and he fell asleep at once. Noura didn't understand what he meant.

She lay awake on her wedding night until day began to dawn. She was excited by this great change in her life, and it felt so odd to be in bed beside a strange man.

The wedding festivities went on for a week, and Hamid slept with her whenever they were alone in the bedroom, whether at siesta time, early morning, night, or in between times. She liked his desire for her, but she herself felt nothing.

"That will come in time. I'm sure it will," one of her girlfriends consoled her.

But her friend was wrong.

15

Colonel Shishakli treasured Farsi's calligraphy. Nasri presented him with a classical poem in beautiful calligraphy almost every week. Hamid Farsi was glad of these commissions, for now many friends of the president also acquired a taste for his work and ordered calligraphy from him. He regarded Nasri as the bearer of good tidings, and unbent toward him, although Nasri hardly noticed.

The second time that Nasri brought the unapproachable President Shishakli a calligraphic inscription when he came to dinner, the president, much moved, was already putting an arm around his shoulders. Since the day when, as a poor child, he had been given a whole honeycomb to eat on his own, said Shishakli, he had never felt as happy as he did now, and he embraced his guest. "You're a true friend."

He asked the other guests to sit down, and then went hand in hand with Nasri into the garden, where he told him at length and emotionally about his terrible luck with politicians. The president spoke like a lonely village boy wanting to pour out his heart to a city dweller, rather than a powerful head of state. Nasri understood nothing about politics, and thought it better to keep his mouth shut.

When they returned, two hours later, the guests were still sitting around the table, stiff with exhaustion, and they smiled subserviently at their president. He took hardly any notice of them, thanked Nasri one last time for the calligraphy, and went off to his bedroom, shoulders bowed. At last the officials who were ensuring that protocol was observed allowed the guests to leave the table. Nasri was beaming, while the others swore quietly to themselves.

Calligraphy – Tawfiq was right there – has a magical effect on an Arab. Even the whore had gone to extraordinary lengths to please him since the day when he first gave her a piece of calligraphy. She wept with joy when she saw the famous calligrapher's signature under the beautifully written aphorism about love.

For the first time he found her ardently loving in bed. He felt he was in Paradise, surrounded by a cloud of perfume and her soft skin. It was a feeling he had never known before – either with one of his wives or his countless whores. His heart caught fire. Should he tell her he was madly in love with her? Better not. He was afraid of her laughter. She had once said nothing could made her laugh more heartily than when married men declared that they were madly in love with her just before orgasm. And as soon as they'd finished they lay beside her, motionless and sweaty, thinking guiltily of their wives.

Nasri said nothing, and cursed his cowardice. Soon, when the whore went to wash and gave him a cool smile – as usual just before he left – he was thankful that reason had prevailed. He paid and left.

Nasri had sworn never to fall in love with a whore. But he gave her a piece of calligraphy now and then, suggesting with a touch of boastfulness that it was he who had dictated the accompanying letter.

Nasri was surprised that the young whore, just like the president, could discuss at length details of calligraphy that had escaped him. When the words were intertwined like an impenetrable forest of fine lines, he couldn't even decipher many of them. The President and the whore, on the other hand, could read every word as if it were the simplest thing in the world. And when they read them aloud to him, he too saw the words emerging from the thicket of characters.

He would have liked to discuss the secret of his craft with the calligrapher, but the questions died away on his tongue. He was afraid of losing his sense of superiority to this man who thought so much of himself if he admitted his ignorance.

Only once did he get a chance to discuss a small part of the secret. One day, when he arrived at the calligrapher's studio to find him absent, the older journeyman asked him, at his master's wish, to wait, and showed him a piece of calligraphy to divert him. It was a painting of vertical, slender lines and curving loops, as well as a large quantity of dots, and it was intended as a blessing on the President. But all he could decipher was the word "Allah."

"I'm no expert," he said, "would you explain the picture to me?"

The journeyman was rather surprised, but with a friendly smile he ran his finger over the glass, tracing the letters of each word, and suddenly a whole sentence slipped out of the tangled lines: Leader of the People, Colonel Shishakli, God's hand is with you.

Nasri was surprised to find how easily the text could be read, but after a few minutes it was blurring in front of his eyes again. Only the single words Allah, Shishakli, and leader were still clear. The rest were lost in the forest of golden letters.

The year 1954 began badly. There was fighting against government troops everywhere. President Shishakli was under pressure, and called off the weekly meetings. Nasri saw him only in the newspapers, where he looked pale and as if he had shrunk inside his uniform, his gaze lost and sad. Nasri thought again of the lonely, vulnerable farmer's son who had poured out his heart to him. "Nothing but thistles and scars," he whispered at the sight of that sad face.

In the spring the Colonel was overthrown in a bloodless coup. The president made a short farewell speech and left the country, his pockets well filled with gold and dollars. Nasri was grief-stricken for weeks. He had nothing to fear, his business manager Tawfiq told him. The new democratic government was going to open up the country, and in times of liberty no one would be attacking businessmen. Personally, said Tawfiq, that primitive peasant who had no idea about anything but was ready to give his opinion on everything had really got on his nerves.

"And from now on," added Tawfiq, laughing, "you won't have to be coming up with an expensive piece of calligraphy every month."

Nasri was indignant to find his business manager so cold and ungrateful. The words that would fire his assistant of so many long years were on the tip of his tongue, but he curbed his anger when he heard the rejoicing in the neighbourhood, where only recently they used to turn out at demonstrations ready to give their lives for the president. He consoled himself with the realization that Damascus was a whore who would open her legs to any ruler. And the next ruler went by the name of parliamentary democracy.

Nasri felt that he had loved the overthrown colonel like a brother without admitting it to himself all these years. He suffered from a recurrent nightmare in which he saw the president opening the door of his house and smiling at a stranger whose face Nasri could not make out. But the smile froze into a mask when the stranger levelled his pistol at the colonel and fired a shot. Every time, Nasri woke up bathed in sweat.

The country did not lapse into chaos, as Colonel Shishakli had assumed it would. In the summer of 1954, the Damascenes seemed to Nasri more peaceful than usual, they laughed a little louder than before, and no one mentioned the toppled president. The farmers had never known a better harvest than they brought in that summer. And suddenly the news kiosks sold over twenty newspapers and as many magazines, all of them competing for readers.

The coup and the president's exile left Asmahan the whore cold. "Men are all the same to me. Once they're naked I don't see any difference between a vegetable seller and a general," she said callously. "Nudity is better camouflage than a carnival mask." A cold shiver ran down Nasri's spine when, on the way home, he worked out the meaning of that remark.

However, she appreciated the calligraphy he gave her, and enjoyed the letters that he claimed to have dictated to the calligrapher. They contained maxims, hymns of praise to sensual enjoyment and the pleasures of life. But none of them contained so much as a word about the deep love that Nasri felt for Asmahan. If that love ever showed through, even in a subordinate clause, Nasri asked the calligrapher for a different accompanying letter. "I don't want her to misunderstand me. Women weigh up every single word, and sometimes they think round corners, not like men. We always think straight ahead, and I can do without that sort of trouble in my life."

Farsi admitted that the remark could be taken as meaning that Nasri couldn't sleep for longing. He had no idea, however, that those lines had been dictated not by the poetic imagination but by a premonition. By this time Nasri's longing for Asmahan was almost tearing him apart. If he so much as heard her name, his heart was warm, and although he swore daily to forget her, he couldn't help noticing that his heart did not obey him. He had yet to learn that you can't decide not to fall in love, just as you can't decide not to die. It was Nasri's bad luck that he couldn't tell anyone, not even Elias the pharmacist, about his ardent passion for Asmahan and his jealousy of her other clients without making himself ridiculous. Who was going to understand that a grown man with three wives could still lose his head like a young man in heat over a whore?

No one knew that since childhood Nasri had been convinced that he must not love anyone, and if he did venture to love then the beloved person would be taken away from him. As a child he paid attention to his father but not his mother. To him, she was only one of several women in the harem building. He did not begin loving her until at the age of nearly twenty he saw how good she was. From then on he honoured her more than anyone. He had married his third wife only because his mother had taken her to her own heart. And indeed Nasimeh had a good character and a wonderful voice, but to his regret she was not beautiful. And what must his mother do, instead of being glad of his marriage? She died a day after the wedding.

He often lay awake wondering what curse he was under, or whether love was a lake that you had to fill with marriage and work if you were not to drown in it. He so often loved women whom he couldn't have. And hadn't he always married under compulsion? His father made him marry his first wife Lamia, with his second wife her brother's gun was the clinching argument, and with his third marriage he wanted to give his mother her heart's desire. You couldn't call it love for any of them.

He kept making up his mind not to love Asmahan so as not to lose her, but as soon as he was lying in her soft arms, immersing himself in the depths of her blue eyes, he lost control of his heart. Once he even broke into song while he was making love to her, although he knew that he had a terrible singing voice.

"I don't mind if you roar like Tarzan, it's funny, but don't look at me in such a soppy way while you do it," said Asmahan. "It makes me feel afraid of you, and then I'd rather be with one of those old gentlemen whose only problem is getting it up."

"Can you write me a letter with hidden words of love that go straight to the heart but don't seem ridiculous to the mind?" he asked Hamid Farsi. He had allowed himself plenty of time this hot May afternoon.

He wanted to give Asmahan a piece of calligraphy based on her full name, and have a particularly subtle letter written to go with it.

"How can words reach the heart without passing through the gateway of the mind?" replied Farsi, shadowing in a book title. Nasri was fascinated to see how the master could place the shadow of every letter consistently just where it would fall if a light had been shining on it from the top left-hand corner. That gave the characters a third dimension, so that they seemed to stand out from the paper.

"In the same way that calligraphy rejoices the heart even if you can't decipher the words," said Nasri. Farsi stopped for a moment and looked up. He was surprised to find that this nearly illiterate man was capable of such an answer.

"That's different," said Farsi, breaking the tense silence. It hadn't lasted as long as two minutes, but it had seemed to Nasri an eternity. "The internal music of calligraphy works on the brain and then opens up the way to the heart – like music when you don't know its origin or what it is about, but you enjoy it all the same."

Nasri didn't understand, but he nodded.

"All the same, it is not a mistake to send a woman you love well-known love poems, the older the better. Then you can say you are sending them because you liked them yourself and wanted the woman to share the same pleasure… it could be something like that, but it won't get past the brain. Language refuses to be smuggled in."

"It's not bad to speak plainly in the middle of the ambiguities of poetry," said Nasri. He had read that in the newspaper that morning, and liked it. The column about addressing the new head of state, who always seemed to speak in double meanings.

"Are you in a hurry?" asked Farsi. The Ministry had given him the honourable commission of redesigning all school textbooks, because in this new democracy they were to be cleansed of any traces of the dictator Shishakli.

When Hamid Farsi began complaining of all his commissions, however, Nasri spoke brusquely to him for the first time. "There's no deadline that should take precedence over an order from an Abbani," he said, "not even a commission for parliament. Just so that we understand each other," he concluded imperiously.

Hamid Farsi obeyed, for Nasri paid ten times the price that any other connoisseur would have been willing to give.

On the fifth day the letter was ready in a red envelope, together with the small framed calligraphic version of a well-known love poem by Ibn Saidun. As usual, Asmahan thought the calligraphy was enchanting, but the accompanying letter moved her to tears. Nasri stood there in her salon, at a loss. He saw the young whore overwhelmed by the beauty of the words. And he saw her emerge from the cage built of the steel of her coldness and fall straight into his arms. "Do what you like to me today. You are lord of my heart," she said, and gave herself to him as she had never given herself before.

Nasri stayed with her until morning. Next day Asmahan refused to take any money for that night. "With that letter you've given me back things that the world stole from me," she said, kissing him fervently on the mouth.

Outside her house, Nasri stopped for a moment, thinking of her beautiful breasts and lips, and breathing in the jasmine fragrance that she had sprayed on her hair after bathing. Hamid Farsi brought him luck, he felt convinced of that.

He set off for the office with a spring in his step, never guessing, surrounded by happiness and the scent of jasmine, how very wrong he was to be proved.

16

Hamid Farsi remained strange to Noura not only on her wedding night, but for all the nights that followed until she ran away. None of the well-meaning women who assured her that you got used to your husband turned out to be right. She did get used to the rooms and the furniture and to being alone. But how was she to get used to a strange man? She didn't know the answer.

In bed, Hamid was kind and considerate, but Noura still felt lonely. She almost suffocated when he was inside her and lay on top of her. She couldn't breathe. And this loneliness and strangeness hurt her all the time.

When all the dishes for the wedding feast had been eaten, all the songs sung, and the last guests had left the house, the frenzied exoticism of the wedding paled to ordinary loneliness. She saw him with new eyes, as if the bridegroom had left the house and a strange husband had taken his place.

She discovered his first weak point very soon: he failed to listen not only to strange women, he didn't listen to her either. Whatever she told him, when she had finished he spoke only of his own projects, large or small. They all obviously occupied his mind more than life with her. When she asked about his plans, he was dismissive. "That's not a suitable subject for women," he said. Any little dwarf of a man interested him more than a clever woman.

Soon all the words dried up on her lips.

He also plagued her with his iron everyday routine. She couldn't get accustomed to that. Although her father was the sheikh of a mosque, he had never taken time-keeping quite so seriously. But Hamid scorned such conduct. It was a sign of the decadence of Arab culture not to take time seriously, he said. He despised nothing in the world so much as the word "tomorrow," so readily used by many Arabs in making promises, doing repairs, carrying out orders, and meeting a deadline. "Don't beat about the bush," he shouted at the joiner one day, "give me a day with a date, because all real days have a beginning and an end. Tomorrow does not."

The joiner had promised three times to make a set of shelves for the kitchen, and in the end Hamid bought one in a furniture shop.

Hamid led his life by the clock, to a strict timetable. He woke up, washed and shaved, drank coffee and left the house on the dot of eight. At ten he phoned and asked Noura if there was anything she needed so that the errand boy could bring it when he came to fetch lunch at midday. The boy was harassed by his master too. At eleven-thirty on the dot he was outside the door, breathless and sweating. Poor errand boy.

At six on the dot Hamid came home to shower. At six-thirty he picked up the newspaper he had brought home from the studio to read it to the end. At seven on the dot he wanted to have his evening meal. He kept looking at the time. On Mondays and Wednesdays he went to bed at nine precisely. On Tuesdays, Fridays and Sundays he slept with Noura and postponed his bedtime by half an hour. On those days he was positively cheerful, to put himself in the right mood and drive the calligraphy that obsessed him out of his head for a couple of hours. Noura learned to smile brightly when her husband came home on those days.

On Thursdays he played cards with three other calligraphers in a coffeehouse in the new part of town until after midnight. On Saturdays he went to the weekly meeting of a calligraphers' society, but Noura never heard about what they discussed. "That's not a subject for women," he said sharply, dismissing the question.

For a while she wondered whether he didn't go to whores on Saturdays. But then she found a document in the inside pocket of the jacket he had worn to one of the meetings. It was two sheets of paper, with the minutes of a meeting of the calligraphers. She read the headings and thought it boring, and wondered why the meeting had been put on record. It was all about Arabic script. She put the folded sheets back into the inside pocket of the jacket so that he wouldn't notice anything.

Before three months were up her intense loneliness had become entrenched in the house. As soon as all was peace and quiet Noura showed her less attractive side. The beloved books she had brought with her changed into insipid writings that had lost all their attraction. And she couldn't buy new books without Hamid's permission. Three times she told him the titles of books that she would like to read, but he just dismissed the idea. Those were modern authors whose works would perturb family life and morality, he said. She lost her temper, because he hadn't read any of them before saying so.

To overcome her loneliness Noura began singing out loud, but soon after that she heard a venomous comment from the house next door that silenced her. "If that woman looks the way she sings, then her husband sleeps with a rusty watering can," someone called across the yard, laughing. It was a little man with a friendly face, and she refused to pass the time of day with him after that.

To take her mind off her troubles, Noura took to cleaning the house again and again. Only when she realized that she was buffing up the windows with a soft cloth for the third time in a week did she throw the cloth into a corner, sit down beside the fountain and weep.

The women who lived in the neighbouring houses in the street were very friendly and open, and when she was invited to coffee with them she found real attention and liking. The women, for their part, liked Noura's elegant way of speaking and her dressmaking skills, and they wished she would go to the bathhouse with them.

They visited each other early in the morning to exchange the rumours of the night, and again after the siesta for the second obligatory coffee of the day. In between they helped each other with cooking or the elaborate process of making candied fruit and preserving fruit and vegetables.

Noura laughed a great deal with her women neighbours. Unlike her mother, they enjoyed life and laughed at everything and anything, even themselves. Above all, they knew cunning ways of making their lives easier. Noura learned a lot from them.

But to be honest, the women bored her. They were simple folk who had nothing to say as soon as the conversation moved away from men, cooking, and babies, on all of which they were true experts.

They couldn't read or write. After several attempts, which failed piti-fully, to interest the women in something about the world outside their routine as married women, Noura fell silent.

The telephone was her salvation. On the phone she could at least keep in touch with the friends of her schooldays. That cheered her life a little, although the time still seemed to pass terribly slowly. Sana, an amusing school friend, advised her, "Write a diary about the secrets of your marriage. Especially about all the forbidden things you long for. But first find a safe hiding place for it!"

Noura found her safe hiding place in the storeroom, where there was an old cupboard with boards at the bottom that could easily be removed.

She began writing, and at the same time observing her husband more closely. She wrote down what she saw and what she felt in a big exercise book. In writing she learned how to ask the most difficult questions, and even if she couldn't always find an answer to them, she felt a strange relief at having put them into words.

With every page she wrote, her distance from her husband increased. Oddly enough, she now saw many features in him that she had not noticed at all before. She found out that Hamid was a bril-liant technician, but unlike her father he was not interested in what the words he wrote said, only in their form. "Proportion and music must both be in tune," he told her one day. "I can't believe," she wrote in her diary, "that a calligrapher is interested only in the beautiful appearance of the words, not what they say." And she underlined it with a red pen.

One day he brought an enchantingly written and framed proverb home with him, and found a place for it in the salon. Noura never tired of praising the beauty of the script, but she could not manage to decipher the words of the proverb. They wound their elaborate way around each other, turning and reflecting. None of the few visitors who came to the house could read it, but they all, including her father, thought the picture that the characters formed wonderfully beauti-ful, saying it satisfied the soul and the mind. When Noura urged her husband to tell her what it said, Hamid only grinned. "Dung makes vegetables grow faster." He took Noura's shock as a sign that she had no sense of humour.

Hamid was surrounded by the walls of his proud silence, as if he were in a citadel where women had no business. His old master, Serani, was allowed in, and so was Prime Minister al-Azm, whose house was very near the studio, and who was a great admirer and a good customer of the calligrapher.

But despite his respect for them, he kept even those men at a distance. In his heart, Hamid Farsi was lonely. Noura was deeply wounded to find that when she tried to get close to him she was repelled as if by thick walls. Her friends tried to comfort her by saying it was just the same with them. Sana had a husband who was consumed by pathological jealousy. "He makes a terrible scene if a man looks at me for too long in the street. Then he stands on his dignity as an air force officer, and I wish the earth would open and swallow me up. He's always afraid that someone else will take me away from him. As if I were a donkey he owned, or a car, or a toy. And he attacks the man at once, the way he's learnt from his father, his neighbours, and those unspeakable Egyptian films where men punch each other in fits of jealousy. And the woman stands to one side waiting, the way a nanny goat, a ewe, or a hen waits to see which billy goat, ram, or rooster wins."

Sana's husband never told her a word about his work in the air force. That wasn't women's business. "But we can be widowed," said Sana bitterly – and prophetically, for a few years later he crashed on the maiden flight of a new fighter plane.

Other friends thought of their husbands as insecure little boys who always needed their sand castles. Noura should be glad her husband was faithful to her, they said. And yet another of them accused her of ingratitude; there was her husband giving her a more comfortable life than she had ever dreamt of, and now she said she was bored.

"What a simple soul!" growled Dalia. "You just tell her that husbands spend more at the brothel and restaurant than on their wives – don't let anyone tell me about ingratitude!"

Even without the dressmaker's support, Noura felt no gratitude to a man who never touched her except when he slept with her, and for months on end didn't ask her how she was. He avoided any kind of touch as if she had an infectious skin disease. Even in the street he always walked just in front of her. She asked him to stay at her side, because she felt it was humiliating to be always scurrying along behind him. He said he would, but in the next street he was several paces ahead of her again. And he would never hold her hand. "A proud man does not do these things," he said briefly.

For years after that she wondered why a man should feel his pride was injured if he held a woman's hand, but she never worked it out. Sometimes she stood in his path so that he would have to touch her, but he always found a way to swerve aside. And if she touched him, he flinched away. He was intent on never showing himself to her naked, and if she herself walked naked from the bedroom to the bathroom he looked away.

Once he scolded her all night because at supper she had touched him under the table. They had been invited to her parents, and her mother was more cheerful than Noura had ever seen her. For the first time she actually stroked her father's cheek in front of guests. Noura was glad of it, and wanted to share her pleasure with her husband. She nudged his leg with her foot under the table. He was startled and alarmed. She had difficulty in keeping the smile on her face. At home he shouted at her, saying such frivolous conduct was like a whore, no decent wife did such a thing in public.

And that evening she shouted back for the first time. She was beside herself. If things went on like this, she said, she would freeze to death at his side. Hamid just laughed unpleasantly. "Then heat the stove. We have plenty of wood." With that cutting remark he left her sitting in the salon.

Her horror knew no bounds when she heard him snoring barely half an hour later.

What was Noura to do? Surely all she wanted was peace. Hadn't her mother said often enough that however bad a marriage was, it was a safe haven? None of that was true. She had never slept so badly, never thought so often of running away.

What exactly troubled her? She didn't know for a long time, not until she met Salman. Only he showed her that her mind was troubled by the certainty that she was wasting her life for no good reason.

Her secret diary was filling up, and Noura felt like a spy who had to observe some alien being. Even when her husband was standing or sleeping beside her, she was aware of the distance between them that allowed her to go on observing him in detail.

He was fanatical in all he thought and did, but hid the sharp edges of his opinions under a thick layer of courtesy. He wanted to be the best at everything, but apart from his calligraphy, he was as inexperienced as a little boy. She often noticed how her father would give way to him so as not to expose him. When she once mentioned that to her father, he replied, "Oh, child, you're right. In many matters he has only his assumptions, which he thinks are knowledge, but if I show him up every week he soon won't want to come and see us anymore, and that would be worse. To see your face means more to me than any opinions in the world, however accurate."

However, it wasn't only in theological, philosophical, and literary questions that Hamid always wanted to be the best, it was the same in many other matters, although he read nothing but the daily paper. After years of fighting to be the most highly regarded of all calligraphers, he had emerged victorious, and like all victors he was intoxicated by his own success.

When he had married Noura, he was so famous that, in spite of his high prices, he could hardly cope with all his commissions. There was no alternative but to delegate much of the work to his assistants. Of course, he did the designs and added the final touches himself. And he still executed the most important commissions, letters and eulogies in the finest of scripts, with his own hands and with enormous pleasure. He asked a high price, but his works were unique. And it flattered him when academics, politicians, and rich businessmen, delighted by the prestige that his work brought them, visited him on purpose to express their gratitude.

"What I provided in the commission," one customer said to him, "was an ugly skeleton of what I wanted, and you have brought it to life with a soul and flesh and blood."

Rich farmers in particular, men who did not know their way around the urban jungle of the capital, asked Hamid Farsi to write letters for them. They never asked the price, because they knew that his letters would open gates – letters each of whose pages was a unique work of art. Hamid never once repeated a pattern. That was also why he did not like letting the completed calligraphy leave his hands.

He would put his mind to the meaning and purpose of a letter for days, and gave it exactly the form that would turn the script into music, riding a wave that took the reader exactly where the man who commissioned the letter wanted.

In his work, he felt very much like a composer. Even his master had praised his feeling for the music of script. While others never developed a true sense of how long an extension should be, how many curves a word could take, and where to place the dots, he had mastered the art perfectly out of his own feeling for the art. His profound insight meant that he never allowed dissonance into the composition of his works.

Arabic script could have been made to be music for the eye. As it is always cursive, the length of the link between the characters plays a large part in the composition. The lengthening or shortening of this link is to the eye like the extension or reduction of the time for which a musical note is held to the ear. The letter *A(lif)*, which is a vertical line in Arabic, becomes a bar line for the rhythm of the music. But as the size of the letter *A(lif)* itself determines the size of all other letters, according to the doctrine of proportion, it also takes part in the height and depth of the music formed horizontally by the letters on every line. And the different breadth of both the letters and the transitions at the foot, body, and head of those letters, from fine as a hair to sweeping, also influences the eye. Extension in the horizontal and the interplay between round and angular characters, between vertical and horizontal lines work on the melody of the script and produce a mood that is either light, playful, and merry, or calmly melancholic, or even heavy and dark.

And if you want to go carefully about making music with the letters, the empty space between letters and words calls for even greater skill. The blank spaces in a work of calligraphy are moments of rest. And as in Arabic music, calligraphy too depends on the repetition of certain elements that encourage not only the dance of body and soul but also our ability to move away from the earthly domain and rise to other spheres.

17

Everything around Noura sank into deadly silence. Evenings became a torment to her. On some of them Hamid spoke not a single word, and if he slept with her he did it with gritted teeth.

Sometimes Noura forced herself to make no sound herself for a whole evening, just to see if he noticed. No reaction. He washed, drank his coffee, slept with her or didn't sleep with her, and snored all night.

And if he did say anything, it was only an echo of the hymns of praise that others sang about him. How long, she wondered, would she be able to endure this life?

Once, by way of protest, she put the dirty dishcloth on a plate, decorated it with a piece of the steel wool she used for scouring pans, and garnished the whole thing with matches, candle ends, and olive pits. She put the plate next to the jug from which he would have to pour himself water. He didn't notice. He sat there without a word, eating his meat pie in silence.

In addition to all this he was miserly. At eleven-thirty every day she had to send an errand boy to take him his lunch in a *matbaki-yya*, a dish in three sections: salad, main dish, and accompaniments. He never ate dessert, and he drank coffee at his studio. Almost half her neighbours sent their husbands lunch in a *matbakiyya*, but unlike Noura all these women were given money by their husbands and could go shopping. They haggled, drank tea and coffee, listened to rumours and passed them on, and laughed a lot with the shopkeepers. Noura loved to go shopping. Even as a little girl she had liked going to the well-known spice dealer Sami, to listen to the fantastic stories he told about every spice.

But Hamid said he could get better food at half the price, and anyway it was not right for the famous calligrapher's beautiful wife to haggle in the market with those "primitives," as he put it.

"He doesn't know anything about it!" she wrote in her diary.

Haggling was right at the top of any Damascene woman's list of delightful activities. Hamid had not the least understanding of that. He sent the cheapest scraps of meat and vegetables home to her by his errand boy, all the stuff that the shopkeepers could palm off only on men. And he bought in quantity, as if she had to prepare lunch for an orphanage, and although it was all of poor quality, Hamid expected her to make the most wonderful dishes out of it. It was her neighbours who came to her aid. They knew secret recipes for making tasty things to eat out of the cheapest ingredients. In return, Noura sewed for them for free, which meant that the women could keep the money they got from their husbands for jobs involving sewing, and spend it on coffee, cardamom, sweets, and cinema tickets.

Hamid Farsi never noticed this arrangement for mutual aid.

He didn't make Noura wear a headscarf. At the time Damascus was in a mood of elation, and only old ladies wore headscarves, while young women hardly ever did, and they wore the veil even less frequently. He was not jealous, but he did not want her to have visitors while he was out.

In fact no one visited except the neighbouring women, whose husbands didn't like them to have visitors while they were not at home either, but no woman in the area obeyed that prohibition.

Hamid didn't notice that either.

The world of family, friends, and neighbours did not seem to touch him at all. He was superficially friendly to everyone and interested in no one. If he found out by chance that one of Noura's girlfriends or neighbours had been visiting her, he rolled his eyes. "They ought to visit you when I'm at home." But apart from her mother, no woman felt at ease in his presence.

"It's sexual conditioning," said her neighbour Sultaneh, a little woman with only one eye. "Men are hunters, always seeking their fortune far away. We women are gatherers and search every inch of the ground for seeds and herbs. Sometimes we find a story that's like a seed, so small you overlook it although it has life in it and is tough enough to survive even if an elephant treads on it. Stories and seeds. That's why women love stories more than men do. That's why they make a better audience."

Noura tried to arouse Hamid's curiosity, and over supper she told him about what happened in the lives of the families living around them, about strange events, and adventurous incidents. But she soon realized that he wasn't listening.

"Keep well away from the disadvantaged and people who have suffered disappointment," was his only comment. "Misfortune is infectious, like a cold." She didn't know where he found all these proverbs that he kept shaking out of his sleeve, and she couldn't take remarks like this seriously. Or not until the day when he so heartlessly and ungraciously threw her friend Bushra out of the house.

Bushra was Badia's daughter, and had grown up – like Noura herself – in Ayyubi Alley. It was Badia who had helped to arrange Noura's marriage to Hamid. She had five sons and Bushra. Her one daughter was the darling of the quarter because of her wonderfully clear, loud laughter. Elias the confectioner would sometimes give her a coloured lollipop when her lovely laugh brought a smile to his face, driving the melancholy away. Noura too loved her, and when Bushra, who was seven years her senior, stroked her face, sometimes even kissed her and called her "my beauty," little Noura was in heaven.

Her parents, her neighbours, and her school friends expected the richest man in the city to choose Bushra for his wife. And at first it looked as if their expectations would be satisfied. Kadri the lawyer, after seeing Bushra pass his window on her way home from school, sent his mother to arrange it all with Badia in the hammam. After that the two women prompted their husbands, who then imagined that with their infallible sense of what was due and right to their tribes they saw how well Bushra, aged fifteen, and Kadri, aged twenty-five, suited each other.

After Bushra's wedding, Noura lost sight of her for seven years. And then, suddenly, the people in the quarter were whispering that Bushra's husband had made a cousin of his pregnant, so he wanted to marry her. The cousin, however, insisted that he must divorce Bushra first. Soon after that, Bushra moved back to her parents' house with her three daughters. She was twenty-two now, and looked pale, but not as if she had borne three children. She was tall and slender like her father, and had her mother's beautiful face.

The little girls amazed the neighbourhood. They all looked like copies of their mother at different ages. The eldest of them was six, the youngest three.

At this time Noura was learning dressmaking from Dalia, and she began seeing more of Bushra again. Together with the forthright Dalia, Bushra was a woman who could tell her something about marriage.

"What would you expect of a husband," she once said, "who slaps you about on the wedding night until you go on your knees and repeat, 'Yes, sir, you are my lord and owner of my soul and I am nothing?' After six years of marriage and three children, he discovered that he loves his cousin, so he is getting divorced from me," she told Noura over coffee one day.

The two of them got on as well as if they had been close friends all those years. About six months later, Noura heard that Bushra was getting married again, this time to Yousef, a friend of her brother, whom she had always liked and who had no objection to her three daughters.

Noura rejoiced at Bushra's happiness, but Dalia did not like the man. He was too jealous, she thought, for a woman of such stature, and had too small a soul. Was Dalia drunk when she said that, Noura wondered, or did she mean it seriously?

Before three years were up Bushra came, unannounced, to see Noura, who was now married to Hamid. Bushra drank her coffee fast, nervously, as if she had to unburden herself of what was on her mind. "He was crazy with jealousy when I had a girl again," she said. "He was sure he would sire only boys and they would look like him. But Dunia is a girl, and she looks like me. He accused me of still harbouring sperm from my first husband in my body, saying it would fertilize me all my life. The doctor assured him that sperm dies after a couple of days at the latest, but it was no good. He accused the doctor of sleeping with me himself, and went for him with a kitchen knife."

Just as she was saying this Hamid entered the house, and fell into a rage as soon as he set eyes on the weeping Bushra. He didn't so much as say good day, but ordered her in an icy voice to leave his house at once and take her bad luck with her.

Noura felt humiliated, and was sure she had lost Bushra forever. She cried all night. Hamid took his blanket, slept on the sofa in the salon, and refused to talk about it next day. As far as he was concerned the matter was over and done with, as if Bushra were a piece of calligraphy that he had delivered.

Many years later, Noura heard that Bushra lived only for her children. She had moved into the first floor of her parents' house, and got a job in the offices of an airline. Soon her laughter was as loud and clear again as it had been in her youth.

On the day when Hamid threw Bushra out of his house, she embraced Noura in the dark corridor by the front door, shedding tears. "He's sick with jealousy too. My poor sister in misfortune," she said as she left.

18

"Working in the café isn't the right job for you in the long term. You're not going to tell me you've learnt something here over the years that will help you to provide for a family later, are you?" asked Karam one warm autumn morning, and he did not wait for an answer. "Hamid Farsi the calligrapher is looking for an errand boy. That squinting lad Mustafa has made off," he added, and took a large gulp of tea. "You ought to apply for the job. Calligraphy, I assure you, is a goldmine." And he raised the glass of tea to his lips again.

Salman froze with horror. He thought the older waiter, Samih, had told tales because of their quarrel the day before.

It had been his first serious quarrel for years. That Monday, as usual, Karam was not in the café. And as always that made the waiter Darwish aggressive. He mentioned his suspicions of what Karam got up to, but only Salman knew the truth. Karam was spending all day in bed with his lover Badri, who like all barbers took a day off on Mondays. However, the café had no day of rest.

The quarrel flared up when the last customer had left. Samih, the eldest of the three waiters, had cashed up at the till, and transferred unpaid bills from his notes of them to the book where they kept the customers' records. As well as those who paid cash, there were regular customers and businesses in the area that paid weekly or even monthly. Salman and Darwish cleared the tables, washed the dishes, mopped the floor, arranged the chairs neatly and put clean ashtrays on the tables. There was nothing their boss hated more than arriving first thing in the morning to find the place in a mess.

Darwish was needling Salman the whole time, trying to find some way of making him lose his temper. The jeweller Elias Barakat had complained of Darwish's arrogant manner that afternoon, and insisted on having Salman to wait at his table. Samih, the older waiter, warned Salman not to stab Darwish in the back, but Salman didn't want to annoy the customer. The jeweller always tipped generously, and he was also a Christian, which was an important reason for Salman to behave well. Samih and Darwish were Muslims, and Salman suspected that they treated Christian customers brusquely on purpose.

Salman waited on the jeweller, who gave him a whole lira as a tip. He'd be back, said Barakat as he left, since this café still had one civilized and well brought-up waiter.

When they were alone, Salman could sense the pent-up dislike of the two Muslims for the "pig-eater," as Darwish had called him. Samih said little, but nodded to his colleague in approval of whatever he said, which spurred Darwish on. It was just before midnight when Darwish hinted that he knew Salman was always getting into bed with the boss to make sure he kept his place, or his clumsiness would have got him fired long ago.

At that Salman's patience wore thin. "You're just jealous," he shouted at Darwish, "because the boss doesn't fancy your bottom anymore, he's found a much more attractive one! You idiot, not even a raven would like the look of my bony behind! Karam fucks a wonderfully handsome man every day, but I'm not about to tell you his name, not even if you're dying of jealousy."

Darwish collapsed like a house of cards and began crying. Samih hissed, nastily, "You devil's spawn, praying to a cross! Did you have to hurt him like that? Don't you know how sensitive he is?"

In fact Samih was not a tale-bearer, but now that the boss was trying to make him like the sound of a new job Salman thought the old waiter had given him away after all.

Why would he go and work for the calligrapher, of all people?

If Karam had said he should go and work for a joiner or a locksmith, he wouldn't have had this sinking feeling in his stomach. But he knew that Karam, and even more his lover Badri, called the calligrapher a serpent and often said bad things about him when they were talking confidentially together. And now Karam wanted him to go and work for the man? Salman couldn't even ask his boss why, because he had often heard those conversations about the calligrapher only by chance. He had eavesdropped on them on the sly and with satisfaction, learning some of the secrets of the city, and with those he had been able to impress even Sarah, who knew everything.

But since Adnan's death there hadn't been many stories Salman could tell her. Adnan the taxi driver, Samira's son, always used to tell the most adventurous of tales to good effect during his breaks in Karam's café. Up to his death, he dropped in two or three times a day to drink tea with a lot of sugar in it. Then one night, as he was driving along a country road, his taxi crashed into a truck parked by the road-side. Adnan and his passenger died at once.

So the last big story he knew was about the lovers Karam and Badri. Sarah never tired of hearing about them. She was positively addicted to their story.

Badri could not be described as a philanthropist. He belonged to an obscure society calling itself "The Pure Ones." It was against Christians and Jews, but above all against a secret organization that went by the name of "The Society of the Wise." Apparently the calligrapher Hamid Farsi had something to do with this society, and its members, said Badri, were serpents. Outwardly they were Muslims, but in their hearts they were enemies of Islam. They used to pray to Greek gods, he said, and they went to bed with their sisters. Sarah laughed herself silly at the idea of sleeping with her own brother, because she had three brothers and couldn't stand any of them.

"That man Badri may have muscles, but there's nothing in his head but bird shit," she said. "All the same, what he and Karam do sounds exciting."

Salman could make no sense of it. On the one hand, Karam couldn't stand fanatics, on the other he wouldn't say a bad word about the Pure Ones so as not to annoy Badri. He was devoted to him, and Badri exploited the fact. Sometimes, after a quarrel, when Karam was weeping with longing for his boyfriend, he had to beg him for forgiveness over the phone until Badri was gracious enough to stop sulking.

When Karam got together with his lover Badri, he was like an affectionate little boy dissolving in gratitude at every touch, and doing whatever Badri wanted without a thought for himself.

In Sarah's opinion, love was a two-faced goddess who liberated you and at the same time enslaved you. She had taken a long walk to the Amara quarter, she said, on purpose to see where Badri had his shabby, gloomy barber's salon. Karam's love, she added, must have blinded him, because that muscle-bound hunk couldn't stimulate anyone in possession of his senses even to pick his nose. "I wouldn't be surprised if your boss were even to die for Badri one day, although the man's as stupid as nails are rusty," she said, and Salman laughed heartily at that expression.

But why, he asked himself that morning, should he go to the calligrapher's?

And as if Karam had heard his unspoken question, he said, "His is a distinguished art. Look at the people who patronize him. There are government ministers and doctors among his customers. And they all want to speak to Hamid Farsi personally."

Salman nodded, but he thought that was too good to be true. The arrogant and moody Hamid Farsi had fired an errand boy almost every year, if the boy, like squinting Mustafa so recently, had not made off already.

"You can crank your lower jaw up again," Karam encouraged him. "This is good news! It's not as if I'm sending you to work in a brothel. Calligraphy is a noble art. The rich love these things, can't get enough of them. And the best of it is, they don't ask about the price. Do you know what Hamid Farsi asks for writing out a maxim like *Bismillah ar-ruhman ar-rahim*? A hundred lira! Admittedly he's a master, but even the masters cook with water. And what do the ink and paper cost him? One lira! As for us here, I don't make as much as that in a week, and I have to put up with my customers' farting and spitting, their bad breath and their sweat. His customers bow down with gratitude. Ours never say anything unless it's to complain."

"But you know I hate school and books," said Salman, trying to build himself a safety raft with a little lie.

"You rascal, are you trying to fool Karam? Sarah has taught you far more than most boys know when they've taken their higher school certificate. And – " said Karam, leaning over to Salman and speaking in a soft conspiratorial tone – "you mustn't let the master calligrapher know how much you can do. You can always say you only went to school until Year Two. And then you can learn his art on the sly. Calligraphers guard their secrets jealously. So you must learn this golden trade in secret yourself. And if he turfs you out you can always come back to me."

Salman breathed a sigh of relief. "And may I visit you?" he asked.

"Are you out of your mind, or what? You'll come here to eat at noon every day, and once a week you can come home to my house to practise calligraphy. No one can get anywhere living where you do now. I'll fit out a little room for you. But not a word to the others about it, because they won't like the idea. Do we understand each other?"

He nodded in silence.

When he thought back to this conversation, Salman had to admit that Karam was right. Apart from Sarah's lessons, and the tips he spent on giving his mother a treat now and then, his time at the café had not been what he had expected at first, but rather dismal. His thoughts wandered around the dark hiding places of his memory. Three times a customer, a rich estate agent who lived by himself, had tried to get him into bed. He ordered small things every day, and touched Salman when he delivered them, his eyes shining with longing. He begged Salman to stay, saying he only wanted to stroke his behind a little. Salman was frightened, and asked Karam for help. Karam smiled meaningly, and from then on sent Darwish, who earned a couple of lira for keeping quiet about it, to the gay estate agent.

Nadia surfaced in his memories as well. Nadia, the pretty twenty-year-old daughter of the carpet dealer Mahmoud Bustani. Her parents had a fine house in Rose Alley, in the middle of the Souk Saruya quarter. Her father came in every day at three to smoke a water-pipe before going to his business. Nadia had been divorced after one year of marriage to a Jordanian prince. She made eyes at Salman until he really did fall in love with her, and she was always there to see him when he delivered orders for her parents or their neighbours. She wanted to know where he lived; he lied, and said Bab Tuma, the centre of the Christian quarter, and when she asked him whether he would convert to Islam for the sake of love he replied boldly that he would become a Jew or even a Buddhist for love if Islam wasn't enough for her. And whenever she asked prying questions about his home, he answered very briefly so that he could conceal his poverty. The beauty of the buildings in the trendy Souk Saruya quarter impaired his honesty. How was he to tell Nadia, or any of the other rich customers in this part of town, about the miserable hovel where he slept at night? There were houses with inner courtyards here, designed by sophisticated architects on the model of pictures of Paradise. Karam had not been exaggerating when he said the rich people of Damascus would be disappointed in Paradise itself and protest, offended, "We were better off in Damascus, so all that piety and fasting was for nothing." Salman thought so too. Paradise was probably made for the poor, and if there was solid housing and enough to eat there, they'd all be happy.

Nadia often complained that he just stood there in silence looking adoringly at her, she would like to hear him say something nice. As he couldn't think of anything, he asked Sarah to help him out, and she dictated the translation of an ardent French love poem to him.

But he was out of luck. Nadia wouldn't even touch the sheet of paper. She had heard from a girlfriend that he lived in a rat-hole, and she had been there and convinced herself of it. "A yard full of beggars! And then you have the impudence to lie to me. You don't love me!" Nadia laughed hysterically, but Salman sensed the suppressed tears of her disappointment. He wanted to tell her he had lied to her *because* he loved her, but Nadia wouldn't let him get a word in. When she told him he was a conceited little liar and it was only her magnanimity that kept her from complaining of him to his boss, he went slowly back to the café.

Karam called Samih to the till and went to the Souk al-Hamidiyyeh with Salman. He bought him two shirts, two pairs of trousers, socks, and new shoes. When they had all those things, they went to the famous Bakdash ice-cream parlour.

"Master Hamid would rather employ simple-minded illiterates than clever people," he said as they spooned up their ices. "He's so jealous that he's ruined the prospects of all three calligraphers who tried to open a shop in this quarter over the last ten years by spreading slander about them. He doesn't want to share the loot he enjoys here, where he has no rivals. But there are crowds of them in the calligraphers' quarter of al-Bahssa.

"He won't give away any of his secrets, so you'll have to spy them out for yourself. You mustn't take off the mask of an indifferent, uninterested simpleton. Perhaps he will forget to be on his guard then, and you must exploit that and crack his secrets. Find out the recipes for his famous inks, and what secret tricks he uses in his writing of script. What exactly makes him such a master? I don't know much about it myself, but I've heard that his calligraphy can be recognized even from a distance. You must find all that out if you're to be successful. But keep the secrets to yourself, write them down and hide your notebooks with me – and not with the Devil, he's in league with him! You must tell no one, not even Sarah. If he catches you, he won't just throw you out before you've learnt all his arts, he will punish you severely. He's done that twice already with incautious apprentices. One of them is now sitting outside the Umayyad Mosque with his crippled hand, begging, and the other sells onions. And neither of them knows why their master crippled them. He's the Devil's twin brother." But the sight of the dismay on his young friend's face told Karam he had gone too far. "However, he won't do anything like that to you. If he touches a hair of your head, there'll be nothing left of his studio and not an intact bone in his body. So you must learn everything, and don't be afraid."

"Suppose I can't learn calligraphy?"

"You're clever, you have a steady hand. And it's not difficult when you know the trick of it. A friend told me that if you have the right pens and the right ink, you've already half mastered the art. So you must take care to notice how your master trims the reeds for his pens until you can do it in your sleep."

"And why are you doing all this for me?" asked Salman, as his eye fell on the two big bags with his new clothes.

"It's nothing, my boy. I have no children, and after all, I owe you my life," he said, affectionately patting Salman's head. "You'll go to the barber today, and then to the hammam, and tomorrow morning you'll come to my place dressed like a prince at nine, and we'll walk round to him. But I'll call him today, because he doesn't like people to drop in unannounced. As I was saying, the French ambassador is more modest than he is," said Karam,

As they said goodbye in the Souk al-Hamidiyyeh, Karam held Salman's hand firmly for a long time. "I'll give you two years, and in that time you must have found out all his tricks. Understand?" he said in an emotional voice.

"Yes, sir, I'll try my hardest," replied Salman shyly. He laughed and saluted Karam to shake of the oppressive sense of gratitude that had moved him to tears. He did not know that he would keep his word.

Salman's mother was more than a little surprised when she saw him early next morning in his new clothes. "You look like a bridegroom. Has Sarah decided to marry you after all?" she asked. The preparations for Sarah's wedding were in full swing.

"No, no, but today I'm going to try to get a new job. With a calligrapher," replied Salman.

His mother took his head between her hands and kissed his forehead. "You smell of good luck," she said.

Hamid Farsi was not as bad as Salman had feared. Karam had known him for years, but Hamid had never been particularly close to him, or indeed any of the other neighbours.

What struck Salman at once, besides the clean and tidy studio, was the calligrapher's clever little eyes. They seemed to be observing him all the time, and going against Karam's advice Salman didn't try to lie and make his family out better than it was. He replied honestly to the master's questions, concealing neither his mother's sickness nor his father's drinking. Hamid Farsi raised his eyebrows, surprised by the frankness of this thin youth, who couldn't be more than seventeen or eighteen, but had already seen the heights and depths of life. He not only saw himself as a child, the boy's jug ears also reminded him of his beloved master Serani, who also had huge ears like sails.

When he asked what Salman hoped to get out of the job, according to his rehearsals with Karam he ought to have said, "To serve you, sir, and earn money," But suddenly Sarah seemed to be prompting him. "Sir, I hardly went to school at all, but I love our Arabic script. I'll never be a calligrapher or a scholar, but I'd like to be a good assistant. I'll try hard and follow your advice, and I'll be your loyal servant any time."

Karam was sure that Salman had messed everything up. But to his great surprise, he heard the most famous calligrapher in Damascus say, "Then let's try it. You are hired at once, and I'll show you what you'll have to do in this studio and who you'll be dealing with. So say goodbye to your old master, without whose word in your favour you couldn't even have set foot in my studio."

Salman went up to Karam and gave him his hand as he had been told. "Thank you very much, master," he said quietly.

"Good luck, my boy, and your hot meal will be waiting for you at my café at twelve every day. And be good, the way you've been good working for me all these years," he said, much moved, as he left.

Outside, he felt that he had been sweating with agitation, and he heaved a sigh of relief. "The crafty devil," he said, laughing, and then he set off for his café at the end of the street.

19

Karam had not been exaggerating. Calligraphy was an entirely different world. Never in his life had Salman thought you could make so much out of written words. He had regarded calligraphers as superior painters who provided signs for shops and buildings. But here a doorway was opening to secrets that felt like magic to him. There was nothing threatening about them in the same way as he had found school threatening, and not for a minute did he feel time hanging heavy and weighing down his heart as it had at school. The days ended faster than he could have wished. Work in the café had left him physically tired, but it had not asked much of his mind. He had wandered everywhere in his thoughts, but he had not thought much about what he was doing.

Here the work did not just call for physical effort, his head too was full to splitting with what he saw and absorbed. In the studio and behind it in the workshop, silence reigned, reminding him of the Catholic church outside the times when mass was celebrated. Not just Hamid Farsi, but all the calligraphers he met were quiet, taciturn men. All the same, Salman's head was so full of ideas that he even forgot his mother and Sarah, Pilot and Karam, because he spent all day thinking of nothing but what was going on around him. He was exhausted in the evening, but happier than he had ever been before.

Salman had to tidy the studio and the workshop every day. His master was more scrupulously clean than a pharmacist, and couldn't bear to see dust. After that Salman could study with the assistants. A saying hung over the workshop door: Haste is the work of the Devil. Nothing here was done hastily. On his very first day Salman watched the journeyman Samad, his master's right-hand man, who was in charge of the workshop, ornamenting a triangle through many reflections for the benefit of his assistants, until it turned into a hexagon with the intertwining words building up around a centre. Salman could still recognize the characters as Samad sketched them, but soon they vanished into an arabesque as beautiful and mysterious as a rose.

Every line was sharp as a knife, but the characters positively leaped out of the paper when the assistant Basem added shadows to the title of the book written out in a sure hand by the journeyman Samad. Salman was allowed to watch. The other men liked him because he did anything they asked at lightning speed.

Hamid Farsi looked in briefly, inspected the book title, nodded, satisfied, and wrote his name under the calligraphic design. He noted something down in his book listing commissions and went out again to go on working on the calligraphy of a complicated poem.

Salman took a piece of scrap paper, wrote his name in pencil and tried to give it shadows. It didn't look bad, either, but the letters did not rise off the page as they did when Basem shaded them.

When he made tea for the assistants in the afternoon, they praised his good taste. He had brewed the tea with the careful attention that Karam had taught him to give the job. "Coffee is a robust drink and can tolerate a few mistakes, but tea is the sensitive son of a mimosa. A moment's carelessness, and it droops and loses its bloom," Karam had told him. Hamid Farsi's assistants watched curiously as Salman made the tea with obvious enjoyment. They were not used to this kind of thing from the previous errand boys. Even the great Master Farsi was impressed. "You'll soon be setting up in competition with your former boss," he said, taking a large gulp of fragrant Ceylon tea.

"You must never forget the angle of the sun," Basem advised him now in friendly tones. "Look, if I paint a line that twists and turns, runs straight and then goes on in a zigzag, and the sun is up there on the left, where will the shadow fall?"

He slowly drew in the shadow as he drank his tea, and Salman saw how it accompanied the line, changing shape as the line itself turned. Master Hamid looked in at the workshop for a moment and nodded, pleased to see his assistant looking after the young lad. Salman jumped up from his stool and stood to attention. Hamid smiled. "Sit down, we're not in a military barracks here, and pay attention to what Basem says."

Over the next few days Salman went on busily absorbing everything he saw and heard. It was all new and mysterious to him. Even paper and ink suddenly became an interesting new world.

Every Friday, when the master – like all Muslims – took his day of rest and his studio was closed, Salman went to the room Karam had made ready for him. It was an attractive little room with a desk, an ancient but comfortable stool, a narrow bed and a tiny shelf. The room was light, there was a big window facing north level with the desk through which the heavy scent of myrtle wafted into the room in spring. There was even electric light.

Salman had his own key, and from now on he could come to his room every day except Mondays. In return he had to pump water from the river, water the shrubs, roses and trees, and then do Karam's shopping and clean the house. That was easy, because the floor was covered with coloured tiles, and except for Mondays Karam himself came to his house only to sleep. A laundry washed his clothes for him.

"You can use the telephone in the kitchen to call out, but don't ever pick it up when it rings," said Karam. He telephoned a lot himself when he was at home.

Karam had given Salman two large notebooks, one for practising calligraphic script, the other for writing down secrets and recipes.

Salman began to look forward to Fridays when he could indulge in writing down his impressions, neatly entering all his remarks and notes scribbled on little pieces of paper in the notebooks. Every time he entered his room he found two or three little poems that Karam had left ready for him. He was expected to learn them by heart. "Poetry opens the heart to the mysteries of language," said Karam, and Salman felt ashamed of himself if he couldn't memorize the poems.

Calligraphy was a new continent in which Salman was travelling. The quiet way the staff talked to each other in the studio was a discovery in itself! They whispered. In the first few days it struck Salman that, used as he was to competing with the noise of the café, he was speaking in far too loud a voice in the workshop. Samad, who ran the place, simply laughed at that, but the three other journeymen Mahmoud, Radi and Said, and their assistants Basem and Ali, tried to draw

Salman's attention to the pitch of his voice by laying their forefingers on their lips.

Apart from Mahmoud, whose manners were rough, none of the others smacked him around the head or used bad language. When Salman used the word "ass" one day, Samad said he should leave such words out in the street, and wait to pick them up and use them again until he had left the studio. The way he put it appealed to Salman, and from then on he stopped at the entrance to the studio and told his bad language to stay outside, promising to collect it again after work. And as if the coarse words had weighed as heavy as lead, he went into the studio with relief.

Hamid Farsi observed him one morning getting rid of his swear words, and when Salman explained what he had been muttering just now, Farsi smiled. But the smile was as cold as the smile of a monarch, and he was absolute monarch here. You couldn't joke with him, or even touch him to get his attention when he was deep in conversation, as you did with the customers in Karam's café. Farsi always sat at the front of the studio at his elegant walnut-wood desk. And they all spoke of him respectfully, indeed reverently, even Samad, who was older than his master. The studio in front of the workshop was forbidden territory to the assistants unless the master had summoned them. Samad, his right-hand man and in charge of the workshop itself, was a man of forty with a handsome face and a cheerful nature. He conscientiously directed and supervised the work of the three journeymen, two assistants, and one errand boy. Everything had its place, and none of the staff seemed to envy any of the others. They all had their fixed wages, on a scale taking their years of experience into account. Those who earned more could do more, and were regularly given the more difficult commissions.

Salman's pay was half what he used to earn in the café. Karam consoled him by saying that all the masters of the craft of calligraphy had begun as errand boys.

Every day Salman went round to Karam's café at lunch time. He had something to eat and drank tea, all free of charge, and then went back to the studio. Samih and Darwish seemed to be changed men, friendly and inclined to indulge him. "Be careful," Karam said. "Don't tell them anything about your work or your master. And not a word about your room in my house. That pair are both stupid, they'd sell their own mothers for bakhsheesh."

Salman felt as if he had been caught somehow red-handed, because he had nearly talked to Samih and Darwish about his master Farsi, who was so rich and yet lived so simply. He didn't drink or smoke, he never played backgammon, never laid a bet, never went to the café. He had lunch sent over by his wife in the middle of the day, and drank nothing but coffee and tea, which he had prepared for him in his own workshop. Only when important customers visited him did he send out to Karam's café for lemonade or coffee.

Salman learned willingly and fast under the supervision of the journeymen. Hamid Farsi seemed to take no more notice of him, and called for him only when he wanted something from the market or it was time to make tea of coffee. That didn't bother Salman, because Hamid seemed aloof with the others as well and took little interest in them, although he knew exactly what each of them could do. He never reproved them at length, but he was pitiless in his judgment of quality. The men trembled when they handed him their work, and if he approved of it they came back to the workshop in great relief. Hamid never showed enthusiasm. Samad, head of the workshop, consoled the journeyman Radi when he once came back from the master looking downcast and dropped to his chair like a sack of potatoes. He had to design a scholar's letterhead all over again because the harmony of the characters did not satisfy Master Hamid.

"If God himself were to write a saying out for him, our master would find something wrong with it," said Samad, helping the journeyman to redesign his style and rearrange the words, and Salman had to admit that the new calligraphic work was much more attractive. A day later Hamid Farsi glanced at it. He nodded, called for Salman, gave him the scholar's address and told him the sum that the customer was to pay. The scholar lived in the nearby Salihiyyeh quarter. He was delighted with the work, and tipped Salman a lira. Salman brought his master the money for the calligraphy and said, innocent as a lamb, that he had been given a lira, shouldn't he share it with the others? Hamid Farsi was visibly impressed.

"But how will you share it out fairly?" he asked, amused. He did not suspect that Salman had already worked out an answer to that on his way. He considered that lira a necessary investment to win him extra goodwill.

"The best idea," said Salman, "would be to spend the lira on Darjeeling tea. It has a delicately perfumed flavour and smells as if you had a garden full of flowers in your mouth when you sip it." At that moment Hamid felt, for the first time, that he liked the thin boy.

His colleagues in the workshop were also pleasantly surprised. They were happy to drink the Darjeeling tea he bought for them, but said that in future, unlike their master Hamid, they would stick to their strong Ceylon.

"It's flowery, yes, but the aroma passes off too quickly," said Samad.

"And it looks too pale," joked Radi. "It reminds me of the fennel tea my grandmother makes for her stomach trouble."

Salman quietly cursed their mothers for bringing such ungrateful folk into the world. Karam just laughed. "You've gone the right way about winning your master's approval, and that's more important than what the others say," he told Salman.

And sure enough, two days later Hamid called for him. "You've been with me for a month, you're making good progress. From next week on you'll be going to my house to fetch me my lunch and take the empty *matbakiyya* from the day before back to my wife. And you can take her any shopping I get you to do. The errand boy before you took an hour and a quarter about it. He was slow and let every street seller and conjuror distract him. I'm sure you can do it in half the time. Anyway, I want my lunch here on the table at twelve on the dot, even if there's chaos in the city," said Master Hamid, trimming the edges of a reed pen as he spoke.

"Don't ruin your life, take it slowly," the journeyman Radi told him as he stirred ink. And Karam whispered to him over his midday meal, "They say he has a pretty wife, so feast your eyes on her curves." He laughed so loud at his joke that Salman kicked his shin under the table in annoyance. "What do you think I am?" he muttered.

"What do you think *I* think you are?" replied Karam, laughing even louder. "A man with a hungry snake between his legs, and along comes a fat little rabbit."

"You're impossible today," said Salman, marching out of the café.

Only outside did he calm down. He went to the ice-cream vendor, bought his favourite ice, Damascus mulberry flavour, and it cooled his seething soul and sweetened the bitter taste in his mouth. Slowly, he set off back to the studio, and as he passed the café Karam called from inside, "See you on Friday." Salman was mollified, and called back, "See you on Friday too."

Next day Hamid Farsi paid off the old man who had been bringing his hot lunch daily. There were up to fifty earthenware pots in the trailer to his bike, belonging to the local craftsmen and tradesman. The old man couldn't read, so the pots were not labelled with names and addresses. But he never mixed up a single one of his customers or their earthenware pots. Now Salman had to do the job for Hamid Farsi.

"But whenever you need me, just call on me," said the old man courteously, and he bowed and went away.

"A good, decent man," said Hamid. He had always used the old man's services when he had no errand boy, or didn't trust the one he had. Samad made jokes in the workshop about his master's avarice. He himself, however, ate only dry bread with olives or sheep's milk cheese during the day, going to Karam's café at most once a week to eat a hot meal. "Our master is disgusted by snack-bars and restaurants," replied Said. Samad smiled. Radi, overhearing, shook his head. "No, he's just miserly," he whispered, rubbing his thumb and forefinger together – which means the love of money, and not only in Damascus.

Karam's café was too expensive for the journeymen Radi and Said. They ate at a grubby but cheap snack bar every day, with the assistants Ali and Basem. Only Mahmoud ate nothing at all during the day. He was a tall man who smoked all the time. He did not enjoy food, and would have liked to nourish himself by smoking, he said if asked to explain his reasons.

One Thursday Salman was told to wait for Hamid that evening.

Around six o'clock he shut up the studio and walked ahead of Salman through the streets at such a fast pace that Salman could hardly keep up. They went from the Souk Saruya to the Citadel, and from there through the Souk al-Hamidiyyeh toward the Umayyad Mosque. Was taking him on this long-distance walk meant to show how short the way was? Just as Salman was wondering about that, his master slipped. He had been about to turn into Bimaristan Street, and missed his footing on the smooth basalt edge of the pavement. It was strange for Salman to see his great master lying helpless among the legs of the passersby. Could Hamid have slipped because he, Salman, had been wishing he would?

"Oh, curses on them all," cried his master, and no one knew whom he meant by that. A vendor of drinks helped him up and offered him a glass of cold water. Hamid Farsi brusquely rejected it and went down Bimaristan Street, walking considerably more slowly now, past the famous Bimaristan Hospital dating from the twelfth century. One knee was bleeding, and his trousers were torn on that leg, but Salman dared not point it out to him. He followed him into Mahkama Street with all its colourful shops, which then led to Tailors' Alley, a street Salman knew well because he had often taken orders to a tailor in the Christian quarter. Tailors' Alley led directly into Straight Street.

The alley where his master lived was off Straight Street. Jews' Street was opposite it, but if you went straight on along Straight Street you reached the Christian quarter. The Orthodox Church of St Mary and the Roman arch stood not a hundred metres from the way into the alley. Salman's street was about five hundred metres from his master's house.

"Here it is. You'll knock three times and wait here," said Hamid Farsi, outside a handsome house, and he pointed to the bronze knocker. "Then my wife will give you the lunch, and you will give her back the empty pot from the day before," he added, opening his door, which like all front doors in Damascus was only closed, not locked.

"And one more thing," said Hamid. "No one must know my address, neither your family nor Samad. Do you understand?" he asked, and did not wait for the answer but disappeared, without saying goodbye, through the doorway and bolted the door on the inside.

Salman breathed a sigh of relief. Now he must explore the way thoroughly, because after his master's fall he hadn't been paying attention to it. So he went back and made sure he had memorized the way to the studio, street by street. It took him exactly twenty minutes, but it made him sweat.

On Saturday, the first working day of the Muslim week, he woke up very early. It was going to be a warm autumn day. His father was still asleep, and his mother was surprised to see him up and about. "So early? In love, or is there an alarm clock inside you now?"

"Today I'm fetching the master's lunch to take it to the studio for the first time. His wife is going to give me the *matbakiyya* from the day before, and I've never seen a Muslim woman so close or been inside her house."

"Muslim, Jewish, Christian, what difference does it make? You're not going to eat the woman. Just collect the *matbakiyya* and take it to your master. Don't worry so much, dear heart," she said, kissing him on both eyes.

At eleven he left the studio and went to Karam's café, drank some tea and quickly left again. Karam held him back by the arm. "Why, how nervous you are. I believe you're going to fall in love today," he said, and stroked Salman's short hair.

Salman's heart was thudding as he stood outside Hamid Farsi's house. He took a deep breath, knocked once and said softly, "Good day." And when he heard footsteps, he repeated in a louder voice, "Hello, good day, mistress… madame?"

A beautiful boyish face appeared in the slightly open doorway. The woman was not reserved and cold. She wore modern clothes, and she didn't have opulent curves, she was rather thin.

"Ah, you're the boy who's coming to collect the lunch at midday now," she said in a friendly tone, and gave him the three-tiered *matbakiyya*. He handed her the washed earthenware pot from the day before.

"Thank you," she said, and closed the door even before he could say "Good day."

On the way back he tried to calm down. He had broken out in a sweat, so he kept on the shady side of the street as he went back to the studio. He arrived just before twelve. Hamid Farsi looked at him sympathetically. "You don't have to run. You saw what happened to me and I'd rather you didn't sweat or get sunstroke and my lunch arrived intact instead." His lunch was salad, lamb in yoghurt sauce, and rice. It all looked appetizing in the little pots, and it smelled delicious. Salman could see why his master thought poorly of restaurant food.

There were aubergines stuffed with ground meat at Karam's that day, a good dish when Salman's mother made it, but in Samih's hands it ended up overcooked and tasted as bitter as the man's soul.

"Well?" asked Karam, when Salman had finished his meal and drunk tea with him. "Did you fall in love?"

The question troubled Salman.

"No, but if such a thing does happen," he said, "of course I'll let you know at once."

Next day, when Salman went to collect Master Hamid's lunch, he got his greeting out even before the woman had fully opened the door. "Hello, good day, madame," he said. She gave him a friendly smile and handed him the *matbakiyya*, as she had the day before, and also a bag of apricots from her mother's cousin, as she explained.

Hamid was having meat pie, baked potatoes, and salad that day. At Karam's there were *bamya*, okra pods, in tomato sauce with rice. Salman hated the slithery okra, so he made do with sheep's cheese, bread, and a few olives.

When he went back to the studio, the smell of apricots filled the whole place and even seeped into the workshop. After that day, Salman always connected their fragrance with the calligrapher's beautiful wife.

Over the first few months Salman learned the secret of making ink. He was only the humblest of assistants, of course, but he memorized the quantities and wrote them in secret on notes, transferring them neatly to his notebooks on Friday at Karam's house.

The studio was using huge quantities of coloured ink for the commissions of an architect who had designed a new mosque. Samad supervised the making of the ink, Radi did the work. And Salman had to fetch gum arabic from the spice market by the sackload.

Samad dissolved it in water and added a carefully weighed quantity of sulphur arsenic and some powder from a bag with no wording on it. When Salman asked what it was, Samad murmured something about sodium. Radi mixed and boiled up large amounts of bright yellow colour every day. For small and very small works of calligraphy, Master Hamid used expensive saffron extracts, but only he could use ink of that noble hue. Samad made orange from arsenic sulphide, white from white lead, and blue from powdered lapis lazuli. Various shades of red were made from powdered cinnabar or lead oxide, for others soapwort, alums, and water were used; for a more intense red, cochineal was added to this extract, a red powder obtained from the insects of the same name.

Samad warned Salman to go carefully with colours, because apart from harmless black ink most pigments were very poisonous. When Radi the journeyman heard that he laughed at Samad's fears. Radi mixed everything with his hands, and would eat afterwards without washing them. A year later he was suddenly attacked by stomach cramps, and as he was very poor he couldn't afford to visit a good doctor. He made do with herbs and other household remedies. Then he turned as sallow and grey in the face as a construction worker. In winter he started vomiting regularly, and soon after Salman left the studio in February of 1957 Radi fell so ill that he couldn't work. His hands were crippled, and when he spoke his mouth was a terrible sight. His gums were rimmed with black. Hamid gave him a small final payment and dismissed him.

But it was not only because of the poison that Hamid didn't like working with colour. As he said to one customer, "Black and white make music, the eye moves between two poles. That creates a rhythm, the music of the eyes, made up of emotion and precision. Colour is fanciful, it easily tempts you to enjoy chaos." Salman wrote that remark down on the margin of an old newspaper, tore the narrow strip of paper off and put it in his trouser pocket before he made the tea.

The only colour that the master really liked was gold on a green or blue background. My golden ecstasy, he called it.

For some time Salman wondered why the master kept sending him to the spice market to buy honey, although he never ate it. He discovered the reason at the end of August: it was for gold ink. That was the boss's business, and only Samad, Hamid's right-hand man, could make or touch it. And no one else was allowed to watch the two of them at work. But Salman stole a look in secret when Hamid was at work in the tiny kitchen behind the studio. The rectangular sheets of gold foil, gossamer-thin, created by rolling and beating out gold, lay between sheets of parchment in a big book with a leather cover.

Hamid would take a porcelain bowl, put gelatin, honey, and dissolved and sieved resin into it. Then he laid the gold leaf in the solution and rubbed it with his forefinger until it too dissolved. After that he rubbed a second, third, and fourth sheet of gold leaf. Next he warmed the whole mixture and let it stand before decanting the fluid. He left the few remains of gold that had not dissolved in the bowl for several days until they were dry again. He added water to the golden fluid and stirred until it was all well mingled, then he scraped the remaining gold out of the bowl, put it in a bottle and poured the gold ink over it.

Hamid always applied the gold thickly, let it dry, and then rubbed the surface with a smooth gemstone until the golden lettering shone.

Salman also made notes about the knives used by the calligrapher. Master Hamid's sharp knife came from Solingen. Samad's knife, of which he was extremely proud, had been made at a famous steelworks in the Iranian city of Singan. He had bought it from an Iranian who was passing through Damascus.

Salman got a sharp knife from a taciturn Armenian cobbler near the street where he lived. He wrote out a beautiful price list in calligraphic script for the cobbler, so that the Armenian would not have to struggle to speak Arabic, which he barely understood, and in return the man gave him the sharp knife.

Salman learned the complex art of making a reed or a bamboo cane into a sharp-edged pen. For many apprentices, the most difficult part was the final cut that determined the length of the pen's edge and the angle at which it inclined to the paper. "Don't saw away like that, cut it," cried Samad one day in horror when the assistant Said was cutting a pen. Samad laid the cane on a wooden board, brought Said's knife down on it once, and the cane was cut. He trimmed the edge and split it so that it would absorb the ink. The tip of the pen slanted at an angle of thirty-five degrees.

The assistant's jaw dropped in amazement.

"Now you can write Thuluth script. If you're hesitant your pen won't speak with a clear tongue that flatters the paper, it will have teeth instead, and you can't even write to your mother-in-law with a pen like that," said Samad, returning to his own desk.

Next Friday Salman practised cutting in his room at Karam's house. He realized that he lacked not just the experience but also the courage to cut the pen with a single stroke.

You had to be careful not to torment the paper with a reed pen, but move it over the surface like a frail and sensitive fairy. Samad had once also shown him the function of every finger of the right hand. "The pen," he said, "lies so that the forefinger moves it from up to down, the middle finger pushes it from right to left, and the thumb takes it in the opposite direction." And Samad had smiled with satisfaction when he watched Salman practising industriously on every spare scrap of paper.

Later Salman was to say that the turning point in his life, the moment that made him a calligrapher, had been on a certain evening in January of the year 1956. He was working overtime to help his master, and all the others in the workshop were doing a night shift as well. It was a commission for the Saudi embassy. The Saudis paid ten times the usual price, but in return they demanded the very best quality. They wanted a large painting made up of proverbs to be given to their king as a present when he visited Damascus.

That night Salman was spellbound by the elegance with which his master Hamid divided up the large surface and conjured the characters up out of nowhere. And by the time day dawned the painting stood there before him like a divine creation. On the way home, Salman kept whispering to himself, "I want to be a calligrapher. I *will* be a calligrapher."

In addition to his calligraphic exercises, Salman taught himself out of a little book that was available to all the staff of the workshop. It said that in their harmony Arabic letters must be based on the geometry that the brilliant calligrapher Ibn Muqla had worked out over a thousand years ago. It concerned the duality of curving and straight lines, of contraction and relaxation, of the visible and the concealed. Soon Salman could distinguish the seven different styles of Arabic script. He found several of them easy. He fell in love with the popular Naskhi style used in most books, but he was afraid to try Thuluth. However, he worked hard to learn, and Hamid even sometimes gave him a word of praise.

He came upon the name of Ibn Muqla on almost every page of this little book. His companions in the workshop did not know much about the great genius, but every week Salman heard his master launch into hymns of praise to that brilliant calligrapher, who had lived in Baghdad and whose doctrine of proportions still held good today.

Hamid Farsi said, of Ibn Muqla, "We are learning the art. He taught it, because God gave it to him. That is how, in his short life, he could do more for calligraphy than hundreds of calligraphers have been able to do since."

On the same evening Salman wrote that down in his notebook, and he added a large question mark to the name of Ibn Muqla.

In the course of the year 1956 Salman learned almost everything about the foundations of Arabic calligraphy, its elements, the equilibrium between the lines and the surface, the rhythm of a work of calligraphy following its rules as music follows its own: the dominance of one part of the words or characters over the others on a page, their harmony and symmetry, about contrast, overlapping and reflection, and above all about the secret of the empty spaces between the letters.

But the most important thing of all that year was that, for the first time in his life, he learned to love a woman.

20

Noura's Uncle Farid was unhappy yet again – it was his ninth or tenth marriage. She was tired of hearing him talk about women. He met the lonely ones when they commissioned him to write letters for them, and then fell in love with his script and his poetic language. Disappointment was not long in coming. Nor did he stop courting other women. "You need maturity in marriage, and your uncle is still a stupid boy," her father said one day when he heard that his brother-in-law had another divorce pending. Noura felt that there was one thing her uncle never stopped to consider, and that was time. He was much older now, and his considerable girth made him look rather ridiculous in his white suit and red shoes. His charming way with women had become the tiresome posturing of a toothless Casanova. When he next visited Noura she sent him away, asking him not to call unless her husband was at home, because she was not allowed to see men when he was out. She knew that Uncle Farid did not like her husband; they were as incompatible as water and fire.

"But Noura, I'm your uncle," purred Farid smoothly. "You can let me in, surely!"

"The same rule applies to all men," she said sternly, closing the door. He never came to see her again, and even after his death Noura did not miss him.

"In prison and in marriage time is the worst of all enemies," the onion seller told her. The old man pushed his handcart down the streets praising the cheap onions he sold in melancholy tones. He had spent three years in prison, and he was unhappily married for the second time. Noura paid for her onions, smiled at their unfortunate vendor, and closed the front door behind her. She was near tears. Her attempts to make time dance past on swift feet had failed again, as they had failed on so many days before. Her long phone calls to her women friends left a stale taste in her mouth.

Time was increasingly turning into a sticky, viscid mass, particularly on the three days of the week when he slept with her: Tuesdays, Fridays, and Sundays. On those days she would have liked to hide away after supper.

She had been fascinated by her husband at first, but that was a thing of the past, and now she saw him with open eyes. He was boring and conceited, but all that still left a corner in her heart that was free of resentment and contempt empty for him – until the night when he first hit her. They had been married just six months. And after that terrible night the empty corner was full of memories of her humiliation, and of a certain smell that his body gave off, like burnt rubber. His former body odour paled to a mere memory.

A strange feeling took over her when he came home. Icy cold filled the rooms; she was freezing and felt paralysed. She remembered a film that had left her feeling like that in the cinema, when a train was frozen in the ice in Siberia. All the passengers had frozen rigid, with ice covering their eyes. For a few brief moments she felt a fire in her burning as if it wanted to make her heart steam and save her limbs from the ice, but then the fire went out, and the chill emanating from her husband entered into her.

Hamid looked after himself carefully, showered every day, and rubbed a mixture of olive oil and lavender oil into his hands to keep them always smooth and supple – for his calligraphy, of course.

That day began with a disaster. A large jar, full to the brim of expensively preserved tiny aubergines stuffed with walnuts, had slipped out of her hand and broken into a thousand pieces on the tiled kitchen floor. The floor and the cupboards were splashed all over with olive oil. She had to throw all the aubergines away in case any little splinters of glass were left, and it took her two hours to clean the kitchen.

Then, feeling exhausted, she cooked Hamid his favourite dish, lentil soup with noodles, sent it off to him in the *matbakiyya*, and rested for half an hour.

When her neighbour Wardeh asked her to a little party Noura was delighted, and thought the day was saved. She was not to know that the real disaster was only just beginning. The sweet rice pudding she ate at Wardeh's house upset her stomach, and she vomited three times that evening. She felt weak and wretched.

But Hamid showed no sympathy. "I want to sleep with you tonight," he said, reaching for her bottom as she served him salad.

When she told him how bad the pain in her stomach was making her feel, he waved the excuse away. "You can be sick all day, but not on Tuesday, Friday, or Saturday night," he said, with a broad smile. "Those are my rights. Didn't your learned father tell you that God gives them to me?"

She wanted to tell him that her father never forced her mother to sleep with him, but her tongue would not obey her. Tears rose to her eyes.

She was afraid of him in bed, afraid with a mortal fear that left her lying rigid, and he was angry. "Am I sleeping with a dead corpse?" She felt angrier with him than ever before, and when she tried pushing him away he hit her. He was in a frenzy, and beat her mercilessly. She was so terrified that she couldn't even shed tears.

In this desperate situation, Noura remembered her mother's advice, which was always to say out loud the things men like to hear, so she began writhing and moaning and asking for more. And that was just what he seemed to like. When he had finally finished, he fell asleep without another word.

His sweat was sticking to her, and smelled of burnt rubber. She got out of bed and crept into the kitchen, where she scrubbed her skin with water and hard soap until it hurt.

From then on Hamid's special body odour made its way through any perfume he used, and it always reminded Noura of that terrible night.

Noura's mother always arrived whenever she was least wanted, whispering advice that no one had asked for. A snake. Noura no longer felt any real hatred for her mother, of the kind she used to feel, only profound contempt. Sometimes she suspected that her mother had fallen in love with Hamid Farsi herself. Whenever she saw him she gazed at him adoringly, touched him tenderly, and agreed to any nonsense he said.

"Your husband is the crown of your head, and you ought to serve him, wash his feet, and then drink the water as a gift from heaven. Proud women end in the gutter, my girl."

Noura turned up the volume of the radio so loud that her mother left the house without saying goodbye. She would have preferred to stay away from her parents for a long time, but Hamid accepted her father's invitation for them to come to lunch one Friday. It was a week before the New Year. The meal was excellent, and Hamid's paeans of praise went on and on. Her mother looked at him lovingly. "Teach your father-in-law to say charming things like that. He never says a word!" When Hamid thanked her for the coffee at the end of the meal she placed a hand firmly on his leg, which not even Noura was allowed to do, but he just smiled at her mother. Noura could have screamed with fury.

"You traitress!" she hissed at her mother in the kitchen, and hated the silly smile that spread over her mother's face. She seemed to be living in another world.

"Your mother has a good heart. She's worried about you," Hamid told her out in the street. Noura felt she was stifling.

"Hello, Noura," called Elias the confectioner. "Aren't you speaking to me anymore?"

Noura felt ashamed of herself for failing to see the old man – toothless now, but still amusing. "Hello, Uncle Elias," she replied, smiling.

"Ah, the master calligrapher has stolen the most beautiful lettering in our quarter and left holes in our alphabet. Would he like to buy his princess a kilo of assorted chocolates? Or maybe 'ish al bulbul, nightingale nests, or perhaps the best barazik, delicious butter cookies with sesame and pistachios? All of it fit to melt a lovely woman's heart."

Elias, like most of the Damascene tradesmen, spoke in a seductive singsong, making his eyebrows dance.

"We don't need any sweets," replied Hamid, narrow-lipped, as he walked on. Noura could only cast an apologetic glance at Elias, and then hurried after her husband.

That night, long before he began going to the mosque every Friday at noon – that was early in 1956 – Hamid forbade her ever to leave the house without wearing a headscarf. And he also threatened to divorce her if she spoke to Christian men in the street. Hamid was like a man drunk. He was shaking all over, and he could hardly get the words out of his mouth.

"So what happened?" asked her neighbour Widad when Noura told her how bored she was. "What do you expect? Even a miracle will lose its lustre if it happens 365 days a year. After five years you'll feel no more for him than if he were your brother. Our husbands can't help it. Time scrapes the gloss off every bridegroom, and there's nothing left but a brittle mixture called 'husband' and 'my children's father.'"

Widad drank in secret to summon up some feeling for her own husband, and when she was drunk she turned him into a wild seventeen-year-old hungry for her body.

Samia, a young neighbour from the north, told Noura that as soon as her husband, a boorish teacher, touched her she sent her mind out of her body to travel far away. She was a mistress of that art by now, and didn't even feel if her husband was still in her or had already gone to sleep.

Noura thought she would try it herself. While her husband lay behind her, pushing himself into her, she wandered around the bedroom, watching herself in bed. Then she went into the kitchen in her mind, drank coffee, and thought of a story from her childhood. When she saw the rolling pin she had used that day to make stuffed pouches of dough lying on the table, the thought suddenly came to her that she could pick it up and stick it in her husband's ass. She felt she could already see the astonishment in his eyes, and burst out laughing.

After a year Hamid wasn't even speaking to her anymore. Everything was going smoothly so far as he was concerned, and he seemed to be happy. She sometimes heard him talking to other people on the phone, and envied them their ability to arouse his interest. Whenever she herself tried to broach a subject he stifled the conversation at birth. "Obviously," he would say, or, "women's nonsense." She had fewer and fewer ways of getting through to him.

Dalia, to whom she poured out her troubles, just shrugged her shoulders. "Sounds as if you're talking about all my customers' husbands. Somehow the system of marriage hasn't matured yet, even though we've been trying it ever since Adam and Eve," she said, and took a large gulp of arak. "People ought not to be allowed to marry for longer than seven months, and when that time's up they should all change partners. That way boredom wouldn't stand a chance." Was she joking? Noura didn't feel like jokes.

She got used to the headscarf. At least with her head tied up like an egg – as her father said, amused – she could leave the house, but only to visit the neighbouring women or do the shopping that her husband didn't get around to.

But she was much better off than other women, said her neighbour Widad. Noura knew that not only Widad but Sultaneh and some of her other women friends were never allowed to leave the house without male company. The front door was as far as they could go. Sultaneh couldn't even look out of the window except on the sly, in case someone saw her. Nor could Widad and Sultaneh phone anyone – they had to wait to pick up the phone, so Noura called them at least once a day.

Even as a young girl Sultaneh had dreamed of going to the Café Brazil disguised as a man, sitting there with the men and then taking off her shirt. She also had the crazy idea of chaining up her husband so that for six months he could move only from the bedroom to the bathroom to the lavatory, to the kitchen, and back again, and then she would ask him, "Well, how do you like my world?"

Noura noticed how bold Sultaneh's tongue was when she was talking about her family. She tore her father's character to shreds, and her husband's too. His well-padded, snow-white body gave off strange smells, she said. "A different stench from every bit of it." Noura didn't have the courage to describe the torments she herself was suffering.

The hours, days, and months followed one another, nipping every surprise in the bud. Noura felt like the donkey working the olive press in the Midan quarter where she had lived as a girl. His eyes were blindfolded as he pulled the millstone round, turning it endlessly from sunrise to sunset. "His eyes are bound so that he'll think he's trotting to some destination, and every day the donkey feels terrible when they take the dirty blindfold off and he finds that he's still in the same place," Dalia had told her then. Noura knew the olive press and the millstone.

"But I'm not a donkey," she said defiantly. "God didn't make me a beautiful woman just so that I could walk on the spot all day long with my eyes bound." Dalia raised her eyebrows. "Oh, my dear, my dear," she whispered, and her anxious glance followed Noura when she left the house.

Noura's school friend Nuriman recommended a consultation with a famous clairvoyant; she wasn't expensive, said Nuriman, and she gave good value. She promised to go with her the first time, because Noura was afraid of walking through the streets in a part of the city that she didn't know.

"She's the only clairvoyant in Damascus," Nuriman whispered on their way to the Muhayirin quarter. They had to catch two different buses and then go some way on foot. In her own case, said Nuriman, the clairvoyant had seen at once that her husband was still bound to another woman by black magic. She had given her the antidote and taught her the right magic spells, and lo and behold, her husband, who had looked at her with as much indifference as if she were a block of wood, came home from work with nothing in his head but to give himself lovingly to her, added Nuriman in a rather louder voice. A significant pause followed. "Soon it turned out that other woman had been sucking him dry and keeping him away from me. She was a distant cousin of his, widowed early, who was hoping he would leave me and go to her. The clairvoyant described just what she looked like and predicted that the jinnee who possessed my husband and had tied a knot in his prick would leave him, take the woman by the ear and bring her to me. And sure enough, she turned up at my door with a red ear and had the nerve to ask after her cousin, saying he hadn't been to see her in quite a while. I wouldn't let her into the house. Let her wait for him in the street and put on her performance there," she said, with a brief laugh.

"And did she wait?"

"Yes, until he came back from work. Then she barred his way and wanted to know why he'd stayed away from her. But my husband pushed her aside and said she could go to the devil, he was better now and wanted to see his wife. She shouted right down the street until she got tired of it and went away."

In gratitude for his cure, Nuriman had taken the clairvoyant the lamb she had promised her.

"Do you think she can get my husband to sleep with me less and talk to me more?" asked Noura, thinking that she sounded ridiculous. Nuriman looked at her in astonishment.

"What? You want less of it? Are you sick?"

Noura did not reply. They had reached the place where the clairvoyant lived. Noura felt very frightened as they entered the room. It was all swathed in black, and it smelled of chicken shit and rancid fat.

The clairvoyant was small and ugly. She wore a stained black dress, and a lot of silver jewellery round her neck. It clinked whenever she moved.

After Nuriman had left, the soothsayer laid out the cards, looking at Noura again and again with her sharp little eyes. "Your heart has seven seals. Your husband loves you, but he has not found the right key. You must help him. He must take seven powders on seven consecutive days, and for each powder you must burn one of seven spells on paper. And here are seven pieces of lead, which you must put under his pillow."

For now, she wanted three lira. That was a lot, but not too much if it would do any good.

After a few days her husband had terrible diarrhoea, and complained of the strange taste of the dishes she served. That was all he said.

Noura visited the enchantress once more, this time on her own, to tell her about a strange dream. On the fourth or fifth day of her husband's "treatment" with powder and the spells, she had dreamt of Omar the vegetable seller. He was a strong man with a bald patch that was always shining, and his vegetable shop was in Straight Street. He was not handsome, but his charm was irresistible. In her dream, she saw him polishing up an aubergine. When he smiled at her, she saw that he was naked. He laid her down on a jute sack, covered her body with rose petals, cut a watermelon open with a large knife, took out a gigantic section of the fruit and put it between his mouth and hers. And as she ate she felt him penetrating her. She went on eating until the last of the fruit fell on her naked belly, and Omar leaned over her and ate the piece of melon, thrusting at her so hard that she fainted away with pleasure.

She had woken up in a very cheerful mood.

When she told the clairvoyant this dream the woman said, "Then my magic has shown you the right man, the one who has the key to your locks."

Noura thought that was very silly, and she decided to avoid the clairvoyant in future. As she was leaving she met a woman who was accompanying a friend to the enchantress's door, but did not want to go in herself.

"She's a charlatan. She lives on other people's misfortune like a maggot in fat," said the stranger. Noura was fascinated by what she said. She wanted to hear more, to comfort herself, and she invited the woman to eat an ice with her. On the way to the ice- cream parlour Safiyyeh – that was the woman's name – told Noura about her own happy life with her husband. She loved him more and more every day, and every day she found new qualities in him. She was a teacher, he was a master locksmith. They had known each other only slightly before their marriage, yet from the first day he had been loving to her, and his tender affection had grown even greater in the ten years since their wedding.

Safiyyeh talked a lot that morning, and Noura listened attentively. To hear that there really were happy couples in Damascus was more exciting than any fairy tale. On parting, she and Safiyyeh exchanged addresses, and promised to visit each other.

"If you ask me," said Safiyyeh, when they said goodbye, "part of your trouble is not being allowed to use your abilities. You're an intel- ligent woman, you should be doing something that fulfils you, not waiting all day for your husband to come home."

But Hamid reacted with a fit of rage when she cautiously hinted that she would like to work as a dressmaker. There was no one in their street who followed that very necessary profession. He shouted at her, and wanted to know who had put the idea into her head.

She did not reply.

Over the next few weeks she visited Safiyyeh several times and saw that the woman had not been exaggerating. Once her husband was at home when Noura arrived, having injured his hand at work the day before. He was friendly and left the two women alone, but he made coffee for them and laughed when his wife inquired, after her first sip, whether there was a coffee shortage in Damascus these days. It was the first time Noura had ever known a man to make coffee for his wife.

Other people's happiness hurt Noura, so she decided not to visit Safiyyeh anymore. It was all so simple. Why did Hamid refuse to take a single step along the path to meet her? He wouldn't even fetch the salt if it wasn't already on the table. "Salt," he said to her, and when Noura did not react, on purpose, hoping he would get to his feet, he grabbed her arm and growled, "Are you hard of hearing? I said salt."

Noura knew that she was at the end of a blind alley. She was in a desperate situation, but she regarded knowing it for what it was as progress.

It was at this time, when she was looking in despair for a way out of her blind alley, that Salman turned up. Salman, a penniless man with a child's beardless face and jug ears! She had thought him about fifteen at first, and was very surprised when he replied, blushing up to both his ears, that he was already twenty. She had to make a great effort not to laugh at the sight of him.

So why did she fall in love with him, of all people? She consoled herself by reflecting that love, like death, has a will of its own. It comes unexpectedly, and cannot be explained. And it sometimes seeks out people you would never have thought of, again like death, which can carry off perfectly healthy people to the next world while the severely ill beg daily for it to come quickly.

That day Noura felt a great need to write down everything going through her mind like waves beating on the shore, all the things she couldn't tell a living soul. "Love is a wild child, there's no hope for it, it comes straight into your heart without knocking on the door."

One interesting aspect of her love for Salman was the fact that it had not been love at first sight, as the old saying goes in Damascus. Early in October, when he first came to her door, she scarcely said "Good day" to him. Every day she gave him the *matbakiyya* and took in the heavy basket of shopping that Hamid had bought. This scene was repeated more than two hundred times in the seven months between October 1955 and April 1956. Sometimes she exchanged a word with him out of civility, or because she felt sorry for him, sometimes she didn't. Sometimes she gave him an apple, sometimes she didn't. He was shy, and far from talkative. And whenever she closed the door he went straight out of her head.

But one day she closed the door and couldn't forget him, and she wished she had not been so cold and condescending to him before.

It was a warm day in the middle of April. Noura thought of Salman all night. Years later, she was to say that her thoughts of him turned into a chisel knocking piece after piece out of the wall at the end of the dark blind alley, and near dawn, soon before she finally fell asleep, she saw a breathtakingly beautiful landscape spread out before her eyes, flooded with light.

Noura asked herself several times next morning: have I really fallen in love with him? She looked at the clock three times, and when she heard the knocker she almost died of joy. She forced herself to keep calm, but when she set eyes on him she knew her fate was decided. He didn't say a word, just cast her an anxious glance and waited for his orders. When she looked into Salman's eyes she felt as if she were beside the sea; there were waves surging through her, and she was a part of those waves.

She took his hand, quickly drew him into the house, and closed the door behind him. "Would you," she asked breathlessly, "would you like a coffee? Or a sweetmeat or a chocolate?" Her intoxicated heart was dancing in her breast.

He didn't reply, but only smiled. He would have liked to say: I'm hungry, do you have a roll and a couple of hardboiled eggs, or a piece of cheese? But he stopped himself.

"Or would you rather have something to eat?" she asked at that moment, as if she had seen his hunger in his eyes.

He nodded, and felt ashamed that she had guessed. She breathed a sigh of relief, went into the kitchen, and filled a large plate with delicious things: cheese, pasturma, olives, preserved peppers, and gherkins.

He was still standing awkwardly in the corridor, leaning against the wall opposite the kitchen. She handed him the plate, and two little flatbreads.

Salman sat down on the floor and carefully put the plate in front of him. She watched him, feeling happier than she had ever been before, and smiling.

That day she discovered, for the first time in her life, that her hand could move of its own accord. Even as she watched Salman from the kitchen doorway, her right hand was on its way toward him. Noura had to follow it, and the hand laid itself on Salman's forehead as if to feel how hot he was. He stopped eating, and shed tears at the same time.

"All of a sudden," he said, and paused as if fighting back his tears, "I know how my dog felt when he came to me and could eat all he wanted for the first time." He told her about his first, nocturnal meeting with the little abandoned puppy who grew into his dog Pilot.

She kissed his lips; they tasted salty. He kissed her back, breathing in the lemon-blossom scent of her cheeks.

And when he took her face between his hands and kissed her eyes, she felt a flame blaze up in her. She held Salman close. Suddenly it occurred to her that he must hurry. She kissed him one last time and stood up.

"The seven locks have just broken open and fallen at my feet," she said. He didn't understand what she meant. Quickly, he took the *matbakiyya* and ran away.

Only then did she see that he had eaten hardly anything.

Noura felt exhausted, as if she had been crossing mountains and valleys. She was surprised that she had felt such extreme pleasure merely from Salman's touches and kisses.

That afternoon she felt guilty. Was she an ungrateful woman living in comfort and betraying the man who provided it for her? She decided to be cool to Salman next day, to give him the *matbakiyya* and close the door, as she had always done before. She would be thankful – just like the lovers in Egyptian films – for those few dreamlike moments, and then read him a lecture about loyalty and duty. But when, in the middle of preparing this speech, she looked at the clock, it was just after eleven, and she longed to see Salman as a drowning man longs for air. And even before he had knocked for the second time, she drew him into the house and to her heart.

From that day on, time flew past as if it were made of pure ether.

21

Master Hamid was seldom agitated. By comparison, Samad said, the Buddha had been a man of regrettably choleric temperament. Only when his sister, a tall, pretty woman, came to the studio did he grow nervous. He didn't like her; she was vulgar and rather provocatively dressed, which embarrassed him. When she was there, the master couldn't sit still, and kept glancing anxiously at the door, as if afraid that one of his distinguished customers might come in and ask who that bold-looking woman was.

His assistants were curiously nervous too. Although she was their employer's sister, they greedily and without inhibition eyed her backside.

Master Hamid gave his sister Siham the money she begged for just so that she would leave his studio as soon as possible. And for some time after that he would curse his useless brother-in-law, a photographer, but apparently a very bad one.

The occasional visit from his mother-in-law, who had kept her youthful looks, also upset the course of his day. He was extremely embarrassed, although shyly friendly. As he always left when she did, Samad claimed that they were going off to a nearby hotel together. But that wasn't true. Hamid used to invite his mother-in-law to a family café not far from the studio, and come back quite cheerful half an hour later.

But in the course of the year, as his mother-in-law turned up more and more frequently, she got on the master's nerves badly. His assistants, of course, sensed it, and Samad said, shaking his head, "That woman will ruin his life yet."

Then, suddenly, she stopped coming at all.

In the spring, Master Hamid had many appointments at the Ministry of Culture, and whenever he was not in the workshop his assistants relaxed slightly. For months they had been dealing with more commissions than ever before, and Master Hamid demanded unconditional dedication to their work.

One sunny day at the beginning of May Hamid was at the Ministry once again, and since there was not much to do in the studio just then, Samad said they could all have an hour off. Salman went to see Karam, who said in great good humour, "Well, my excellent calligrapher, does your boss want to order something to eat?"

"No, no, he's back at the Ministry, and Samad gave us all an hour off as a reward for finishing all the work that's to be collected this afternoon." Salman said nothing for a moment, wondering whether he ought not to tell his fatherly friend Karam about his love for Noura, which was now three weeks old. He felt great confidence in Karam, and an equally great need to tell him everything. "Do you have a little time to spare for me?"

"For you, all the time in the world. What's it about?"

"There's a woman, don't ask me her name. I don't know it myself, but she's very beautiful and I... I'm not sure, but I think she likes me," said Salman, hesitantly.

"So where's the problem?"

"Perhaps I'm just imagining that she loves me. Maybe she only wants to drive her boredom away. And she's a Muslim."

"Well, it's not difficult to find out about the first problem. The second is a delicate matter, and you must approach it slowly, but there's always a way."

Salman smiled bitterly. "The woman is married – to a powerful man," he added quickly.

"Good heavens! What a fellow you are! First you tell me a harmless story, then every sentence is another hammer-blow. Do you love the woman? That's what really matters. Everything else will follow if you love her and she loves you. Married, Muslim, Christian, Jew, man, woman. None of that's important except to inflexible minds." Leaning over the table, he went on. "As you know, I love Badri, whatever he does or doesn't do, says or doesn't say. And he loves me, not the way I'd like, but as far as he can. That's my bad luck, but I love him. Even if it cost me my life, I wouldn't move a centimetre away from him. Love doesn't judge positives against negatives, what's safe against what isn't, what's harmless against what's dangerous, or it wouldn't be love, it would be a tradesman's balance sheet. So what does your heart say?"

"I love her very much, but I don't really know whether she loves me back. She certainly likes me, but I don't think she'd like it if she knew I live in Grace and Favour Yard."

"In that case you should leave her at once, because she wouldn't be worth your love. Although I'd guess that the woman doesn't care a bit where you come from. Who you are is what matters, and she's struck lucky with you. But if I may give you some advice, don't think too much, act – and you'll soon find out whether she loves you or just wants to amuse herself. Didn't your Jesus say: knock and the door shall be opened? Or was that the Buddha?"

Salman didn't know. The hour was up, and he had to go back to the studio. But Karam held him back by his arm. "I have something for you," he said, pointing to a bicycle standing by the pavement. It was a robust transporter bike, with rather wider tyres than average and a small, firmly mounted carrier above the front wheel, the kind that many grocers and bakers used for delivering goods to their customers. "Made in Holland," said Karam. "I got it in payment for the debts a no-good man ran up with me for a year. He assured me he was writing sensational books, but he was really writing poetry that would make our lame sprinters break all Olympic records if you read it to them for an hour and then opened the door to freedom. That bike covers no more than a quarter of what he owes. He'll have to have paid off half of it before I let him order a tea here again."

Salman was overwhelmed by this present, and hugged his friend. "I thought you could save at least half an hour in the middle of the day with the bike, and enjoy the time with *her*," he whispered into Salman's ear. "You mustn't tell anyone in the studio about your bike. Leave it with my friend the potter Yassin. You know his shop. You can pick it up whenever you like, and you can go from there back to the studio on foot. If one of Hamid's assistants sees you, say the bicycle belongs to Karam but you have the use of it now and then."

Salman thought of nothing but Noura all the time, and at quarter to eleven his patience gave out. He snatched up the bag with the roasted coffee that Master Hamid had bought his wife from the nearby coffee-roasting shop. "But it isn't eleven yet," Samad objected.

"Let him walk there at his leisure for once," Radi defended him, and Samad finally said he could go. Salman walked the first five steps slowly, then he raced to the potter's yard, got on his bike and rode away.

On the bike, it took him exactly ten minutes.

"You've robbed me of over twenty minutes of burning, tantalizing waiting," said Noura, pressing close to him at once in the dark corridor just inside the front door. He kissed her for longer than he had ever kissed a living soul before. Soon she couldn't keep on her feet, and she led him to the room opposite the kitchen. It was a kind of lumber-room with a broad old sofa in it. Noura had cleaned the room and cleared away a great many pots and pans, lamps, household utensils, and countless cartons of old junk.

For a long time Salman had seemed to her like a being from another world. Since that first kiss in the middle of April, he had made no attempt to sleep with her. She was burning for it, but he caressed her as tenderly and thoughtfully as if her skin were a delicate rose petal, and he was afraid of crushing it in his fingers. It made her crazy for him.

That day, when she couldn't stand it anymore, she forgot his concern for her and her own fragility. She pulled his trousers down and made love to him without more ado. For the first time in her life she felt what many of her friends had told her about total ecstasy.

She felt her veins catch fire. It was as if hot steam were surging through her body. Her heart beat fast, and she saw the most beautiful face in the world held in her hands, the face of a man making little sounds of joy like a dolphin, and in her concern for him she held him very close. "You taste of roast pistachios," he said, surprised, when he had licked her breasts.

Then he lay on the sofa beside her, and only now did she notice that he was not circumcized. "Did the circumcizer forget you?"

"No, we don't get circumcized," he said.

"Why not? It's a sign that a boy has grown up. Why isn't it a sign to you Christians?"

"Maybe Jesus wanted his followers to stay children forever."

22

Nasri Abbani would never have believed that passionate love could end so abruptly. He had been in love with fifteen-year-old Almaz for over a year. Even when he was with other women, he closed his eyes and saw Almaz. She had a divine body, with such a smooth, soft skin that his fingers could hardly get a grip on it. And she smelled so feminine! She was a mistress of the art of flirtation. She could turn men's heads as she swung between hinting at possibilities and refusing herself in a way that was all her own, something Nasri had never known in any other woman, a refusal that neither insulted a man nor entirely rejected him, but only said: you haven't tried hard enough with me yet.

She was the daughter of one of his tenants. Still a child though she was, she was far in advance of all his three wives together. She had a wonderfully comical sense of humour and was never at a loss for an answer. Her sharp tongue – and this particularly impressed Nasri – left deep wounds in her enemies. She was three fingers taller than him, and she also had a lovely face more like a Swedish beauty than an Arab.

He had known her when she was still playing with dolls. Even then she had that sensual expression that conveys flattery and provocation at the same time. Her parents appeared to understand nothing at all of what was going on.

Whenever Nasri visited her father, who wasn't much older than he was, she seemed to have been just waiting for him. She positively clung to him. He gave her generous presents, and never forgot to bring her favourite sweetmeat with him, pistachio rolls. Once, in the cold month of January 1955, he wanted to discuss a project with her father, but found only Almaz at home. Her parents had travelled north for a few days to go to a funeral, and an aunt came in the evening after work to spend the night with the girl. When Almaz bit into her pistachio roll that day, licked her lips and looked sideways at him with half-closed eyes, he lost control and his reason.

He got her pregnant.

His brothers and his assistant Tawfiq were beside themselves, and he would happily have settled the matter with money, but Almaz's father was a hot-tempered man. Either Nasri must marry the girl, or he swore he would empty his double-barrelled shotgun twice, first in Nasri's mouth and then in his own. He would sooner die than put up with such disgrace, he said, and he was not to be moved by either persuasion or blackmail.

Tawfiq, Nasri's business manager, was the first to give way. Better to marry Almaz and reinforce the clan with her children than unleash a scandal with an uncertain outcome, he said. The worst wife is better than the finest whore, because with a whore you squander not only your money but, above all, your seed.

"Well, I'm doing better there than my brothers," said Nasri, annoyed. "I'll increase the Abbani clan four times over. I'm a real Damascene stud bull," he cried, recollecting the International Damascene Fair last autumn, when he had come face to face in the Netherlands House of Industry and Agriculture with a formidable animal who, according to the information provided by the Dutch, had sired over three thousand calves.

So Nasri gave in and married Almaz in March. He felt a strength of love for her that rejuvenated him, while his other three wives made him feel older with their sorrows and complaints.

After the wedding Nasri and Almaz flew to Cairo, and then his heart was in trouble. Once made up and wearing pretty clothes this young woman, who had been no further afield than her parents' rural home on the outskirts of Damascus, proved to be a woman of the world. She gave orders to the men in the hotels and on the boats during their trips on the Nile, and made them run to do her bidding. They all wanted to serve Almaz. It left Nasri speechless. In bed, however, soon after the best moment, when he was drowsing beside her, exhausted and drunk with pleasure, she put on a performance that, for quite a long time, he could not understand. Only later did he recognize it as a mixture of pathological jealousy and a pronounced desire to dominate. She urged him to criticize his other three wives, and was always wanting him to promise that she came first in his affections, she was the mistress of his heart, and he would go to see the other wives only with her consent.

He could not and would not promise that, but he was ready to compromise. So he complied with her wish to make their two weeks of holiday into a month, but he was not putting up with her domineering nature. In the Abbani household, he said, a husband was always the master. She should be glad she was his favourite wife, but she couldn't ask for more.

He phoned Tawfiq and said he had caught Egyptian fever and must recuperate in a sanatorium on the Red Sea. Tawfiq was to make sure his wives had all their hearts could desire.

But extending the holiday by no means solved the problem. Almaz's jealousy continued to get on his nerves, and when he said a friendly word to a woman, maybe a waitress or a street seller, she made a terrible fuss. As she saw it, all women had only one aim in life, and that was to destroy her happiness with Nasri.

When they came back to Damascus they moved into a grandly furnished house in elegant Baghdad Street, but on the very first night Almaz started complaining that it was all so cold, so European. She wanted a fountain and a garden with orange and lemon trees, jasmine and grapevines, flowerbeds and beds of herbs. She could live in a place like that, but not in this unwelcoming building.

And then Almaz put on uncanny amounts of weight during her pregnancy, probably owing to the large quantities of cakes and other sweet things that she consumed, as well as the stuffed dough pouches that her mother sent her every week, as if her daughter were in danger of starving to death.

Nasri knew how pregnancy can alter women. Only his first wife Lamia had gone unaffected until the last few weeks. His second wife Saideh put on some weight, and her dislike for him grew steadily up to the time of the birth. She would not let him sleep with her for three months before it because his prick, as Saideh had read somewhere, would batter the head of the baby inside her.

His third wife Nasimeh did not usually think much of sex, but when she was pregnant she was lustful and wanted to sleep with him every day.

Almaz, on the other hand, went through a strange phase. She put on so much weight on her breasts, belly, and behind that her friends and relations hardly recognized her.

She didn't breathe these days, she puffed and panted, she didn't so much eat as devour her food, and she hardly moved at all and didn't do a hand's turn around the house. She enlisted the aid of her relations, and paid them generously out of his pocket. Only the smell of her was as feminine as ever, and still attracted him.

And with every kilo she put on, she was more jealous than ever because he seldom slept with her. She suspected all his wives and all the whores in the city of having conspired against her. Her digs at him burned in his wounds as if she had sharpened her tongue with pepperoni oil.

After the birth, his friends consoled him, all that would be over. The extra weight, her venomous tongue, and her bad temper would go away. But when Nariman was born in September, Almaz was more unpleasant than ever. Her daughter was now the centre of the world, and all and sundry should become her slaves on the spot. The worst of it was that her relations enthusiastically took her side. Almaz's parents mutated into babbling idiots, and sometimes, when Nasri observed them, he was close to calling the mental hospital and getting his in-laws taken away.

And then he and Almaz had to move to the Old Town, because her parents had inherited a house there from an aunt, and didn't want to sell it to a stranger. A number of houses in the city stood empty at that time. Damascus and its immediate surroundings had no more than three hundred thousand inhabitants, but covered as large an area as Cairo. As Nasri would not agree to rent it, or to live on his in-laws' charity, he bought the house from them.

It was south of the Umayyad Mosque, in a side street close to Straight Street. It had a small but beautiful inner courtyard with a garden, a bitter orange tree, a sweet orange tree, and a fountain. Everything about the house was small and full of nooks and crannies, but not only did it have an upper floor, like all the Arab houses in this part of town, it also had an attic storey above that. You reached the attic from the first floor up a tall wooden ladder.

Their move in November cost Nasri the last of his strength, since Almaz hardly did anything, and nothing pleased her. When he poured out his sorrows to his friend Elias the pharmacist, Elias laughed cynically. "If you marry any more wives there'll soon be a housing shortage in Damascus."

Nasri couldn't laugh at this joke.

Almaz's parents seemed to have taken up residence in the house. Whenever he came home to it they were there. Several times he was on the point of getting divorced from Almaz, but his brothers and his business manager recommended him to keep his temper in the interests of the clan.

So after a long interval he went back to visiting Asmahan, his favourite whore. However, she had changed completely. Not only did she want him to love her passionately, she was also making him the crazy proposition of giving up her life as a whore to be available only to him.

Asmahan represented danger, because she had fallen in love with him. Over all the years when he had been unable to sleep at night for thinking about her, she had remained cold – and now that he wanted no more from her, she was pestering him.

There was nothing for it but flight.

Of course Almaz found out about his visits to Asmahan and asked him to explain himself. He knew perfectly well, she said, that she needed his loving care, and if he was still going off to see whores, she would get her revenge on him some day.

Her parents, who were present, froze rigid with shame. They would have liked to get up and go, but Almaz wagged her forefinger at them to make them stay where they were.

"Women talk a lot of nonsense. I don't have anything to do with whores," said Nasri patronizingly.

Elias the pharmacist warned him not to take her threat lightly. Nasri, however, felt sure of himself, since his relationship with Asmahan had been on ice for some time.

Almaz soon seemed to calm down, but she remained cool. If he visited her once every four days he found it tedious. He disliked her parents so much that he often lost his temper and sent them home, but sometimes he actually found the fuss they kicked up consoling. They clowned about with baby Nariman all day, and were slaves of their own daughter.

Usually, however, the spectacle repelled him. He moved his bedroom to the first floor and left the ground floor under his wife's rule. Upstairs he was left undisturbed.

Almaz did not lose any weight at all after Nariman's birth, and moved about like a sumo wrestler. Only her enchanting odour and her daughter reminded him, painfully, of her former beauty.

One October day he was sitting on the tiny terrace in front of the attic with his father-in-law, drinking a little bottle of arak with iced water. It was warm and summery. They looked out across the rooftops of the city as it slowly grew quieter while sunset came on. Pigeon breeders sent their birds up into the air, directing them from their roofs by whistling, and the pigeons circled and performed acrobatic dives and turns as they flew. At this evening hour the carpet of sound that filled the sky above Damascus grew calmer and more melancholy.

They ate roasted peanuts, drank the chilled, cloudy arak out of delicate glasses, and discussed happiness and women, this year's harvest and the war on the Suez Canal.

When the bottle was empty, the nuts were eaten, and they had exchanged stories and rumours, Nasri's father-in-law set off on his way back to the ground floor. He spoke the name of God as a charm to protect him, because he was afraid of the rickety old wooden ladder that led down to the first-floor terrace where washing was hung out. Nasri put the chairs and the little marble table away in the attic, which consisted of only one room with a window looking east, opposite the door.

That little window gave him a glimpse of the house next door. It was not at a very good angle, but he could make out the kitchen window on the ground floor and part of the inner courtyard, with a fountain and trees, as well as a lumber-room on the first floor of the house.

He looked idly through the half-closed shutters of his window – and then he saw her. She was bathing at her leisure, singing softly to herself. What a sight! What beauty! Nasri gazed and gazed, and had to swallow because his throat was so dry that it hurt. At that moment his wife called him down to supper.

He took no notice of either the food or the conversation.

Next morning he woke very early, crept up to the attic and watched the house next door again. It lay there perfectly peaceful in the light of dawn.

The unknown woman had taken possession of him. She had a delicate face with big, beautiful eyes, and was a little shorter than Nasri and almost boyishly slender. He had never had a woman like that yet. Who was she? Why was there no man in the house? Was she a widow? Or one of the several wives of a man who visited her only once a week?

Whoever she was, Nasri wanted her.

But he had to be patient, because he was about to go to Saudi Arabia, Jordan, and Morocco with Tawfiq on important business. His presence was essential.

Two weeks later he boarded a rather elderly Syrian Airlines plane for the flight back to Damascus. Tawfiq, who was with him, had some excellent contracts in the bag and was beaming with satisfaction, while Nasri Abbani was in a bad temper and looked as if he hadn't had enough sleep.

When Nasri went up to the attic immediately after his return to look for his unknown beloved, it seemed as if the earth had swallowed her up. Where was she? He would have to spy on her cautiously without letting the jealous Almaz notice anything.

While he was thinking about that, Almaz came heaving herself upstairs and wanted to know what he was doing up there.

The best time for him was during the siesta, when Almaz slept soundly. Even if Nariman cried she had no chance of attracting her mother's attention. If her grandparents weren't there she had to calm herself down on her own, because Almaz lay sleeping like a log, snoring so loudly that it sent the flies in the bedroom looking for escape.

What could Nasri do? Now and then the voice of reason spoke, blaming him for acting like a boy in love. There were whores all over the New Town, each lovelier than the last, and here he was waiting, with his heart thumping, for a sight of a woman neighbour. But he ignored the voice of reason. Defiantly, he whispered, "So what about it? Love makes us children again."

One icy December morning, pale with his grief, he went into Hamid Farsi's studio. The calligrapher had customers, a married couple who had come to collect a framed calligraphic work. Nasri said a civil good day and waited patiently. His mind was elsewhere, and he did not take in much of the lively conversation, except that the couple thought the picture was too expensive.

"Your coffee," said someone beside him. It was a thin young man with jug ears, serving him the sweet coffee.

The coffee tasted insipid, and the troublesome customers wouldn't stop haggling. Hamid Farsi was obviously annoyed. Nasri tried to read his thoughts: first the customers commission an expensive work from the best calligrapher in the city, and then they get faint-hearted when it comes to paying!

After a full quarter of an hour Hamid agreed a price with the husband that was ten lira less than the sum he himself had asked. The delicate little red-haired wife was not satisfied. She hissed something inaudible to her husband, and when he did not react she rolled her eyes and showed Nasri her annoyance. He refrained from giving her the smile of solidarity that usually unites customers against the person they are dealing with. These miserly people were getting on his nerves.

When the deal was finally done, the calligrapher put the money in his desk drawer and turned to Nasri with a broad smile.

"Where have you been all this time? I haven't heard anything of you for ages. I even looked in to see you recently to make you a proposition!"

"You came to see me?" asked Nasri in surprise, put out because they had not told him at the office.

"Yes, we are planning to found a School of Calligraphy. We already have generous support from the Ministry of Culture and the leading families of Damascus – al-Azm, Bakri, Sihnawi, Barasi, Asfar, Ghazi, Mardam Bey and many other personalities, for instance Shukri al-Quwwatli, Fares al-Khuri, Khalid al-Azm, Fakri al-Barudi and Sabri al-Assali have not only welcomed our idea, they are backing us with large donations. And I thought you ought not to be missing from that catalogue of honourable men. Arabic script must be close to all hearts. Our beautiful art must not fall into neglect and decline, it must be studied, cleansed of unnecessary accretions, further developed. If we don't do anything about it our script will soon be written by European machines." The calligrapher noticed that Nasri seemed preoccupied, so he would have to entice him. "Of course there'll be a marble slab immortalizing the names of all who made the school possible. And if I know you and your generosity, yours will be up there at the top."

Now Nasri knew why they hadn't told him about this at the office. It had been agreed not exactly to turn down all requests for donations but to leave them unanswered long enough and often enough to wear out the petitioners – and there were a great many in Damascus – until they gave up asking of their own accord.

But this was different. He imagined first, and enjoyably, the envy of his two brothers when they found his name among donors including the great men of politics and culture, then he thought of the annoyance of his teachers who used to tell him that the Arabic language would be put to shame by the damage he did to it every day. For a moment he thought, with particular relish, of Sheikh Rashid Dumani, the teacher he particularly hated. He would make sure he was invited to the opening ceremony.

"A good idea," he said, "and I'd be happy to be part of it. As it happens, I have a newly renovated house standing empty in elegant Baghdad Street – you can have it rent-free for the next ten years. The donation will run out then, and the school can rent or buy the house. Just so long as it is in the same spotless condition in ten years' time as you'll find it today. What do you say?"

"You leave me speechless," said the calligrapher, unable to restrain his tears. Nasri felt nothing when he saw the emotions of a man who was usually so cold welling up. The house was empty, like four others that he owned, and if an empty house could win him renown while scholars lived a life of poverty, it just went to show, yet again, that school was not the way to fame and fortune.

"Do you have teachers and enough students?" asked Nasri, to break the oppressive silence.

"Teachers, yes, and we must pick our students from all over the country. Only the best will be fit to say they studied with us, and soon the school will be world famous, for we set store by the quality of training in calligraphy according to the criteria of the legendary Ibn Muqla. Students will come to us from all the Arab and Islamic countries, making Damascus their centre. When can I see the house?"

"There's not much to see; it's a modern European building. Seven rooms on the ground floor, five on the first floor, and five more on the second floor. There's a kitchen, two bathrooms and two lavatories on each floor. Go to see my business manager today and sign a contract. I'll call him and give him instructions. When are you thinking of opening the school?"

"If God wills, in May, but the official ceremony will be in March, so that we can begin advertising in February and send out invitations." Hamid stopped for a moment and turned to the workshop. "Salman," he called, and the young man who had served Nasri his coffee appeared, "run over to Karam's, will you, and fetch us two cups of coffee."

"Not for me, thank you, I must go in a moment, and I'll have to drink coffee again where I'm going... so thank you, no more today, please, but could I have a word with you in private?" said Nasri, glancing at the young man with the jug ears.

"We can go out for a moment. There are several cafés that open very early in the Salihiyyeh quarter," said Hamid.

Ten minutes later they were sitting almost alone in the Café al-Amir. "It's about a woman," said Nasri when the old waiter had grumpily brought them steaming cups of coffee. "A woman who has stolen my heart. I need a letter. She's a young widow and lives very quietly. That's why I need your help. Your letters have always worked magic. No one in this city writes better."

"How old is the woman? Is she well-to-do? Does she read poetry?"

"You see that salesgirl in the textiles shop opposite? She's about her size and shape, but her face is much prettier. Like a beautiful boy's. I don't know whether she reads poetry."

The calligrapher glanced at the girl in the shop. "She's pretty too," he said, smiling. But Nasri shook his head, and described the charms of his beloved as far more erotic than the salesgirl's. He mentioned those details that, visibly or invisibly, made the difference, the way the lady of his heart moved, the radiance that came from within. And he explained the subtle difference in the radiance of a woman who had been satisfied. "This woman has never yet known satisfaction," he said in a conspiratorial tone, "while the salesgirl over there is positively replete with it."

Hamid looked at the shop across the road, interested, but for the life of him he couldn't see how his rich customer recognized the girl's sexual satisfaction.

"I'll write you not only that letter but all your letters for the next ten years, free of charge!" the calligrapher promised.

Nasri phoned his manager Tawfiq and explained that he was now a patron of the arts, and the house in Baghdad Street was to be at the disposal of the School of Calligraphy free for the next ten years. He expected cries of indignation, but Tawfiq reacted calmly, almost cheerfully. "That sounds good. Who else is making a donation?" And when Nasri enumerated all the well-known names in a loud voice, mentioning that his would head the list on the marble slab, Tawfiq was afraid he was drunk.

"Tawfiq is expecting you," said Nasri, smiling, as he came back.

"There's something I must ask you," said Hamid, "although I don't want to pry too much into your relationship with the lady you love. But I have to know, so as to decide what kind of letter to write. What is her life like?"

Nasri broke out in a cold sweat. He would never have expected the very correct calligrapher to ask a question so close to the bone all of a sudden.

"Oh, she lives not far from here, close to the parliament building," he lied.

"No, no, you misunderstood me. I'm not interested in where she lives, but I have to know how and with whom she lives. I suspect you will have to give her the letter in secret, and if there's any danger of someone else in the house seeing you, I'll make the meaning of the letter clear but without giving you away. If it's possible for you to hand this lady the letter personally I can write more directly than if a messenger is delivering it. In that case it would be better to use invisible ink. So I have to know whether she lives alone or with others."

"No, no, she lives in a house by herself. I don't know yet exactly how I'll get the letter to her. What did you mean by invisible ink?"

"Well, one can write with various fluids that can be read only after treatment with warmth or chemicals. You can write with milk, lemon juice, onion juice. And there are inks that cost a good deal more, but the writing remains legible only for a certain period of time."

"No, I'd rather not have that. I want to let the woman have beautiful letters written in your hand. With my name, Nasri Abbani, at the bottom. One does not hide a name like mine," said Nasri proudly.

"No invisible ink, then. That's all right, I'll think it over a little and you can have your letter in three or four days' time."

"Wait before you phrase it. I'll call you tomorrow at the latest, once I'm sure what I want the letter to say," said Nasri as he left. He had to hurry, because his wife Lamia had to go to the eye specialist. Little veins had been breaking in her left eye for months, and now it was dark red and looked as if he had been beating her. She was afraid she had eye cancer. It was a form of hysteria. To women, every tiny abnormality that could usually be cured with herbal teas threatened them with cancer, and these days they didn't go to consult their grandmothers, who knew just what herb to use for which disorder, they went straight off to the specialist.

23

Hamid was surprised to get such a friendly reception from Tawfiq, Nasri's business manager. The grey-haired little man with the attentive eyes had an intelligent smile, and his questions were not sly or suspicious. They were sharp as a knife, and contained cleverly hidden traps, but when he heard that the famous Hamid Farsi himself was to be at the head of this new school, and the calligrapher Serani, a legend in his own lifetime, its honorary president, the business manager became almost servile in his polite expressions. He gave Hamid the contract and wrote, where the amount of rent ought to be, "The contracting party to pay no rent for the duration of this agreement." However, he drew the attention of Hamid Farsi, although in a kindly manner, to the paragraphs stipulating that the tenant could be given immediate notice if he used the house for other purposes, or let it fall into ruin. "With so many buildings and so many tenants as Mr Abbani has, otherwise we'd be renovating the whole time and couldn't do any other business."

Hamid, expressing his full understanding, signed with a flourish.

The next day Nasri phoned the calligrapher to tell him what he wanted to be in the letter. "There should be something about gold in it. You must say that I'd be ready to give her weight in gold if I could see her beautiful eyes and kiss the birthmark on her belly. Or something like that. Anyway, I'd like gold to come into the letter."

"Lucky woman!" cried Hamid into the phone. "Half the girls in Damascus would be at your feet if you were to give them their weight in cotton, let alone gold."

"You're right, but the heart is a wild beast and has never understood reason."

"You put that very well. I'll use it: the heart is a wild beast. Beautifully put," repeated the calligrapher in a singsong voice. "I already have a draft in mind, and I think you'll like it. Two pages, normal notepaper format, but on superfine handmade paper from China, white as snow so that the black of the script will unfold regally on it, and it's just this moment occurred to me to write the word 'gold' in gold leaf. You can collect the letter in two days' time. And by the way, did your friendly manager say that we've already signed the contract? He's given me the key. Yesterday night I was so curious that I went to Baghdad Street to look at the house. A pearl of great price, you weren't exaggerating. The marble slabs will be ready in early January."

"Several slabs? Do you have so many donors?"

"Yes, but I want one of them to name only the noblest donors and benefactors of the school. You will of course come first. The rest will come after you."

Nasri had decided to sail his letter through the air to the beautiful woman. Days before, he had given up the idea of going to her house and delivering the letter direct, or having it delivered by a messenger once he had found her street.

He tried to locate the woman's house precisely, and found it very difficult to identify her front door from his attic window. However, he had noticed the unusual brown paint of the guttering, and hoped that once in her street he would be able to see which house it was.

But he had not yet even left Straight Street to find out where his mysterious neighbour lived when he heard the voice of his distant cousin Bilal Abbani. Bilal was a man of little intellect but a busy tongue. He had been paralysed after an accident, and now spent twenty-four hours a day sitting at his window. "Well, whom have we here?" that horrible voice croaked. "Why, if it isn't my cousin Nasri Abbani! What are you doing in our street? Done someone down again and bringing the compensation payment, are you?" And he laughed such a dirty laugh that Nasri wished him dead. "Good day," was all he called as he hurried past under Bilal's window. Ten paces further on the second surprise was lying in wait. The sister of one of his tenants recognized him and rushed to take his hand. She wanted to kiss it in gratitude, and called out loud to someone inside the house where she rented a room. "Here's the generous Mr Abbani, come and look at this fine example of a man!" He freed his hand and walked hastily on, cursing his luck, as she called to her women friends who had come hurrying up, "He's shy, you see, a real Abbani."

Not five metres further on a beggar hailed him. "You here, Mr Abbani? What a surprise," he cried hoarsely.

Nasri had no idea how the beggar, who was clutching him firmly by the sleeve, knew his name. Furiously, he freed himself again, in such agitation that he not only failed to find the beautiful woman's house, he didn't even know how to find his way out of the street again.

No, he thought, this street is a minefield. His cousin was one of the mines, his tenant's sister another, the beggar and all the many people lurking behind windows and looking through doors left ajar, ready to tear his reputation to shreds, were a whole battery of mines. Nasri remembered the story of a lover who waited forty years to hand the woman he adored a love letter. By that time she had four sons and twenty grandchildren.

He would have to find some other way. Why not fold the letter into a paper swallow and let it fly from his attic into her room or her inner courtyard, he asked himself as he saw two boys near the Umayyad Mosque, skilfully sending their folded swallows sailing through the air.

The visit to the eye specialist didn't take long. Dr Farah examined the reddened eye for exactly five minutes, reassured Abbani and his wife, prescribed her a heparin derivative and charged thirty lira. "That was expensive," marvelled his wife Lamia as they went out. Nasri pointed to the plate on the doctor's door. "Someone has to pay for his travels to all these wonderful countries." Lamia had just read the last line under the doctor's name on the doorplate. It named hospitals in New York, London, Lyon, Madrid, and Frankfurt in evidence of his qualifications.

At home with his wife Lamia, he began folding paper swallows and sailing them through the air from the first-floor balcony. His four elder daughters jumped around him excitedly, the two younger girls pointed to the paper birds laughing and marvelling at them. They sometimes dive-bombed down on the balcony, sometimes sailed in elegant wide arcs to get stuck somewhere among the trees of the large garden, or simply landed in a belly-flop.

Paper swallows, Nasri decided, were unreliable. One of them was even caught by a gust of wind and carried into the garden next door. He imagined his letter landing not in his lovely neighbour's court-yard but in a nearby garden, where it could be found and read by the wrong person, maybe even his cousin Bilal. Nasri's secret would be out. He felt fury like a stone in his throat.

What on earth, Lamia wondered, had come over the man? She had never seen him playing with their daughters before. And now, suddenly, there he was romping with them on a sunny but very cold December day.

It was his third daughter, Samira, who found a much simpler trick than the complicated swallow. She folded the sheet of paper three times lengthwise. The folded paper strip looked like a ruler. Now she bent it into a V-shape in the middle and let it fall from the balcony. And lo and behold, the paper turned gently in the air like the rotor of a helicopter and fell slowly to the ground not far from the balcony. Nasri was delighted. "That's the way to do it!" he cried. And he too folded the paper lengthwise, weighted it with a coin that he fixed with some glue to the middle of the V shape, and now the paper sailed vertically down and dropped reliably just where he wanted it, under-neath the balcony.

24

A week after the signing of the contract, about forty men were sitting in the largest room of the new school. There were no chairs or tables yet, so they all sat on rugs provided by Hamid Farsi. They were drinking tea and listening to Hamid, their president, whom they addressed as Grand Master. He was explaining the most important points in the planning of the new school. His voice was triumphant, his bearing that of a proud general before a battle for which he was well prepared. On the wall behind him hung the design of a large notice, at present still on paper: Ibn Muqla School of Calligraphy.

"This will enable our Society to make great progress. It will be the first college in Syria for training calligraphers in the art developed by our honoured master Ibn Muqla three years before his death in the year 937. Our enemies will not rest, so the opening ceremony and the names of our patrons should intimidate and subdue them. And before they get over the first shock the second school will already have been founded in Aleppo. A head start is the secret of victory. Then, while they are arguing about the schools in Damascus and Aleppo, we'll have opened the third in Homs and the fourth in Latakia.

"These schools will be the seeds from which a new future for calligraphy will grow. We will preserve tradition here in Damascus, and in our search for innovation we will experiment and develop the art until we have a dynamic modern alphabet, while incidentally – I would say at four-year intervals – we send out a group of young and very well-trained calligraphers out into the country. In twenty years' time, I expect us to have raised calligraphy to what in essence it is, a divine and pure art.

"The attacking strategy of the bearded fools who call themselves the Pure Ones consists of telling us that we offend religion because we want to reform Arabic script and the Arabic language. Do not let them browbeat you, dear brothers. It is just because we love Islam and revere the Quran that we do not want that loveliest of all languages to moulder away. He who cares for language cares also for the mind, and God's is the greatest and purest mind of all. God is feared by the stupid; God and his Prophet will be loved and honoured by us to the end of all time.

"My dream is of an Arabic language that can express all nuances of sound on earth from the North to the South Poles. However, we have a long way to go before we achieve that. So set out on your way, soldiers of civilization, and sharpen your pens. We are going on the attack."

Applause echoed through the whole house. Hamid had risen to his feet, and he acknowledged the praise of his friends, much moved. Even his worst enemies would have had to admit that Hamid Farsi was the first to have succeeded in giving their Society an official school.

Twelve men formed the Council of the Wise, the highest committee of the Society, thirty-six were the circle of Initiates, and together they headed the Society of the Wise, a secret association of calligraphers. It had been founded in the year 1267 by Yaqout al-Musta'simi, one of the most brilliant practitioners of his art. He was both a calligrapher and a librarian, and in the cold February days of the year 1258 he had witnessed the destruction of Baghdad by the Mongols, who set fire to all the libraries in the city and threw so many books into the Tigris that its waters wore black for seven days, as if in mourning for the downfall of Arab culture.

Yaqout himself had no time to weep. He did not content himself with founding a great school of calligraphy in Baghdad, he also sent out five of his best and most esteemed pupils to all points of the compass with instructions to set up societies of calligraphers and found schools all over the Islamic world. Hamid hoped to revive the spirit of Yaqout.

25

It was an icy cold December day, and the rain had not stopped until dawn, after turning all the hollows in Grace and Favour Yard into puddles. Salman woke very early, feeling tired out. The night had been a short one for all the staff of Hamid's workshop. He had fallen into bed, ready to drop with exhaustion, but he could not sleep. He thought of Noura, heard the rain drumming on the corrugated iron roof above the room where he lay, and envied her husband, who could lie beside her now. The memory of her soft skin warmed him. But he was also overcome by great fear in the darkness. What if Master Hamid found out?

He jumped out of bed, washed quickly and ate the bread and jam his mother had spread for him. The bread was fresh, with an earthy aroma. His mother was smiling for the first time in a long while; the strange fever that for months on end had made her life so difficult had passed off.

His father had already gone to work. Salman put five lira in the pocket of his mother's cardigan. "Buy something your heart desires and then you'll be really well again," he said. She kissed him, took his head in her hands, breathed in with enjoyment and beamed at him. "You smell of happiness," she said. He laughed, hurried out and was just in time to catch the bus. He arrived at the workshop on the dot.

Master Hamid Farsi was in a bad temper. His sister Siham had been there again early that morning asking for money because, she said, her husband needed to have an operation. Hamid had shouted at her that he was not a charity organization, her husband ought to be working instead of doing nothing but smoke hashish and drink, but in the end he had given her the money. The master's ill humour infected his assistants. Even the lively Radi couldn't manage a joke, and the journeyman Mahmoud was grumpy. Unlike Samad, he always gave Salman boring jobs that taught him nothing.

Their main task that day was to prepare a great many notes, each with a character written out large and a quotation from the Quran, or a saying of the Prophet's, beginning with that letter. The journeymen worked as if they were on a production line. Ten copies for each letter of the alphabet had been ordered, and as soon as the ink was dry Salman had to fold the papers and put them into little fabric bags. Later the customer, a well-known midwife, would sew up the little bags and sell them for large sums of money to superstitious women.

Salman remembered a joke that Benjamin had told at school, about a stupid priest in the village where his parents lived. The priest, who was well known as an exorcist, was summoned one day to drive the Devil out of the soul of a young man possessed by the Evil One. He placed the Bible on the young man's head as he knelt on the floor and began to read. "I and N together say 'I.N.' T.H.E. together say 'the.' B.E.G.I.N.N.I.N.G together say 'beginning.' G.O.D. together say 'God.' C.R.E.A.T.E.D. together say 'created.'"

"How much longer are you going on reading like that?" asked the Devil in a frightful gurgle of a voice.

"Right to the end of the Bible," said the priest calmly, and he went on with his reading. "T.H.E. together say 'the.' H.E.A.V.E.N. together say 'heaven.'"

"That's enough!" shouted the Devil. "That'll do. I'm off, but not because you're holy, I'm off because you're so boring."

Salman laughed to himself, but he didn't like to tell the joke because the others were Muslims. Luckily it was time to fetch the *matbakiyya* for Master Hamid, and above all to see Noura.

When Salman took the meal back to the studio, Hamid, who had left with a rich customer, wasn't there yet. He put the *matbakiyya* down and went over to Karam's café. For the first time in his life Salman was feeling such indescribable happiness that he now knew what Sarah had meant by feeling that you were in Paradise when you were loved. He could happily have embraced all the passersby he met on the way to the café.

Karam seemed to have caught some kind of fever. Every day he wanted to know more about the School of Calligraphy. It got on Salman's nerves, because all he himself knew was that it was going to open its doors in May. There would be a great ceremony early in March, with famous personalities from the worlds of politics and culture, large donations from all over the country were already coming in, and a second school was to be opened in Aleppo with the excess funds. The whole business strengthened some kind of society to which Hamid was very close, and weakened another one.

There was no more for him to tell, because the master was very vague when he talked about it. However, Karam went on asking questions, because he suspected secret plans behind the School.

"Secret plans? You're crazy. You're getting to talk like Badri, who suspects a Jewish conspiracy behind every change in the weather. There aren't any secret plans. All Hamid wants is to make his name immortal!"

The expression on Karam's face was very intent. He said nothing.

Unlike Karam, Hamid was in a good mood now. Salman had never seen his master so cheerful and forthcoming as he was these days. He worked hard enough for two. As always, he carried out all his commissions precisely, and spent hours on the telephone talking about the School, the necessary permits, the furniture, press advertising and other business matters. Sometimes he stayed in the studio until midnight, but he sent all his assistants home shortly after five in the afternoon.

26

Salman's job, working on his own this morning, was to add the shadowing to a large saying written out by Samad. This was the first responsible piece of work to be entrusted to him alone, so he wasn't listening to the master's phone conversation.

"Salman," said his master, startling him in the middle of his work, "you can take my wife the basket of nuts from Adel the vegetable seller, and on the way to my house I want you to pick up the spices I ordered from Halabis. Tell her I'm lunching with the minister of culture, so there's no need for her to send me lunch today," he added in a loud voice, as if he wanted all his men to know. Salman was surprised, since his master could have told his wife all that on the telephone. Sure enough, he did ring his wife later, repeated it all and told her she was to visit her parents that evening. He would fetch her from there when he came back from the Ministry, where he had to join an important meeting with experts.

Soon after ten Salman had finished his shading, and Samad praised his neat work. As he knew that the master wouldn't be coming back today, he sent Salman home.

"Deliver those nuts and the other things, and then you can enjoy an afternoon at home. That'll do for today, and tomorrow morning make sure you're here refreshed and on the dot," said friendly Samad. He himself still had work to keep him busy until late in the afternoon, and then he too would be going home.

Salman left the bicycle and went to Noura on foot. He balanced the big, heavy basket on his head as he made his way through the crowd of passersby, carts, and donkeys. All the donkeys were hard of hearing and lame today, and the sole idea in their heads was to get in his way.

Noura kissed his eyes. "Not only do you have wonderful ears, you have the most beautiful eyes I've ever seen. They are round and clever like the eyes of cats," she said, when he was caressing the tip of her nose.

Years later, he remembered that Noura had been the first woman in his life to think anything about him was beautiful. Sarah liked him, but she had never paid him a compliment about his eyes. They were in fact beautiful, he thought. But how Noura could think his ears wonderful was a mystery to him.

"Show me how to play marbles. I always envied the boys in my street because we girls could never play marbles," she suddenly said, bringing him a little wooden box of marbles.

They played. Noura turned out to be good at the game, but she couldn't defeat Salman. "You just need practice. I had a tough schooling in Grace and Favour Yard and scraped my hands until they were sore," he said when she admired his skill.

He crouched behind her and took her right hand in his to show her how to hold the marbles. A wave of warmth surged through her body, and her heart beat fast with longing for him, but she pulled herself together so that she could learn the game.

They were both naked.

"If your husband arrives he'll knock me into hell within five minutes," he said as she picked up the marbles.

"He wouldn't do that. He doesn't like getting his hands dirty on account of the calligraphy. No, he'd speak the divorce formula three times: you are divorced, you are divorced, you are divorced. And then he'd be rid of me. It's not like with you Christians. The rope to which every Muslim woman is tied is her husband's tongue. He'd need a witness, and with you here he'd have culprit and witness in one," she said, pushing Salman down on the sofa and patting his behind.

"No, I wouldn't do as a witness. You're forgetting that I'm a Christian," he replied, kissing her on the shoulder.

"I'm not forgetting it, but now you must forget my husband," she said, and kissed him back. And Salman forgot everything.

27

The rain refused to stop, and the faces of the Damascenes, who had beamed happily at first, for rain in this drought-stricken region promised a better harvest, grew gloomier the longer and harder rain went on falling on the mud-brick houses. After five days the floods came. The Old Town was soon under water. The river Barada, which shrank to a narrow channel in summer, became a raging torrent. It burst its banks long before reaching Damascus, destroyed gardens, and carried a number of huts away with it. Many of the romantic restaurants and cafés on the riverbank were flooded up to the first floor. From Victoria Bridge to Martyrs' Square, the city had become a great lake. Worst affected was the Souk al-Khatatin, the Street of the Calligraphers in the Bahssa quarter. And because the floodwater had arrived overnight, when no one expected it, the calligraphers had suffered great losses.

Hamid was glad that his own studio – in the Souk Saruya quarter, which was on rather higher ground – remained intact, and now he and a few of the other calligraphers whom the water had not reached got all the commissions that their colleagues could not fulfil.

After exactly seven days the rain stopped. The sun shone down from a bright blue sky, dazzling the people of Damascus.

When Salman rode through the Old Town on his bicycle just after eleven, the flat roofs were steaming under the burning sun like fresh flatbreads.

He had to make detours again and again to avoid the knee-high muddy water. He marvelled at all the children noisily and cheerfully playing in it as if they were at the seaside. Noura had made a little dish of green beans with meat and tomatoes for them to share. It tasted delicious, but he had no time to spare and swallowed his helping in a hurry. "I'm sorry, but I have to leave again soon because the flood has made many roads impassable," he said, to excuse the way he bolted the food in such haste.

"How mean of you! I was going to eat you up myself as dessert," she said, affectionately nibbling one of his earlobes.

"You can always make a start on my ears. There's plenty of ear-space there," replied Salman.

When he had left, she looked out at the street through the grating over the window and watched him riding past people and bringing a smile to all faces. It was as if Salman had a magic paintbrush and could tickle the human heart with it.

Noura knew no one else who spread so much happiness, and she marvelled at her earlier blindness.

"Take care of yourself," she whispered.

Mahmoud showed him how paper was marbled. That would have been interesting if Salman's teacher had been one of the other journeymen. But Mahmoud kept pinching his arm and rapping him on the head – neither of them for any reason – and was not very good at telling him how the process worked.

It was Radi who explained the mysteries of marbling paper in the midday break. The studio used large quantities of marbled paper for the borders of calligraphic works.

In the middle of December Sarah visited Damascus. She was pregnant, and looked more beautiful than ever. She was radiant with happiness.

It was a sunny day, but there were several puddles still left from the last rain. An old man looked through the gateway into the yard, wearily crying his trade: "Any old clothes, old shoes, old iron?" His tone of voice showed that he didn't expect much from the inhabitants of this place. One mother, whose four-year old child was crying, called out to him, "Will you buy this little devil?" The boy froze, looked anxiously at the dirty man with his big sack, and shot indoors like lightning.

"Oh, madame, I have plenty of those. Nine in all, and every one of them a machine munching up all they can lay hands on," he replied, waving a dismissive hand.

Salman found Sarah sitting in the sun outside her parents' door.

He took a stool and sat down beside her, feeling as close to her as he had in the old days, and so they talked openly about her life with her husband, Salman's mother's sickness, and what had happened to several inhabitants of Grace and Favour Yard. Sarah knew that since the tragic death of her son Adnan, Samira had aged many years and turned very devout. She did not see men anymore, and saw her son's death as her punishment here on earth.

Sarah, living far away in the city of Homs, seemed to know more about Salman's neighbours than he did himself. She told him what had happened to Said. He had seen the good-looking boy grow up to be a large, fat man. Said walked like a woman. There had been whispering about him for a long time, rumours that he was developing in an odd way.

"Said is a male prostitute," explained Sarah. "First it was just a few customers at the hammam who courted the pretty boy and gave him lavish tips. Then one of them seduced him, and another blackmailed him, and a third," she said sadly, "didn't have to blackmail him at all." As a girl, she had liked handsome young Said very much.

"That's bad," whispered Salman. He remembered many guests at the café whose tips were always accompanied by some fumbling. They were lonely men, whether rich or poor, and Salman tried to make it obvious, without insulting them, that he was not the boy they were after.

"Well?" she suddenly interrupted his thoughts. "Have you fallen in love yet, or are you still living like a monk?"

Salman smiled. "Even monks can't resist love. I read that not so long ago," he replied. "Her name is Noura. She'd keep any monk from his prayers."

"Oh, why not slow your tongue down – or are you still in the early phase of love, when you're blinded by hormones?" responded Sarah, ready as ever with a reply.

Salman shook his head. "I'm not exaggerating. Have you seen the actress Audrey Hepburn on film?"

"Of course. I've seen *Roman Holiday* and *Sabrina* twice each, but what about her?"

"Noura could be her twin sister."

"Really? Or are you kidding me?"

"No, really," he replied, and said no more for a moment. What Karam had said came back to his mind. "But what's more important than her beauty is that I love her, I'd love her even if she had only one eye and a club foot. She lives in here," and he tapped his breast. "She's almost as wonderful as you," he added.

"And you're the greatest charmer ever – how can anyone fail to like you?"

"Oh, I could mention a few specimens of the human race who manage that. There are plenty of those in the café as well as the studio," said Salman.

"And what does this beauty of yours do?" asked Sarah, just as Said came into the yard, greeted them wearily and went straight to his apartment, where he had lived alone since the death of the widow who had adopted him.

"She's really a trained dressmaker, but her husband is a rich calligrapher, and he won't let her work at her profession," said Salman, unable to suppress a grin, because he could guess what Sarah was going to say next.

"Salman, Salman, what on earth are you doing? Is she married to your master or to one of his enemies?"

"She's his wife. And if I were to love the wives of all his enemies I'd need a harem to keep them in. He has many, many enemies."

"Oh, my dear boy, how you've changed. You talk like a journalist," she marvelled.

"I haven't changed myself, it's love that has changed me, and I don't care in the least that she's a Muslim."

"Oh no! What concerns me is to make sure that you don't end up lying in the gutter with a hole in your head one of these days. Telling you to keep your fingers off the woman would be stupid, because your fingers can't help it. But do be careful! I shall pray to the Virgin Mary every night before I close my eyes to protect you," she said, caressing his head, and then she stood up. She and her mother, who was already waiting, were going to visit a sick aunt.

"Like your May bug long ago," whispered Salman, but Sarah couldn't hear him anymore.

On Wednesday he was to take Hamid his lunch for the last time that week, because his master was going to the north of the country for three days on Thursday. Salman told Noura that they could meet at Karam's house, where he spent all day alone on Fridays working.

"We can spend all day together without being disturbed," he said hopefully, in pleading tones.

She got him to give her Karam's address, writing down the bus lines and tram lines she should take, and kissed him goodbye. "Shall I bring us something to eat?" she asked. He said no. There was always plenty of food in Karam's house.

"Just bring me yourself, because I'm hungry for you," he said, kissing her. She laughed. If anyone were to ask him what was the most beautiful thing in the world, he would say without a moment's hesitation that it was Noura's gurgle of laughter.

She gave him the *matbakiyya* with the food in it, and a bag containing an ironed shirt and clean socks for Hamid. He had an important appointment to meet an influential scholar that evening, and there wasn't time for him to come home first.

"I've thought of something else," said Salman as he was about to go. Noura laughed, because she knew his tricks by now.

"Yes, that it's forever since we kissed," she said, imitating his voice.

"No, seriously. Do you know anything about calligraphy?" he asked.

"Only a little. But Hamid has a very good library. Can I look anything up for you?"

"Who is Ibn Muqla? All the calligraphers revere him. Your husband speaks of him as if he were a saint. And what kind of a society is it that your husband belongs to? But you mustn't ask him that yourself, because it's a secret society. I overheard him making a telephone call."

"I don't know anything about a secret society. Hamid and a secret society? That's so unlikely! But I'll try to find out something about that, too, and have something to tell you when we meet on Friday," said Noura, giving him a long kiss on the lips. "Why do you always taste so good?"

"Samad's teaching me the art of reflection in calligraphy at the moment, and when I first kissed you all your fragrance was reflected in my mouth. You're tasting yourself," he said confidently, and he left. A boy had made himself comfortable on the carrier of the bike, but when he saw Salman coming with the *matbakiyya* he jumped off and ran away.

28

Noura hadn't been out of the house so early since her schooldays as she was that Friday. She hesitated for a long time, wondering whether to wear a veil for the sake of caution or not, and decided against it.

A strong wind was blowing dust, scraps of paper and leaves along the road ahead of her. Pigeons and sparrows flew low through the streets. Was she a sparrow or a pigeon, she asked herself, and didn't know why she wanted to be neither one nor the other. A woman neighbour had once said she thought Noura was more like a cactus than any member of the animal kingdom. "I'm the Rose of Jericho," whispered Noura. The wind has its way with the desert rose for years, and then it thinks it has mastered the Rose of Jericho. But the first drop of rain reminds the rose that it was once a little green oasis.

Her husband had better look out for himself. She had already tasted that first drop of water.

At six-thirty she caught the bus at the stop opposite her street. The face of Damascus was innocent at that early hour of the morning. Even the Damascenes who were out and about still looked sleepy and peaceful as small children. She saw Tamer the beggar, whom she hadn't met for a very long time. People said he had suddenly disappeared, but there he was before her all at once, alive and well, washed and with his hair combed. His face was still wet and his hair was dripping. Tamer played his *nay* flute outside Hejaz railway station. He played beautifully; he had been a highly respected member of the Syrian Radio orchestra until something threw him off track. Now he lived in the streets.

When Tamer played, if you closed your eyes while you listened you heard the wind singing in the desert. This morning the melancholy sound of his reed flute made its way to her even through the racket of a bus full of schoolchildren.

She suddenly thought of her diary. She would certainly have written about Tamer the beggar if she hadn't burnt the exercise book a week ago. Since Salman's first kiss she had written in the diary only occasionally, and if she did she said nothing clear and direct. No one else must know the secret of her love for Salman. And she was no longer interested in writing about her husband, so she wrote only about her own emotional turmoil. Again and again she had written that she was determined never to see Salman again. But as soon as it was eleven o'clock, she found herself hoping he would arrive a little earlier than usual today. An animal force drew her heart to him. Not only did she feel a deep desire to protect Salman, as if he were a vulnerable child, the smell of him, the taste of his mouth, and the look in his eyes also roused her to physical craving such as she had never known before, had never even heard or read about. She kept the secret to herself. There was no need even for him to know that more than once, on their very first kiss at meeting, she had been transported to the Paradise of pleasure and lingered there for a long time in ecstasy. And afterwards she would swear to herself, yet again, to call a halt to their love. Her reason warned her than an affair between a Muslim married woman and a Christian could end only in catastrophe. And where else was this love going to lead them? But that question in Noura's mind spoke as softly as a little girl might ask for the time of day in all the tumult of a wild folk-dance.

She had so often prepared a sensible conversation with him in which she would calmly and objectively set out all the reasons against that animal longing, but as soon as he knocked on the door she changed her mind. She decided to tell him later, when they were lying side by side, relaxed and mellow with exhaustion. Yes, that was the moment for it. But when the time came she had forgotten all about it: "forgotten on purpose," as she wrote in her diary. However, when the diary did nothing but torment her, like a pitiless mirror of the vows she had made and failed to keep, and she couldn't help realizing that, although she did not mention Salman by name, anyone would recognize him after reading two lines, she decided it was foolish of her to put him in mortal danger. She burned the exercise book in a copper bowl and sprinkled its ashes round a rose-bush.

In the bus, she couldn't help smiling at all her childish decisions to give up seeing Salman. She reached her destination after almost an hour, pressed down the handle of the garden gate, as Salman had told her to do, and walked quickly to the house. Suddenly the front door opened. Noura was scared to death, but Salman smiled at her and drew her inside the house. She stumbled into his arms, and before she could even get her breath back she sank into his deep kiss.

"Breakfast is served, madame," he said, taking her coat and putting it over the chair in his room.

She was deeply moved. There was a lovingly prepared breakfast waiting in the kitchen: jam, cheese, olives, fresh bread, and tea. All very modest, but it was the first time in her life that a man had made breakfast for her.

Seeing Noura's emotion, Salman felt awkward. There was so much he wanted to say to her, but all he could get out was the silliest possible phrase: "Let's eat!" Years later he was still annoyed with himself because, instead of any of the poetic opening remarks he had carefully prepared, that prosaic "Let's eat!" was all that remained.

Later, Salman didn't know how many times they had made love that morning. Finally he kissed Noura once again. "If I am ever asked whether I believe in Paradise, I'll say I not only believe in it, I've been there already." He caressed her face, she kissed the tips of his fingers.

When she got out of the bed and put on her wristwatch, she whistled silently through her teeth. "Four hours of love, Madame Noura, congratulations on your long stay in the Paradise of the senses," she told herself ironically.

"You're not going now, are you?" asked Salman in concern.

"No, no, but I'd like to be dressed before I read you something very sad," she said. "I can't read something like that lying down, and certainly not naked or in night-clothes. I get that from my father. He was always very correctly dressed when he read, as if he were going to meet the author of the book or the hero of the story. And when I've finished reading it, I'll go back to bed and we can make love as wildly as a couple of monkeys."

Salman jumped up. "Then I must get up properly too. I'm the host, and it's not right for a guest to sit there reading in an elegant dress while her host lounges around stark naked."

He quickly dressed, tidied his bed, and sat down opposite her.

"Well, I couldn't find out anything about the secret society. You must have misunderstood, or maybe you got something mixed up. My father didn't know anything about it either. I pretended to him that I'd read a journalist's story about a secret society of calligraphers. He told me not to take journalists so seriously, because it must be a tough job having to write news stories every day, and a newspaper that didn't exaggerate would very soon fail. However, I did find out something about Ibn Muqla. It's a very sad story that my husband once wrote and published in a journal. I copied it out for you, all I've done is to convert Islamic dates into Christian dates. Would you like to read the story yourself, or shall I read it aloud?"

"Read it aloud to me, please," said Salman.

"Ibn Muqla," she began to read, "was born in the year 885 or 886 in Baghdad. No one knows which for certain, because he was born into a very poor family. He died in July 940, and the date is known so precisely because he died while he was being held in prison, and because he was famous at that time throughout the entire Arab and Islamic world. His name itself is a curiosity. *Muqla*, a poetic word for 'eye,' was the affectionate nickname given to his mother by her father, because he particularly loved this daughter. She married a poor calligrapher, and the family was then called not after her husband or his clan, but simply after her, which was rare in Arabia at that time and still is. Muqla's children and grandchildren were all calligraphers, but without a shadow of doubt Muhammad Ibn Muqla was the most famous of them all.

He was the greatest Arabic calligrapher of all time, an architect of script. He not only developed and improved several styles, he was also the first to draw up a doctrine of the dimensions of written characters, keeping them in harmony and symmetry with each other. His proportional doctrine holds good to this day, and can easily be used to check whether the proportions of a work of calligraphy are correct or not.

Alif, the Arabic letter A, is a vertical stroke, and Ibn Muqla chose it as the criterion for all written characters. Ever since then, every calligrapher has begun by establishing the length of the Alif in his chosen script. The calculation is worked out by means of vertically placed dots. The size of the dot, in turn, depends on the pen that is used and is made by pressing the pen down on the paper. All the other letters, whether horizontal or vertical, are adjusted to the size worked out by Ibn Muqla and determined by a certain number of dots. In addition, the curves of many letters lie along a circle with a diameter corresponding to the length of the Alif. Maintaining these proportions is like maintaining the rhythm in a musical composition. It is the only way to make the script harmonious, so that it becomes music for the eye. After years of practice, every master calligrapher automatically knows the rules. However, the dots always allow a quick check of whether the proportions are correct.

Ibn Muqla was a gifted mathematician, calligraphic scholar, and natural scientist. He also studied the works of both theologians and atheists, writers like Ibn al-Rawandi, Ibn al-Muqaffa', al-Rasi, and al-Farabi. Most of all, he was fascinated by the polymath scholar al-Jahiz. But unlike al-Jahiz, Ibn Muqla enjoyed being close to the rulers of his time. Al-Jahiz could not endure more than three days at the court of Caliph al-Ma'moun, the great patron of science and literature, son of the legendary Haroun al-Rashid.

Ibn Muqla was First Vizier – the equivalent of a prime minister today – to three caliphs in succession. But his proximity to them, which he sought again and again, was his undoing in the end.

Ibn Muqla realized that Arabic script was not of divine origin, but the work of the human hand. He was fascinated by its beauty, but he also recognized its weaknesses. So at quite an early date he began devising ways to introduce cautious reforms into the alphabet, the source of the script itself. He experimented, made notes, and waited for a suitable moment. At this time Baghdad was the capital of an international empire, the centre of the secular and religious power of Islam.

Many calligraphic scholars and translators of Ibn Muqla's day criticized the lack of letters that would allow them to reproduce, in Arabic, certain sounds and names from other countries and other languages. This criticism encouraged Ibn Muqla to go further. And now his study of natural science helped him to find the crucial idea. He knew, of course, that religious fanatics regarded Arabic script as sacred because the word of God was written down in Arabic in the Quran. Yet he also knew that Arabic script had been reformed several times already.

The most radical change had been introduced, also in Baghdad, almost a hundred years before Ibn Muqla's birth. Up to the time of that reform the Arabic language had no letters with dots, and since many letters resembled each other uncertainty, misunderstanding, and misinterpretation were always likely to occur during the reading process, even when scholars read aloud. Several minor reforms had been tried in the attempt to improve Arabic script, but the greatest and most radical reform came twelve centuries ago.

Fifteen letters, over half the Arabic alphabet, had dots situated above or below the characters added to them. As a result, mistakes in reading could be almost eliminated. At the time Caliph Abdulmalik bin Marwan and al-Hajjaj, the bloodthirsty governor of his eastern province, stifled all the conservative voices that were raised against any kind of reform. The caliph had the Quran recopied in the reformed script, and after that anyone could read the holy book without making mistakes.

Religious texts were not the only kind to gain in clarity. The Arabic language of poetry, science, and everyday life also became clearer and more precise. But without the strong hand of the caliph, such a step could never have been taken.

Ibn Muqla knew that. And he himself needed the support of an enlightened and farsighted caliph to push through the great reform of Arabic script that was now overdue.

Ibn Muqla loved calligraphic script like his own child. He gave all he had in its service, and in the end he lost everything.

Did he want to gain power, as his enemies claimed, when they published hostile accounts of seditious plans, filling page after page with their flimsy reasoning?

No, Ibn Muqla had already achieved so much before he introduced the radical step leading to reform and to his ruin.

He was tutor to the last Abbasid caliph, al-Radi Billah, and taught him philosophy, mathematics, and language. Ibn Muqla was to the caliph what Aristotle had been to Alexander the Great, but Caliph al-Radi Billah lacked the great soul of the Macedonian conqueror of the world.

When Ibn Muqla was still at the height of his power, he had a palace built for himself in Baghdad. Legends accumulated around it. The words carved into the great stone blocks on the interior of the garden wall were a saying of his own: 'What I create will outlast time.'

The palace had a huge garden that Ibn Muqla, who loved the animal kingdom, had converted into a unique kind of zoo where all the animals could move about freely in separate enclosures. To give the birds a sense of freedom, he had his zoo covered with a silken net stretched high in the air above the garden. A large team of keepers and veterinarians, under the direction of a Persian scientist called Muhammad Nureddin, was responsible for looking after the animals.

Ibn Muqla hoped to understand creation through study of the animal kingdom, and his staff began experiments in interbreeding. These animal experiments aroused interest but also opposition and contempt in the caliph's palace. Ordinary people remained unaware of all these discussions and experiments, hidden as they were behind thick palace walls.

It was true that Ibn Muqla's employees soon achieved some small degree of success with the interbreeding of birds, dogs and cats, sheep and goats, donkeys and horses, but many of the experiments led to the birth of creatures with deformities.

Progress in natural science encouraged Ibn Muqla to take another step, one that could have brought him worldwide renown. The twentieth Abbasid Caliph, al-Radi Billah, had a great liking for him. Ibn Muqla saw him as the man to stand by him in his attempts to reform the written language. The caliph was twenty-four years old, an open-minded man who wrote poetry himself and loved wine and women. He banished conservative scholars from Baghdad, his capital, and surrounded himself with liberal theologians, but like all the later caliphs he had less and less say in what went on at his court. Palace bureaucrats, princes, high officers of state, and the caliph's wives all engaged in intrigues and conspiracies, to ensure that no reformer could stay near the caliph too long.

Ibn Muqla's reputation, knowledge and wealth aroused much envy and hostility. At this time he was in his late forties, and he saw that the caliphate was rotten through and through. He feared that he would not be able to put his revolutionary plans into practice. Baghdad had become a place of unrest, revolution, and plotting. Ibn Muqla himself had a proud nature and a hot temper. He often reacted irritably, impatiently, and brusquely to the court officials, making himself unpopular among those close to the caliph.

Yet in spite of all the intrigues and conspiracies against him, he had become vizier to young Caliph al-Radi. Ibn Muqla felt confirmed in his belief in his own genius, and that made him arrogant.

Loyal friends, rightly anxious on his behalf, advised him to leave the palace and bask in his fame as a brilliant calligrapher, but Ibn Muqla had his own ambitious plans for the Arabic alphabet, and he needed the caliph's support for them against the power of the mosques. However, he was mistaken in his assessment of the caliph, and he paid a high price for that.

Ibn Muqla had studied the Persian, Arabic, Aramaic, Turkish, and Greek languages, as well as the changes undergone by Arabic script from its first beginnings to his own day. Careful studies enabled him to invent a new Arabic alphabet that, with only twenty-five letters, could express all the languages known at that time. With that end in view, certain 'dead' letters must disappear and several new ones be introduced. In case resistance to his ideas was too great, he planned to retain the characters of the old alphabet and add four new ones, P, O, W and E, with which Persian, Japanese, Chinese and Latin words, and many languages of Africa and Asia, could have been reproduced better.

He knew that the mere idea of making any changes to Arabic script had been considered a mortal sin under all the caliphs. They had kept as many as four thousand women and eunuchs in their palaces to minister to their pleasure, they quite often liked wine better than theology, but they were unyielding when it came to matters of religion. They had famous philosophers and poets lashed or barbarically executed for suggesting the least reform to the structure of government or religion, or expressing the faintest doubt of the Quran.

The caliphs did not scruple to consider themselves the 'shadow of God on earth', and their caliphate the perfect expression of divine rule. So they, and even more so their administrators, were implacable if anyone wanted to introduce any change whatsoever.

With his revolutionary reforms of Arabic script, Ibn Muqla wanted to make the Arabic characters unambiguous, and he had no idea that in so doing he was supporting the ruling Sunnis in their struggle with the Shiites. Extreme Shiite groups such as the Ismailites had always regarded the Quran as a book written on several levels and capable of various interpretations. Certain extremists went so far as to claim that what the common people understood of the Quran was merely *al saher*, the surface, the husk, which concealed a more important and complex kernel, *batin*. They were therefore called the Batinites. According to their doctrine, every word in the Quran had a double meaning. The Sunni doctrine was diametrically opposite, and said there were no double meanings in the language of God.

The caliph in Baghdad, his advisers, court philosophers, and theologians were Sunnis. They disguised their campaign against the Shiites as the struggle of a devout caliph, God's chosen ruler, against apostates and unbelievers. They were delighted that Ibn Muqla had developed a precise system for the dimensions of written letters and a simple, beautiful and flexible script, Naskhi, which copyists – for *naskh* means to copy – could now use to write out the Quran fast, clearly, and without flourishes. To this day it is the script most often used for printing books.

The words of the Quran were now clearly legible, and Ibn Muqla's scripts were the best weapon in the Sunni armoury against Shiite opposition. The caliph and his theologians, however, did not realize that Ibn Muqla wanted to introduce yet more radical reforms to Arabic script.

Caliph al-Radi loved Ibn Muqla, and praised him publicly, but when the calligrapher confided a detail of the secret of his new alphabet to him, the caliph was shocked. He warned Ibn Muqla that his enemies were moving against him, but Ibn Muqla interpreted this warning as a hint from an ally, stuck to his plan, and began to form groups of like-minded people. Some scholars and well-known translators shared his views of the necessity for radical reform of the Arabic language and its script, but they suspected it would be dangerous to support the idea, because conservatives would see it as an attack on the Quran. So the majority of reformers held back. However, Ibn Muqla scorned the danger, for he felt sure of the sympathies of Caliph al-Radi.

Ibn Muqla's enemies, learning of his plans, told the caliph about them, presenting them in connection with his animal experiments, the only aim of which, as they saw it, was to mock God by making Ibn Muqla himself figure as a creator. And now this man also wanted to change the holy language of the Quran! The young caliph told Ibn Muqla to abandon his project.

But Ibn Muqla, who was very devout at heart but not fanatical, assured the caliph that he would sooner die than doubt a word of the holy book. In fact, he said, the simplification of Arabic script would give the language and the Quran yet wider distribution.

The two friends parted, each in the erroneous and dangerous belief that he had convinced the other.

The caliph wanted to protect the scholar whom he respected so much from intrigues, and thought that now he had seen the mortal danger threatening him.

Ibn Muqla, on the other hand, considered himself in the right as a reformer, and thought his was the only way to make Arabic script worthy of an international empire.

He wrote several treatises in which he enumerated the inadequacies of the Arabic language and its script, and put forward ideas for their improvement.

At first Caliph al-Radi did not reject reform. But the scholars had threatened to withdraw their support for him and remain true to Islam if he agreed to Ibn Muqla's ideas. The caliph, who had already seen the murders of his father at the hands of an angry mob and his uncle as the result of a palace conspiracy – he himself had only just escaped an assassination attempt – knew what that meant.

Then those intriguing against Ibn Muqla told the caliph that he had been plotting against him. The angry caliph ordered his arrest, without questioning him personally. He lacked the courage to punish his vizier the great calligrapher himself, and delegated the task to an emir at court whom he thought reliable, never guessing that this man was the leader of the conspiracy against Ibn Muqla. He had Ibn Muqla lashed, but he refused to say where he had hidden his new alphabet after writing it down. In revenge the courtier had Ibn Muqla's right hand cut off. He seized his property and had his palace, including the zoo, burnt down. It is said that everything was consumed by the flames except for the section of wall that bore the word 'time.'

What the fire did not destroy was stolen by the hungry people of Baghdad. The conspirators announced publicly that Ibn Muqla had been plotting against the caliph. A palace historian refutes this lie by telling us that he was not executed, as was usual in such cases, but was even treated later by the caliph's personal physician, and dined with the caliph himself.

Ibn Muqla lamented his mutilation for the rest of his life. 'My hand was chopped off like a thief's, the hand with which I twice copied the Quran.'

He was now fifty years old, and had no intention of giving up. He skilfully bound his reed pen to the stump of his wrist, and in that way he was able to practise calligraphy again, if not as beautifully as before. He founded the first great school for calligraphers, with the aim of passing on his knowledge, forming his most gifted students into a circle of initiates who would understand his reforms, remember them, and pass them on if anything happened to him. His disappointment on finding that his scholarly friends had distanced themselves from him when he was punished left him an embittered man. Now he wanted to implant the secret knowledge of his script in the hearts of young calligraphers, so that it would be preserved after his own death.

But he did not guess that he was taking another step into a trap set by his enemies, who misrepresented his plans for the school as another conspiracy against the caliph.

The caliph was angry because Ibn Muqla would not listen to him, and he ordered his judge to keep him prisoner in a house far from the city, and make sure that he could not dictate his secrets to anyone again. The calligrapher was to live there at the expense of the palace until the end of his days, but he was not to speak to any one except his guard.

One of his archenemies had his tongue cut out, and flung him into a prison on the outskirts of the desert, where he lived in isolation and misery. Protests from the poets and scholars of the time did no good.

Ibn Muqla died in July 940. The greatest poets of his epoch made moving speeches at his graveside. If he had really been conspiring against the caliph or the Quran, as his enemies claimed, no poet would have dared to praise him, let alone show that he mourned him, for the poets and scholars of the time all worked at the caliph's court and lived by his grace and favour.

'What I create will outlast time,' runs the most famous saying of Ibn Muqla's to have come down to us, and to this day it tells us of the vision of a man who knew that the rules he created for Arabic calligraphy would live as long as the script itself," Noura ended her reading. She put the sheets of paper together and laid them on the table.

There was silence in the little room. Salman wanted to say so much, but he could not find the words.

"He was never a conspirator," said Noura softly. Salman nodded, and at that moment they both heard the garden gate creak.

"Someone's coming," cried Noura, quickly putting her coat on. "Go and see who it is, and don't bother about me. If it's Karam I'll be gone," she said, pale in the face and nodding toward the window. She had opened it even before Salman reached the door of his room. As it was on the ground floor, she had only to climb over the window sill.

"Well, my little calligrapher," said Karam at the front door, "I thought I'd just look in. There aren't many customers in the café today," he said, putting a bag of bread on the kitchen table and glancing at Salman. "Why, you look pale! Are you hiding something from your friend Karam?" Without more ado, he opened the door of Salman's room and stopped in the doorway. Salman expected to hear a cry. His heart was hammering in his chest.

Disappointed, Karam came back into the kitchen. "I thought you might have a visitor. I've no objection, but you mustn't keep secrets from me. So why *are* you so pale?"

"You startled me. I thought you were an intruder."

Salman went back into his room, closed the window that Noura had left ajar, sat down at the table and put the stack of paper containing the story of Ibn Muqla into the drawer. Karam was on the telephone, probably to Badri, but it didn't sound as if the latter felt like coming round to see him.

He searched the room for any traces that might give Noura away, and was deeply grateful to her for having tidied up in the kitchen so well and so quickly, leaving no sign that they had breakfasted together there.

Suddenly, however, he saw the silver comb that Noura wore in her hair on the floor. He picked up the pretty thing and held it to his face.

He could have wept, he felt so sorry to have caused Noura so much trouble and alarm with his invitation. Yet his heart laughed at Karam's disappointment.

He opened the drawer to leaf through the article about Ibn Muqla again. Then he discovered the last page, a page that Noura had also been going to read him: a poem which a woman of the eleventh century had written about her lover.

Quickly, he stuffed all the sheets of paper back into the drawer.

And there was Karam standing in the doorway again. "You're very industrious today. Have you had anything at all to eat?" he asked.

Salman shook his head. "I'm not hungry," he said, and bent over his notebook again. Karam stood behind him, reading aloud from the piece of paper that Salman had in front of him: "Script is in universal equilibrium between the earthly and the heavenly, horizontals and verticals, curves and straight lines, the open and the concealed, the broad and the narrow, joy and grief, the hard and the soft, the sharp and the playful, rise and fall, day and night, Being and Nothing, creator and creation."

He stopped. "A wonderful saying. Where did you find it?" he asked.

"In a big, fat book where Master Hamid records his secrets," said Salman. "He locks the book up in a large cupboard with other important things."

"What kind of secrets?" asked Karam.

"His recipes for invisible inks, two books about secret scripts, the folder with sheets of gold leaf, his expensive knife, his recipes for ordinary inks, and the book where I found those words."

"And what else is in it, as well as clever sayings?"

"I don't know. I only managed to glance at it. It's very thick," said Salman, tidying his papers to hide his nervousness. Then he put a hand thoughtfully over his mouth, as if he had just remembered something. "Oh yes, there's something in it about letters that are dead and letters that are alive, but I didn't understand it. Sometimes there are pages written in a secret script. The letters are Arabic, but the language isn't, and it isn't Persian or Turkish either," he added.

"Letters that are dead? Are you sure?" asked Karam in surprise.

"Yes, but why are you interested in that?"

"Well, it's always good to know what innocent people are planning. Letters that are dead?" repeated Karam, and there was a devilish glint in his eyes.

But now Karam had to go back to the café, and he finally left Salman alone. Salman went into the kitchen and climbed on a chair to look out at the street through a little window above the shelf of spices. He saw Karam going down the street in the direction of the tram stop.

He made himself tea and gradually calmed down. When he called Noura it was already after four.

"This is Salman," he said, excitedly. "Is everything all right?"

"Yes, dear heart. But I lost my silver comb when I jumped out of the window into the garden."

"No, no, it had fallen under the bed earlier. Shall I keep it as a memento of our first adventure?"

"It's yours. I bought it years ago with a tip from a rich customer of Dalia the dressmaker. But tell me, what was that sudden visit to check up on you all about?"

"I don't understand it myself. Was it chance or an ambush – did he want to catch us out of pure curiosity, and if so why?"

"Maybe to blackmail me. Or maybe he's just a poor, lonely man who…"

"No, no. Karam thinks nothing of women, if you see what I mean," Salman interrupted her. "I'm sure of that, and it's exactly what makes his sudden descent on us so odd. He said he was bored in the café."

They talked for a while longer, developing their theories, and dreaming to themselves, but then Salman thought of something he wanted to tell Noura.

"Pray that my interrogation goes all right," he asked her. He would have liked to tell her about this in bed, enjoying her consoling kisses, but he had forgotten.

"What interrogation?" asked Noura.

"Someone's been informing on the boss, telling his fanatical enemies about the forthcoming founding of the School of Calligraphy even before it's been officially announced. And Radi, the nicest of the journeymen, warned me that he's heard Master Hamid and his assistant Samad suspect me of being the informer."

"But you're a Christian! How could they be stupid enough to think you'd be hand in glove with a set of radical Muslim fanatics? Don't worry, though. Hamid may be impossible as a husband, but he's a clever, cautious man. I won't pray; the whole thing is probably just a bad joke. You wait and see," she said, before hanging up.

Salman worked for about an hour, but then he felt so restless that he couldn't concentrate. He put his books and notes away in the drawer, and slipped the silver comb into his trouser pocket. When he opened the door of his room to go out he almost died of shock, for at that very moment Karam was coming through the door again. "Somehow I just don't feel like sitting in the café today. I thought I'd come back and make us something to eat. You've done quite enough work," he said with a chilly grin.

"Thank you very much, but I have to go home. My mother isn't feeling well," said Salman. And for the first time he felt afraid of Karam.

Outside, the evening air was cool. The tram drove through the Damascene evening, and he thought the city did not look at all as it did in daytime. People were hurrying, laden with shopping bags, full of plans, glad and tired at the same time as they made their way home down the streets.

For a moment he forgot that he was in a tram. He felt as if he were on a carousel turning and turning as it passed lighted rooms, colourful shops, cheerful children, old men and women bowed by the weight of their years. He closed his eyes for a moment. When he opened them again he was looking straight into the laughing face of a drunk, who turned round and asked the driver in a loud voice, "Going to Argentina today?"

The driver seemed to know the man. "Not today, no. We're going to Honolulu today. Argentina won't be on our route again until the 30th of February," he called back.

Only a few passengers were going, like Salman, to the city centre. There he boarded another tram to reach Bab Tuma in the Christian quarter. It was rather crowded, and Salman was glad to find a seat. Men and women in their best clothes were joking together on their way to a party.

Somehow he couldn't get the devilish glint in Karam's eyes out of his mind. He wondered why his friend was taking such an interest in the calligrapher's secrets all of a sudden. But as he was on the point of thinking further about that, the tram shot full tilt around a bend. The driver, infected by the partying mood of his passengers, began singing along with them, changing gear in time. A beautiful if rather plump woman lost her balance and landed, laughing, on Salman's lap. Other people were suddenly thrown into each other's arms. The driver saw his tottering passengers in the rear mirror, braked, and disentangled the screeching crowd.

"The poor boy, you'll crush him!" cried a man in an elegant dark blue suit with a red carnation in his buttonhole.

"Oh, come on, he's enjoying it," responded another man, this one in dress uniform.

The woman, giggling, tried to climb off Salman's lap. He liked the scent of her perfume, a mixture of lemon blossom and ripe apples, when her cheek brushed his face briefly. He breathed its fragrance in. The woman was on her feet again, looking at Salman in some embarrassment.

Years were to pass before he remembered the devilish glint in Karam's eyes again, making an effort to go back in his mind to the Paradise that he had known in Noura's arms. He could remember the evening tram ride as well, and at that later date he understood why the Devil had made Karam's eyes glint.

On the night after his adventurous tram ride, Salman heard that Shimon the vegetable seller had fled to Israel. He wondered why. Over the next few days he kept looking up to Shimon's room from his own window, hoping to see light there, but it stayed dark.

Not until a month later did a married couple rent the two-roomed apartment, and the owner of the shop was complaining even years later that Shimon still owed him three months' rent.

Salman and all the neighbours in Grace and Favour Yard knew, however, that the miserly owner was lying. The proceeds of the dried herbs, olive oil and exotic fruits that were now his property would have paid the rent for a year.

29

Master Hamid underestimated the fanatics. He himself was not a religious man. He did believe that some mighty being was responsible for all creation, and he was proud to the farthest corner of his soul that God felt such a particular liking for Arabic that he had dictated the Quran in that language to his Prophet Muhammad. Apart from that he was indifferent to all religions, and saw piety and extremes of faith as the basis on which simple-minded attitudes were built. However, he respected Jews more than Christians, because he saw many parallels between Judaism and Islam, while Christians arrogantly insisted on holding to their belief that God had fathered a son who drank wine and got himself crucified. And in addition the man Jesus required his followers to love their enemies!

Hamid seldom went to the mosque. But that suddenly changed in early January 1956, when his revered master and teacher Serani recommended him to go to the Umayyad Mosque on Fridays. It was a meeting place for highly respected theologians, politicians, the best-known businessmen in the city, and influential heads of clans. Serani was anxious about Hamid, who had been his favourite pupil. "People are whispering about your plans, and their whispers are gradually assuming a shape that I do not like. Come to the mosque on Friday with me, and they will see that you are a good Muslim." Hamid was touched by the old man's concern for him, and he decided to pray in the great mosque every Friday.

Soon after that, in the spring of 1956, he appreciated his master's wisdom. Great men of theology, science, and politics invited him to drink tea, approved of his radical support for the wearing of the veil and headscarf, and had to admit that they had previously entertained an entirely different idea of him.

In May, he boasted to those he met here that he had just declined a large commission for the Catholic Church, and would soon be going on pilgrimage to Mecca for the first time. Only his assistants didn't believe in this new piety of his.

"There's probably a big commission for the Saudis in prospect," surmised Samad in private. The other journeymen also doubted the new devotion to religion of their boss, a man who, as Mahmoud claimed, went to an exclusive little brothel in the new part of the city with three other calligraphers every Thursday.

"He plays cards on Thursday," objected Samad.

"Yes, but not at a café, at Madame Juliette's. So my cousin told me. He's worked for one of those calligraphers, and he lives near the madam. They play cards there every Thursday, and the winner of the game can choose a whore at the others' expense."

In the autumn of 1956 Hamid Farsi felt that he had convinced all the prominent men of Damascus, as well as the sternest theologians, of the importance of paying attention to the art of calligraphy. He did not say a word about reforms to them, although most of them, for all their friendliness, kept their distance from his project. Yet he felt sure that the conservative theologians had their hounds, the Pure Ones, firmly on the leash.

However, he was overestimating the influence of the liberal theologians on the fanatics in the underground. Two weeks after Farsi had signed the contract to rent the building for the School of Calligraphy, a bearded man walked into Nasri Abbani's office and asked sardonically where the owner of this outfit was. Tawfiq had some difficulty in suppressing his laughter. "I'm the errand boy around here. How can I help you?"

"Your master has made a mistake. We have nothing against his clan, but he has been giving money to support Hamid Farsi in his devilish work. Tell him to withdraw that support, and give the money to poor Muslims instead, or donate it for the renovation of our mosques, and then nothing will happen to him." The man showed no emotion as he spoke, and he frightened Tawfiq badly. He had feared cold characters like this since childhood. They understood very little, but shrank from nothing because, in their blindness, they thought they had one foot in Paradise already. No scientific knowledge in the world could equip warriors better.

"Now listen to me: my boss has given his support to a School of Calligraphy, not a brothel, " replied Tawfiq in tones of superiority, to cover up his fear.

"We think, however, that this calligraphy of his is only a cloak to disguise the work of the Devil. And I didn't come to discuss the matter with you or with him, but to give a warning," said the man, suddenly agitated after all. He turned on his heel and left.

Tawfiq stood in his office, shaking. It took him a little while to get over the fanatic's appearance. Then he took a deep breath and called Nasri. Nasri was in high good humour.

"Let them go to the Devil. A shower and a shave would do them more good. If calligraphy is blasphemy and the work of the Devil, then I don't know what God still stands for," he said.

Tawfiq nodded. His old distrust, however, reawakened as soon as he had hung up, and he thought of a saying of his dead father: "You can't take your eyes off that Nasri for a moment, or he'll be getting a woman pregnant and taking his business to the point of ruin."

Nasri's loyal assistant thought for a long time, trying to work out ways of averting misfortune from his master. He phoned Islamic scholars, professors, journalists both liberal and conservative, and they all laughed at his fears and assured him that calligraphy was the highest form of art ever produced by Arab culture. "And now those barbarians want to forbid us the divine game of letters as the work of the Devil," protested Mamdouh Burham, editor in chief of the conservative *Al Ayyam* newspaper. "They're hostile to all the pleasures of life anyway, and to that extent they're anti-Islamic. Our Prophet, God's blessings be upon him, was a man who enjoyed sensual pleasure," he concluded.

Only one man gave an answer that went beyond mere reassurance. He was Habib Kahaleh, the experienced journalist and chief editor of the satirical magazine *Al Moudhik al Moubki*. "It is not Arabic script or calligraphy," said that elegant man, "but – so I have heard – the calligrapher's secret plans that upset the fanatics, and if that is the case you needn't worry about Nasri Abbani. Their main target is Hamid Farsi."

He recommended Tawfiq to forget the crazy fanatic. But the dead eyes of the bearded man followed Tawfiq into his dreams.

Unlike Tawfiq, Nasri Abbani forgot all about the phone call at once, ate dessert, drank a coffee, and went up to his room on the first floor.

He took a folder out of his briefcase, opened it, and the two-page letter lay before him. A work of art. The description of the woman was perfect. And if you narrowed your eyes, the lines turned into a blazing flame.

What divine script! Nasri could hardly bring himself to fold that superfine paper. The fold itself seemed to him brutal, but he did it in exactly the right way for the edge of the paper to meet the central fold. He took the heavy gold coin that he had bought in Goldsmiths' Street near the Umayyad Mosque, placed it right on the middle point of the strip that the letter had now become, fixed it in place with a little glue, and the coin was in place. He climbed on the bed, held the strip aloft, and let it fall. The strip rotated like a propeller as it moved almost vertically toward the floor.

Now he was waiting patiently for his mother-in-law to finish washing the dishes and clearing up the kitchen. After an eternity, she too went to bed. He knew that Almaz had been snoring for a long time already beside her daughter Nariman, who grew more and more like her every day.

All was more silent than a graveyard when Nasri slowly went to the wooden ladder, climbed it cautiously and without a sound, and quickly closed the attic door behind him.

Outside, the sun was spreading a bright carpet over the city. It was pleasantly warm, but the cold night air still lingered in the attic. Nasri shivered, and went over to the window. He glanced out at the courtyard below, where the woman was sunbathing in a large chair beside the fountain. She was reading. When he opened the window, she looked up and smiled. Nasri could have died with delight. He responded with a nod, and showed her the paper. The wind had died down. He let the paper strip sail down and saw the surprise on the woman's face. She laughed, and clapped her hand over her mouth. The propeller landed two metres from the wall, not far from the fountain.

The woman sat up, smiled at him again, and got to her feet to pick up the strip of paper. Then Nasri heard footsteps and a bang. It sounded like someone hitting a door with a hammer. He quickly closed the window, waited for a moment, and stepped out on the little terrace in front of the attic. At that moment he saw his wife come into the stairwell that led from the first floor to the ground floor. He waited by the ladder to see if he had been wrong. But no one appeared up the stairs.

A hallucination, he thought, the result of his pangs of conscience, and he smiled, because he had not in fact felt any pangs of conscience at all since childhood. He stepped on to the first rung of the ladder, and as he felt for the next rung with his other foot the wood collapsed under him and he fell, flailing about in the air for something to catch hold of, until he struck the ground hard with his left leg.

Darkness full of pain came down on him like a plank. When he came back to his senses, he was lying in hospital. His left leg was in plaster, and he couldn't move it.

30

Hamid Farsi was standing in front of his assembled employees in a
towering rage, for only they knew about Nasri Abbani's generous gift,
and the two marble slabs that the journeyman Samad had chiselled
to his master's design in the workshop. It was also he who had drawn
Hamid's attention to the errand boy Salman as a possible informer,
for of all his staff the errand boy had more chance to overhear conversations with the customers than anyone else.

"But he's a Christian," said Master Hamid, dismissing the idea.
That did not deter Samad. "Christians or Jews, they're all traitors.
They sold their Jesus for thirty pieces of silver. Let Mahmoud get to
work on him, and he'll sing like a canary."

Master Hamid, did not reply, but he finally agreed.

The unfortunate errand boy arrived at work next day bruised all
over, with his hands and one eye swollen, and a wound close to the
base of his left ear was thickly encrusted with a brown scab. However,
Mahmoud had not been able to get him to say anything at all. Samad
stood in front of his master with his head bowed.

With apparent innocence Hamid asked Salman what had happened to him, and Salman, for fear of Mahmoud, said he had fallen
off his bicycle and down a steep slope.

It was the day before Christmas. Hamid looked at the thin boy
sympathetically. "You celebrate the birth of your Prophet tomorrow,
don't you?" he asked. Salman nodded. "And after that everyone cel-
ebrates New Year's Eve. Stay at home until the second of January and
get better," he said, taking his wallet out of his pocket. He gave Salman
his full month's wages and sent him off. At that moment his sister
Siham appeared at the doorway of the studio. "You get out of here,"
cried Hamid, much annoyed. "I have no time for you today and no
money either," he added, pushing her out. His sister muttered something, struck the glazed door with her fist, and left.

"And Mahmoud can be errand boy today as punishment," shouted Hamid loud enough for everyone in the workshop to hear him.

For Mahmoud his journeyman, a grown man, that was indeed a severe punishment. But worse was to come in January.

When Salman called Noura from a phone kiosk and told her what had happened she said she wanted to see him. Salman was ashamed to think of her seeing him like this, but she insisted on a meeting.

They sat in a café in the new part of the city, near the Fardous cinema. Salman said nothing, but Noura was horrified. What had they done to Salman? How could her husband be so cruel? She wept at the sight of him, and she kissed his eyes, unafraid of being seen. The café owner looked sympathetically at the couple. Noura felt bitter hatred of her husband. After their meeting she went to see Dalia. She told her nothing about what had happened, but for the first time in her life she drank some arak. After that she felt better. When she said goodbye, the dressmaker hugged her and held her close. "Look after yourself, my child," she said softly. Noura nodded, and walked slowly home.

On the third of January, when Salman was back at the workshop, Karam asked him at lunchtime whether he had heard that Mahmoud was sick. Salman shook his head.

"Very sick indeed, so I hear, and after tomorrow he won't be able to work again," said Karam, with a smile full of meaning. Salman's mind was elsewhere that day. Noura had mentioned, in passing, that she knew someone who, at the price of a hundred lira, could get you genuine papers and give you a new identity.

How can anyone, he wanted to ask, get genuine papers in another name? He had heard only of good forgeries and bad ones. "It seems," Noura went on, as if she had heard his unspoken question, "that he has access to the data in the office for the registration of residents, and he can bring the dead to life or duplicate people."

Salman was still thinking about the implications of this tale of a second identity, and he wasn't greatly interested in whether that lout Mahmoud was sick or not. Not until the next day was he to discover that he had not really been listening to what Karam said properly, let alone understanding it.

On the night of the second of January the calligrapher's journeyman had been set upon by four muscular, bearded men. They beat him mercilessly, and at every blow they cried *Allahu Akbar*, God is great, as if they were performing a religious rite. And then the largest of them crushed his right hand with a sledgehammer.

If a passerby had not discovered Mahmoud whimpering quietly in the dark entrance of a warehouse, he would have died of internal bleeding. And as if that were not enough, an unknown man phoned Hamid early next morning and told him that his journeyman had tried to rape a young woman. Under this provocation, he added, her brother had broken the hand that had touched her.

Hamid brought the receiver down on the rest as quickly as if it were burning. He said not a word about the attack, but a day later the whole studio knew about it. Master Hamid had gone to a meeting with the minister of culture, and when the telephone rang it was Samad who answered it.

The caller was Mahmoud's wife. In tears, she told Samad that her husband, thanks be to God, was no longer in danger of death, but he would never be able to use his right hand again. She wept bitterly, because everyone in the hospital knew that Mahmoud had been beaten up because of a rape, and now they were both equally despised.

Samad made two or three consoling remarks, and hung up. Salman was torn between gratitude to Karam, who must certainly be behind this act of retribution, and abhorrence at the brutality of the punishment, which also affected Mahmoud's family. They would be destitute now. What kind of cruel game was Karam playing?

On that sad day the journeyman Radi vomited for the first time. They kept his sickness secret from their master. Radi's prospects did not look good, but he recovered to some extent over the next few days. Salman made herbal teas to help Radi when he was pale and had stomach cramps.

Hamid did not lament the loss of Mahmoud for long. A week later he sent his assistant Samad out to seek the services of a capable young calligrapher whom he had heard of. Samad was to settle the matter over a good lunch. Hamid gave him twenty lira, saying, "See that he's well fed. The stomach rules the mind."

Two days later the new journeyman arrived. His name was Bashir Magdi, and he dreamed of redesigning all the scripts used in printing newspapers and magazines some day. He was a cheerful companion, and liked Salman from the first. Only Hamid had some reservations about him. "You're not producing rough work to be thrown away here," he told him, "you're doing work to last forever. Let time, not haste, dwell in your characters."

But Bashir couldn't work slowly. Two months after joining the workshop, he threw in the towel and went to work at a major newspaper. He became its chief calligrapher.

Salman's mother was not at all well. She ran a high temperature over the Christmas season, and then recovered slightly, only to take to her bed again, drained of strength again. Salman bought her expensive medicines, but they could only alleviate the pain, they couldn't cure his mother.

Every Friday he took her to see Dr Sahum, who treated the poor free that day. His practice was crowded, and you had to wait a long time, but Dr Sahum was friendly to all the patients down to the very last. In the end he couldn't say exactly what was wrong with Salman's mother. General exhaustion? A viral infection? And then he took Salman aside and told him that his mother did not have much longer to live. She was not yet forty years old.

What a wretched existence, Salman thought on his way to work. Someone like his mother, born in poverty, sold off to a strange man whom she neither loved nor respected and who neither loved nor respected her, she had spent her life in pain and was now dying a slow, tormenting death.

"Sometimes I think God avenges himself on the wrong people," he said to Noura.

In the morning, after cleaning the studio thoroughly as he did every week, Salman was to deliver a framed work of calligraphy, already paid for, to a customer. He wrapped the valuable calligraphy in newspaper and set out just before ten. When he came to Victoria Bridge he saw Pilot sitting placidly in front of a blind beggar. "Pilot, oh, my dear dog, who'd have thought it?" he whispered in agitation. He wanted to run straight to him, but he feared for the expensive piece of calligraphy. So first he went to see the architect three streets away and delivered the work of art. His instructions were to wait for the architect to receive the calligraphy in person and thank him for it. Hamid was a proud calligrapher who often told the tale of the Egyptian ruler Muhammad Ali and the Persian calligrapher. Muhammad Ali, the great pasha of Egypt, asked the Persian calligrapher Sinklakh to copy a famous religious poem in fine calligraphy to be hung in the Great Mosque that the pasha was building in Cairo at the time. The calligrapher spent two months on his work of art. When he had finished it, he told his servant to take the scroll to Egypt. At court the servant was to announce that he had the calligraphic poem with him, and if the pasha did not stand up to receive the scroll with due honour, the man was to turn and bring it back again. Sinklakh demanded respect for calligraphy. But not only Muhammad Ali, his entire court also rose and applauded when the servant entered the hall with the great scroll.

In the architect's office, the secretary wanted to take Salman's package from him at first, but he stuck to his guns until she finally fetched her boss. He was delighted with the calligraphy, gave Salman a tip, and sent the master calligrapher his heartfelt greetings and thanks, as was right and proper.

Salman rushed out and ran all the way back to Victoria Bridge. Thank heavens, the dog was still there. He was lying down now, watching the passersby. Behind him, the young blind beggar was singing, in a heart-rending voice, of his sad fate. Suddenly the dog sat up. He looked older now and scarred, but the bold, mischievous expression he had worn even as a puppy was the same as ever. Dogs can sometimes look at you in a way that makes you think they understand everything, thought Salman.

Pilot ran to Salman, bounded around him, wagging his tail, and almost knocked him over. He had recognized him, and was barking with joy at their reunion. "Pilot!" cried Salman, "Dear Pilot!" The beggar stopped singing. "Aini," he called, "come here, Aini, heel!" But the dog took no notice. "Help, someone's trying to steal my dog," shouted the beggar at the top of his voice. "Please, help a blind man and God will reward you!"

"Stop shouting like that," Salman called back. "No one's trying to steal anything from you. This dog is mine. I saved his life when he was abandoned, and he grew up with me until someone stole him. His name is Pilot." Salman saw uncertainty and fear in the young beggar's face. "See how he listens to me. Pilot! Sit!" And the dog sat down, wagging his tail, and stayed put, much as he wanted to go to Salman. The beggar sensed that the dog was obeying.

"He's my dog, and I've been looking for him for years. How much do you want for him?" asked Salman.

"Maybe he was your dog once," said the beggar pitifully, "but now he's my eyesight. His name is Aini to show that he is my eyes, and he looks after me all day long. You can't take him away from me. Once some bad boys tried to rob me, and he protected me bravely – can you see his scars?"

"But…" Salman began to protest.

"No buts. Aini and I have been living happily together for years. He's my brother, he cares for me, he even sheds tears with me when I'm sad."

"All right. I understand," said Salman. "I'll leave you the dog and give you a present too. Call him Pilot from now on, and I'll show you a coffeehouse, a very fine one in the rich Souk Saruya quarter, not far from here. Pilot once saved the life of the owner, Karam. He knows the dog and loves him. You'll get a hot meal there at noon every day, and Pilot too, all right? Karam is a generous man, but he'll do it only if you call the dog Pilot."

"That's fine. I'd call myself Pilot for a hot meal. I haven't had one for days. What's the name of the café?"

"The Café Karam. I'll be there between twelve and twelve-thirty," said Salman, patting Pilot, who was dozing now, reassured by the friendlier sound of their voices.

But Karam was like a changed man. He wouldn't have anything to do with either Pilot or the beggar, and refused in no uncertain terms to give the man a meal.

When Karam saw Salman coming, he shook his head, then grabbed him by his shirt and dragged him into the café, while Darwish was asking the beggar, if rather more politely than his boss, to go away and not bother their customers with his dog. Surreptitiously, he gave him a falafel roll.

"Are you crazy, sending that lousy beggar and his mangy dog to the café?" Karam hissed at Salman.

Salman was both shocked and ashamed. He wanted to ask what was so bad about letting a beggar sit in the café for once, but Karam gave him no chance. "You keep your mouth shut! Do you know what kind of people come here? People from the best circles, former ministers, the present prime minister, his cousin, jewellers, professors, scholars, the sheikh of the Umayyad Mosque and several generals are among my regular customers, and you can think of nothing better than to send this impudent beggar to me. Get out and take this loud-mouth away from my café," he cried angrily. At the same moment Salman heard the beggar call to his dog. "Come along, Aini, this place stinks of greed and decay. God punish the man who led us here. Come on, Aini, come on," he called, and he walked away.

Salman was weeping with rage. He hated Master Hamid, who hadn't given him a moment's peace that morning, he hated Karam for making such an outcry, but most of all he hated himself.

He never saw Pilot again.

Salman used the bicycle only for his daily journey to his master's house and back. He would have liked to show it off in Grace and Favour Yard, but he was afraid someone might give him away, for Basem and Ali, who worked at the studio, lived less than a hundred metres from the Yard.

On the bike Salman saw the city of Damascus in a different way; it wasn't like being on foot or sitting in the bus. He suddenly noticed how many foreigners worked in the city. One day he saw a farmer walking along behind his strong, heavily laden mule. You could hardly see the animal under the long trunks and branches of the timber it was carrying. The farmer kept calling wearily, "Firewood! Watch your backs! Firewood!"

Salman had been told by his father that farmers sold the wood of old, sick trees because it fetched good money. They themselves burned only dried cow dung and straw.

The farmer reached a road junction where three men, leaning on gigantic hatchets, were smoking and telling jokes.

When a woman bought two of the tree trunks, one of the men came over and chopped the wood up. He came from Albania and earned a meagre wage here.

The knife-grinders of Damascus came from Afghanistan, the watchmakers were Armenian, the carpet dealers Persian, and the men who sold nuts in the streets came from the Sudan.

Early in February the weather improved, and after a few sunny days the Damascenes breathed a sigh of relief. Salman's mother also felt better. She got up, some colour came back into her cheeks and she made a thousand plans. But the doctor warned her not to overtax her strength.

One morning his mother surprised Salman at breakfast. "Do you know what I've always dreamt of?" she asked, a little shyly. Salman shook his head.

"Going for a ride on your bike. I mean, I can't ride it myself, but if you were to take me on it I'd be so proud of you. Will you do that for me?"

"Happily," said Salman.

And one afternoon they did it. After work, he rode the bicycle through the front gate into Grace and Favour Yard. He fetched a quilt, laid it on the load surface of the carrier, and invited his mother to sit on it.

Then Salman rode proudly all round the big courtyard with her. The neighbours, men and women alike, came out, sat outside their doors on stools, and watched the happy woman on the front of the transporter bike. Barakat, the baker's journeyman with the beautiful daughters, all of them married now, threw Salman's mother a little red windmill fastened to a stick. She laughed, held it up, and the wind blew the small red sails round and round. For the first time in his life, Salman heard his mother strike up a cheerful song.

Salman rode round with her more than twenty times, sometimes with a crowd of children in his wake, shouting happily and singing. Anyone who also had a bike rode behind Salman, and they all kept ringing their bells. It looked like a wedding procession. Kamil the police officer, Sarah's father, stood in the middle of the yard directing the traffic by whistling.

Salman noticed how handsome and youthful Sarah's father looked by comparison with her mother, who seemed old and tired these days – and who was very jealous. He remembered what Sarah had told him, years ago: "My mother swallows her jealousy every evening and decides to trust my father, but at night the jealousy comes out of her open mouth again, and as soon as my father leaves early in the morning it jumps right back on my mother's shoulder and whispers that her suspicions are justified. And she feeds the horrible clinging thing like a pet. By evening it's the size of a rooster. And when my father comes home from work, tired, my mother is ashamed, she gives him a kiss, guilty as she feels, slaughters her jealousy and eats it up again."

Salman rode around in circles with his mother until, exhausted but happy, she asked him to stop. He rode back to their apartment door with him, and she got off the bike and hugged him. "It was even better than the dream I've been carrying around with me ever since my childhood."

A week later she lapsed into a coma. Salman sang her own songs softly by her bedside, but she no longer reacted. Sometimes he imagined she had moved her hand to show that she wanted him to go on singing.

At the end of February, a day after Salman had lost his job, she died in the night. She lay there perfectly still, with the hint of a smile on her lips. Salman was woken by the noise his father made, crying like a child, kissing his wife again and again and begging her to forgive him. They found the little red windmill under her pillow.

After the incident with the beggar, Salman stayed away from Karam's café for a week. He didn't even go to Karam's house on Friday.

Days later, he was going to take the bike back to the yard of the pottery when he saw Karam there. Salman padlocked the bike and was about to disappear fast. "Hey, wait, where are you off to?" shouted Karam in friendly, almost imploring tones.

Salman did not reply, but stopped and lowered his gaze. "You must understand me," said Karam. "I can't take in all the hungry folk in the world."

"No one asked you to. I just wanted to see Pilot again, and I couldn't manage to tell you in advance that day. I'm sorry, but you mustn't go saying I ruined you."

"No, you haven't ruined me. I'm really sorry, and I ask you to forgive me. Shall we be friends again?" he asked. Salman nodded, and Karam hugged him and held him close.

"Hey, not so tight or someone will be setting Badri on me," joked Salman.

They walked side by side to the café. "Well?" asked Karam. "So what's new on the amorous front?" However, Salman wasn't going to say a word to him about his passion for Noura. Not out of suspicion, simply because he did not want to share that precious thing, his love, with anyone.

"No, it's still one-sided on my part. Maybe she likes me, she's friendly to me, but very faithful to her husband, and she wouldn't start anything with a man whose ears stick out," he said, but inside he was grinning so widely that he almost got hiccups.

31

It was his letters that made Asmahan forget she was never going to love anyone. But it was a long time since she had been mistress of her heart, and her self-imposed sober good sense vanished as soon as Nasri stepped into the house. Once again she became the young girl who, over ten years ago, had waited longingly for the words of the boy she loved then, and lay awake at night if one of his letters was late.

She had been ten or eleven when she fell hopelessly in love with Malik, the pale boy next door. He wasn't yet fifteen, but he held the secret key of poetry, which he used to unlock the worlds behind written characters and show them to her. That was long ago.

Asmahan's mother came from a rich family. She had been the third woman in Syria to take her higher school certificate two years before Asmahan's birth.

Her father's family were merchants in the city, with trading links dating back to the Middle Ages with Venice, Vienna, London, and Lübeck. He was director of a tobacco factory, and although he was a Muslim he sent her and his other four children to elite Christian schools. Hers was in the Salihiyyeh quarter, three streets away from her present house. The school was run by stern nuns who wore strange clothes and snow-white headdresses with large, angular wings bending up on both sides. When the nuns walked the wings of their headdresses bobbed up and down as if they had swans on their heads, flapping to keep their balance.

The school had a large library, but the schoolgirls were not allowed to touch the books. Nor could Asmahan choose what she read at home. Her father kept his books in a handsome glass-fronted book-case. She learned all the titles on the spines of the books by heart, but she never thought of trying to take one of the books off the shelf and reading it. It was Malik who told her that banned books, more than any others, hold everything that it is valuable to know. One day she found the key to the bookcase and took out a book. Its title, *The Secret of Words*, had fascinated her. Malik knew the book, and he told her to go on reading, because even what she didn't understand would gather inside her, like a flower-bud, waiting for the right moment to unfold its petals.

It was to be five years before she had read all the books in her father's library. She always took a book to her secret meetings with Malik, and read him a poem or an anecdote about love. Malik seemed to turn even paler than he already was as he listened. Sometimes he shed tears when the poem was about the torment of love.

Asmahan never again met a better listener. She felt that Malik was drawing her words into his ears with an invisible magnet, so avidly that he almost tore them out of her. So her tongue tingled in a strange way when she spoke to him.

And after she had read to him, he told her what the allusions in the lines of poetry meant, and she felt as if he were taking her by the hand and leading her into secret gardens of pleasure. Malik could not only read the visible words, he could also see their hidden roots.

Almost every day she slipped through a secret gap in the hedge into the garden of his parents' house, and they met in the toolshed. The big garden had become a jungle of trees and shrubs run wild, because his parents hated gardening and had no wish to tend roses, grapevines, orange, and mulberry trees. They had inherited the place and let it go to rack and ruin. Even before they immigrated to America in 1940 the house, once grand, was well on the way to falling into ruin.

But that was only much later, when Asmahan was already married and Malik had been underground for three years.

They met almost daily for five years. Her mother and her brothers and sisters never noticed anything until Malik's death.

It was like addiction to a drug. He was always sitting there as if expecting her arrival, yet every time he was visibly relieved when she did appear.

As soon as they were sitting on the big old sofa that must once have been very luxurious, with its red velvet upholstery, he would touch her lips with his delicate fingers and begin reciting poems about the beauty of women. It was some time before she realized that they were his own poems composed to celebrate her beauty. She forgot the stack of flower pots, the rusting tools left there by former gardeners, the watering cans, and the hose. Touched by his words, she moved as if in another world that belonged only to the two of them.

Once he brought with him a large book whose pages were full of ornamentation that she could not understand, in the shape of inter-twining script. Here and there she could make out a word, a letter, but the whole thing remained a mystery. The characters formed an elegant jungle of black ink with white spaces in between.

He kissed her for a long time that day, and she felt dizzy. He took her forefinger and ran it along the letters on the page, and she felt this script flowing into her. The book lay on a low old table in front of her. Malik bent closer to the paper, and sought his way through the laby-rinth of the lines, curves, and dots. He looked divinely beautiful in the light falling through the coloured glass window. When she kissed his earlobe, he smiled and ran his finger along a word that she now saw set free from the jungle of characters, and she could read it: Love.

Another day she saw him sitting in the garden shed with a big book in front of him. He stood up at once, smiled at her, took her hand and led her to the sofa, where he kissed her so hard that she was in turmoil. He frightened her, for he seemed to be in a frenzy. She lay under him, and he kissed her not only on her lips, throat, and cheeks, as if he were groping like a blind man his kisses some-times went down to her belt, and he found her watch and kissed that, he kissed her dress, her knees, her underclothes, all the time making sounds like the soft wailing of a baby hungrily searching for its mother's breast.

Then he smiled, sat up, waited until she was sitting up too, took her right forefinger in his hand and wandered over the words of the first large ornament in the book.

They were lines in a passionate erotic poem, and she quickly real-ized that this was a forbidden book of love. The man who wrote them had lived in the fourteenth century; he collected daring, openly erotic poems from all over the world, and concealed them by the art of calligraphy. Only experts could read the secrets hidden in the lettering. For those not initiated, the script looked merely like beautiful ornamentation.

Page after page described forbidden love, amorous practices, and the growing longing for the touch of the beloved. And again and again, the poems celebrated the physical beauty of men and women in every detail. Often there was an easily legible religious saying on the page above the erotic poetry to camouflage it. Malik guided Asmahan's finger on until she felt a violent longing for him. She put her arms round him and listened to the fast beating of his heart as she lay over him.

She loved him with eroticism and innocence at the same time. Days, months, and years went by as if in a second, so that later she could not tell those years apart. She woke up only when he suddenly fell severely ill.

Hadn't she known, all these years, that he was incurably sick? Had she never feared for him? Why had she made so many plans in her daydreams, knowing that his heart disease was past curing? Had she perhaps idolized him so much to keep him alive for longer?

It was a complete surprise when his sister came to the front door of her house one day and muttered, with her eyes cast down, that Malik was dying and wanted to see her. Asmahan immediately ran without stopping from the street where she lived to the Italian hospital, far away in the city. His room was full of people. Malik saw her and smiled. In the silence that suddenly fell he whispered, "There she is. There she is."

The disapproving glances of those present drew her attention to the fact that she was wearing her slippers. "Come here, I want to show you something," said Malik, barely audibly, but even from the doorway she could understand it as clearly as if the words had been whispered into her ear. Her feet were rooted to the spot as if the glances of the others had weighted them with lead.

"I want to be alone," she heard Malik ask his mother, who was holding his hand. Her eyes were red and swollen. Asmahan sat on the side of the bed, and when he put his hand out to her she looked around, embarrassed. But the room was suddenly empty, as if swept clear by some magic hand.

"I wrote this for you," he said, and took out of the little bedside locker a small rectangular package clumsily wrapped in paper and tied up with thick string. Asmahan undid the many tight knots with trembling fingers, and tore the paper in her impatience. A small, framed work of calligraphy came into view. It looked very complex, and it resembled a rose.

"When you can read that you will think of me," said Malik, fighting for breath.

"Love is the only disease of which I do not wish to be cured," she read six months later, when she was able to decipher it. The small framed saying accompanied her all her life, like an icon.

Two days after her visit to the hospital, she woke from a nightmare as day was about to dawn. She heard someone calling to her, ran out of her room on to the small terrace, but her parents and her three younger brothers were still asleep in their own rooms on the other side of it.

Only later did Asmahan learn from Malik's sister, who had slept on the floor beside his bed during all his nights in hospital, that at that hour of the morning, when he was dying, Malik had called her name aloud.

Malik was not twenty when he died, Asmahan was just fifteen years old. A week later she had a fever and lost consciousness. When she came back to her senses, her mother knew all about her relationship with Malik. How she had found out remained her secret. She consoled Asmahan and asked whether everything was all right with her "down there," and was visibly relieved to discover that Asmahan was still a virgin.

Asmahan swore to herself that she would never love anyone again. She declared her heart dead, never guessing that hearts have no way of understanding a declaration.

Men's glances, bent on her with desire the older and more feminine she grew, left her cold.

"What does 'only fifteen' mean? She has more experience of love than I do. She's in urgent need of a husband," said her mother that same evening to her father.

A year later Asmahan married her cousin, ten years her senior, a heavily built forensic surgeon with uncouth manners, who knew more about corpses than living bodies and minds.

Early in 1950, Asmahan's father had a remarkable letter from Florida. The letter came at just the right time, for her father had lost all his money in speculations. He was living on his salary as director of the tobacco factory, but he would soon have to run up debts to finance his expensive lifestyle. After six months the house was heavily mortgaged. And now this letter came like divine intervention at the last minute. Her father's uncle was a rich hotelier, and had no children. After several divorces, and legal proceedings in which he had lost a lot of money, he hated the Americans. Now, fearing that at the end of a long working life the United States would inherit his still large fortune, he sent for the only nephew he knew from the days before he emigrated. He wanted him to go to the States, acquire a green card, and inherit his property. An airline ticket convinced Asmahan's father that this was not just a joke.

Three weeks later he had the papers he needed, wound up his affairs in Damascus, and emigrated with his entire remaining family.

There was a moving farewell in Beirut harbour. Everyone was in tears, except for Asmahan's husband, who laughed and joked the whole time. Asmahan felt revulsion for the man. She waited until the ship went out of harbour and then said what she thought of him. All the way back to Damascus they quarrelled, and shortly before they arrived she said she wanted a divorce.

"Not until I find a more beautiful mistress," he said, laughing coarsely. "But if you're in a hurry you can find me one." And he shook with laughter so much that he almost lost control of the car.

A week later Asmahan had her first lover. At a reception given by the then minister of culture, Fouad Shayeb, she was envied by the women there, and courted by all the powerful men. She had only to choose between them.

She enjoyed her champagne and observed the men strutting like roosters. They seemed to her just little boys, vain, mindless, unreliable. And she saw how small and stooped her arrogant husband suddenly was in front of the minister of health, and he in turn before the prime minister, and the prime minister himself before the head of the armed forces, a dwarf with a huge, scarred red nose and a figure decorated and hung about with brightly coloured orders and other trumpery that clinked with a metallic sound when the dwarf moved. He looked like the ape Asmahan had seen at a fair when she was a little girl. The ape had worn an over-decorated Napoleonic uniform, and could stand upright when the command was given, salute, and grin horribly all the time.

"One of these apes will wipe that smile off your face," whispered Asmahan to herself as her husband laughed out loud again. She smiled at their host, a charming little man from the Christian village of Malula. He was very knowledgeable, and a good speaker. She liked him, but he was far too cultivated and at the same time not powerful enough for the task Asmahan had ready for her future lover. The one man for that was one whose laughter that evening was even louder and more primitive than her husband's: the interior minister Said Badrakhan. He was a bold adventurer from one of the richest families in the north, and his conduct matched his origin.

He was the instrument to sweep her husband away like a chessman swept off the board. And so he did. Six months later the whole world knew about their affair. Her husband agreed to a divorce to avoid even greater scandal. The interior minister let him know that if he touched a hair of Asmahan's head, he would be unable to dissect any more corpses in future because he would be one of them himself.

She moved out, and her lover gave her the little house near the parliament building. Two months later Said Badrakham died in a mysterious road accident. It was certain that the brakes of his car had been tampered with. The files covering the incident disappeared, and the government did not react to rumours that he had been killed on the orders of the President because he had drawn up a file at the Interior Ministry on the venality, dissolution, and other flaws of the head of state. His widow, however, spread the story, through a journalist, that his affair with a young whore had cost him his life, because the young woman's ex-husband had hired killers to avenge his honour.

The entire business left Asmahan cold, and whether by chance or not, on the very day after the funeral she slept with a man for money for the first time. He was a member of parliament, and very generous.

It was also he who advised her never to ask a fixed sum. "Look around you, and you'll see that the really superior goods in shop windows never have price tickets on them. Be choosy and clever at picking your clients, and they will come and reward you more than well if you make them happy."

The words of the member of parliament were to prove prophetic. Asmahan could soon hardly move for clients of the very best class. It was said of her later that she made more money in a week than the prime minister made a month, or a high school teacher's earnings for a year, and Asmahan invested the money well.

Three months after the divorce, Nasri entered her salon, and from the first he was special. He was up to every trick, he knew half the city above and below ground, as he once said to her, joking. Nasri was extravagant, generous, and had excellent taste. Asmahan had resisted showing him her feelings for a long time, but Nasri's letters, with the works of calligraphy, were waves beating high against the dam she had erected and bringing it down.

She forgot her vow never to love anyone, and fell hopelessly in love with him after the third or fourth letter. And it was those letters, bringing her to life, conveying a sense of great lightness, that made life hard for her. She could no longer lie indifferent in the arms of the other men. She assumed a smile like a mask, but some of her experienced clients saw through it. They were not pleased, and no longer said when they left that they felt they had been in Paradise, they talked to her almost like doctors, telling her she was tense, stiff, her heart wasn't in the job.

She could not imagine a day without seeing Nasri, smelling him, giving herself to him. And he came regularly in the middle of every day.

However, he reacted almost with shock when she said she could imagine living with him and for him alone. He wrote her no more letters, he visited her less frequently, and the more she telephoned him the more elusive he was. Those were four of the worst weeks of her life. Nasri seemed to have disappeared. She was very worried, and went to his office one morning. There he sat, laughing with a grey-haired assistant. When he saw her his expression changed. The assistant went out of the office without a sound, and fast, like a man getting to safety from the threat of a thunderstorm.

"What are you doing here?" asked Nasri brusquely.

"Looking for you. I was worried. Aren't you glad to see me?" She gave him a pleading glance. He did not reply, but smiled uncertainly and blustered about business that kept him occupied, but he promised to come and see her soon. However, he did not.

When she went to his office once more – again after a long time – Tawfiq, the grey-haired assistant, took her firmly by the arm and would not let her in. "This is a decent business firm, not a brothel," he said, pushing her in the direction of the stairs and closing the door.

The words she had once heard a drunken old whore say echoed menacingly in her ears: "When someone first rejects you you're past your peak, and the road downhill goes faster than you think."

"No," she cried as she came to herself. She ran downstairs and out of the building. She swore revenge, and went back to her work, hoping that her clients' requests and paeans of praise would help her to forget the wounds she had suffered. She did not have to wait long. The first client to visit, a famous confectioner, praised her effusively when he left, saying he felt more satisfied than with anyone else.

Soon the flattery of her clients drove the old whore's words out of her mind. But she decided that the next time someone rejected her she would stop at once, and move north to the Mediterranean, where she would make herself out a young widow and open a beach café. She would amuse herself and never work as a whore again, but wait with curiosity for whatever surprises life brought. I have money enough to be secure, she thought proudly.

32

Nasri was not to be intimidated either by his broken leg or the jealousy of his fourth wife Almaz. At the beginning of February he was able to walk without crutches again. An iron spiral staircase now led from the first floor up to the attic.

He did not tell Hamid a word about his accident, but spoke enthusiastically of the wonderful effect of the first letter, and commissioned a second. He dictated a few details to the calligrapher, about the woman's laughter and her delicate hands, and was about to go when the calligrapher said, "Thank you for not backing out."

"Backing out? Why in the world would I back out?"

"Because of the shameless blackmail the so-called Pure Ones are exerting. They sent one of their bearded fanatics to see your business manager. He phoned me at the time, sounding concerned, and I assured him that we now have President al-Quwwatli aboard the project, as well as all the Christian patriarchs. I have no idea how the news even reached their stupid minds."

Nasri had been hearing about the Pure Ones for years; his youngest brother secretly sympathized with them. He himself couldn't stand them. They looked like caricature ugly Arabs, and he thought their propaganda ridiculous. They were a danger to the public. They wanted to do away with the republic, democracy, and political parties, and return to sharia and the caliphate. As a party they stood no chance in the open-minded and ethnically mingled society of Syria, so they maintained an underground army that acted with uncompromising hostility, blackmailing, agitating and mounting assassination attempts, while the distinguished Pure Ones delivered lectures on the glorious past of the Arabs to which they wanted to return.

"But listen to me. They don't know Nasri Abbani. I now consider your school a positive necessity." He stopped, because he didn't care for his own emotional tone. He in fact regarded calligraphy as a harmless art.

"Well, in your skirmishing with the bearded fellows don't forget my letter. Another bearded man urgently needs it," he said, laughing smugly, and he gave Hamid his hand and left before the calligrapher had really worked out what he meant.

Three days later, Nasri sent the next letter sailing through the air. The beautiful woman was sitting in the inner courtyard, copying something out of a large volume into a notebook. She smiled when she saw him up at his little window. Nasri had sent her down another gold coin and suggested meeting her at a place of her own choice.

The woman laughed, picked up the letter and disappeared.

From mid-December Hamid Farsi had been travelling all over the country again. He was collecting money and convincing influential patrons that they should support his School of Calligraphy. Lavish donations flowed in, and he was beginning to consider opening a second school in Aleppo, the northern metropolis, directly after the opening of the first in Damascus. After that five more branches were to be founded in the main cities of Syria. But central control was to be from Damascus.

Far more important to him than the donations was the confirmation of his vision that the time was ripe for a radical reform of Arabic script. When he had explained his ideas a year earlier to the Council of the Wise, the highest organ of the Society of the Wise, they had laughed at him. Some cowards saw his plan as endangering the Society, and would rather have snored in peace for another hundred years. But when he stood by his plans, and announced that he himself would take the responsibility – even if it cost him his life – those hands that had pointed suspiciously to him at first now applauded.

The country was experiencing an upturn, and all ways were open, even those that you could only dream of a few years ago.

In the middle of February Hamid boarded a bus going from Damascus to Aleppo. At nine o'clock the bus, which was really scheduled to leave at eight, finally set off. It made its way through the city until it joined the national highway going to Aleppo at the northern exit from the city.

In Port Said Street he saw Nasri Abbani deep in conversation with the well-known pharmacist Elias Ashkar outside the latter's shop. They seemed to be on very good terms. Hamid wondered why he himself could not build up such a close relationship with the remarkable and generous Nasri Abbani, who whether intentionally or unintentionally had given great support to the Society of the Wise.

Several members of the Society distrusted the rich and worldly Abbani, others wanted to take his money but not put his name on the tablet of honour.

At the meeting where this was discussed Hamid was beside himself. Were the Council of the Wise, he asked, going to act like women gossiping about some piece of news over coffee until they had made it a scurrilous rumour, or were they concerned with realizing their ideas? "We don't want to marry Nasri Abbani, we want to get his support for our side, so whether or not he visits whores is nothing to do with us. Or do any of you know how often this minister or that general, scholar or businessman cheats on his wife, his customers, or God?"

His audience clapped. For a moment he found them so repellent that a shudder ran down his back. A wall as cold as ice separated him from all the members there, just as it separated him from Abbani, whom he had defended.

Hamid intended to stay in Aleppo for three days and go on from there to Istanbul, where he was to take part in a congress of Islamic calligraphers, and negotiate over an important commission. A new mosque was to be built in Ankara, with money from Saudi Arabia, and famous calligraphers were to be involved in the design. Three Arab masters had been invited, and Hamid thought he stood a good chance.

The day after he left, the employees in Hamid Farsi's studio began working shorter hours and taking ever longer breaks.

Samad was a good technician who knew all the tricks of calligraphy, but never went outside the prescribed regulations. "Without crossing boundaries you'll never be a master," Hamid told him. But Samad lacked both ambition and imagination. Nor did he want, like Hamid Farsi, to live only for calligraphy. He loved his wife and his three sons dearly, cooked and sang for them, and these four people gave him all that he felt it was worth living for. Calligraphy was a wonderful way of earning money, no more. Of course he did not say so out loud, for that would have lost him his job on the spot. And he would never earn as much anywhere else as he did with Hamid, whose right-hand man he had become over decades of work.

Samad let his colleagues know that he valued their work, and so they liked him. On the other hand, they feared Hamid. They were always glad when their master had business outside the studio. This time Samad sent them home early in the afternoon. Only one man had to remain on duty by the telephone until six, to take any orders that came in.

Hamid returned in a bad temper. The meeting in Aleppo had not gone as he had expected, and in Istanbul an Egyptian had been given the commission to work on the mosque. "The Turks wanted me, but the Saudi representative didn't because he thought I was a Shiite. He just couldn't get his head around the fact that a man's name could be Farsi, meaning Persian, and he could still be a Sunni," he said indignantly. He did not say a word about the meeting in Aleppo. The calligraphers there had protested in no uncertain terms against the idea of a School of Calligraphy in Damascus. Why not base it in the north, away from the centre of power? And who held power in the Society? The country, they said angrily, was democratic, but the Society was still stuck in the caliphate system, where a Grand Master could leave his legacy to a successor of his own choice. It wouldn't do. Hamid stood his ground, however. And finally the masters of calligraphy had calmed down and unanimously agreed to support his project for the School of Calligraphy in Damascus.

"In Aleppo they quarrel heatedly, but they don't leave their friends high and dry, which is more than can be said of Damascus," the head of the section there had said arrogantly. That barbed remark hurt.

Only later was Hamid to understand that the meeting in Aleppo had not gone as badly as he thought directly after it. He had met the calligrapher Ali Barakeh, a small young man who supported the Grand Master without reservations, and listened unmoved to the attacks from other quarters. Ali Barakeh idolized Hamid Farsi and hung on his every word. So Hamid made up his mind to name him his successor, also hoping to win sympathy in Aleppo that way. But then it was already too late.

When he entered his studio after returning to Damascus, and found everything neat and tidy and well organized, he was reassured. He felt a desire to write down his thoughts and impressions of Aleppo and Istanbul. He told Salman to make him a coffee, opened the locked cupboard, and took out the thick book in which he recorded his ideas and his secrets. Even as he opened the cupboard he sensed that something about the lock was wrong.

Nothing inside was missing, but when he opened the black, linen-bound book, he saw that a stranger's rough hand had damaged it. There was a tear in the binding. Someone had forcibly opened the book. A tear of that kind couldn't be repaired. If a book was badly bound, pages dropped out; if it was well bound, like his thick blank book here, it always opened at just this place. His book had been given to him by his master Serani, and had been made by the legendary bookbinder Salim Baklan.

Hamid exploded. He shouted furiously in such a loud voice that the whole studio shook. He summoned Samad, blaming him and calling him to account. His assistant stood before him, head bent, wondering which of the men in the workshop had been unnaturally edgy over the last few days. It didn't take him long to work that out: Salman.

When Hamid finally stopped shouting because he was breathless, and the locals were beginning to gather outside the shop window, Samad looked at him with scorn. "You're making me look ridiculous in front of our neighbours, God forgive you. But it wasn't me. Anyone can break into anywhere these days, but now that I look at the cupboard, it was a pro. And I can't help it if a professional criminal breaks in by night and steals your book, or the gold leaf, your knife, or anything else. You could always buy a steel safe, but I've heard that the king of the Damascene burglars can open any safe in the city with his eyes blindfolded." Samad paused. "But if you listen to me, I'd say fire the errand boy. I get a feeling that there's something not quite right about him."

Hamid looked up. His eyes were burning.

"Fire him, then," he said in a cracked voice.

33

Over the next few days, Hamid Farsi was happy to find what swift progress preparations for the School of Calligraphy were making. Decorators, electricians, locksmiths, and joiners were working round the clock to have the building finished and gleaming with fresh paint a week before the opening.

The opening ceremony itself was to be on the first of March. Of the hundred and twenty prominent guests invited, only four had declined. And the editorial teams of all the newspapers and magazines published in Damascus were going to report the occasion. Even the most important Lebanese newspaper, *Al Nahar*, planned to write about it.

Two days before the opening of the School of Calligraphy, Nasri, in a state of desperation, received his third letter from the hand of Hamid Farsi the master calligrapher. Had he failed, wondered the calligrapher, to make any headway with his beloved yet? The text written by Hamid was full of sad reproaches to her for playing a game of hide and seek, and asked her reason for declining to meet him. In addition Hamid had copied out two seventh-century poems from an old collection of lyrics. They spoke of the lover's longing for a single meeting. Perhaps Nasri would touch her heart with this third letter. Hamid genuinely hoped so.

Nasri had to go to his office first and discuss something with Tawfiq, and then he went to see his wife Almaz, who had a heavy cold. She wouldn't be trailing around after him today.

That night he was going to see whether the beautiful woman was even at home. He climbed to the attic and looked down into her inner courtyard. There were lights on in it, he could see everything clearly – and what he saw took his breath away.

The beautiful woman had a companion – none other than Hamid Farsi.

Blind with fury, Nasri climbed down the spiral staircase again. What a despicable trick! He had told Hamid that the woman had not agreed to see him, he had paid good money and given her gold, and now that hypocrite was making use of his chance and might be blackmailing the young woman.

Nasri thought of nothing but revenge all night. And when he finally thought of a way to injure Hamid the grin on his face in the darkness was so broad that it almost illuminated the room. "Hamid, Hamid, you've made the biggest mistake of your life."

But the mistake was Nasri's.

34

Tears ran down Salman's cheeks as he and his father followed his mother's coffin. Only when four men lowered the modest wooden casket into the grave did his tears dry up. He felt a strange fear. The thought that his mother would never stand up again weighed heavily on his heart.

Only their neighbours from Grace and Favour Yard accompanied his mother on her last journey, and old Father Basilius added to the general misery. He was in an extremely bad temper, reproving two mass servers who kept fooling about, he mumbled his way through the funeral service as if it were a tiresome duty, and then hurried straight home. It was too cold and the whole occasion seemed too shabby for him.

Karam parted from Salman at the graveyard, and hugged him. "God be with her. I feel for your grief, but believe me, it's a release from all her torments," he said, looking into the distance. Salman did not reply. "Oh, and I've found you a good job with Elias Barakat the jeweller. You know him, and he likes you a lot." He kissed Salman's forehead and was gone.

All the others present expressed their sympathy, but to the end of his days only what his neighbour Maroun said remained in Salman's memory like a solitary peak rising from a flat plain. "I won't try to console you. I mourn my own mother to this day. Mothers are divine creatures, and when they die so does the divine spark in us. All consolation is hypocrisy." When Salman looked up at him, tears were running down the man's cheeks. He had never before seen Maroun's face as wise and beautiful as at that moment.

When Salman went home alone that cold afternoon, the apartment felt terribly empty. His father was spending the rest of the day with Maroun, Kamil, and Barakat in the wine bar on the corner of Abbara Alley.

Wandering around the place, Salman found his mother's old slippers still under the table where she had left them last time she stepped out of them before finally taking to her bed. He picked them up and began weeping again.

It was not until nearly midnight that his father staggered home to bed.

Two days later Salman phoned Noura from the post office. When he heard her voice he felt relieved. And Noura herself felt, yet again, that Salman was as fragile as a vase made of thin glass with a crack in it, so that it threatened to break apart any moment. When she hung up, she wondered if she would be as sad if her own mother were to die. No, certainly not, she told herself, and felt ashamed.

Salman had invited Noura to his home. She had always wanted to know where it was and what it was like, but she had been too shy to ask him. Now she was going to see him there one afternoon. In the Christian quarter no one was particularly interested in who visited whom. Christians' houses were open to all, and men and women visited each other. She had often noticed that when she was a little girl, since many Christians lived in the Midan quarter where she had grown up. When visitors came, the women sat with the men there.

Salman didn't mind what the neighbours said. The only one among them whose opinion had ever meant anything to him was Sarah, and she had left long ago. His father was out all day and quite often all night as well. What he did interested no one, least of all Salman. His mother had been the bridge between them, and now they were the two banks of a river and never met.

On the day when Noura was going to visit him at two in the afternoon, he got on his bike just after eleven and rode off to see Karam.

Karam was charming and captivating; it was just like the old days. But when the conversation came round to the burglary in which Salman had helped him, he proved slippery as an eel.

Salman could have kicked himself for his naiveté. He had really thought that Karam wanted to know all those things out of sheer curiosity. Salman had made an imprint of the old-fashioned lock of the cupboard for him. After a few days, Karam handed him a duplicate key that Salman could use to unlock the cupboard – with some difficulty – when the master was away, and take out the beautiful big book containing the calligrapher's secrets.

It had been impossible to copy everything out in a short time. So the only way to get a copy made in 1950s Damascus was by a photographer. It was when he thought of that, at the latest, that Salman was really furious with himself, because he had still suspected nothing and just thought it was all rather amusing and exciting. Four hundred and twenty pages. The photographer had a very good camera and took two hundred and ten photographs, each showing a double spread from the book. Salman stood watching, and his heart fell when he heard the spine of the book crack audibly in the middle because the photographer needed a flat surface.

"Don't worry, it will be all right," Karam reassured him.

It was not all right.

For Karam to get two hundred and ten expensive photographs taken to satisfy his curiosity and to risk his, Salman's, job was something he couldn't get his head around, as he told Karam now in a steady voice. Karam was full of flattery again, and encouraged him to go and see the jeweller straight away. He said a lot of fine-sounding things about the sacrifices great and small to be made for friendship. For the first time Salman felt that there was often no real joy in Karam's laughter; it was only an act on the part of his facial muscles as they drew back his lips and bared his teeth.

A little boy came into the café and ordered something at the counter. "Hassan, the new errand boy. He's a distant relation of Samad's," said Karam. Salman glanced at the little fellow biting cheerfully into a falafel sandwich.

Salman decided to retrieve his implements and above all his important notebooks from the room in Karam's house. Their ways must part. Above all, he must not go along with any proposition made by that enigmatic man again. He would rather starve than visit the Café Karam. For nights on end Salman lay awake in bed. It was not just his disappointment that robbed him of sleep, one idea tormented him more than any other: could it be that Karam was malicious enough to have made use of him from the start, as a spy on Hamid Farsi and as the lover of Hamid's wife? Was that his gratitude for being saved from drowning? Karam had often shown that he thought nothing of gratitude. He would flatter you and then go behind your back. And what if he had deliberately used him to seduce Noura? Would that cloud his love for her? He could find no answer to that question, but he decided to tell Noura everything, all muddled up together the way it was as it seethed inside his head. Sarah had once told him that keeping silent in love was the first rift, and would grow unnoticed into other silences, until love broke to pieces.

But now he must pretend to Karam to suspect nothing until he had his notebooks safe. In the first two books, Salman had written down all that he had learnt in Hamid's studio: technique, the master's advice, the making of inks, the composition and secret of colours, and how to make corrections. But the third notebook was particularly dear to his heart. In that one Noura had written the answers to the questions that – intrigued by the information about Ibn Muqla – he had so often asked her. Noura was glad to be asked to perform these tasks, not only because her husband's library made the search easier for her, most of all because they made time pass quickly. And Salman was someone who listened avidly and gratefully to everything she had to say about the famous calligraphers of history, both men and women, and the secrets of the old masters. He would kiss every one of her fingertips afterwards, and caress her earlobes so tenderly that sometimes she couldn't stand it any longer, but threw herself on him and made love to him passionately.

It was just before one-thirty when Salman reached his apartment. He opened the windows and doors, swept the rooms, wiped the floor with a damp cloth, placed a plate of fresh biscuits on the table and prepared the water for particularly good tea, a variety he had bought from the best tea merchant in Straight Street, opposite the entrance to the spice market, the Souk al-Busuriyyeh.

Noura's heart was beating fast when she came through the gate of Grace and Favour Yard and saw Salman. He was standing at the door of his apartment on the left-hand side of the large rectangle that was the poor quarter of the yard.

He smiled and came to meet her, greeted her formally and with reserve, and accompanied her to the front door, where he stood aside to let her go in first.

She was amazed to see how fresh and clean the apartment was, and how meticulously tidy. He read her expression correctly.

"Two hours in the morning, quarter of an hour in the afternoon," he said with a grin. She took off her coat, and he was fascinated by her new cotton dress. "You're as beautiful as the women in the fashion magazines," he said, embracing her lovingly. She was going to thank him for the compliment, since she had made the new dress herself, but her lips found better occupation. They clung to him and did not let go until she came back to her senses naked and sweating in bed beside him. "Aren't you going to lock the door?" she asked, rather late in the day.

"No one in this street locks the door, and nothing has ever gone missing yet."

When they were both dressed again and sitting at the kitchen table, drinking tea, she gave him a long, thoughtful look. "I want to leave Damascus with you," she said at last. "Since I fell in love with you I've felt less and less able to put up with him. We have no chance here, he'll kill us. But we are sure to find a place where we can live and love each other, undisturbed, by day and night." She smiled at her own naiveté. "I mean after we've earned a living, of course. Me with dressmaking, you with calligraphy."

Salman said nothing, almost alarmed by the beauty of the dream that Noura had conjured up in so few words.

"And even if they were to catch me," she went on in the silence, "I wouldn't be sorry if I could only have spent a week in Paradise with you first."

"No, they won't catch us," said Salman. "We'll live as unobtrusively as possible. And the larger the city where we go, the more invisible we'll be."

"Aleppo," said Noura at once. "It's the second largest city in Syria." He tried suggesting Beirut, for he had heard that the capital of Lebanon looked kindly on all runaways and exiles, but she convinced him that their papers would not be checked as often in Syria as outside the country, and consoled him by describing the wonderful cuisine of Aleppo, which cast the cookery of both Damascus and Beirut into the shade.

"I need two passport photographs of you, with both your ears showing."

"Both my ears?" He sounded surprised. "A normal photo won't be big enough, I'd need a panoramic photograph to have room for both of them," he replied, and despite the fear still sitting at the table with them she laughed. She could hardly hold her tea glass, but put it down on the table and coughed because she had swallowed the wrong way. Salman's laughter cleansed her heart. His was not a gurgling, trilling or musical laugh, it was all his own. He laughed almost breathlessly, like an asthmatic, took a breath and laughed again like a wave breaking. He infected everyone with his laughter, even the chairs, she thought, as she knocked against one while she laughed and it made a bumping sound rather like a chuckle.

"And speaking of photos, I'd urgently recommend you to collect all the negatives of the photographs of the book from the photographer before Karam thinks of it. That occurred to me last night. My husband mentioned the burglary at the studio a couple of days ago, and he said in passing that there were treasures from ten centuries in his book, treasures of knowledge, philosophy, technique, and the history of calligraphy. You risked everything, so why not take them too? Who knows, they may come in useful some day."

"But how are we to convince the photographer? The negatives belong to Karam, and he left them at the photographer's only for the sake of security, in case anyone came searching his house or the café for them."

"Does the photographer know Karam well?"

"No, he doesn't know him at all. He's one of many photographers in the new part of town. Karam didn't want the pictures taken by anyone who might recognize him later."

"Wonderful, then you just call him saying you're Karam, tell him you need the negatives and you'll send your wife to collect them. Tell him her name – Aisha – and say she will give him the number of photographs, two hundred and ten, as a password. If he wants to know more you can describe my hair and say I wear glasses," Noura went on.

"Glasses? Why glasses?" asked Salman.

Noura laughed. "That," she said, "is the secret of the calligrapher's wife. And you will be waiting in a side street to take the package of photos," she concluded, giving him a long goodbye kiss. At the door, she turned back once more. "I like your neat, tidy place here. You're going to be a good husband for a very busy dressmaker."

As she stepped out of Abbara Alley into Straight Street, she was wondering whether she had done right not to tell Salman anything yet about the three letters from the tiresome old goat who was pestering her. She had been about to do so several times, but her tongue had stopped the words and sent them back down her throat. They were hard to swallow.

She consoled herself again by thinking that there would be plenty of time in the future to tell this tedious story. Just now more dangerous prospects stood ahead, and at the thought she clenched her right hand to a fist in her coat pocket. She was determined to go the way she had chosen to the end.

Two days later, Salman rode his bicycle home. A package in the basket danced about at every uneven place in the road. When he left the bicycle outside the apartment door Barakat, the baker, who was standing in the yard, greeted him.

"Anything edible in there?" asked Barakat cheerfully.

"No, something legible, that's all," replied Salman, laughing.

"I'll leave it to you, then! Have fun," said his neighbour.

Salman opened the large case he had bought for the journey. It was still empty. He weighed up the heavy packet in his hands for a moment, and then put it in his case unopened.

Not until about three months later was Salman to open the package, and marvel at the amount of secret and dangerous knowledge that lay before his eyes.

When he told Noura, at their next meeting, of his suspicion that Karam had put him in her way on purpose, she listened attentively. Salman looked as if the idea troubled him very much.

"And what if he did?" said Noura, smiling at him. "If I hadn't fallen in love with you Karam would have had no chance, however subtle the man he sent to visit me. Never mind Karam, Badri, Hamid, the Societies of the Wise and the Unwise, the Pure and the Filthy, let's leave them to get on with their conspiracies while we go away together," she said firmly. Salman breathed a sigh of relief.

35

The opening ceremony on the first of March was grander and finer than Hamid could ever have expected. Only one small thing clouded his delight; Nasri Abbani had not turned up. But Hamid soon forgot him.

His distinguished guests uttered fulsome praise. Even President al-Quwwatli, the head of state, was present, but preserving a discreet distance. In view of all the scholars there, he didn't want to make a speech.

It was rumoured that the Saudis, with whom his family had been closely connected for centuries, had asked him not to speak at the opening so as not to give a political dimension to a private School of Calligraphy. When Hamid heard that, his chest swelled with pride.

The minister of culture praised the industry, vision, and persistence of the first director of the school, Hamid Farsi, who, he said, had visited him almost every week until he finally had written permission to open it from the ministry of culture.

"I asked Mr Farsi," joked the minister, "how long there had been plans for this school, and he replied: since the year 940. I thought I had failed to hear him properly, and he must have said 1940. What, for a whole seven years? I asked appreciatively. Hamid Farsi smiled, and out of courtesy he did not correct me. But my well-read colleague, an admirer of Mr Farsi, told me later that he had meant the year of the death of the greatest calligrapher of all time, Ibn Muqla, who died in 940. It is therefore a particular honour to open this school, which will revive his name."

Long and loud applause thundered through the hall.

When Hamid went to the speaker's rostrum, the photographers' cameras flashed in competition. He thanked the minister, and promised to do everything possible in the cause of calligraphy. His speech was short but powerful. "Ladies and gentlemen," he concluded, "here in Damascus, I promise you, here in the heart of Arabia, calligraphy will flourish and make Damascus the capital of a strong nation once again."

The applause moved Hamid to tears.

When he slowly and with relish read out the list of patrons, it struck him again that Nasri Abbani was not present. Why had he failed to turn up?

The guests ate and drank, talked and laughed loudly until midnight. Again and again a camera flashed, because many of the guests wanted to take souvenir photographs of such legendary personalities as the brilliant Fares al-Khuri, the only Christian prime minister in the history of Syria.

After the ceremony, when all the guests had left the School, Hamid was surrounded by deep silence. He walked through the empty building, letting the images of the last few hours run past his mind's eye. His great dream had come true, but was he a happy man now?

Why had Nasri Abbani stayed away from the ceremony? Everyone was wondering. Nasri Abbani's former teacher, Sheikh Dumani, a senile old man whom Hamid had invited, was surprised to see that his worst pupil in fifty years of teaching headed the list of patrons of culture and calligraphy. "His handwriting was as illegible as if he'd bribed the chickens to do his homework for him," slobbered the old man toothlessly. "As usual, he'll have been held up somewhere by his prick," he announced to the assembled company, suggestively cradling his balls in his left hand.

"Well, that danger doesn't threaten you and me," remarked old Fares al-Khuri cynically, and the men around them laughed.

But why hadn't Nasri come? Were those idiotic Pure Ones behind the fact that Tawfiq, Nasri Abbani's right-hand man, had suddenly called a day before the ceremony, saying that he was getting many threats, so his boss would like to cancel the contract to rent, "for reasons of the security of his property, you understand." Hamid did not understand, and his lawyer reassured him: the contract was valid, and no power on earth could cancel it now.

Nasri Abbani not only failed to come to the ceremony, he would not see Hamid in the next few days and did not return his phone calls.

What had happened?

Hamid had no idea.

36

On the tenth of April 1957, Noura and Salman boarded the bus from Damascus to Aleppo.

They took three large cases and a bag containing food and drink for the journey.

"Hold out your hands," said Noura when they were finally seated, and she put a heavy velvet bag into them.

"What is it?" he asked.

"Seventy gold coins that Hamid gave me on our wedding day. My wages in advance for four years of cleaning, cooking, and ironing. And putting up with his moods. The other thing," she said in a soft, sad voice, "is something that no money can pay for."

She looked out of the window at the labourers tearing tramlines up from the ground. The third tram route was being built. "You don't see donkeys for hire about anymore these days," she said, shaking her head. What problems she's had, thought Salman. Here she was running away from her native city and her marriage, and she thought about donkeys. He put his arm round her. "I'll always be your donkey," he said, but his joke could not cheer Noura up.

Only two hours before leaving she had gone to see Dalia. The dressmaker had looked up from her sewing machine and understood at once. "I'm going away," whispered Noura.

"I suspected as much when I saw you. Have you thought it all over?" asked Dalia. Noura nodded.

They both cried when they said goodbye. Dalia knew she would never see her young friend again. Later, she was to say that she understood for the first time that day how you can go into deadly danger not because you hate life, but because you love it.

Finally Noura went to her parents' house. She knew that her father had been in bed with a cold for some days. She gave him an envelope with letters in it, told him briefly what kind of letters they were, and asked him to look after them well. Then she was on her way again. He ran after her in his bedroom slippers. "Child," he asked in alarm, "has something happened?"

She shed tears.

"Can I help you, my dearest child?" he asked, feeling so weak at the knees that he had to lean on something for support.

"Read my letter and see what you must do. I can help myself," she said, and saw that he too was weeping. His tears drew her down into the depths like leaden weights. In her mind she freed herself from him, and hurried out.

"God be with you on your way," he whispered, hoping she would turn at the end of the street and wave, as she always used to do, but Noura had already disappeared round the corner and into the main road.

Slowly, Rami Arabi went back to his bedroom. He opened the large envelope with trembling fingers. It contained Noura's farewell letter, and over thirty notes he had written her with his witty sayings and turns of phrase. His heart guessed that the return of his own words meant a deep separation. But Nasri's letters were the real shock.

He was horrified, he reached out for support, picked Noura's letter up again and read it carefully. She wrote about her disappointment, the torment of an unhappy married life to which he had delivered her up. She assured him that she would not hate either him or her mother for that, but she was taking her life into her own hands, since as parents they had failed in their prime duty to protect her.

Rami Arabi knew his daughter too well to misunderstand. She had written all this down for him before she went away because she felt like a sponge soaked with bitter words. She had to squeeze the sponge out before she could take up whatever her new life had to offer.

When he had read it all for the third time, he looked at those seductive letters in her husband's calligraphic handwriting. His hands were shaking. He felt paralysed.

"The bloody pimp!" he heard himself cry out loud.

Her mother did not hear about Noura's visit and the letters until that evening, when she came back from the weekly meeting of a women's religious society. She asked her husband to read the farewell letter aloud to her, and the frankness of its wording told her that Noura had gone already. She let out a scream, and wailed so loudly that three women from the house next door came round, thinking that their neighbour Sahar's husband had breathed his last.

Salman had been back to the café owner Karam's house that day, had picked up his notebooks and writing implements, and left a circular calligraphic work behind for Karam. After work that evening, Karam was surprised to find the key in the front door of the house. He thought Salman had come back, and looked forward to seeing him.

When Karam had been to Grace and Favour Yard to see him in the middle of March, but did not find him there, a woman neighbour said Salman was learning the art of fine Damascene cuisine from a master chef. The Al Andalus restaurant, she added, was very elegant and very expensive, and was near Bab Tuma.

Salman seemed glad to see Karam there. Now that he had discovered cookery, he said, he got along with a spoon better than a reed pen. He had a lot to do just now, he added, because there were two weddings ahead to be catered for, but as soon as he had a moment he would be back to see Karam and perhaps practise a little calligraphy. His boss Carlos, who was quarter Spanish, quarter Jewish, quarter Arab and at least a quarter Christian, loved calligraphy and thought that, with cookery, riding, and fencing, it was an art that you must master before you could call yourself a man.

This was an emotional meeting for Karam. For the first time he discovered that Salman could also speak very eloquently. When he said so, joking, Salman laughed and said yes, he might be right. All these years he had had a kind of knot tied in his tongue, and now love and spices had freed him of it.

He's not a boy anymore, he is a man now, said Karam to himself on the way back to his café. He felt deep affection, far from any pity or pangs of conscience, for this brave young man, an affection that blossomed in his heart like a lily, and was far more than his love for Badri's divine body. For the first time Salman seemed to him irresistibly attractive. Next time they met, he was going to say so. Again and again he hoped for a telephone call or a spontaneous visit to the café, but March came to an end without granting the enamoured Karam's wish. Badri's feelings were hurt because Karam talked of nothing but Salman, and he was not mistaken in his assumptions, for the heart of a lover betrayed has an invisible compass.

So that April day Karam opened his front door and called out to Salman, but silence swallowed up his voice. Walking slowly, he went to the room where Salman always worked. The door was not closed. The drawer in the desk yawned open, cleared out, in the empty room. Only a piece of calligraphy the size of a hand lay on the desk. Karam could not decipher it.

Two days later he showed it to Hamid's journeyman Samad, who was having a bite to eat in the café at midday. "Can you read what this tangled stuff says?" he asked, putting the stiff sheet of paper in front of the expert.

"It's not tangled stuff, it's Kufic script with reflection. It's neatly written, the proportions, angles, and curves all correct, but the script lacks elegance. Who wrote it?"

"A friend," replied Karam proudly.

"No, that can't be so," said Samad.

"Why not, may I ask?"

"Because no friend can have written that. It says: The heart of Karam is a graveyard."

All the colour drained from Karam's face. Even his dark eyes seemed to have turned pale grey. He dragged himself into his office behind the bar. His staff swore that when he came out again his hair was no longer blue-black but ashen grey.

Salman disappeared quietly, as was always his way. He did not say goodbye to anyone. He merely wrote a long letter to Sarah, and asked her to tell a white lie to cover up his and Noura's tracks.

He sold his bicycle for good money to a vegetable seller in the distant Amara quarter of the city.

Apart from Sarah's mother hardly anyone in Grace and Favour Yard noticed that Salman had gone away. Only when his father fell seriously ill with liver disease two months later did several neighbours realize that it was a long time since they had last seen Salman. Many of those who lived in the Yard were already looking forward to the chance of getting a good two-roomed apartment soon. But Salman's father recovered and lived for many more years, although he never drank a drop of alcohol again.

At about this time Sarah's mother Faizeh came back from Homs, where her daughter had had her first child, a little girl. Faizeh told Mahmoud the butcher and her neighbour Samira in confidence that Salman was working as a chef in Kuwait for a good salary. "But that's strictly between ourselves," said Faizeh in conspiratorial tones. In Damascus, that was as good as a request to spread the news with great speed, and Mahmoud the butcher and Samira did valiantly.

Within twenty-seven hours and thirty-three minutes, the news reached Karam in his café. He did not believe what he heard, but rang Al Andalus, the grand restaurant in the Christian quarter, and asked the owner about his friend Salman.

"I'm afraid he's not here now. I'd happily have made that witty young man my deputy. None of my staff ever learned as quickly as he did – he sang as he worked, and he was so enthusiastic about everything. He had a very good nose too, and a good nose is worth gold in our profession. A pity, but I can't grudge it to him. I've heard he's earning more in Kuwait than I do in my restaurant."

Karam hung up, weeping with rage at the oil sheikhs, the Pure Ones, his own stupidity, Badri, and Salman's hard heart that had given him no chance to put his mistake right again.

The story of Salman's new career as a chef in Kuwait had undergone several metamorphoses after the twentieth or thirtieth time of telling. Sometimes Salman was cooking for the Emir of Kuwait, sometimes he was owner of a chain of restaurants in the Gulf region. Some people said he had converted to Islam and married a cousin of the ruler, others were sure that he had been made into fish-food.

In the autumn, anyway, when the story found its way back to Sarah's mother, it had been through so many changes that not even Faizeh herself would have known it again.

37

Years later, Hamid was to tell anyone who had ears and the patience to listen, that his wife's flight had opened his eyes. On the day of her disappearance, he admitted, the decline of the Arabs had become clear to him. He no longer wanted to be part of it. He had wanted to shake people awake, but now he would leave them deep in their slumbers and regret nothing. A race that punishes its reformers and persecutes, banishes, and kills its prophets, he now saw, was fated to fall.

Hamid found his wife gone when he came home in the evening. There had been a great deal to do at the School of Calligraphy, and he had spent a long time that afternoon bringing tough negotiations to a successful conclusion. He was commissioned to carry out all the calligraphy and ornamentation for the Saladin Mosque financed by Saudi Arabia. The negotiations had not been easy, particularly as calligraphers from the other Arab countries were prepared to do the work for a fifth of what he was asking. Three of the most famous Syrian calligraphers also went away empty-handed. Hamid offered to employ them himself in return for a good fee, and they gratefully accepted. It had been an excellent day.

So he went home happy and content that warm April night. The School of Calligraphy had begun teaching at the beginning of April, a month earlier than planned, and he had carried his point in the Society of the Wise in the face of all who envied him and would have disputed the position of Grand Master with him. An overwhelming majority of members showed their absolute confidence in him. His adversaries had not chosen their moment well. Hamid was not just the best calligrapher but the hero who had brought the Society further than anyone else before him.

On the way home he whispered to himself, several times, "Hamid, you did it!" And then he took a deep breath and cried, in slightly too loud a voice, "Yes, I did!"

Now he was going to enjoy his wife and the night. He had bought her a thin nightdress of translucent red silk, and he wanted her to put it on and indulge all his whims.

In an expensive delicatessen he had two hundred grams of pasturma, air-dried beef ham with a piquant coating of sharp spices, sliced paper-thin for him. He also bought expensive cheese and olives, and for his wife an Italian jar of mini-artichokes preserved in olive oil. At the fruit-seller's on Straight Street at the corner of his own street he bought an expensive pineapple for the first time in his life.

"Never mind the price," he told the fruit and vegetable vendor, "today is a special day."

Whistling his favourite tune, he opened the door.

He could never forget that moment of menacing silence. Curiously enough, he guessed at once that Noura was neither visiting neighbours nor at her parents' house. Something terrible must have happened. He went into the kitchen, put the paper bags down on the table, and called, "Noura!" His heart was thudding.

No answer, no note, nothing. He went into the courtyard and dropped into a chair by the fountain, feeling weak. At that moment he grasped the catastrophe.

"There are moments when you know what you have done wrong. I was close to death when, in a single second, I understood all that was wrong in my life. I was born into the wrong society at the wrong time," he repeated later. His audience felt sorry for him, but no one could understand.

Many of his own decisions now seemed to him mistaken. Yet he wanted only one thing, to honour Arabic script, that divine invention that made a few written characters into oceans, deserts, and mountains, that moved the heart and inspired the mind. And did it not endow everything recorded in ink on paper with a long life? Only gods can do that. He should have realized. Script was a goddess, and only a man who gave up everything for it would be let into Paradise. What place was there for a wife and children? And hadn't he been born into the wrong family, for a start? Who but a madman would cuff his son around the head for having a divine gift? Was his father sick? And his mother, who had never loved or defended him, was she not sick as well?

What idiocy it was to want to lead a married life. Of course he needed a woman. Not that he was an addict like Nasri Abbani. No, somehow love play did not satisfy him half as much as working on calligraphy.

He sat for half an hour in his deserted house, wishing some neighbour would tell him that Noura had had an accident, or had fallen down in a faint and had been taken to hospital.

But no one knocked at the door for hours on end, although he put on all the lights and turned up the radio, letting the neighbours know that he was there.

Hours later, the idea of an accident struck him as absurd, and that hurt, because he realized how helpless he was. He was also sure that his parents-in-law knew nothing about any accident, or they would have phoned him.

How long had he slept? He didn't know. From that day on he abandoned the discipline that had woken him at six every morning and sent him to bed at ten in the evening at the latest. Day and night became indistinguishable.

A vigorous knocking woke him. He looked around him, startled, and shook his hand, because he had had a nightmare in which a large wasp stung him right between his forefinger and middle finger. He was lying on the bed, fully dressed. For the first time in his life he had gone to sleep unwashed, still in his street clothes.

It was still early, but day was already dawning outside.

Noura's father stood at the door, pale-faced, his eyes red with weeping. He was uglier than ever.

"*Assalam alaikoum*," he greeted Hamid dryly. Sheikh Rami Arabi had never been a dissembler, as Hamid knew. He came straight to the point. Without a word, he flung the letters down on the little table in the inner courtyard and stood there. Of course Hamid recognized his own hand. How in the world had Noura's father come by those letters? And suddenly it was all clear to him. Hamid understood what the scholar, without any words, was telling him. His knees gave way under him, he dropped on the nearest chair. How was he going to explain himself to his wife's father? He hoped the whole thing was only a nightmare.

"Please sit down. It's a terrible misunderstanding, and I can explain to Noura," he said in a broken voice. For a moment he was secretly relieved that Noura had gone for refuge to her parents, and sent her father here ahead of her. However, he maintained the façade of the shocked husband. "She ought to have discussed it with me before alarming you unnecessarily. Those are letters for a customer that I…" he began trying to explain.

But Sheikh Arabi shook his head, dismissing the idea. "Noura is not with us. She's run away… I gave you a flower to be your wife, and what did you do to her, you man without honour?" said the sheikh, his voice choked with his unspoken grief. He cast his son-in-law a contemptuous glance and left.

Hamid Farsi was stunned.

That fornicating goat Nasri Abbani had tricked him. He had seduced his wife Noura with those letters, and who knew how many people he had told about it, all to destroy his, Hamid's, reputation and humiliate him. Had Nasri Abbani planned it all from the first?

But the calligrapher and his neighbours, whose ears were pricked, still did not believe that Noura had run away for good. He phoned the studio and said he wouldn't be in that day. Such a thing had never happened before. From now on until the closing of the studio, however, it became almost the general rule.

Hamid washed and shaved, put on his summer suit, and went purposefully off to see his parents-in-law in the Midan quarter. Sheikh Arabi was not at home. Only his wife Sahar, her face tearstained, looked round the door.

"What have you done? I loved you like a son," she said, concealing her other feelings, for once she had thought herself eternally in love with this wiry and strong-willed man. If he said a word to her, or just lightly touched her, she felt moved to the depths of her heart. But she had sacrificed that heart to save the honour and reputation of the family. And now everything in her died, and she felt that she had acted correctly, for all this man's aura had done was dazzle her. She would have been lost with him anyway.

She did not seem about to let him in. It was not usual in this traditional quarter for a woman to receive another man in her husband's absence. Even male cousins and sons-in-law had to wait until the master of the house came home.

"Let me explain," he said, taking her hand. But she withdrew it quickly and closed the door. Hamid called again, through the door, "But when did she leave?"

"We don't know," said Noura's mother, weeping. He knocked quietly, but in vain. The Arabis' neighbour Badia appeared in the doorway of her house.

"What's happened? Can I help you?" she asked the calligrapher, whom she knew well. She guessed it was something bad, for Noura's mother wouldn't say a word to her, for the first time; she had just kept muttering, "A disaster, a disaster," and disappeared from view.

"No, thank you," said the calligrapher briefly, and he dragged himself away to the main road, where he hired a cab to take him home.

It was worse than he had thought.

"I'm an ass," he cried when he was sitting alone by the fountain that evening, thinking of Nasri. He wailed so loud that the neighbours heard him. Up to now none of them had known about Noura's flight. Only in the course of that evening did certain news reach the house next door, but then by dawn it was setting out its rounds, a fully matured rumour, through the bakeries and snack bars of the quarter.

Nasri Abbani might have been swallowed up by the earth. Weeks after Noura's flight, Hamid still couldn't find him. And in his wounded imagination he staged whole films in which the rich Abbani seduced women and then sold them to oil sheikhs.

Hamid went to the studio only once or twice a month. Even then, when large commissions came in and he was urgently needed, he dismissed them from his mind.

At the end of May, Salim, a barber whose shop was not far from Hamid's studio, told him he had heard that Nasri Abbani had not fixed on Hamid by chance; he had been planning to drive him to ruin from the first. Nasri Abbani, he said, had received instructions from high places not only to approach Hamid with commissions for extravagant works of calligraphy, seducing him gradually with his generosity, until the point came when he could produce written evidence of his lack of character. Salim added, in conspiratorial tones, that the roles were well allotted. While Nasri Abbani was ruining Hamid's reputation with those letters, a gang of experienced criminals had abducted Noura. It was a ruse that had been employed three or four times in Beirut, Cairo, and Baghdad to get rid of unpopular colleagues or political opponents.

"And what can be more humiliating for any Arab man than to have the story spread that he was pimping for his own wife?" asked Salim, but he did not wait for an answer. He rose and said goodbye to Hamid with a soft pressure of his hand. "The Abbani clan ruined my own father too because he trusted its members unsuspectingly. They're in league with the Devil! Or do you think it's just chance that Nasri, that fornicating goat, owns half the building sites in Abu Roummaneh without ever having lifted a finger?"

Hamid could have wept with fury. The man was saying exactly what he had worked out for himself. Nasri Abbani was a snake. And now he understood why he had stayed away from the public opening ceremony of the School of Calligraphy.

To get the better of Nasri, that wily criminal, and call a halt to his own running costs, Hamid decided in July to close the studio for the time being. Samad reminded him in vain of several major commissions that must be delivered in the autumn. But Hamid was not changing his mind.

That was on the day when the rumours in Damascus struck up another song about Noura, like a chorale directed by an invisible hand. This one said she had been seen on a British passenger ship leaving Beirut for the Gulf.

In a fit of rage, Hamid fired all the employees in his studio, from Samad to the young errand boy Hassan, every one of them. And as they left he told them what he had thought of them all these years: they were incompetent craftsmen, and therefore hopeless as candidates to learn the art of calligraphy. He told Samad contemptuously that he and the errand boy Hassan had better go looking for the nearest car repair workshop, where they could finally make themselves useful to their fellow men.

Not only Samad but all his assistants were deeply insulted. They thought their master had gone completely crazy, not even preserving a minimum of courtesy and gratitude. Only the thin little boy Hassan followed his master's advice and looked for a car repair workshop where, small and half-starved as he was, he faced up to the heavily built owner and said boldly that a master of calligraphy had prophesied that he would be a good motor mechanic. The oil-smeared man laughed, showing his yellow teeth. "Oh, calligraphers talk a lot of nonsense, but who cares? We could do with an errand boy. Can you make tea?"

"The best tea you ever drank, sir," said the boy proudly.

"Then come on in. One lira a week, and after that we'll see," said the owner of the car repair shop.

38

On 13 April 1957, nine days after Noura's flight, ten bearded men stormed the School of Calligraphy late in the morning. They locked the door from the inside, tore the telephone wire out of the wall, and broke all the furniture. It was a Friday, and only the secretary had come to the School to deal with all the paperwork that had accumulated during the week. She had the shock of her life. The men looked as if they had come straight out of a bad film about Arabs. One of them shouted at her, "How dare you work on a Friday, you unbeliever!" He struck her a blow that knocked her to the ground. Another snatched her jacket off the coat stand and flung it over her head. "Cover your head, whore!" he cried. She couldn't even scream. They gagged her and tied her to her office chair. After that the men rampaged through the building, and she heard furniture, mirrors, glass tables, and bookcases being smashed to smithereens. When they came back to her office, they took a broad brush and painted their hideous sayings and threats on the walls in dripping red. Then the horror was over.

At the beginning of May the School closed down for the protection of its students. Hamid was sure now that Nasri Abbani had been one of those pulling the strings that led to the closing of his School of Calligraphy.

39

Some people said he was in Beirut, others claimed to have seen him in Istanbul, still others said that he had gone to Brazil to join his friend, Colonel Shishakli, the former president.

No one would have bet a single lira on the chances that Nasri Abbani was still in Damascus.

He loved his native city in the same way as he loved women: addictively and beyond all measure. He was a true Damascene who thought the city was Paradise. Every time he had to leave Damascus it felt like a kind of torture, and he was sure his journey would end in darkness and cold – and a life of toil and tribulation. Nasri was not capable of that sort of thing.

It was his manager Tawfiq who advised him to take the calligrapher's humiliation seriously. He believed him, said Tawfiq, when he said he hadn't touched the woman, but his belief didn't count. In the city everyone claimed, as if they had seen it for themselves, that the calligrapher had written love letters for that famous philanderer Nasri in return for money. And as if it wasn't enough that Hamid Farsi's wife had run away, his great dream of the School of Calligraphy had finally come to nothing as well. As a result the cuckolded husband was blind and unpredictable in his fury. "I'm not interested to know whether you stuck your prick into the woman or a wasps' next, but I do feel a burning desire to make sure that lunatic doesn't stick something sharp into you," added Tawfiq.

What a tone his accountant was taking! For the first time, Nasri felt that he had underestimated Tawfiq all along. He was more than a mere financial brain blindly making his way through life calculating profits, he was an experienced man with strong nerves. Ever since Nasri had felt it wise to hide from Hamid, he had noticed a change in his manager's attitude. He was as civil as before, but less patient, and his voice was not louder but more commanding. It bore a distant resemblance to the voice of Nasri's father.

"This is a matter of life or death," Tawfiq had said, emphasizing the fact that he expected his orders to be followed, although with the courtesy of all Damascenes he called them suggestions. And against his inclination, Nasri had to obey.

The first six weeks of his life in hiding were extremely difficult. He had to relearn everything. How to be awake while others were asleep, how to spend long hours and days in closed rooms because no one was to know he was sitting just next door, how to say nothing for hours or even days on end. It was Nasri's first experience of such things. His isolation filled his time with little barbs, making it an instrument of torture. All his life he had merely skimmed the newspapers; now he even read the advertisements and death announcements, and there was still time left over.

He thought about things that had never crossed his mind before, and achieved insights he could never previously have guessed at.

From hour to hour his torments increased. His eyes hurt whenever he looked at anything, his ears hurt whenever he heard anything, his heart threatened to stand still and then, next moment, to explode, and he had droning headaches as if his brain were too small for all his thoughts. Suddenly words grew inside him just as an embryo grows hands and feet. And his tongue flung the words at the wall, at the window, or if he was lying down at the ceiling. His heart calmed down and the headaches went away. It must have been like this at the dawn of humanity, he thought, the isolation of men and women made language grow in them so that their hearts would not explode or their brains die of sorrow.

Every chance meeting in the street could cost him his life. He could not allow himself any careless act, however small. He always had to be faster than anyone who might give him away, and cleverer than that damned intelligent calligrapher.

The few people he still saw acted differently to him now. A childhood friend declined to meet him, and a high-ranking officer who had crawled to him when President Shishakli was still in power wouldn't even come to the phone. A young officer in the room outside his sent Nasri away, saying that his commandant didn't know anyone called Nasri Abbani.

He lay awake for hours, thinking. He wasn't even embittered by the attitude of these friends who had cultivated not him but his aura; basking in it, they had hoped to brighten the darkness of their own lives a little.

In hiding, and pursued, he kept remembering his great-uncle Ahmad Abu Khalil Abbani, his grandfather's brother, who had also gone on the run from his pursuers. Even as a child he had been fascinated by the theatre, and he had made that low form of art, performed at the time in coffee houses and dance halls to entertain the customers, into a great dramatic art. He had founded his own theatrical ensemble, staging his own plays and many others translated from the French. As the first modern man of the theatre in Syria, he had suffered arson attacks, humiliations, murder threats, and persecution. He had invested all his money in his beloved theatre, and the mob, egged on by fanatics, had burnt it down. The drama was still taboo thirty years later, and until 1930 the Mufti of Damascus banned men and above all women from performing on stage, which explained why the few singers and actors who ever appeared at all were Christians and Jews.

Ahmad Abu Khalil Abbani had to hide until at last he and his ensemble took refuge in Cairo, where he founded another theatre and trained a generation of Egyptian, Syrian, and Lebanese actors. But here too arsonists set fire to his theatre in the year 1900. He returned to Damascus, an embittered man, and died of a broken heart in 1903.

Nasri, now in hiding himself, wept when he remembered his great-uncle's portrait. It used to hang in his father's salon along with many other pictures. The endless sadness in his eyes went to Nasri's heart.

For the first two weeks in hiding Nasri lived with his first wife Lamia. But when the first rumours of his whereabouts circulated in that part of town, Lamia's women neighbours advised her to send him away for fear that his dissolute conduct might put the children in danger too.

Lamia was pale, often cried in the night, and jumped at the slightest sound. It was hell. But he did not go until his children, in tearful chorus, recited the request they had learnt by heart, asking him to spare them and go away. He cursed Lamia and his father who had forced the marriage on him, and went by night to the house of his third wife Nasimeh, because he knew that his second wife Saideh's house was full of guests. Her whole family had come from the south to visit, and when they came they were so glad to see Saideh that for love of her they wouldn't let any member of the family go home.

Nasimeh, his third wife, whose tongue had once spoken so sweetly that he could forget how ugly she was for minutes at a time, now used this good opportunity to call him to account. She reproached him daily for spoiling her life, failing to complete his studies of architecture, and neglecting to build any of the houses she had wanted. After seven days he could stand it no longer and beat her. She screamed so loudly that the neighbours came, thinking Nasimeh had been attacked. She sent them packing again without giving Nasri away, but she told him to get out of her house at once. Nasri would have liked to apologize to his wife and thank her for her courage, because from his hiding place he had heard everything, but Nasimeh left him no choice. "Either you leave my house within three hours or I won't acknowledge you anymore," she cried, weeping. In her family, as she had always proudly told him in the old days, no man had ever raised his hand against a woman.

After her family had left he called Saideh, his second wife, who was glad that he wanted to come to her and said she had been longing to see him.

She welcomed him with a lavishly laden table and a long night of love. She had always known, she said venomously, that Nasimeh was not a woman but a man. Only men would be interested in such fantasies as building houses. As for Lamia, she had always been rather hysterical. On the other hand, she said, he could stay with her forever, so that she could enjoy his company every night. She wasn't afraid. For the first time in his life Nasri admired her, and found her more attractive every day.

And as the house was in the Salihiyyeh quarter, he could go to the nightclubs when Saideh was asleep.

This arrangement worked well for some weeks. But Saideh was not brave, as he had assumed, it was just that she didn't take Nasri's danger seriously, and apparently she told everyone that he was hiding with her. So her friends and relations came to see him, and Nasri soon felt they were gaping at him as if he were a monkey in a cage.

It was all rather annoying.

But what led him to leave the house hastily and without saying goodbye was a phone call from Tawfiq, who had heard in a café where Nasri was hiding. "You must leave the house at once. And don't go to any of your other wives, because Hamid has his sights set on all four houses now. Take a taxi to my place. I'll come straight home and we can discuss the situation."

Nasri's swift action saved his life, for exactly an hour after his hasty departure Hamid Farsi stormed into the grand house with a knife drawn, pushed the screaming Saideh out of his way and searched the rooms. Hamid was trembling all over when, disappointed, he had to leave. "So he got away from me this time. But I'll find him yet and murder him," he said breathlessly, slamming the door behind him.

Tawfiq's wife had prepared a lavish meal, but she herself withdrew to be with her children. And as if nothing had happened, while he poured tea at the end of the meal Tawfiq launched into a brief account of the business he had successfully done for Nasri. All of it excellent news! Nasri swallowed the cutting remarks that were on the tip of his tongue along with a large gulp of tea.

Only one comment escaped him. "There'll be no point in any of those deals if he gets his hands on me."

It was Tawfiq's opinion that Nasri should leave the city at once, but on that point Nasri was not open to persuasion. So Tawfiq tried to think of the safest place for him in Damascus and its immediate surroundings, and that was with Nasri's Uncle Badruddin, who owned a villa that was like a castle in Dummar, a village nearby.

Nasri agreed; he had no choice. When, just once, he went to the Café Havana in broad daylight out of desire for the noise of the city, the whole thing nearly went wrong. He drank a coffee and was letting his eyes and ears feast on the busy life of Damascus when he suddenly saw Hamid Farsi on the other side of the street. Hamid seemed to be watching the café, and if a tram had not come down the road and blocked his view of the café just then Nasri would have fallen into his hands. Instead, he slipped out the back door, jumped into a taxi, and fled to Dummar. The calligrapher was becoming some kind of giant kraken with tentacles reaching out to him everywhere.

Uncle Badruddin was a rich gentleman farmer of the old school who thought city folk were much to be pitied. Even as a child Nasri had thought him rather limited in his outlook. When his uncle visited them in Damascus, bringing his apples, and began philosophizing on modern times and why they were so bad – "people have forgotten their Mother Earth," he used to say – and when the conversation turned to the way young folk behaved, the inconstancy of married couples, the stink of the newfangled factories, or the wars flaring up all over the world, everyone had soon felt bored. Nasri could stand it for ten minutes at the most. His uncle couldn't even tell a story, only preach sermon after sermon about the decline of morality.

By now he was around seventy, and as well as the limitations of his mind, his fear of the Last Judgment (which he expected any day now) had intensified. Anything in the nature of a storm, a war, or an epidemic was reliable evidence, as he saw it, that the end of the world was imminent.

It had become no easier to be close to him, and as he had not a single tooth left in his mouth you not only got an earful from him, you also got a face full of spray.

"The end is coming, and the world will fall into the sun and burn up like a piece of paper over the fire," he announced one evening. After such apocalyptic predictions Nasri found it harder than ever to get to sleep. All kinds of ideas raced through his head until at some point in the night he would wake up bathed in sweat.

He himself soon didn't know how long he had been staying with his uncle, who wore him out with his rustic hospitality. "Why are you picking at your food like a schoolboy? Help yourself! We have plenty here, we don't want a guest to go hungry to bed, not like other hosts today. Eat all you like, we're not watching," he cried, and Nasri was sure his uncle was counting every mouthful he took.

Nasri seldom ate dessert, and as he saw it fruit was for children and invalids. What he needed was a good strong coffee with cardamom. His uncle, on the other hand, expressed it as his opinion that coffee was poisonous, and since he would eat and drink only what came from Syrian fields, coffee was out of the question for him anyway.

Nor could Nasri smoke, and he had to drink his arak in secret straight from the bottle, without water and without ice cubes. It was misery.

The days and weeks lost any distinguishing features. A time came when Nasri woke from a nightmare and hurried out into the still cool night. He ran as if his uncle were after him. He did not slow down until he was on the main road and saw the lights of a bus on the way to Damascus. Nasri waved, the bus stopped, he climbed in and sat down. The bus was almost empty. A few farmers on their way to market in Damascus had loaded their vegetables and chickens on board.

Soon he fell into a deep sleep. He didn't wake up until the bus braked suddenly on the outskirts of the city to let a small flock of sheep cross the road. The shepherd shouted angrily at the lead ram, which had stopped in the middle of the road and was bleating at the city as it woke from sleep.

"Even a castrated ram will fall in love in Damascus," said Nasri to his neighbour.

After three days in the city, he suggested, those sheep would be playing backgammon and drinking arak. "That's why they go to slaughter quickly. Any sheep that gets away becomes a citizen of Damascus," replied the man when the shepherd's stick came down on the skull of the ram.

The sky above Damascus was already growing lighter.

Nasri stole into his office and phoned Tawfiq. "Where will you go now?" asked his confidant. His voice sounded weary.

"To see my whore. No one will think of looking for me there," said Nasri.

On the way to Asmahan he wondered why he thought all his wives so ugly. He was sure that each of them was beautiful in her own way, but not to him, or not now. Why do people get ugly when we stop loving them? To him, Asmahan was pretty as a picture and very attractive, but his manager thought she was terrible. So, Nasri concluded, just before reaching her street, he loved Asmahan. Probably because she didn't belong to him. Like the desert, she belonged to everyone and no one. From the pavement opposite the little house he saw an elegant elderly client leaving. He quickly crossed the road and pushed the doorbell.

40

Asmahan had heard of the flight of the calligrapher's beautiful wife. Nasri's part in it became harder to work out from week to week. He himself, however, had disappeared. And suddenly there he was in front of her. He must have been watching the house for some time, because the doorbell rang only a moment after Habib the old jeweller had closed the door behind him. She thought the elderly man had left some tablets, his glasses or his walking stick behind, because he was always forgetting something, and she suspected he did it on purpose so as to take her in his arms once more, for free. Habib was miserly. She opened the door, laughing. There stood the pale-faced Nasri.

"Let me in, please, there's a madman trying to kill me," he said breathlessly. She let him in, and for a moment she even felt a little sorry for him. Nasri told her his problem at once. He wanted to hide out for a while on the first floor of her house, where none of her clients were allowed to go. The calligrapher, said Nasri, would have hired killers by now.

"And when they find you," said Asmahan, "they'll kill me too. At least I'd like to know what for! Did the calligrapher write the love letters you gave me as well? Couldn't you find a single word of your own for me? Did you pay him to express your love?"

In her agitation she fetched a piece of paper and put it down in front of him with a dramatic gesture. "Write me a short letter here," she said. Nasri was upset, he raged and roared, but it was no use. She knew now that he had been lying to her. Her pity turned to deep contempt.

Then the doorbell rang. Asmahan smiled, for she knew exactly how she could get rid of him forever. An old story, told to her once by a school friend, had shown her how to humiliate vain men.

"You must hide, quick." She pushed him into a small cupboard where he could sit on a stool among buckets and brooms. What kind of life was this? Only recently he had been one of the most highly regarded citizens of Damascus, and now he had to hide from the world among all this junk!

And as he was thinking of his sad fate he heard Asmahan laugh. The broom cupboard was separated from her bedroom only by a thin wooden partition. He had to listen to Asmahan and the unknown man making love and obviously enjoying it. When the sounds of love-making had died away at last, he heard the two of them talking about him. The man was telling Asmahan, in detail, what rumours about Nasri and Noura were going the rounds. Nasri almost exploded, and his heart was so full of shame that it felt like jumping out of his chest.

"That bastard pays for letters," said the man, "so that he can seduce women, and his own wives are seduced daily by one or another of their neighbours with no need for letters at all."

"Is that true?" asked Asmahan. "And have you been making up to them yourself?"

"No," said the man in her bed, "but a friend of mine has been through all four of Nasri's wives."

Nasri was on the point of exploding. He could have wrung Asmahan's neck, but what he was hearing took his breath away.

For he was beginning to realize that Asmahan's client was someone high up in the Secret Service. Like all men of his stamp, he was inclined to show off, but he was astonishingly well informed.

"By now," he added, "even my own men are looking for Nasri."

"Why? Has he been making love to their wives as well?"

The man laughed. "No, not that, but the calligrapher is after him. And as the Secret Service doesn't have much to do in a democracy, they like to get private work on the side. I always earn a little out of it myself without having to get my hands dirty. Well, what's one to do? I long for the old days of strong government, although that's slandered as dictatorship now. My men were overworked back then."

"And these days they're hired to look for Nasri Abbani and murder him?" asked Asmahan.

"No, they're only looking for him. The calligrapher wants to keep the pleasure of murdering him for himself. It's his honour that's been dragged in the dust. My men can investigate all they like, but they have orders not to lay hands on him. If one of them does more than

I've allowed, he'll be fired on the spot. I have reasons enough to fire the entire army in my desk drawers." The man laughed so much at his own joke that Nasri's ears hurt.

"And what does anyone who gives away Nasri's hiding place get?"

"It'd be twenty thousand to twenty-five thousand lira. The calligrapher's in a hurry, and he's a very rich man."

Nasri was in a trap. The longer he listened the more frightened he felt. How could this jumped-up calligraphic painter whose school he had supported be after his life? And how had it happened that Asmahan suddenly had the upper hand and could make herself so much richer with a single remark? What had become of his life?

After a while all was quiet in the room next door to the broom cupboard, and what seemed another eternity later Asmahan opened the cupboard door. She was tearstained and drunk. "Get out of here this minute, before I weaken and call the calligrapher," she said.

Nasri was close to tears himself. "Let me explain," he begged her.

"Go to hell," she shouted, and pointed at the front door of the house.

Nasri went from Asmahan's house to the nearby Al Amir hotel, summoned Tawfiq, and told him what had happened. They discussed what he should do now.

Tawfiq urged him to move to Beirut, but Nasri hated Beirut. He couldn't stand the sea or the Lebanese way of life.

"Then all we have is my late sister's apartment," said Tawfiq, who had heard from some of the porters of the buildings belonging to Nasri that strangers were giving them money and asking whether the owner was hiding out in one of his empty apartments. "It's a modest place, but comfortably furnished. It's going to be sold," Tawfiq went on, "but that can wait a few months until we're over this crisis. It's also an anonymous kind of place, in a modern four-storey building with sixteen apartments, all just the same, and their tenants or owners are changing all the time. A real no man's land," said Tawfiq, getting to his feet. "What's more, the building has two ways out to two different streets. I'll fetch the car," he said, and went to the door. He turned. "Take care," he said in a paternal, almost affectionate tone, and he set off. Quarter of an hour later Nasri, looking out of the window, saw Tawfiq parking his Citroën outside the hotel entrance. Nasri paid for the room, and camouflaged by a pair of sunglasses, he slipped into the car.

The apartment was on the third floor of a modern building close to Mount Qasioun. Looking out from the balcony, Nasri saw a small, dusty square and the main road of the quarter running downhill to the city centre. He had a good view of Damascus.

"I could hold out here forever," he told Tawfiq before his manager left the apartment. Nasri felt deeply grateful to him. That very day Tawfiq had apparently had the apartment cleaned and the fridge filled with delicious things to eat. He also found sugar, coffee, cardamom, tea, and various other comestibles in the kitchen, and a note: "Call me if you need anything."

Nasri did in fact call him two hours later, thanked him and asked if he could bring Elias Ashkar the pharmacist to the apartment, because he missed him. He was a reliable friend, he added, and a very civilized man.

Tawfiq was not enthusiastic. "He's a Christian," he pointed out.

"So what?" said Nasri, suddenly angry with the man to whom he had every reason to be grateful. "He can be a Jew or a fire-worshipper for all I care. He's as decent a man as you or I," he added, thinking that the pious Tawfiq would not much like that comparison.

"As you like. I'll bring him to see you tomorrow evening," said Tawfiq. His words were forced into a corset of civility and regret.

"And tell him to bring a bottle of lion's milk," added Nasri, knowing that obedient as he might be, Tawfiq, being a good Muslim, would decline even to buy arak, known jokingly as lion's milk.

The two visitors came that evening. But Tawfiq, visibly nervous, was quick to leave and drove home again. Elias Ashkar felt honoured to visit his friend of so many years in hiding, and hugged Nasri with tears in his eyes. "I miss our morning coffee together," he said, much moved.

Elias could only confirm what Nasri had long known, that the calligrapher was sparing himself no effort or expense to get hold of him.

"Why don't you have him killed? There are so many unemployed criminals ready to murder anyone you like for a hundred lira. Then you'd be left in peace," said Elias, when they were both drunk. The bottle of arak was almost empty.

"No, one doesn't do that kind of thing. His wife has run away from him, the School of Calligraphy is in ruins, he's closed his studio – and is he to die as well?" Nasri shook his head. "He's a poor devil, and he'll soon find out that I have nothing to do with any of it. Tawfiq is going to see him tomorrow and try to make him see sense. The goldsmith Najib Rihan is arranging the meeting."

Nasri still felt a trace of gratitude to the calligrapher, and when the arak had banished his remaining fear he told the pharmacist what an effect Hamid's letters had on whores and presidents alike.

When the pharmacist went to the bathroom, Nasri glanced at the newspaper that his friend had brought him. He saw an advertisement: "Fashion Show. Paris models display the '56/'57 winter collection of the Paris fashion house of Carven in the Hotel Semiramis." He smiled, remembering last year's fashion show in the same hotel, organized by the very same fashion house of Carven. It looked as if the paper were a year out of date.

It was late when the pharmacist left the building. He looked around the shadows of the entrance for a long time before weaving his way out into the lamplit street.

Three days later Tawfiq came with news that the calligrapher was now entirely unhinged. Persecution mania, he said. Although he had declined the goldsmith's offer to act as a go-between, he, Tawfiq, had gone to see Hamid Farsi, who had told him in all seriousness that Nasri had been the man pulling the strings of a conspiracy aiming to disgrace him publicly because he, Hamid Farsi, wanted to carry through revolutionary reforms of Arabic script. It wasn't about Noura, it was only about his humiliation, and for that he was going to kill Nasri.

Nasri was furious. The pharmacist had been right, he said, the calligrapher was a disaster that ought to be prevented. He would have to be killed to keep him from killing Nasri.

Tawfiq did not reply to that. When Nasri stopped to get his breath back, he stood up. "I must get back to the office. We have a big deal to do with the Japanese today," he said, leaving. Nasri was angry with his manager, and cursed him and all Japanese.

When he went to the window, his blood froze with fear. There on the other side of the street, not ten metres away, stood Hamid Farsi leaning against a poplar, keeping watch on the building. Tawfiq left and went to his Citroën. Hamid waited a little longer, until a bus cut off the sight of the place where he was lurking, and then scurried across the road to the building as nimbly as a weasel.

Nasri froze. He knew that neither his door nor most of the others had nameplates on them. But perhaps the calligrapher had found out exactly where he was hiding. He went to the kitchen and looked for a large knife, but all the knives were small and old, with wooden handles beginning to crumble. But then he saw a long, sharp kebab skewer. "You just come here. I'll spit you on this," he whispered, grinning nastily at the idea of holding the calligrapher over a flame with onions and peppers, like *shashlik*. With the skewer in his right hand he tiptoed to the door of the apartment, and listened for noises in the stairwell. In the apartment to the right of him a girl was crying loudly, in the apartment to the left of him the lid of a pan fell to the floor with a crash. Below him a woman swore. He thought he heard footsteps. Then it occurred to him that too much silence in one of the apartments might seem suspicious. He walked casually into the living room, turned the radio on, and when he came to a song of lamentation he thought: that's the kind of thing housewives like. He went back to the kitchen, ran water, tapped a board with a cooking spoon, and knocked a water glass against a metal bowl.

He felt ridiculous, and could have wept if fear had not driven his self-pity out of him. He stole over to the window and watched the street. Then he saw Hamid Farsi coming out of the building again and returning to his observation post behind the poplar.

Nasri called Tawfiq, who said nothing, as though he had guessed as much. "I have news for you," he said then. "It's curious, and only you can decide if it is good news for you or not." Even before Nasri could ask what this was all about, he heard Tawfiq say, "Your wife Almaz came here. She wants you. You're to go to her, she says, and keep watch on Hamid Farsi from her house."

Nasri thought about it.

"Not a bad idea," he said then. "Tell her I'll be with her tomorrow about midnight."

He thought of the many stories about clever women that he used to hear even as a child. He smiled and shook his head as he imagined the absurdity of keeping watch by night on his own pursuer Hamid Farsi.

Only a woman could think of such a trick, he thought.

Next evening Nasri kept watch on the man who was after him where he stayed by the old poplar until late into the night.

Just before midnight he left the building through the back exit, took a taxi, and drove through the city in the late summer night. He reflected on his life, as the lights of his beloved city soothed his soul. He wondered whether it wasn't time for him to start an entirely new life. The first step in this new life would be to divorce all his wives. It would not be simple, and it would also be very expensive, but he never wanted to be stuck with wives he didn't love again.

Nasri was determined as never before to put this plan into practice. He had no idea how little time he had left.

41

Hamid Farsi was desperately searching for Nasri Abbani. At the end of July he had been sure that his enemy was in the city, because three detectives independently of each other had seen him in the Café Havana on Port Said Street, close to the Abbani building.

So Hamid lay in wait for the fornicator near the Librairie Universelle bookshop, opposite the café. One afternoon he suddenly saw him sitting in the window. But Hamid wasn't skilful enough; Abbani saw him and made his getaway through the back door.

Hamid hired a detective agency to watch the houses of Nasri's wives. It was expensive, and again and again there was a false alarm. Once a detective called him to say he was sure Nasri was now living in hiding with his second wife in the Salihiyyeh district. Hamid hurried off, knocked, and forced his way in. The woman fell to the floor. He felt sorry for her, but Nasri was nowhere to be found.

He had no luck with the third wife in the Midan quarter either. As for the fourth wife, she wouldn't even listen to him and she was certainly not letting him into the house. She stood there, a broad figure, cursing him and her own husband, and slammed the door. He heard her calling "Pimp!" in a loud voice from behind the closed door.

That cut him to the heart.

Nasri had not turned up at his office either. His deputy warned Hamid that if he found him prowling around outside the office again, he would set the police on him.

Hamid was not in the least afraid of the police. He feared only that they might frustrate his plan of revenge. From that day on he avoided going down Port Said Street too often.

He stuck close to Tawfiq. That was the advice of an old Secret Service man, and one day Tawfiq drove his old Citroën to a building at the foot of Mount Qassioun. Hamid was sure the man would lead him, unintentionally, to his master, but he couldn't find a trace of Nasri anywhere. He spent two days and a long night watching the building. No luck.

And then, a week later, Karam called him. The café proprietor said he had important news for him.

Hamid set out at once for the café, where Karam told him that for the last few days Nasri Abbani had been hiding with his fourth wife Almaz.

"And how do you know that?" asked Hamid suspiciously. He was afraid that the café owner was trying to trick him. Over the last few weeks his exposed nerves had been vulnerable to both useless detectives and men with malice in mind. The latter called at night and gave him an address where, they said, Nasri was staying. The addresses were once the brothel and twice well-known nightclubs, and in all three cases Hamid looked ridiculous.

"Listen: my niece Almaz is Nasri's fourth wife. She's horrified by the way that fornicating goat would leave no whore in the city alone, and now he's getting the Saudis to send him women at great expense." Nasri, he said, had come back and was acting as if nothing had happened.

"You know her house in Dakak Street," said Karam. "You went to see her there once, she told me. The buildings in her street run almost parallel to those in yours."

Hamid was astonished. Yes, he had once briefly encountered that fat woman with her loose tongue, but he would never have thought that the wall of the house in Dakar Street lay right next to his own.

"Nasri lived with my niece in Baghdad Street first," Karam went on, "in the very same house that was going to be the School of Calligraphy later, but my niece soon discovered that her husband was sleeping with two of her women neighbours. That was too much of a humiliation for Almaz, and she didn't want to spend a day longer in the house. That's why they moved to the Old Town in such a hurry. Almaz had her mind set at rest for a while, until Nasri discovered your wife."

"But how could he have seen my wife?" asked Hamid, his throat dry.

"His house has an attic with a view down into your inner courtyard."

"Attic? What attic? Our house is the tallest on three sides, with nothing but the sky above. And on the fourth side there's only a high mud-brick wall without any windows in it. I've never seen anyone there," said Hamid. He was beginning to feel that this was an absurd conversation, and he couldn't imagine Nasri, who after all knew that he, Hamid, was after him, hiding so close to him.

"You don't understand because you're a decent man. Unlike Nasri. You keep your eyes lowered because other men's wives are taboo. You don't even know how many women there are in the houses you look down to from your terrace. But he uses a tiny window as a peephole. Take a good look when you go home today," said Karam, and he stood up, because one of his staff was indicating that he was wanted on the telephone.

Hamid too rose, thanked Karam, and went straight home. Once there, he did indeed see the inconspicuous little window in the wall. The attic must be up there, above his house. The wall was so weather-beaten that you could see hardly any difference between the plaster and the two halves of the wooden window frame when they were closed. At the moment they were open. Hamid imagined that a woman had waved to him. He did not react.

He had to admit that he had never noticed either that house or the other neighbouring buildings. So far as he was concerned, his own house ended on the ground floor anyway. He never went into the rooms on the first floor or up to the flat roof where his wife used to hang out the washing. He had never looked into the other inner courtyards. They were none of his business, as his grandfather and his father had drummed into him: other people's houses were private.

Hamid stood under the window and looked up. Any piece of paper weighted with a small pebble could land here, he thought.

He went back to his chair beside the fountain and looked up once more. The window was closed again now, and he could hardly see it.

Next morning he went out of the house early and did not come back until evening. Could it be that that bastard had always seduced Noura in the morning? He remembered how Abbani had once told him he didn't wake up until nine, since he was out and about almost every night. He took his evening meal early with whichever of his wives it was his turn to visit.

THE CALLIGRAPHER'S SECRET

However that might be, if it had been only a case of the licentious ways of a fornicating goat, Nasri would have known at their first meeting, at the latest, that Noura was Hamid's wife, and he would have stopped asking her husband to write letters for him at once. Or had the whole thing been planned far ahead? Had Nasri sought out Noura from the first, he wondered, to humiliate him? He felt boundless hatred for Nasri Abbani, to whom he had given nothing but beauty, and who had then struck a mortal blow to his reputation. And suddenly the generosity of Abbani's donation to the School of Calligraphy seemed to be part of the diabolical plan to make his dream collapse like a house of cards. His enemy was no bearded idiot. No, his enemy was a smiling man who was only waiting to plunge a sharp knife into his body.

Next morning Hamid rang Karam several times, to no avail. He walked through the Old Town and felt, for the first time, the glances of others burning into his skin.

He turned back halfway, slammed the door behind him, and crept into the dark bedroom.

Suddenly he heard the phone ring.

He went into the salon where the telephone stood. It was Laila Bakri, a school friend of his wife's, ringing to ask if Noura was back yet.

He closed his eyes and saw sparks in front of a dark sky. "What's that to do with you, you stupid whore?" he shouted into the mouthpiece, and hung up.

42

Five months after the disappearance of his wife, Hamid Farsi stabbed Nasri Abbani with a sharp knife as the latter was coming out of the Hammam Nureddin in the spice market, late at night, and walking along the dark street that led to the house of his fourth wife Almaz.

Nasri died without knowing that his wife Almaz, with Karam's help, had given him away. She was bitterly disappointed by the way he slept around. After coming into her life at a moment of weakness, he had left her with only one option after making her pregnant – unless she wanted to die – and that was to marry him. And then he betrayed her at every opportunity he had.

After the wedding she began to love Nasri passionately. His generosity to her alone would have been reason enough. But the more she loved him, the colder he grew. And when she once told him after Nariman's birth how much she loved him, he replied dismissively, "All right, all right, you'll soon get over it. It's like a fever, normally harmless. You should put your mind to losing weight instead."

From that day on her love evaporated.

When Karam visited her one day, he told her about Asmahan the high-class whore whom Nasri had been visiting every day for years. Apparently, said Karam, she had fallen in love with him, and as he did not return her love she had stopped being willing to see him as a client.

And then came the scandal over the calligrapher's wife. She had had her suspicions for some time, because Nasri climbed up to the attic more and more often, and she felt even more deeply injured than by the whore Asmahan. Now it was from her own house that Nasri planned his new seduction.

She had meant to teach him a little lesson with that fall, but Nasri had forgotten it even before the plaster came off his leg. And then he had installed an iron spiral staircase up to the attic, with ulterior motives in mind.

She summoned her uncle Karam, and he came at once, as always when she needed him. He was not a real uncle, only a distant cousin of her father's, but he was friendly, often helped her, and asked nothing in return. She liked his deep voice, and he gave her good advice, on the sole condition that she didn't say a word about it to her husband, because he didn't like him.

While her parents tried to calm her down, Karam was firmly on her side. He was implacable. Karam indicated that the scandal over the calligrapher's wife was something to do with pimping, and her husband was involved in it. But he advised her not to show that she suspected anything, for Nasri could throw her out, and then she and Nariman would have to live in poverty. The Abbanis had all the judges in the city behind them.

Nasri would soon die, said Karam, and it would be better for her to seem loyal to him and offer him a hiding place now that his other wives had proved so cowardly. Then she would be sure of a good inheritance for herself and her daughter.

"I'll tell you straight out, Hamid will catch up with him. It's only a matter of days or weeks. He got away from Hamid only at the last moment three times. But before he dies you must have made sure you've secured everything for yourself."

So Almaz immediately rang Tawfiq and told him briefly that she was going to visit him at the office within the next half hour. He was to send the other staff away, she said, because she wanted to speak to him in a private. She had an idea that she didn't want to discuss on the phone.

Karam smiled, gave Almaz a hug, and left.

Taking his victim by surprise, Hamid had stabbed him twelve times in the region of the heart. Every single thrust of his knife, which was sharp as a razor blade, would have been fatal, as the forensic expert said at the autopsy. Nasri Abbani didn't even manage to take his pistol out of his pocket, and even if he had done so, he had never in his life fired a pistol.

For many years, Hamid was to think of the last minutes in the life of Nasri Abbani. "Hamid, you're crazy," gasped the dying man. "Killing me when I've never done you any harm."

"What about my wife, you bastard?" Hamid had shouted. Abbani, lying in a pool of blood, raised his hand like a drowning man. His lips trembled in the wan light of the street lamps.

Rashid Sabuni, one of the best-known lawyers in Damascus, had no difficulty in convincing the judge and jury that life imprisonment for this brutal murder, committed with intent, would be the minimum sentence demanded by justice.

Not just the number of stab wounds, all the other evidence was against Hamid Farsi. The café proprietor Karam Midani also incriminated the accused. He had met the calligrapher again and again, he said, and since the disappearance of Hamid Farsi's wife he had had only one thought in his head, to kill Abbani.

Hamid shook his head, horrified. He thought he must be losing his mind. He accused the witness Karam of being a member of the secret society of the Pure Ones, and a homosexual notorious all over the city. Karam had egged him on to follow Nasri, and had even offered him a pistol. Hamid was so beside himself that he tried to attack the witness physically. Two police officers forcibly escorted him out of the courtroom.

His lack of respect throughout the trial for the judge, and his total failure to show any remorse, earned him a life sentence.

However, he spent less than two years of it in the Citadel prison in Damascus, where right at the start, to the fury of the Abbani family, he was given one of the finest three cells, known by the inmates as "the villa." He was spoilt, and well treated, and was allowed to do calligraphic work for the prison governor. Protests did no good, because the al-Azm clan, of which the governor was a member, was even more powerful than the Abbani clan.

Nasri's younger brother Muhammad, confused by grief and rage, used underworld connections to hire a murderer held in the same prison as Hamid Farsi to kill him. However, the man was overpowered by the guard in charge of those three cells. After three hard blows in the face the criminal, a man getting on in years, was shaking with fear and disclosed the name of the man who had hired him.

A charge of incitement to murder was brought against the Abbanis. They were glad to get off just by signing a document. Next day their lawyer explained exactly what it was to which, in their fear of retribution and scandal, they had put their names. Their horror was boundless. They, the undersigned, took the entire responsibility on themselves if anything unfortunate were to happen to Hamid Farsi, their brother's murderer.

The Second Kernel of the Truth

*Others read in order to study,
while we must study so that
we can read.*

Taha Hussein (1862–1973)
Egyptian writer

*Truth is a jewel, and makes the life
of its owner rich but dangerous.*

Yousef S. Fadeli (1803–1830)
Syrian alchemist

1

Only in prison did Hamid Farsi really come to think about his life, which now seemed strange and far away. He felt relieved to be in this cell, but that very feeling disturbed him. "Sentenced to prison for life," he repeated, to present his disaster to himself as dramatically as possible, but he could not find anything dramatic about it.

Lying on his bed, he was amazed to realize how quickly all that he had built up had fallen into ruin. His reputation as a man, his fame as a calligrapher, his certainties and his pleasure in life were all gone as if they had not until very recently been impregnable defences.

In the afternoon, drinking tea with Governor al-Azm, he said casually, as if speaking to himself, "Life is nothing but a struggle against decline and decay, and we always lose in the end."

Noura's flight had been the beginning of his downfall. It was a mystery to him why she had not run away with Nasri, but had left that fornicating goat behind for him to deal with. As if she wanted him to kill Nasri, as if Nasri had to pay for something. Maybe Nasri had never told her that he had four wives until he had slept with her, and the information came as an unpleasant surprise.

Had she perhaps wanted to teach Nasri a lesson? Had she underestimated him, Hamid? Did she maybe think that he would just slap Nasri around a bit to make him look ridiculous? Or had she wanted Nasri to kill him? Hamid had never understood women. His grandfather had once looked at the clear, starry sky above Damascus and told him that only when he had counted every star there would he be able to fathom the mind of a woman.

The Citadel prison occupied a large site in the extreme north of the Old Town. The citadel itself had been destroyed and rebuilt several times since the days of Saladin, and during the four hundred years of

Ottoman rule it had not been under the direct authority of the governor of Damascus, but along with its garrison was directly answerable
to the Sultan in Istanbul. The Ottoman sultans knew that the restless city of Damascus was more easily governed without the powerful
Citadel. Sure enough, the Sultan's loyal elite troops came out of the
Citadel whenever there was a revolt in the city to subdue the rioters.

The French then posted their own garrison in the Citadel and for
twenty-five years used it as a prison for Syrian insurgents. Since independence it had served for several decades as the central prison, but
out of indolence the Damascenes went on calling the prison just "the
Citadel." That was to come in useful, for fifty years after independence
the building was renovated and once again was officially known as
the Citadel. The prison was moved elsewhere.

The Citadel was one of the few in the east that had not been built
on a hill but level with the rest of the city. In its days as a prison a
tangle of rusty barbed wire and shapeless rails secured the walls and
obscured the view of the building.

Hamid's cell was on the second storey of the north wing. That was
an advantage, because this side was spared the blazing heat of the
summer sun. From the grating over his door he could look out at
the inner courtyard of the Citadel, as well as the roofs and streets of
the Old Town. Somewhere among them lay his beautiful house. The
small barred window opposite the door showed him a section of the
rooftops of the Souk Saruya quarter where he had once had his studio.

Out of eight hundred prisoners, Hamid was one of three with
special privileges. The cell next to his was occupied by a rich Damascene merchant's son who had committed seven murders. He was a
quiet man with a pitifully pale complexion who had slaughtered his
wife's family in a quarrel. The third and rather larger cell contained
the son of an emir unknown to Hamid, serving life imprisonment for
the vicious murder of a cousin. If the murdered man had not been the
president's son-in-law, he assured people, he would not have spent a
single day in prison. He was unpleasantly talkative, loud-mouthed,
boastful, and crude. Hamid avoided him.

Hamid's cell was a spacious room. But for the barred door and
window you would have thought it was the attic room of a fine house.

He was allowed his calligraphy instruments, because the prison governor, a distant relative of Prime Minister Khalid al-Azm, revered his art. He had told him over tea on his very first day that he was extremely sorry to see him in prison over a woman. He himself had four official and five unofficial wives, and he wouldn't dream of quarrelling with another man over any of them.

He regretted, he said, that he could not set Hamid free, but as long as he, Governor al-Azm, was in charge of this prison he would be treated like a nobleman, for calligraphers were the true princes of Arab culture. "What am I, with my degree in law from the Sorbonne, by comparison with you?" he added with a show of modesty.

Hamid was not in the mood for bombastic speeches, and the man talked on and on without stopping like a garrulous drunk. However, he was soon to find out that Governor al-Azm was as good as his word. Both the guards and the older inmates, the men who really ran the prison, treated him respectfully. He did not have to do menial work or stand in line for anything. A guard knocked on the door twice a day and asked in subservient tones, if with a touch of irony, whether there was anything he wanted apart from his freedom.

Pots of jasmine and roses, his favourite flowers, were quickly brought in to adorn the walkway in the open air that separated his cell from the handrail around the inner courtyard. He could also send out for ink and paper of the best quality.

Not a week went by before his first commission came from the governor. He wanted a saying from the Quran written out in Kufic script, which Hamid did not particularly like. "And it's wanted in a hurry," added the guard bringing the message, as he did later with all the other commissions for works of calligraphy intended by the governor for his distinguished friends at home and abroad.

On his first and only exploration of the lower floors of the prison, where he was allowed to go accompanied by a guard, Hamid realized what luxury he and the two scions of powerful clans enjoyed in the Citadel. All the others lived in dank, dark misery and the stench of decay.

What kind of men were they? The prisoners included professors, writers, lawyers, and doctors who could not only speak for a full hour on Arabic poetry and philosophy, but also loved French, English, and Greek literature. In here they were prepared to murder a man brutally for a cigarette, a bowl of soup, or for no reason at all. They seemed to have stripped off the veneer of civilization like a thin raincoat as soon as they entered the prison.

He never wanted to go down to those lower levels again.

Besides his most important calligraphic instruments and the certificate that testified to his mastery of calligraphy, he had with him a unique thirteenth-century document the size of a hand, several books of theoretical and secret writings about the art of calligraphy, and three rare eighteenth-century calligraphic works that his master had given him. He also had a photograph dating from the old days brought from his studio, where it had always hung above his desk. Time and damp had left stains on the picture, turning its black to light sepia. He hung it on the wall beside the window of his cell.

The photograph had been taken after a party at his grandparents' house, when he himself was still a small child. Neither his sister Siham nor his younger brother Fihmi had yet been born. Never before had he looked at the photograph as often as he did now.

2

His grandfather sat on a chair like a throne in the front row, with Hamid, his favourite grandchild, on his lap, and they were both looking at the camera with a triumphant expression. Grandmother Farida, with some flowers beside her, was sitting on a small bench at a certain distance from them as if she did not belong with her husband. Behind his grandmother, in the very middle of the picture, stood his youngest uncle, Abbas, and to the left of him was Uncle Bashir. Hamid's father stood by himself on their left. He was the firstborn son. Instead of taking over his father's business, as was usual for an eldest son, he had decided in favour of calligraphy, but all his life he was only an average craftsman. There was a dull look in his eyes. And some way from him, as if to demonstrate the distance she preserved from this family, stood Hamid's mother, her expression gloomy as she gazed into the distance.

Centre right, behind his grandfather, stood Aunt Mayyada with her husband Subhi in his uniform. He was still a French Air Force officer at the time. Later, as an experienced airman, he was recruited by the new Saudi army for good money and with the prospect of Saudi citizenship. So he immigrated to Saudi Arabia, but Aunt Mayyada thought life there was tedious, and she couldn't stand the heat and the isolation. She and her children came to Damascus every year. She soon had nine children, and they stayed in Damascus longer and longer as time went by. After a while there were rumours that her husband had married a Saudi princess. The royal house thought well of Subhi, who was high up in the Defence Ministry.

Later on, when Aunt Mayyada was growing old, she came to Damascus by herself. Her sons and daughters stayed with their father or with their own families, and Hamid gradually realized that his aunt lived alone. Her husband sent her a generous allowance, but he never visited her or his native city again.

Mayyada was fond of Hamid, but he did not keep in touch with her much because his parents disliked her. However, when he needed her help she was there for him, for instance in arranging his second marriage.

"Grandfather was right. Aunt Mayyada brought bad luck. Whatever she touched went wrong," whispered Hamid. He turned his eyes to the picture again. Between his aunt and her husband stood their first-born son Rushdi. He was three years older than Hamid and had a bad squint. At the time Hamid thought Rushdi was joking and squinted to make other people laugh, but when the boy pulled both his ears and still kept squinting horribly Hamid realized that it was no joke. Rushdi's four sisters were not at the party, and so not in the photograph either. They were visiting their other grandparents, who unlike Grandfather Farsi liked girls.

To the right of brother-in-law Subhi, Aunt Sa'adiyyeh and her fiancé Halim were posing as if about to appear in the newspaper. Halim was a well-known folksinger of the time, and the pin-up of all the young women in Damascus. After three years of marriage he returned Hamid's aunt to her parents, still *virgo intacta*, as the women said, blaming him. He divorced her and fled abroad with his gay lover, a Canadian diplomat. Aunt Sa'adiyyeh was pretty as a picture, and soon married a young film director. She immigrated to the United States with him, and the family never heard from them again.

To one side and in front of Halim the singer stood Aunt Basma, who was only twelve at the time. Hamid's grandmother had had her when she was forty and did not like her at all. Basma was the black sheep of the family. Even in the picture Hamid could see that she was not enjoying the occasion. She did not look friendly or in party mood, but stared indignantly at the photographer as if she wanted him to explain why the family had gone to such expense that day.

Basma had fallen in love with a Jewish doctor in the middle of the 1930s and immigrated to Israel with him, not that the country was called Israel yet; it was still Palestine, and was under British occupation.

Grandfather took this as a personal insult and publicly disinherited her, in front of respected businessmen and sheikhs as witnesses, to retrieve what he could of his honour.

Because Grandmother was superstitious and feared the number thirteen, the family's old cook Widad stood next to Aunt Basma. Hamid remembered her well; in the kitchen she always had an apron covered with greasy marks round her waist, but in the picture she wore an elegant black dress.

To Hamid now, the photograph bore witness to another world, like old pictures of American Indian chiefs, harem ladies, or Hawaiian dancing girls. And soon after it was taken that world had disappeared forever. The photograph captured a moment of happiness. It was one of the few times in Hamid's childhood and youth when he had tasted infinite joy. Grandfather loved him and told everyone that when Hamid was fifteen he was going to pass the carpet business on to him, for unlike his own sons, his grandson had inherited his sharp mind. He would let no one treat the boy harshly; he spoilt him and played with him like a friend. It was he who initiated Hamid into the mysteries of mathematics. Those hours full of strange calculations left him with a love of numbers for life. And if Hamid did not understand something, and asked, his grandfather would explain patiently as if he had all the time in the world.

Hamid wanted to stay with his grandfather forever, so there was a drama at the end of every visit because he didn't want to go home to his parents' house, which was chilly as the grave. There was a sour smell about it, while his grandparents' house smelled of jasmine and roses.

His grandfather Hamid Farsi was his protector until the day he died, which particularly annoyed his mother, who hated her father-in-law. She stood as far from him as possible in the photograph, with her lips firmly compressed, as if she and not Hamid had been slapped shortly before. You couldn't tell from looking at him in the picture, but one ear had been burning like fire. However, his triumph over his mother helped him to forget the pain.

On that day, when his grandmother was celebrating a round-number birthday, his mother was in a particularly bad temper. While the photographer was making preparations in the courtyard for the big family picture, she took him into one of the small, windowless rooms of the big house and slapped him because he didn't want to stand between her and his father, but insisted on sitting on his grandfather's lap.

The cook heard him screaming, opened the door, and told his mother to stop hitting him at once, or she would tell Hamid Bey, the master of the house, that she was tormenting his darling grandson.

As his mother stormed out in a huff, the cook washed his face, carefully combed his hair, and whispered encouragingly to him that Grandfather was specially fond of him. Then she gave him a caramel.

He was four or five at the time, old enough to understand what was going on.

3

As the firstborn, Hamid bore his grandfather's name, a custom that had existed since the Middle Ages. He never guessed that his name was to govern his fate.

A year after the family photograph was taken, his brother Fihmi was born. He looked very like their mother, blond and blue-eyed and well-rounded, while Hamid had inherited the darkness of his grandfather's complexion, eyes, and hair.

Fihmi was their mother's darling, and there was no room left in her heart for anyone else. When he was two, still not talking yet and hardly able to walk properly, she took him from doctor to doctor – and as you could count the real doctors in Damascus on the fingers of one hand at the time, that meant from quack to quack.

But none of them did him any good. It was to turn out later that Fihmi suffered from an incurable brain disease. He was beautiful as a doll, and their mother let his curly hair grow long, so that he looked like a pretty girl. Almost every week she paid good money to have him photographed, she adorned the pictures with olive branches, and sometimes even lit a candle in front of them and burned incense in a dish.

Nor did Siham, who was born a year after Fihmi, have any love from their mother. The girl would have been neglected if a widow from the house next door had not stepped in. She treated Siham like her own daughter. Sometimes her mother forgot to fetch her home, and she would spend the night with the widow, who had always wanted a child but never had one.

And then came the day that was to turn the life of the whole family upside down. While Hamid's mother was enjoying a cosy chat with the widow next door, he stole into his parents' bedroom, where his brother was asleep in the big bed. He wanted to play with him and

347

maybe tease him a little. Hamid shook the little boy, but he didn't want to wake up. When he pinched him rather hard, Fihmi began screaming in such a loud voice that Hamid was frightened and held his brother's mouth closed. The child wriggled and hit out. Exactly what happened then could never be explained, and Hamid did not tell anyone about it, but in any event his brother fell head first on the tiled floor, and suddenly lay perfectly still. Hamid, in the grip of terrible fear, ran to his own room and pretended to be playing marbles. Soon after that he heard his mother utter a scream that went to the marrow of his bones. She screamed so loud and long that soon the whole neighbourhood was in the house. No one bothered about Hamid.

Fihmi's death hit his parents hard. His father blamed his mother, saying it wasn't the fall that had killed the boy but all the pills prescribed by the quack doctors. "He had to suffer more than if you had entrusted him to the will of God," he shouted. The fall, he claimed, had been the work of an angel's hand to spare the child further torments.

When Hamid heard that, he thought for a moment that he had indeed felt the strong, invisible hand of an angel that day. But he kept it to himself, because he was afraid of his father's despair, and his mother was absorbed in her own grief. She had eyes for no one and nothing else, wept and wailed and blamed herself. Because she had been drinking coffee with the widow next door when Fihmi died, she cursed coffee and never touched it again until her own tragic death.

And now poor ill-starred Fihmi finally became a saint to whom his mother prayed day and night. Her grief-stricken veneration of him went so far that she had his likeness imprinted on a gold medallion that she wore on a chain around her neck, which to Hamid's father was like a ridiculous imitation of a Christian custom.

At the age of six, Siham was already so mature and tough-minded that she took no more notice of her parents or her brother. She was repelled by her mother's religious mania, which was gradually beginning to infect her father, although he had resisted it at first. After a while they were both praying, burning candles and incense, and talking of nothing but angels and demons.

Siham laughed disrespectfully when her parents' mania spiralled out of control, and although she earned many slaps, she did not keep quiet. With the years, her heart grew colder than the block of ice that was delivered every day to keep the vegetables and meat in the larder fresh.

The thin little girl grew into a tall, very feminine woman who turned all men's heads. Her parents lived in fear that their daughter would bring shame on the family, and agreed at once when a photographer of modest means asked for Siham's hand in marriage. Siham was just sixteen at the time. Years later she told Hamid that she had fixed the whole thing, and had got the photographer wrapped around her little finger at their very first meeting. "I wanted to get away from that damned tomb," she had said. Her husband, who was not particularly bright, genuinely believed that this beauty, who let him photograph her in the poses assumed by American movie divas, had fallen in love with him although she treated him like a dog. Hamid took great pains to avoid her house; he could not stand either his sister's coldness or her husband's subservience to her.

His own disaster left her cold as well. She was interested only in getting her hands on everything she could. She had been full of respect and slimy servility to him when he was at the height of his fame, and kept coming to his studio to ask for money for some tasteless object or other. And he always cursed his soft heart when she giggled boldly, triumphantly put the money in her purse, and sashayed out of his studio chewing gum.

Now that he was in prison she was too embarrassed to come and visit him, but had no scruples about laying hands on his money and his goods.

To dispel these gloomy thoughts of his sister, Hamid scrutinized his father's face in the photograph closely with a small magnifying glass.

Could anyone tell from the picture that he was in great financial straits at the time? He had broken off his training with the famous calligrapher al-Sharif a year earlier, out of sheer laziness, and set up on his own. He had no idea yet of the great difficulty of getting commissions as an independent calligrapher in Damascus without a certificate from a master of the art. Simply to show off, he rented a studio in the al-Bahssa district, the calligraphers' quarter of the city at that time, but he had to give it up again, and in addition the area suffered a flood. From then on he worked at home. The room that he grandly called his studio had one window looking out on the courtyard and another between it and the children's room, so Hamid could watch his father at work for hours on end without being noticed.

His mother might not have been there at all. She was obsessed by Fihmi. She spoke of nothing but her dead darling, and tried to get in touch with him at expensive séances with mediums who were charlatans. The house was going to rack and ruin. And since Hamid's father was a man of weak character he did not get divorced, but clung all the more to his wife as she slid toward derangement. He could hardly support the family on the few small commissions that he still received.

About a year after Fihmi's death, Hamid's mother had fallen victim to full-blown madness, and his father followed her example a little later. Hamid had to keep quiet, because if he expressed the slightest doubt his mother would be beside herself with fury, striking out and screaming. Once she hit his right ear, which bled profusely, and was deaf for weeks. Even years later his hearing in that ear was poor.

If he wondered now why he had not wept at his parents' funeral, it was not because of the ridiculous nature of the few blackened remains that he had been handed after their death in a bus accident, or because of the hypocritical words about his father spoken by the sheikh, who had been well paid to officiate. The real reason, it struck him here in prison, was that they had made him weep so often that in the end he had no tears left for them.

4

Thunder was rumbling in the distance. Hamid's temples were throbbing, as they always did when a storm was coming. The thunder and lightning moved closer, and when the storm was right above Damascus his headache died away. There was a power outage, the whole city was left in darkness, and in his cell he heard the curses of the people of Damascus in the nearby streets, shops, and cafés surrounding the Citadel.

He lit a candle to look closely at the faces in the photograph again, wondering whether what he knew about his family sprang from his imagination or from memory. He wasn't sure.

Soon the lights came back on, but only in the office building and the three privileged cells. The lower floors remained plunged in deep darkness, from which screams rose to him like the cries of the damned being tortured in Hell. One voice made his blood run cold; a man was begging for mercy. His voice was as terrified and hopeless as the lowing of a young calf just before it goes to slaughter. His cries were drowned out again and again by the laughter of the other prison inmates down there. The man begged the guards to protect him, but he called for them in vain.

His mind in turmoil, Hamid went back to the photograph on the wall and examined it once more. The bearing of his grandfather Hamid Farsi bore witness to his pride, his love of life, and his melancholy and pain. He seemed to be proud of his noble origins and his achievement. Hamid remembered that his grandfather, who was not religious, often talked about an old Sufi master called al-Hallaj, who considered that God and man were equal and their union made them an inseparable entity. The Sufi scholar had been crucified in Baghdad for his opinions in the year 922.

And he, Hamid? What guilt had he brought on himself? Had his downfall not begun when he decided to reform Arabic script?

Reforming the script and its language would be a blessing to mankind. Why did he encounter so much opposition, so much obstinacy, as if he hated Islam? He who had always lived an upright and devout life, so devout that his grandfather had once advised him not to be so hard on himself? Mankind, said his grandfather, had invented Paradise and Hell and set them up on earth.

Hamid looked around him. Wasn't he shut up in hell here, while his adulterous wife was amusing herself somewhere out in the wide world?

His grandfather had been something of a playboy, a man of many aspects. He was the most successful man in Damascus, yet at the same time bitterly disappointed in his sons, so that he had told Hamid he must grow up quickly and save his reputation or all that he had built up would be lost.

At the time Hamid wasn't even seven years old, but he decided to eat twice as much as usual so as to grow faster.

Later, Hamid discovered that his grandmother disliked him because she couldn't stand all the things that her husband enjoyed: parties, women, laughter. "If I don't care for someone," said his grandfather once, "she'll be bosom friends with him next day."

Hamid held the magnifying glass closer to his grandfather's face. He saw pain in the corners of his eyes and mouth. And indeed, he had had to bear pain as heavy as mountains. He was Persian by origin, and as a child of four had fled with his father to Damascus from Iran, where he had seen fanatics murder his sister and mother because someone had informed on his father for sympathizing with a rebel Sufi sect.

As if by a miracle, Ahmad and his son Hamid escaped to Damascus from their pursuers. At the time the city hospitably took in many refugees, including him and his father. Ahmad Farsi, a carpet merchant, was already very rich at the time. With the gold dinars he had brought with him, he bought a fine house near the Umayyad Mosque, and a large shop in the Souk al-Hamidiyyeh, and grandfather Hamid Farsi went on running the business after his father's death.

Ahmad and his son soon became Syrians. Ahmad hated religious fanatics of any and every sect worse than the Devil, "for the Devil is a prince of noble form," he said, "and it was not he who took my daughter and my wife. A fanatical neighbour strangled them both with his own hands."

He never prayed.

His son, Hamid's grandfather, only ever went to the mosque to meet one of the more religious businessmen there. He kept open house for everyone, and entertained Jews and Christians at his table as if they were members of his own family.

In the picture Grandfather wore a waistcoat and tie, and he had a gold watch in his breast pocket. You could still see the watch-chain in the picture, although it was made of fine gold thread. At the time when the photograph was taken, Hamid Farsi had been the best-known carpet merchant in the city.

When his grandfather died, his grandson Hamid walked behind the coffin feeling numb. He was eleven or twelve, and already apprenticed to Serani the great master of calligraphy. He could not grasp the fact that death was final, or understand why it was in such a hurry to take those you loved best away. It could have removed a number of unpleasant neighbours from the street instead.

Not until much later did he realize that he had buried his happiness that day. Unseen, it lay in his grandfather's coffin. Never again did he feel the tingling that refreshed his heart as soon as he set eyes on his grandfather. Of course he had achieved a great deal, and less gifted calligraphers envied him, but none of them knew that he, the famous Hamid Farsi, was an unhappy man.

After Grandfather's death, his three sons quarrelled. Hamid's father inherited nothing but five carpets. Grandfather had bequeathed the house to his middle son, and the youngest son inherited the business in the Souk al-Hamidiyyeh. Grandfather had either overlooked his firstborn son, Hamid's father, or had never forgiven him for going his own way instead of working in the family business.

Hamid's father had been a religious child. The script in the Quran and on the walls of the mosques fascinated him long before he could read it. He wanted to be a calligrapher from the first, and he finally got what he wanted, but in all he did he was never more than an assiduous imitator, and his talent was only moderate.

Hamid's mother claimed that Grandfather had disinherited her husband because he despised her and would rather have married his son to a cousin, which confirmed his mother in her opinion that her husband's family – apart from him – were all villains and malefactors.

Siham, Hamid's sister, thought their father had been disinherited because just before Grandfather's death he had forced Hamid the younger to apprentice himself to a calligrapher instead of going into the family business. He apparently said, "That useless Ahmad has broken my heart three times: he married against my will, he refuses to take over my business, and he won't let my favourite grandson go into the carpet business either. This is enough."

Whatever the true reason may have been, Hamid's father went away as good as empty-handed. However, he did not want the Farsi family to lose face, so he did not protest. He watched with satisfaction as his two brothers came to no good and finally sank into ruin. He felt particular superiority in that it was not he himself but God who had avenged him.

Bashir, the elder of Hamid's two uncles, fell sick of a muscular wasting disease soon after Grandfather's death. Soon he could no longer walk, and he cursed his wife day and night for tormenting him. Hamid's father refused to go and see his severely ill brother, although the house was less than a hundred metres away from his own street.

Uncle Bashir was a sad sight. He sat on a shabby mattress surrounded by rubbish, the house was in a bad state, and his wife was either out or on the point of going out when Hamid went to see his uncle. She was not beautiful, so she made herself up elaborately, but she had a beautiful body and always smelled of an exotic perfume called *Soir de Paris*. Once Hamid took one of the little blue bottles that stood under the big mirror in the bathroom. Whenever he smelled it, it reminded him of his aunt.

Without his parents' knowledge, he kept stealing away to see Uncle Bashir. Not out of pity, as he assured his sister, but because his uncle fascinated him. From where he sat he could follow his wife down the streets and into strange houses, where she gave herself to all sorts of different men so that she could buy pretty clothes, jewellery, and perfume.

The tales that Uncle Bashir told were gruesomely erotic. But he told them as if Hamid's aunt were not his wife but the heroine of a story. He narrated her adventures with verve, and was full of concern when she was in danger of being abducted, or a jealous lover threatened her with a knife.

"As soon as she goes out of the doorway she's the heroine of my story," said his uncle, when Hamid asked one day why he was so pleased when, in his tales, his wife made love to other men and drank wine, while he had just been reproaching her in real life for not wanting to cook him a hot meal.

"Here she's my wife, and she makes life hell for me."

He never repeated a story, and if he noticed that his words were holding Hamid spellbound he would break off in the middle. "Well, that's enough for one day. We don't want you feeling randy about your own aunt. Off you go home, and don't come back until you've forgotten her."

Of course Hamid was back next day, all innocence, to hear more about her adventures.

Now he brought his face closer to the photograph. He looked hard at Uncle Bashir, who stood behind Hamid's grandmother with his chest thrust out, beaming like a hero and laughing with bold confidence. How weak human beings were. A virus, some kind of short-circuit in the brain – and a hero becomes a picture of misery.

5

Hamid let his gaze move on to his grandmother. She was not sitting, as usual at the time, on a chair next to her husband, but by herself on a bench. A bouquet of flowers lay on the bench, as if to indicate that no one was to sit beside her. It was her birthday. She was a daughter of the grand Damascene al-Abed clan, and loved flowers and poetry. Her father Ahmad Izzat Pasha al-Abed was the best friend and adviser of the Ottoman Sultan Abdulhamid.

Grandmother venerated the Ottoman sultan and hated everything republican. As a result she did not get on with her brother, who had been appointed the sultan's ambassador to the United States but then changed sides overnight and became an ardent republican. He was the first president of the Syrian state.

Ahmad Izzat was rich as Croesus, and had a beautiful house built for him by a Spanish architect in Martyrs' Square in the city centre. Grandmother Farida had grown up there, surrounded by a large staff of servants. Like her father, she spoke four languages: Arabic, Turkish, French, and English. She was the first Muslim woman to join the Syrian Women's Literary Club, founded by Christian women from prosperous families in 1922. Under its first president, Madame Moushaka, it supported the opening of reading rooms for women in public libraries, a purely masculine domain at the time. Soon Farida was responsible for correspondence and the organization of readings. She invited women writers from all over the world to Damascus, and proudly used to show any visitor letters from the English author Agatha Christie, who had once been in Damascus herself and had appeared at Grandmother's salon.

And she was boundlessly proud of her enlightened father, whose picture in her salon dominated all the other photos. She would often stand in front of it, lost in thought, apparently carrying on a conversation with her dead father, a small, bearded man with clever little eyes and a big nose. In the picture he wore his dress uniform, and had a red fez on his head, as was usual at the time. His chest was covered from shoulders to belt with large eight-pointed stars, various crosses, and medallions hanging from coloured ribbons. To Hamid he looked funny, and far from majestic with all that metal about his person, and if he had not been afraid of his grandmother he would have told her so.

"An ape in uniform," whispered Hamid, a remark that he had carefully kept locked inside him for many years.

Grandmother Farida always gave visitors the feeling that she was granting them a short audience. She was beautiful but seemed to be under great stress. Hamid could not remember a single normal answer to his many questions. For instance, there was the time just before her death when he asked her for a drink of water. "The water in the eyes of the beloved," she replied, looking into the distance, "comes from the clouds of his heart."

Grandfather Hamid greatly respected his wife Farida, and much as he loved cheerfulness, he was faithful to her all his life and put up with all her whims. When he kissed her, once a year, she would speak to him angrily in French, rubbing the place as theatrically as if to wipe traces of grease off her face and adjusting her dress. You would have thought Grandfather had done something indecent.

When the photograph was taken, his grandmother had eyes only for Abbas, her youngest son. All the others merely had walk-on parts in a play in which she and Abbas took the leading roles. She did all she could to appear young, which could sometimes be embarrassing. The old lady often made up her face heavily, like a young woman of doubtful reputation, but there was no hiding the wrinkles left by time, and rouge unevenly applied gave Farida the look of an ageing clown. As for Abbas, he knew just how to exploit his mother's crazy devotion to him. He supported everything she did until the day she died, as if he had neither eyes nor ears.

"That strutting peacock Abbas," whispered Hamid disapprovingly, and looked through the magnifying glass at the laughing young man, the only man in the photo not wearing a suit, but an elegant white jacket with an open-necked dark shirt. His hand was on his mother's shoulder, and she was looking up at him as if he were her bridegroom.

A year before Grandfather's death, Farida ran a high temperature and suddenly died.

And not three years after Grandfather's death, Uncle Abbas had ruined the business. He took to the bottle, fled from his creditors in Damascus, and died a beggar in Beirut. He was buried there anonymously, because no one wanted to transport the body to Damascus.

Hamid's father was convinced that God was striking down all his enemies. By that time he was already under his wife's spell, and his brain was clouded by incense and superstition.

Strange, Hamid often thought, how his family was coming to ruin in the third generation. The last Farsi in Damascus would die with him, and die where? In prison. A guard told him that he too was the third generation of what had once been a distinguished clan. And where had he landed? In prison too. It was an eternal rule, said the man, coughing: the first generation builds up the family fortunes, the second consolidates them, the third destroys them.

Hamid's glance wandered over the photograph once again. What had become of his aunts? He didn't know. Grandfather had not loved any of them. They wanted no more to do with the family after the quarrel over the inheritance, and his mother's attempt to gather them around her and try to challenge the will in court came to nothing.

The photograph had been taken near the great fountain that Grandfather loved so much. Hamid remembered seeing and admiring fish there for the first time in his life.

The house was still standing. When Hamid went to see it again, three years before his own misfortunes, the inner courtyard seemed to have shrunk by comparison with his memory of it. The present owner, a friendly man, invited him in for coffee when Hamid asked if he could look at the house of his childhood days.

The owner now, a customs officer, knew nothing about the Farsi family. He had bought the house through an estate agent who didn't want to talk about the heavily debt-ridden former owners. And the house had brought him bad luck as well, he said; one of his sons had strangled himself by accident playing in the orange tree. After that he had had all the trees in the courtyard felled. Now he wanted to sell the house and move to a spacious apartment in the modern part of town, with his wife and other five children. Was Hamid interested?

No; he never wanted to see the place again.

6

The thunder was moving away from the city, going south, and rain was falling even harder. The light flickered. Hamid got up and, to be on the safe side, lit the candle again.

He examined his father's unmoving face. That was how he had looked at the funerals of Hamid's grandparents, and at Hamid's first wedding, with a face like a mask of tanned leather. He always wore that mask-like expression, whether he was doing calligraphy or tying his shoelaces.

Hamid remembered the moment when he had shown his father his first piece of calligraphy. He had been nine or ten years old, and had been practising on his own for years in secret. He forgot to play and sometimes even to eat, but he never spent a single day without practising calligraphy.

His father was beside himself with fury and envy of the beauty of the Thuluth script in which his son had written out a poem. Hamid had no idea that he had picked the most elegant and demanding script of all. Only masters of calligraphy ever used it. Not his father.

"You copied that from somewhere," said his father, dismissing it and turning to his work on a large cinema poster for an Indian feature film.

No, he said, he had written it out all by himself. They had learnt the poem in school, and he had wanted to give it to his father.

"You only copied it," said his father, putting down the brush with which he was filling in the large letters on the poster after tracing their outlines in ink first. He slowly stood up and came toward Hamid, and at that moment the boy knew that he was going to hit him. He tried to protect his head. "Liar!" shouted his father, bringing his fist down. But Hamid wasn't going to lie to escape any more blows.

"I wrote it out all by myself," he cried, begging for mercy, and then he called for his mother. She appeared briefly in the doorway, then just shook her head and went away again without a word.

"You can't have done. Even I couldn't have done it," said his father. "Where did you copy the poem from?" And he went on hitting the boy mercilessly.

One blow struck his right eye. At the time he thought he had lost it, and everything went dark.

Hamid shook his head as he stared at his father's face. "A vacuous face," he whispered. He saw himself sitting in the dark little broom cupboard, where his fear of rats made him forget his pain. No one came to comfort him, no one brought him a piece of bread or a drink of water. Only a tiny rat put its head out of a hole for a moment, squeaked, looked at him with melancholy eyes, and disappeared again.

He could hardly sleep that night, because his mother had told him that rats ate the noses and ears of children who told lies.

"I wasn't telling lies," he whispered in a soft, pleading tone, hoping that the rats would understand him.

He did not drop off to sleep until day began to dawn, and then he dreamed he was walking around in a jungle where the trees, creepers, and bushes were made of nothing but large, brightly coloured letters of different sizes. Each flower, too, was an artfully formed character. He was to tell people about that dream often later, not only because it was the harbinger of a new life for him but also because, since that day, he had disliked large coloured scripts, and loved only black ink.

However, the dream went on. Somewhere behind him someone was calling his name. Hamid turned briefly and went on. He did not notice some tree roots sticking out of the ground, and he stumbled and woke up.

His father was standing at the door of the little room.

Hamid felt his nose and ears, and was relieved to find that the rats had believed him.

"Come out of there and write that poem down again," he told him. Only later was Hamid to find out the reason for this change of heart. The rich cinema and theatre owner for whom his father was designing a series of posters had told him that some people had talents that no one could understand. The day before, at his theatre, he had listened to a boy who could sing the old songs and play the lute better than the majority of those asses who went about in black suits and called themselves musicians.

Hamid's right eye hurt terribly, and Siham laughed at his appearance. "You look like our neighbour Mahmoud," she said to needle him. Mahmoud was a drunk who often got into brawls, which always left their mark on him. Siham shouted, "Mahmoud, Mahmoud," from the inner courtyard until she got a slap in the face. She howled, and went to her bedroom.

His father gave him a piece of best-quality paper and a reed pen. "Sit down here and write," he said, when Hamid caressed the paper. The new reed pen was much better than his own, which he had cut from a reed with a kitchen knife. It lay comfortably in his hand, and its tip was sharp as a knife.

The only trouble was that his father was standing right beside him.

"Father, please will you take a couple of steps back," he said without looking up. He spoke in a formal tone that he had never used to his father before and never used again. Many years later he realized that his future as a calligrapher had been decided in that short moment. And as he spoke, he looked at the sharp cobbler's knife with which his father had trimmed the reed pen. It lay on the desk beside the inkwell. If his father beat him so badly again, he told himself, he would ram that knife into his belly.

As if stunned, his father took two steps back, and Hamid swiftly wrote out the poem. He had watched for years as his father did calligraphy, and had never understood why, in all his work, he hesitated, made mistakes, had to wipe ink spots away and remove the last remains of them with a knife. Then he would moisten the place and smooth it with a little piece of marble, let it dry and rub it smooth again.

Hamid looked at the poem one last time, narrowing his eyes. That was the only way he could assess the proportions of black and white accurately without pausing on any of the letters. He heaved a sigh of relief. The rhythm was right, the end result was even better than the first time.

"Here's the poem," he said. There was no pride in his voice, only defiance. His father froze. He could not write as beautifully as that himself. The script had something that he had always been looking for and never found. Music. The characters seemed to be following a melody.

"It was coincidence that you did that so well," he said when he had control of himself again. "Now write: 'You should honour and serve your parents.' In Diwani script if you can."

"Yes, but keep away from the desk," said Hamid, when he saw that his father was coming closer again.

"As you like, but write what I dictated."

Hamid took a new sheet of paper and dipped the pen into the silver inkwell. His father's ink had a musty smell. He was to remember that all his life, and he used to give his apprentices the job of stirring all the inkwells in his studio every day. If you don't stir ink, it goes mouldy, and then it can't be used. He always put a drop of camphor solution in his inkwell. The smell was invigorating. Other calligraphers perfumed their ink with jasmine, rose, or orange blossom.

Under his father's stern gaze he thought for a moment, then closed his eyes until he had found the form that would fit the words best: a wave of the sea.

Then he wrote out the saying, and you might have thought that the characters formed the picture of a wave breaking.

"I must show that to Master Serani," cried his father. It was the first time Hamid had heard the name of the greatest Syrian calligrapher of his time.

His father suddenly hugged him, kissed him, and wept. "God has given you all that I wanted for myself. Only he knows why, but I am proud of you. You are my son."

At last the great day came when Serani could see them. Hamid was to wear a suit for the first time. It was a light summer suit that his father had bought in one of the best clothes shops in the Souk al-Hamidiyyeh. Or rather, he had bartered for it; he did not pay money but did a deal with the shopkeeper: he would paint him a new shop sign in exchange for the suit. The old sign had been up for fifty years, and the paint was flaking here and there, so that you could hardly decipher it.

"How long will you have to work to pay it off?" Hamid asked his father on the way back.

"A week," said his father. Hamid glanced back at the shop sign, then at the suit in the big bag he was carrying, and shook his head. He resolved that when he was his father's age, he wouldn't even have to spend a day working for a new suit.

Master Serani had a large studio near the Umayyad Mosque, where he employed three journeymen, five assistants, and two errand boys.

On that day Hamid realized what an insignificant figure his father cut. He had stopped twice outside Master Serani's studio already, not daring to go in either time, and turning back. His hands were sweating. Only at the third attempt did he venture to open the door and humbly wish the master good day.

Then he stood with his head bowed in front of the great calligrapher where he sat enthroned on his large chair. Serani was rather a small man. He had carefully combed his sparse hair, and his narrow, straight-cut moustache gave a touch of melancholy to his face, but his eyes were bright and lively. No one else had such eyes, eyes in which sadness, a keen mind, and anxiety mingled. Later, Hamid was often to find this first impression confirmed. Master Serani seldom laughed, he was very religious, and courteous but reserved, and when he spoke his words were worthy of a philosopher.

Only one detail of his outer appearance seemed comic to Hamid; his right ear, which stuck out, was almost double the size of his left ear. It looked as if someone had been dragging the master round and round by his ear.

"What brings you to me, Ahmad?" asked Serani, after briefly responding to his father's greeting. His voice was civil and quiet, but designed to sound unfriendly and negative. Master Serani and his father had once been pupils of the famous calligrapher Mamdouh al-Sharif, and they had never got on well. Hamid's father, who had wanted to earn money quickly, soon left the studio. He contented himself with commercial calligraphy that relied for its effect more on a colourful appearance than on art. Serani, however, was al-Sharif's best pupil, and stayed with him for over a decade until he had learnt all the mysteries of script. By the middle of the 1920s his reputation had reached Istanbul and Cairo, from where he received major commissions for the restoration of historical artworks, mosques, and palaces.

"It's about my son Hamid," said his father.

Master Serani looked at the thin, small boy for a long time. Hamid did not fear the master's gaze, and looked back. It was like a test, and Hamid had obviously convinced Master Serani. His gaze became milder, the trace of a smile flitted over the kindly, narrow face of the famous man, who was thirty-six at the time but looked like a fifty-year-old. "Then show me what you can do, my boy," he said in a gentle voice, and he rose to his feet and took a reed pen out of a cupboard.

"Which script do you prefer?" asked Serani.

"Thuluth, master," replied Hamid quietly.

"Then write me the sentence with which everything begins," said Serani. It was the most frequently repeated sentence in the Arabic language, written out again and again by calligraphers. All prayers, books, letters, speeches, law books, and Muslim writings – whether Arabic or otherwise – began with it: *Bismillah ar-rahman ar-rahim.* In the name of Allah the all-merciful, the compassionate.

Hamid closed his eyes. Hundreds of variants of the phrase raced through his memory, but he could find none that he really liked. He did not know how long he had been thinking when he heard his father's low voice: "Get on with it, the master doesn't have all day..." But evidently the master looked at him angrily, for he fell silent again. About a year later Hamid was very glad to hear the master say that only when a calligraphic work appeared in your head as a clear image could your hand carry it out.

At last Hamid found the form to express the musical sound of the devout prayer. As if on an accordion, the words were melodically extended and compressed. He opened his eyes and began to write. He wrote each word without lifting his pen, then dipped it in the inkwell and wrote on. The ink had a pleasant lemon-blossom fragrance. Master Serani loved those little blossoms, which were distilled in Damascus.

When Hamid had finished writing, the master picked up the sheet of paper, examined it carefully, and gave it back to the boy. He was wondering how a thistle like Ahmad could have brought such a flower into the world, and was convinced yet again that God's will was unfathomable.

"Write your name in the bottom left-hand corner, and the date by Islamic reckoning, and in a year's time we'll see what progress you've made."

He was accepted into the studio. His father shed tears of joy. Hamid saw it as a mercy in every sense, for from now on his father was kinder to him. From the first day with the master, he had to learn not only calligraphic techniques and recipes for ink, but also how to cut reed pens, as well as studying geometry, symmetry and perspective, light and shade, the doctrine of harmony, and other important prerequisites of the art. Most important of all was a thorough study of the history of calligraphy, and all the styles of Arabic script. And if he had a brief break from work, the master handed him the Quran or a collected volume of Arabic poetry and said, "Here you can discover the secret fruits of the language."

7

Serani was famous among calligraphers for never praising anyone, but he was the most courteous man on earth. His studio was like a beehive. As well as the journeymen, assistants, errand boys, and customers, two or three of the sons of rich families came to him to be introduced to the art of calligraphy. It was regarded as part of a good education at the time for boys to learn not only to ride well, but also to master Arabic script perfectly.

Hamid learned eagerly, and his master was lenient over obvious mistakes, but implacable if he saw something concealed and botched up. He particularly despised scratching letters out. "If something can't be licked off it must be done again," he taught. Serani never scratched a mistake away with a sharp knife, but licked the fresh ink off the paper like lightning if he noticed a mistake. At first Hamid was shocked and disgusted to see not only his master but all the journeymen licking up ink, but practising in secret he soon learnt that it was the best and quickest way to correct mistakes. Later he found out that all calligraphers did it, and they would say, joking, that a master calligrapher could be considered really experienced only when, in the course of the years, he had licked up a whole bottle of ink.

But a calligrapher who scratched out a great deal was considered unsure of himself. Hamid's father scratched away on every calligraphic work he produced.

Master Serani never worked out the length of time that he or one of his assistants would need for a piece of calligraphy, but repeated again and again, "Let time make itself at home in your work." With an attitude like that he was never going to get rich, but his calligraphy adorned the major mosques, ministries, and palaces of the city.

Hamid never visited his master at home, and even after years did not know where he lived, although from the first Serani had treated him as his personal pupil. He was his best student, and far too good for the menial tasks performed by Ismail the errand boy.

Ismail went to their master's house several times a day, to do the shopping for Serani's wife and take a hot lunch in a *matbakiyya* to Serani at work. He told Hamid how simply their master lived.

Serani's standards were so strict that it was ten years before he would let any of his journeymen have the much-desired document certifying that he had completed his training, which calligraphers regarded as a master's diploma. Many journeymen left his studio embittered and abandoned the career; others, feeling that they would never gain their master's seal of approval, founded their own calligraphy workshops, with varying degrees of success.

Hamid received no special treatment. He had to learn everything thoroughly, and besides his own calligraphic exercises he had to help every day with the commissions being carried out by the workshop, for Serani regarded Arabic calligraphy as a communal art. He used to say that a European practised his art on his own because he thought he was a universe in himself, but that was the conceited notion of unbelievers. A man of faith knew that he was only a part of the universe, and so each of the master's assistants was to join in the work of calligraphy at present being created.

These tasks were not difficult, but they called for patience and stamina, and Hamid possessed both those virtues. Although he fell into bed exhausted in the evening, he knew that working in Master Serani's studio was Paradise compared to school. Everyone here spoke softly, and an apprentice was seldom beaten or scolded. Hamid only once earned a slap from Hassan, the oldest of the journeymen, when he upset the big jar containing freshly prepared ink. But Hassan was a decent man; his hand had gone out to strike Hamid, but he did not complain of him to their master. Once again, following the old recipe of an alchemist, he boiled a mixture of gum arabic, soot, and charred rose petals with water for hours, sieved it, thickened it until the solution was a soft dough, dissolved the whole thing, boiled it again, sieved and thickened it again, until the ink was smooth and black as night. The experienced journeyman carried out this whole performance in secret, so that their master would not hear about

Hamid's accident. When Serani asked for it three days later, the ink was ready and even perfumed with lemon blossom.

Nor did the others bear Hamid a grudge when he once ruined a reed, cutting it up too small. He had not known that the reed, which looked cheap, had been processed for three years in Persia before it came on the market. Master Serani always bought the most expensive implements for his workshop. "A calligrapher who stints on his purchases will be sorry for it later."

It was another world. And Hamid was intensely grateful when he heard about the dirt and the harsh treatment that other boys had to endure in learning a trade. He felt like a prince.

Every morning the schoolboys in his street watched him leave home, and he smiled happily because he no longer had to go the same way as they did to the inferno that was school. The teachers in elementary school, which he had hated, made their canes whistle through the air all day above the children's heads. They were giants and the pupils delivered up to their mercies were tiny.

Hamid had enjoyed hearing the history of past times and reciting the Quran, and he had been top of the class in arithmetic, but not a day went by when he wasn't hit by one of the teachers or an older boy. He had always been small and thin. One bigger boy in particular persecuted him during every break. This boy was nicknamed Hassun, goldfinch, although he was not in the least like that delicate little bird. He was a colossus who looked down on Hamid and three other small boys and took away their sandwiches every morning. If they resisted he dragged them off one by one to a dark corner, where no school supervisor could see him, and crushed their balls until they were almost fainting with pain. Every night Hamid thought of the way he was going to punch his tormentor's ugly face next day, but as soon as the bell rang for break he could already feel how his balls would hurt, and gave up his sandwich of his own accord.

For all its drawbacks, the school had a good reputation, which meant that he had never been able to convince his parents that it was hell on earth. His father was sure that it was a factory turning out the men of tomorrow.

Hamid looked at his father in the family photograph. "A factory making men," he whispered bitterly, shaking his head. He walked up and down his cell, looking briefly at the dark sky through the barred window. Why had he been shut up here behind bars? It had been a fair fight. He had only defended himself against the powerful Abbani, who always got what he wanted without caring whether he was wrecking other people's lives or not. He had not acted with malice, as the Abbani family's wretched lawyer had made out.

Karam the café proprietor had told him that the philandering Nasri Abbani was living in hiding with his wife Almaz, but that he went to the Hammam Nureddin every Tuesday evening.

When Hamid and Karam met in the Café Havana Karam warned him that Nasri was armed, and advised him to take a pistol with him. He even offered to get hold of one for him. But Hamid did not want a pistol. Pistols were not for men. Any child could shoot down a hero from a distance with a pistol. Only a knife could redeem his honour.

And then that same Karam gave evidence against him in front of the judge. He was a man of bad character. No one knew just what part he had played in the story.

He, Hamid, had faced Nasri and told him he was going to kill him for the injury to his honour, and instead of apologizing, Nasri had asked since when rats like Hamid Farsi had any honour? He wasn't even an Arab but a Persian mongrel, a refugee. As he spoke he put his hand in his jacket pocket, but the unwieldy revolver was stuck there. Should he have waited for the bastard to riddle him with bullets? No – he had gone for him with the knife.

What was so cold-blooded about that?

Hamid smiled bitterly. It had been a matter of life or death. Why was he not allowed his victory? In answer to that question, not only did the judges and lawyers shake their heads, so did Master Serani when he visited him in prison. "You fell into a trap," he said quietly. He saw a conspiracy behind the whole thing. He had heard that the café proprietor had provided Abbani with his revolver, although Abbani himself didn't want the gun and had never in his life held one. He had also been dead drunk that evening, as the autopsy showed.

Hamid's master really believed that Abbani had been innocent, and

Karam and the Pure Ones were behind it all. That wouldn't have mattered if his teacher and master had merely been wrong about Abbani. But he also asked Hamid to return the certificate making him Grand Master of the Society of the Wise so that it could choose a successor, in order to avoid a split. Half the calligraphers admired Hamid and would have left it to him to choose his successor, the other half wanted to expel him from the Society, but they were prepared to refrain from doing so if he would return the certificate of his own accord.

"Tell them I have already found a successor, and I will give the certificate to him," said Hamid.

Serani left, bowed down by grief. He turned one last time to wave, hoping that Hamid would change his mind and call to him, but he stood there like a statue, frozen and motionless.

Agitated, Hamid paced up and down his cell. He remembered that Nasri had been stinking of liquor, and was babbling rather than speaking. Karam's part in it all was an enigma. Had he lured him into a trap, or had Karam himself been blackmailed and forced to give evidence against him? Perhaps he had been paid for it? Karam had egged him on to attack Abbani because the latter had, allegedly, raped Karam's niece Almaz. Her family had been relieved when the man made up for it by marrying their pregnant daughter. And it was from this niece, Abbani's fourth wife, that Karam had heard when and where he could find the philanderer. Karam denied it all in court, and the widow made herself out a loving wife on the witness stand and praised her dead husband's fidelity until the judge sent her home. The judge himself, as Hamid's lawyer whispered to him, had often been to the brothel in Nasri's company.

"How else could I have found out where to find that strutting rooster Abbani if Karam hadn't told me?" shouted Hamid, but the judge never seemed to have heard of logic. He said he was sticking to the facts, and the facts were that Hamid, it was well known, had been looking for Nasri for months, and had asked several men and women about him. That was the most important argument for finding him guilty, and it supported a verdict of premeditated murder.

Nothing was any good.

Hamid struck the wall with his fist. "Bloody justice! She's a whore too, led around with her eyes blindfolded."

He sat on the edge of his bed, bent down, and drew out a longish, large wooden box. He opened it and took out the sheet of paper on which he had written when he first visited his master's studio.

He could still hear the words his master had said to his father back then, when they were leaving. "Ahmad, God gives the gift of talent to his elect, we cannot and need not understand why, and that gift, you may believe me, is no cause for rejoicing. It is a heavy duty. What I am saying verges on blasphemy, and I say it all the same. It is both a gift and an imposition. Go home and be glad you don't have it, and look after the boy. I don't want to hear of you mistreating him. Do we understand each other?"

His father had nodded without a word.

Master Serani did not want anyone else to supervise Hamid. He made him his personal pupil, and was very well satisfied with his progress. It was about five years before the Damascenes began speaking of "that infant prodigy of calligraphy," which Hamid thought was going too far. He couldn't hold a candle to his master, yet people said that the calligraphy of master and pupil could no longer be told apart.

His master handed over more and more important commissions to him now. At sixteen he was already in charge of the studio when Serani was away, and that was about half the time. More than one of the journeymen was as old as Hamid's father, but that made no difference to Serani. Nor did the fact that being singled out like that made Hamid unpopular. In addition, his own perfectionism made him disinclined to overlook any carelessness from journeymen working to routine, and that did not make them like him any better.

Serani knew that his assistants were unhappy about it, but it was as if he was spellbound by his pupil. "Hamid is my deputy. Anyone who doesn't do as he says can leave," he said curtly.

Hamid put the leaf with that first work of calligraphy back in the wooden box, and was about to slide it back under the bed when he saw the thick notebook with the black cover in which he had entered his thoughts and secrets. It was a journal of his work and a diary combined, and on the advice of his master he had not given it any title, to avoid arousing too much curiosity.

At the time, Serani had bought him the large, thick notebook from the famous bookbinder Salim Baklan, whose workshop provided artistic covers for the most expensive printed copies of the Quran. "A book bound by Baklan is indestructible," said Serani.

The binding had been broken when the pages were wrenched apart by force. When it happened his assistant Samad had laid the blame on the errand boy Salman, who had come to him through Karam.

Hamid shook his head to dispel his thoughts about the dubious motives of the café proprietor, and returned to the notebook. He had noted down the subjects of his exercises and his feelings every evening. Later, he confided to his diary his ideas about script and his secret plans.

He could write frankly because he had a special drawer in a large cupboard in the studio, and kept the key to it on a chain around his neck. But even if he sometimes left the drawer unlocked, no one ever touched anything in there.

He couldn't keep anything at home, because nothing escaped his sister Siham, and no lock could withstand her curiosity for more than three days.

When he set up independently and had his own studio, he kept the notebook in the cupboard behind his desk. It was his most precious possession. It not only contained all his ideas, thoughts, and plans for a reform of calligraphy, but also the names and opinions of his friends in the Secret Society of the Wise. He kept it secure and unobtrusive among many other notebooks and works on ornamentation and calligraphy, for this cupboard was always kept locked because it also contained gold leaf and expensive writing instruments.

None of his assistants had ever touched the cupboard. He was sure of that. For a while he left secret marks that would have shown him if anyone had opened its door. But apart from him, no one seemed interested in what it held.

Only that little Salman was noticeably curious. He absorbed every remark about calligraphy and busily made notes on scraps of paper, but otherwise his talents were only moderate. Later, after suspicion had fallen on him and he had lost his job in the studio, he was said to have gone to work in a restaurant. If he had been after the secrets of calligraphy, he would not have become a restaurant chef.

The others in the studio were good fellows, and three of them even good craftsmen, but none of them really deserved to be called a calligrapher.

"The pen is the tongue of the hand." He quietly read aloud the saying that Master Serani, at his request, had written on the first page of the notebook.

Calligraphy, he himself had enthusiastically written, is the art of using black to bring pure joy to the desert of white paper. It gives it form and value.

He leafed through a few pages of technical comments on the correct proportions of the characters, then came upon an episode that had impressed him at the time. He had recorded it word for word.

Master Serani had told him: "The Prophet set great store by script, and the Quran, the word of God, is written in it. The first words heard by the Prophet Muhammad were:

Read in the name of the Lord who made thee,
who created mankind out of liquid blood,
read, the Lord is generous,
He taught us to use a pen for writing,
He instructed man
in what
he did not know before.

After the victory of the battle of Badir the Prophet offered every prisoner freedom if he could teach ten Muslims to read and write."

Hamid leafed through a few pages about the making and care of writing instruments. He remembered this time of his life very well. He had been studying about a year when he showed his master a saying that he had written out the night before as ordered by a customer. Serani praised his work. An older colleague was envious, and made poisonous remarks all morning, until Serani took him aside and told him to stop. Hamid was on the other side of a screen and had heard it all.

Sitting on his bed in the cell with the notebook in his hands, he remembered Serani's words as well as if he had only just spoken them. "You are hard-working, but he is gifted. Just as bees do not know who led them to create the perfect hexagons of their honeycombs, Hamid does not know who makes his pen follow those invisible lines and shapes. So do not be envious; there's nothing he can do about it."

At the time, Hamid had had an idea. He was lying in bed early in the morning. As always, he was left to his own devices, for his father and mother took no notice of him in those days. His mother was always awake at dawn, but she never once woke him. His father snored in bed until ten. So Hamid learned to get up early and fetch warm fresh bread from the bakery, to make his favourite flatbreads with thyme and olive oil. He ate one in the kitchen, and wrapped the other in a paper bag for later. He washed thoroughly, perfumed himself with a drop of lemon-blossom oil, and set off for his master's studio, whistling. He was looking forward to the work, and to not having to go home until evening.

He told Master Serani his idea, and when Serani, admiring it, nodded his head, Hamid wrote down the sentence: "The letters are dancing, and the lines become music for the eye."

Master Serani had corrected only one word. "Not for the eye, music for the soul." Both then and later Hamid thought that too high-flown, so he did not change it in his notebook.

He smiled.

He had covered three pages with reflections on the degree of difficulty of the various letters. For him, the letter H was difficult to control. However, Master Serani said that anyone who could write an elegant U need fear no other letter. The journeyman Hassan, he had said in the notebook, thought that R gave him the most trouble, because it only looked easy to write, yet its elegance determined the form of an entire word.

Poor Hassan, thought Hamid now, he had died when a horse ran wild and kicked him on the temple in his parents' stable. He leafed quickly on until he found the photograph that he had stuck in the middle of one page: Master Serani and his assistants on an outing to picnic beside the river Barada. Hassan was holding his *shashlik* skewer up to the photographer like a sword. A pity, he had been a good soul, and did not deserve to die like that in a stable.

Hamid turned back to his pages on the degrees of difficulty. A couple of pages later he had noted down an argument between Serani and two of his colleagues. Hamid had been going to withdraw to the back rooms of the workshop after the errand boy had made coffee for the guests, but the master insisted that his best pupil should stay to hear the discussion. So he sat in a corner of the large room and listened to their debate.

His entry, however, showed that his mind had not been entirely on the argument. Only a few scraps of the conversation, and some striking sayings, had been caught in the coarse sieve of his attention. They were loosely set down side by side like pebbles. In those days Hamid had been in love with a pretty Christian girl. She worked as a maid-servant in a big house, halfway between his home and his master's studio. She was five or six years older than Hamid, and very courageous. He had kissed her a couple of times, and she always waited at her window for him to pass by. However, a week before the dispute mentioned in the notebook, she had suddenly disappeared. All he knew about her was her name: Rosa.

He had written, "The Quran, after all, is written in Arabic," and after it in brackets: Sheikh Mustafa.

"The Quran was revealed in Mecca and Medina, recorded in Baghdad, recited in Egypt, but written most beautifully of all in Istanbul," had said Master Serani.

No one could have understood the splintered ideas he had noted down while he was lost in the ocean of his grief for Rosa. He had written them down at the time just in case his master asked about them later, but he never did.

Only later did he find out for himself that, although the Arabs and the Persians had contributed to creating script, it was the Ottomans who had done most for Arabic calligraphy. Ottoman calligraphers developed script to artistic perfection. They also invented several new styles such as Diwani, Diwani gali, Tughra, Ruq'a, and Sunbuli.

In the middle of an otherwise blank page, Hamid found the words, underlined in red: "I am going to invent a new style." He later proudly showed this remark to his master, who only shook his head. "These are the high-spirited leaps of a foal. Learn to breathe properly as you write first. You get so excited that you pant like a puppy in the blazing sun," he said kindly.

"Proximity sometimes magnifies incidentals and makes us overlook what is essential," he had written a few pages further on, quoting the unfortunate journeyman Hassan, "so no wonder that prophets, writers, painters, musicians, and calligraphers have suffered most from their surroundings."

How right the poor man was. Hassan must have known more than he showed. An unpretentious farmer's son with a razor-sharp mind, and unlucky. He had remained a bachelor because he limped; he had broken his right leg as a child, and someone had botched the job of setting it in plaster so that the bone would knit properly.

Hamid had been just twelve when he was to help Hassan with a complicated ornament one day. That morning they heard a loud argument between two of their master's friends about Arabic script. Serani himself remained neutral, agreeing politely now with one, now with the other, and they could tell from his voice and his remarks that he would have liked to cut the debate short.

Hassan took the side of the guest who was against regarding the language and its characters as sacred in themselves. "You can use the same characters to write both the best and the worst words," he said. "And Arabic characters can't have been invented by God. They're full of drawbacks."

Hamid had written that on a blank page as well, underlining it in red, as if he had already guessed that it was the seed of a doubt that would change his life.

8

Hamid had read many books about various scripts, describing and listing all the sounds and words that could be only poorly expressed in Arabic script, collecting examples of the weaknesses of the script and the language, and containing proposals put forward over many centuries by reformers.

He looked at a title that he had written out carefully in the Naskhi style: "Reform of Arabic script. A treatise by the slave of God Hamid Farsi." He had learnt the description "slave of God" from his master at the time, when he was sixteen, and he used it until he set up independently and decided that it was hypocritical modesty.

Now he reread the plans that he had formulated several times over a period of two years, writing them down on loose sheets of paper before transferring them to the notebook, and was proud of their fresh approach and their precision. He had set out his proposals for reform on fifty pages, in tiny but legible script, establishing the fundamental principles of three new styles.

Arabic script had developed no further for over a thousand years, and calligraphy had not changed in a hundred and fifty years. Only a few improvements of his own master had been recognized, and a horrible Egyptian script whose inventor, Muhammad Mahfouz, had designed it for King Fouad I in a spirit of pure opportunism. Emulating the Europeans, he proposed to introduce capital letters, and he also wanted to reshape each letter so that it represented a crown. As a result he called his laboured invention Crown style. He thought that hardly anyone would notice this retrograde step.

In his notebook, Hamid had set out two great weaknesses of Arabic script that only a calligrapher could solve: "Arabic characters," he wrote, "are written in four different ways, depending on whether they are at the beginning, in the middle or at the end of a word, or stand on their own." That is to say, a student must learn over a hundred different forms of letters. He went on, "Many Arabic characters resemble each other, and are distinguishable only through the addition of one, two, or three dots. A new script should be devised in which every letter is written in only one way and cannot be confused with any other," he noted, arrogant and radical as all revolutionaries are.

In the course of his work he recognized the third weakness of Arabic script. "Some letters are superfluous, others are lacking." He called his proposals: "The Effective Alphabet."

He experimented for countless days and nights, learning many alphabets. By now he was nineteen, and he was waiting for an opportunity to put his proposals for reform to his master. He felt sure of himself, yet he could already see Serani's sceptical expression. He was very conservative, and it was difficult to win his approval for any innovations. He firmly rejected the idea of separating the letters in writing, which was coming into fashion just then. It was nothing but a cheap attempt to curry favour with Europeans, he said, calligraphy for tourists who couldn't read Arabic, in fact calligraphy for the illiterate.

"No, Arabic art consists of giving form to entire words, not to separate letters. If a Frenchman incorporates a Chinese word in a surrealist picture, do we call it Chinese calligraphy?" he asked ironically.

There were many calligraphers, and Hamid despised them, who provided pictures of exactly that kind for oil sheikhs, the majority of whom were now illiterate. Huge oil paintings with a jumble of letters in the shape of deserts and oases, or camels and caravans, compositions that spared the sheikhs any implied reproof. They would hang these representational paintings in their own rooms, which was forbidden by Islam.

Master Serani rejected not only this bad habit but also imitation of the Japanese and large-scale calligraphy with brushes, also coming into fashion at the time.

"As if a donkey had dipped his tail in ink and wiped it over the paper," he said scornfully when his journeyman Hassan showed him the work of a colleague executed in this way.

So Hamid prepared himself for a difficult confrontation with his master. Serani had always been the father figure Hamid dreamed of, and he did not want to keep the subject that entirely obsessed his heart and mind secret from him any longer. He would accept a disagreement, perhaps even dismissal.

But it did not turn out that way.

At this phase, Hamid felt like a tent pitched in a storm. He reacted impatiently and with irritation to the apprentices' jokes and mistakes. One night he could not sleep, and his restlessness drove him out of bed. He decided to go to the studio. He was the only one, apart from Master Serani himself, who had a key to it.

At this hour the first signs of dawn were already tentatively appearing in the dark streets. When he saw light in the studio in the distance, he was surprised, and feared one of the journeymen might have left the light on all night.

To his great surprise, he saw Master Serani sitting at his desk, reading his, Hamid's, notebook.

"You have been very bold and reaped a good harvest. I have read through your proposals for improvements twice. The book was on my desk. I wouldn't leave it lying around if I were you. It contains jewels for connoisseurs, and they are a knife in the hand of the ignorant," he said.

Hamid suddenly felt cold. He poured himself some of the hot tea that his master had just made, and sat down on a small chair opposite him.

"As if an angel's hand had led you to me," said Serani, looking thoughtfully at Hamid. "It's incredible; I woke after two hours of sleep and felt that I had to come here. Sometimes such a feeling is a premonition of disaster. I come in and see your notebook lying on my desk. I open it, and what do I read? Exactly what I myself wrote in secret twenty years ago. I read your fifty pages twice, and compared them with what I said. Here, this is my notebook; you're welcome to read it, for you are no longer my pupil but my young colleague," he said, taking a large but rather thinner notebook out of his desk drawer. Every page was hand-ruled and carefully covered with writing. Hamid leafed through it, but he was so excited that he could hardly read anything.

"Our notebooks are identical in both their good and their bad points. I find exactly the same mistakes as I made myself in your work as well."

"What kind of mistakes?" asked Hamid, his throat dry.

"Wishing to reduce the alphabet – what you call an 'effective alphabet' is what I called just 'an alphabet.' You want to prune away twelve characters; I would have removed fourteen. Today I think – perhaps it's my advancing age speaking – that would not be an improvement after all, but an act of destruction."

"Destruction?" Hamid was wide awake now. "And what about all the duplications of some letters, and the superfluous letter LA, made of two single letters that already occur in the alphabet written together as a single sign?"

"I don't want to discourage you. The Prophet added the letter LA to the alphabet, and so it will stay until the end of the world. If you will take my advice, do not reject a single letter, because if you do the whole Islamic world will be against you, for those letters are in the Quran. The Arabic language has only twenty-nine letters, and the more of them you destroy, the more uncertain and imprecise the language itself will be. But there is nothing for you to be ashamed of. That was the third proposition in my own notebook. At the time I was even more radical than you. I wagered that the Arabic language could be reproduced perfectly with only fifteen letters. Today I can only laugh at that. Do you know any English?"

Hamid shook his head. The only European language he had learnt at school was a little French.

"English has many letters that appear in a written word but are not pronounced; others disappear from the mouth as soon as two of them are contained in a word, like *gh* in *night* and *light*. Delightful, don't you think? Two letters sitting quietly side by side and watching the others. Others again sometimes wear the mask of other letters, either singly or in pairs. O, for instance, often likes to camouflage itself as U. Incidentally, a friend of mine counted over seventy different ways of writing letters that give you an I in English. And the I itself is not short of different forms. There are also letters like C and H that, once they merge, produce a new letter that is not in the English alphabet. That's riches. The clever English never throw a letter away, but sometimes combine several letters to make a new one. They keep everything, so that they can read texts of the past or the future. A wish to do away with letters was also one of the sins of my youth…"

Serani smiled, embarrassed, and flapped his hand as if driving away his mistakes like troublesome flies. He poured more tea.

"The French disguise the three letters A, U, and X, when they meet, as the letter O," said Hamid, searching his scanty knowledge to keep up.

Serani leafed through Hamid's notebook for a long time, drank his tea, and said nothing, as if he had not heard him.

"Exactly. One never removes a letter," he said at last, as if he had been looking for a conclusive argument all this time, "when the millennia have shaped it, but the French and English don't even have a Quran, and the Quran, as long as you call yourself a Muslim, is the word of God. So be careful, my boy, because at this point matters become dangerous. They did then, they do now. One must be on the watch for fanatics. A colleague of mine paid with his life for wanting to imitate the Turks and suggesting abolishing Arabic characters and introducing the Roman alphabet. He wouldn't listen to me." A look of grief came into Serani's face. "No," he said quietly, "such a thing would have to be prepared for in secret over a long period, one would have to win over more and more scholars who could later defend a cautious reform publicly with all the force of their authority. Nothing can be done without them."

"But they will never agree to such a revolution," replied Hamid.

"Who's talking about a revolution? Nothing will be overturned. It's just that the alphabet will be extended so that Arabic becomes the most elegant and efficient language in the world. That's why I think well of your second proposal: you write that our alphabet needs four – I myself would say six – new letters so that it can give perfect expression to Turkish, Persian, Japanese, Chinese, and all the languages written in the Roman alphabet. No one will touch the Quran and its characters, but a modern script becomes increasingly important for our modern way of life. You are on the right road there. And it will be a good idea to devise new forms for letters so that they no longer cause confusion, but that can't be done in a day. It will take a century and great care for the best shape of the letters to crystallize."

"And suppose scholars say that goes against Islam because the Arabic language is sacred and can contain no more letters than the Quran?"

"They'll say that anyway, but you can silence them by reminding them that Arabic has already been reformed two or three times. The characters used to write out the first copies of the Quran looked different, had no dots, and were reformed several times in the course of a thousand years before they assumed the shape they take today. You can also point out that Persian is written in an extended Arabic alphabet of thirty-two letters, and ask if that has made the Persians less devout and worse Muslims."

Serani rose and went to the window. He watched the street sweepers doing their work at this early hour closely for a while. "Perhaps what I am about to say will offend you, so promise me to say nothing for a day before you answer me. I know how much trouble you take, and you are closer to me than my only son, who doesn't want to know anything about calligraphy. But you have something that I never had. Your divine talent has made you proud, and pride leads to arrogance. Calligraphy, however, is an art of modesty. Only a man with a humble heart can open the last gates of its mysteries. Arrogance is a sly quality; you don't notice its influence, but it will lead you into blind alleys."

Hamid caught his breath. He was near tears. Suddenly he felt Serani's small hand on his shoulder. He started, because he had not heard his master's footsteps.

"Take this notebook of mine and read it today. You are excused from work. Read it. You will see that I have spent over twenty years trying to devise just one new style. I have not succeeded, not because I have no imagination, but because the old Ottomans left hardly anything for us to do. And what are you about? You write that you have devised seven new styles and three of them are fully developed. But let us look at them closely. The style that you call Morgana looks like a drunken version of Thuluth. Your Pyramid style forcibly reduces all the letters to triangular shape. Fantasia has no structure, and what you call Modern I resembles a rope cut into pieces. There is no internal music to the characters. Salim style is inelegant. And finally, the style to which, in friendship to me, you have given my name. It looks strange to me. A calligrapher need **not** devise so much novelty. If you concentrate on a single innovation, a single style, you will realize how difficult genuine invention is. And if it is successful, it immortalizes you."

Hamid had begun weeping quietly. His tears were because he was angry with himself and disappointed in his master. There was so much that he wanted to say, but he held his tongue all day. After that he could not help seeing that his master was right, and was grateful to him for advising a day's silence, for he would have lost his mentor Serani forever if he had told him what he thought at once.

A month later, just as Hamid was about to leave work, Serani kept him back. He closed the studio, made tea, and sat down.

He said nothing for a long time.

"From the very first moment," he said at last, "as I have told you before, you were like the son I always wanted. Nine years ago you came to me, today you are head of the workshop and my right-hand man, and even more. The other journeymen are good fellows and industrious assistants, but the fire has not caught their hearts. Today I would like to give you the title of a master. It is the custom for the man chosen for that distinction to write out his own certificate, as his last piece of work for his own master, so to speak. The only prescribed part of it is this official text, which should be roughly in the middle. Otherwise you are free to design it and choose its wording as you will. You can quote the maxims of the Prophet, or passages from the Quran, or words of wisdom that are important to you, and incorporate them in the whole certificate. Look at the collection of certificates in this volume before you design your own."

Serani gave him a small piece of paper, which said that Master Serani gave him, Hamid Farsi, this certificate because he had shown proof of all the requisite qualities for a master of calligraphy. "Prepare the certificate at your leisure, and bring it to me for my signature at the beginning of next month. And as soon as I have signed it, take it home with you. You are still very young, and the envy of the others could injure you. Let it be a secret between us."

At that moment Hamid was the happiest man on earth. He took his master's hand and kissed it.

"For heaven's sake," said Serani, half joking but also slightly shocked. "What's come over you? Even as a little boy you never kissed my hand."

"Because I was too stupid to understand who you are," said Hamid, suddenly shedding tears of joy.

When he had finished the certificate a month later he brought it to the studio wrapped in a large scarf, and hid it in his drawer until all the other assistants had gone home.

"Today you can make the tea," said Serani, and he went on working until Hamid brought him the fragrant Ceylon tea.

Then he examined the certificate with visible satisfaction. "Good heavens, can you design one for me as well?" he joked.

"Yours is heavenly. This is only dust," replied Hamid.

"I was always a creature of the earth, so I like dust. Curiously enough, all the sayings you have chosen are to do with change. In my own time, as you can read on my own certificate, I wrote only of thanks and more thanks. I was rather naïve at the time, and could think of nothing but my gratitude."

Serani signed the certificate with the words: "Salem Serani, the poor slave of God, hereby confers and confirms the title of Master."

"Now," he said, "sit down with me today as a master calligrapher for the first time. There is something very important with which I must burden you."

And his master began telling him about the Secret Society of the Wise. About the heaven of ignorance, the purgatory of semi-wisdom, and the hell of wisdom.

A week later he was solemnly admitted to the Society.

He leafed through his notebook, and found the pages that, like all members of the Society, he had written in the secret Siyakat script.

Hamid remembered the first meetings he had attended. He was fascinated by the encyclopaedic knowledge of the men he met, but they seemed to him rather apathetic, and the majority were elderly. And then those emotional sayings: "This world is hell for the wise, purgatory for the semi-wise, and Paradise only for the ignorant." It was apparently something said by Ibn Muqla. Here in the Council of the Wise, the committee of the Society, he noticed nothing reminiscent of hell. All the masters were well-to-do, many of them married to younger wives, and they cast respectably rounded shadows of their well-nourished existence.

He had understood why there was a vow of silence, for since the founding of the Society deadly danger had been lying in wait for all its members, and they must do all they could to protect themselves from being given away.

Their greeting consisted of a code to assist them in the recognition of foreign calligraphers. This was a ritual from the past, and had no significance in modern life, because the branches of the Society were confined to a single country in each instance, and the number of members was limited. They all knew each other, had contact with members in other cities, and always provided letters of recommendation for visiting foreign calligraphers.

When Hamid learned about the secret Siyakat script developed by calligraphers for the Ottoman sultan, he was so fascinated that he wrote pages in his diary in it. Under the sultans, Siyakat looked like a sequence of Arabic shorthand characters, and it was very complicated for the world of its time. All the sultan's reports were recorded in this script to shield them from the eyes of the curious, but every gifted calligrapher could lift the veil of secrecy.

The Council of the Wise later agreed to Hamid's suggestion of abandoning Siyakat, because the secret script made communication between friends more difficult, but did not prevent it from being deciphered by experienced potential enemies.

At the time he felt buoyed up by a wave of enthusiasm, and he realized that he was in a position to make many changes. But soon he felt a cold wind blowing. His proposal to exploit the general sense that the country was making a new beginning to make radical reform of the script a subject of public discussion was brusquely rejected. It was too early, said the others, it would endanger the Society.

Later, when the minister of culture did put through some radical reforms, the members of the Secret Society were jubilant, but no one recalled that he, Hamid Farsi, had made these suggestions long before the minister. Nor did any of them say a word of apology to him.

Now he read what he had angrily written at the time. "The Arab clan system allows no one to admit mistakes, yet civilization is no more than the sum of all mistakes that have been corrected."

He shook his head. "Theirs was not the counsel of the wise, but of simple shepherds," he whispered. And they opposed the next steps, so that apart from the founding of the School of Calligraphy not one decision had been taken in favour of his ideas within a ten-year period.

"Envious, every last one of them," he said, closing the thick notebook.

And in the Society they only smiled pityingly at the two styles of calligraphy that he had developed over the years. Hamid defended his innovations, wrote a round letter to all the members and introduced his two new styles. Damascene Script, very elegant, was open but had much to do with the geometry of the circle. Young Script was very slender, smooth, free of all flourishes. It moved with verve, keen and full of energy. It preferred slanting to vertical lines. He asked for criticism, hoping for encouragement and praise, but he received not a single answer to his letter.

That was when his isolation had begun to taste bitter.

9

Hamid closed the notebook, put it back in the box, and pushed the box under his bed again. He stood up, went to the opposite wall and let his gaze travel over the work of calligraphy hanging there. The wording, "God is beautiful and loves beauty," was traced in gold leaf in Thuluth script on a dark blue background, and it dated from the year 1267. The picture was no larger than the palm of his hand, but it was unique and of incalculable value. He had sent, unobtrusively, for this jewel of calligraphy to be brought with seven other calligraphic works from his studio to the prison. No one knew that the small picture concealed a secret: a document certifying his membership of the Secret Society of the Wise and his appointment as Grand Master two years later. The document had been given to him by his master in a secret ceremony of the Society. In his own time, Serani had received the document from his master al-Sharif, and he in turn from his own master Siba'i. The list of all holders was hidden in the frame of the picture; it went back to the year 1267 and was evidence of the association's existence right back to Grand Master Yaqout al-Mustasimi. He had founded the Secret Society of Calligraphers, and in the document he described himself as a humble pupil of the master of all masters, Ibn Muqla.

In the twentieth century, the Secret Society still aimed to remain true to the ideas of its founder. At the time he had sent out twelve of his best students and loyal supporters to twelve regions of what had then been the great Arab empire, reaching from China to Spain. The seat of the Master of all Masters had been in Baghdad at the time, but was later moved to Istanbul, where it remained for four hundred years. After the collapse of the Ottoman empire, and the decision of the founder of the modern Republic of Turkey, Mustafa Kemal Atatürk, to write Turkish in the Roman alphabet after 1928, a bitter quarrel flared up between the masters in Damascus, Baghdad, and Cairo, all of whom wanted the seat of the Society to be in their cities. The matter remained undecided for another half a century, but the principles of the organization were still the same. In each of the Arab countries, depending on its size, there was a Grand Master in the Council of the Wise and three, six, or twelve other masters, who headed small circles of calligraphers known as initiates. Each of the initiates must exert his influence over a circle of other persons known in the Society as "the semi-wise."

The business of the Society was to work not publicly, but in secret through the circle of initiates and the semi-wise to root out weaknesses of the Arabic language and its script, so that one day it would truly deserve to be called divine. Many masters had lost their lives through treachery. The word "Martyr" stood beside their names.

Hamid remembered the moment when he had knelt before his master. Serani stood in front of him, and placed his left hand on his head. He laid the forefinger of his right hand vertically on Hamid's lips. "I am your master and protector, and I command you to repeat in your heart that you will spend your life in the service of script, and never give away the secret."

In a daze, Hamid had nodded.

He and his master had to say a prayer of thanks together, and then Master Serani led him to a table on which a small loaf and a dish of salt stood. The Grand Master shared bread and salt with him. Only now did he bring out the small gold ring and put it on the ring finger of Hamid's left hand, saying softly, "With this ring I bind your heart to our aim, given to us by the great master Ibn Muqla." After that Serani turned to the Council of the Wise and took his leave of them, promising to pledge himself always to the Society and to stand by the new Grand Master.

The twelve masters came up to Hamid, kissed the ring and embraced him, each whispering as he did so, "My Grand Master."

A few days later Serani told him, when all the others had left the studio, "I am old and tired, and glad that I have found you for the Society. It is my greatest achievement. I had the same fire in my heart as you when I was young, but increasingly I feel the ashes of the years stifling its embers. I have not much to my credit; perhaps most important were a few small improvements to Taalik style, but in thirty years I have doubled the circle of the initiates in this country, and trebled the circle of the semi-wise. Now it is for you to educate, encourage, and instruct these two grades between the Masters and the great mass of the ignorant, sending out initiates again and again so that they can enlighten the people and, with them, defend the cause of Arabic script against the sons of darkness who call themselves the Pure Ones.

"You are the Grand Master now. God has given you a wealth of talent for that position. Your office pledges you, young as you are, to love and protect the twelve masters as if they were your own children. You must always maintain equilibrium between the security of silence and the necessity of disturbance. You must not intervene when the semi-wise enlighten the ignorant and win one or another of them over to membership of their own circle. For they do not know what might harm the Society, and can easily be excluded again if they offend against our principles. But it is you who must judge if a semi-wise man may be elevated to the rank of initiate or not. And you must be even more careful in choosing a successor in the Council of the Wise for a member whom death has taken away. Do not let a master's fame dazzle you as you make your decision. You are the head of the Society, and ultimately you will administer the oath of loyalty to the initiates and masters, thus putting yourself in danger.

"For another five years, you can consult me. I know all the masters and every initiate personally. After that you will know them for yourself.

"I am tired. I have noticed it for some time, but my vanity stood in the way of admitting it. Seeing you, however, I know what fire and passion mean. So I hand on the banner willingly to you. From now on, I am only a toothless old lion."

Serani was not even fifty yet, but he did look battle-weary.

They sat together for a long time that night. "From tomorrow morning," said Master Serani, smiling, as they parted, "you must begin looking for a master pupil of your own. You can never start too soon. It took me twenty years to find you. And do you know what was the crucial factor? Your questions, your doubts. No one can learn such questions as you asked me. The characters were and are accessible to all students, but only you asked questions about their content. You had no answers, but answers are never more important than questions," he said forcefully. "Do not look among your pupils for the one whom you like best and who is the most agreeable company, but for the one who is the absolute master. Never mind how much you may dislike him, you're not going to marry him, just confirm his acceptance into our Society."

"Master, how am I to know who will be the best successor to me if several men not only have fire in their hearts, but are equally good at calligraphy?" Hamid asked.

"He will be the one you begin to envy, the one you think secretly is better than you," said Serani with a kindly smile.

"You mean that I am... no, no." Hamid dared not think that sentence out to its end.

"Yes, yes, you are better than me," said Serani, with a kindly smile. "Where likeability is concerned, my journeyman Mahmoud comes out a hundred times ahead, Hassan ten times ahead, but you know them. Hassan comes to grief with Diwani style, Mahmoud with Thuluth style, and neither of them can stand geometry. It is as if a mathematician didn't like algebra," he added. "And what about you? You write characters following the invisible diameter of a circle to the nearest millimetre. I once gave both Mahmoud and Hassan a ruler and asked them to show me a single letter in a poem written by you in Diwani script that deviated by more than a millimetre from its line. They knew as well as I that you do not use a ruler, and do not trace circles in pencil before you can fit the letters into them. They came back to me an hour later with pale faces, their eyes cast down."

The list of calligraphers hidden behind the picture contained the names of Arab, Persian, and from the sixteenth century, above all, Ottoman masters who had brought Arabic calligraphy to its finest flowering. Hamid was only the third Syrian master since the fall of the Ottoman empire.

He had spent a decade looking for a successor, but none of his colleagues or his own journeymen was more than an average calligrapher.

But only a month before his wife ran away, an old master drew his attention to Ali Barakeh, an extraordinary calligrapher from Aleppo. His hand was bold and his script full of virtuoso music. Hamid sent for photographs of his calligraphy, and on close examination of them he felt sure that Ali Barakeh would be the man to follow him, if he had the heart of a master to match his technical achievement in script.

When, after the foundation of the School, the Society was in a state of crisis, Ali Barakeh stood behind him like a rock. His decision to make the young calligrapher his successor was made.

The tragic events of his life, however, had prevented him from telling Barakeh in good time. In prison, Hamid waited until, early in January, the governor expressed a wish for a large-scale calligraphic work. It was to be given to a large new mosque in Saudi Arabia in the summer as a present from the al-Azm family. The prison governor offered him the large joinery workshop as a studio for work on the calligraphic saying, which would be eight metres long. The fine, durable cedar wood on which the saying was to be inscribed had been brought in from Lebanon. Three master joiners, under Hamid's supervision, had worked it to a huge surface, smooth as a mirror, with an elaborately carved frame.

Hamid now wished he had the assistance of that calligrapher from Aleppo, who had done outstanding work in many of the mosques of his native city, and he showed a few photographs of it to the governor. Governor al-Azm was enthusiastic.

So Hamid wrote Master Barakeh a letter with a letterhead in the form of a complex ornament that only a master could read. The letter itself contained the courteous official invitation. However, the ornamentation concealed the secret message telling Barakeh that Hamid Farsi wanted to give him the document that would make him Grand Master of the Secret Society of Calligraphers.

Ali Barakeh sent the prison governor a friendly letter by return of post, saying he would feel honoured to provide a religious maxim for the mosque in the holy land of Islam. Such was the honour that he would ask no fee, only a modest place to spend the night and a single meal a day while he was working on it.

He hoped the governor would understand, he wrote, that he could not begin until April, for the mosque in Aleppo on which he was working was to be consecrated at the end of March in the presence of the President of Syria. At present he was working twelve to fourteen hours a day so that the calligraphy would be ready in time. However, he would devote the month of April to this wonderful commission from the Damascus prison.

The governor was delighted. He sent for Hamid to come to his office, and showed him the letter. In the ornamentation that surrounded it like a decorative border, and could be deciphered by no ordinary mortal, the master from Aleppo wrote that he would feel it an honour to receive the greatest prize of his life, although by comparison with him, Grand Master Hamid, he was a mere dilettante.

When Hamid was sure that his successor would come to Damascus, he sent the guard to his sister Siham telling her to come and visit him at once. Siham was more than a little surprised to find a Hamid who seemed to be powerful even behind prison bars.

Hamid made his demand at once. "If I have calculated correctly, you have laid hands on a million lira of my property. Bring me fifty thousand here, and I will forgive you everything. And don't sell my house, because I am going to live in it when I get out of here. You can let it, I'm happy with that, but bring me the money. I need it for a noble purpose. If I do not have it within a week, I shall instruct my lawyers to recover everything you have taken from me. And remember, I shall be out quite soon. The governor says I shall be pardoned after serving seven years. Do you hear that? And what are seven years? Bring me fifty thousand lira and I will consider that we are quits."

"I'll do my best," Siham said evasively at last, and she left.

Ten days later the governor summoned Hamid to his office again. He gave him a large bag made of bamboo and reeds.

Hamid rewarded the guard, and when he was alone again slit open the bottom of the bag and smiled. "That daughter of the devil," he said, laughing. Siham had sent him the money, but only forty thousand lira. However, even that was a fortune at the time.

He planned for his successor Ali Barakeh to set up a secret punishment squad to oppose the Pure Ones, the worst enemies of the Society, fighting back against them even to the death. "It is not right for us to go on waiting like obedient sheep for them to mow us down. They must learn that for every death in our ranks, there will be one in theirs," he whispered.

Early in April 1958, Ali Barakeh was to arrive in Damascus. Hamid had already entered his name and year of birth, 1929, on the list hidden in the picture frame in February. Now he was sure that he would at least save his secret and be able to realize some of his dreams through that capable calligrapher.

But it was not to turn out as he intended.

10

Governor al-Azm sent a guard to bring Hamid to him. He was forth-coming as always, just like all those upper middle-class men whom Hamid could never puzzle out. They smiled all the time like Chinese, even when they were sticking a knife in your belly or when they had to swallow a bitter disappointment. Hamid had never been able to do that. Master Serani often used to warn him that his thoughts could be read on his face as if it were a book written in distinct characters.

He had met members of those elevated social circles only as cus-tomers. He knew that such men, with our without the title of Pasha or Bey, were not interested in him, only in his art. They admired the art, not the artist.

Hamid did not behave with quiet deference when he met them, but was proud to the point of arrogance to show these silk-clad person-ages that he had gained all he had for himself, instead of inheriting wealth as they had done, and that if they were not going to accept him as one of their own, they must at least show him a minimum of respect. He knew that the al-Azm clan, whose leaders were all cus-tomers of his, had been in league with the rulers of Syria against the ordinary people, and the other clans were no better. So he sometimes reacted aggressively when one of these fine upstarts remarked, of his work, that he had a great gift; it was as if such condescension belittled his work. To be called gifted was praise to the ears of children and amateurs, but not to the best calligrapher in Damascus.

Today, as usual, Governor al-Azm came round his desk to welcome him.

"A small but fine piece of calligraphy," he said when a guard had brought tea. "If possible in green and gold. Those are my cousin's favourite colours. Ali Bey is a great admirer of your art. He is parlia-mentary president, and in a week's time he is coming out of the hos-pital. A stomach ulcer, or you could say it was politics. I hate politics, but he always wanted to be a politician. When we were little boys playing together, guess what part he always wanted to take?"

Hamid shook his head. He had no idea what the governor was talking about.

"He always wanted to play the president. But never mind that now – he is a great connoisseur of calligraphy, and always regrets never having the time to draw and paint himself. However, he admires you enormously, and thinks, as I do, that the greatest crime is really to keep you in prison. As I told you recently, he plans to get you pardoned after seven years. After all, he is the president's son-in-law. I wasn't really supposed to tell you about the pardon… now, where was I? Oh, yes, if possible write something so that it looks like a falcon or an eagle. My cousin is very fond of falconry."

Hamid rolled his eyes; he hated both the vegetation style and the animal style of calligraphy, in which the letters mutate into trees, landscapes, lions, and birds of prey. He thought it ridiculous to distort characters until they slavishly served to make a picture. The results could be improved on by any novice painter or photographer.

Governor al-Azm noticed Hamid's reluctance. "It was only an idea. I don't understand much about these things. Write just as you like." The governor hesitated slightly, pouring Hamid tea. "And then there's one other little thing," he said quietly. "My aunt, the mother of my cousin Ali Bey and sister of Prime Minister al-Azm, has donated money for the restoration of the little Omar Mosque – did I tell you about that aunt of mine?"

Hamid did not know why the governor was telling all these stories, and shook his head.

"She's a hundred and ten, and still goes shopping every day, has her siesta, and drinks a litre of red wine every evening, and six months ago she grew a second set of milk teeth. If I hadn't seen them for myself I'd never have believed it. Little snow-white teeth growing in her gums. But however that may be – legend says that a Sufi master dreamed that Omar, the third caliph, wanted to build a mosque in that little square close to Silk Street. At that time, in the eighteenth century, the area was a sink of iniquity." The governor laughed knowingly, and took a gulp of tea. "There's to be a marble plaque at the entrance commemorating her generous donation, and it would be an honour for my family if you would design it on paper. I have three stone-masons here who could engrave your calligraphy in marble, two of them serving life sentences, the third five years."

On the way back to his cell, the guard told him his brother had a son, now seven years old, who had been born covered with hair and sexually mature. Hamid felt he was in a madhouse. He shook his head as the guard locked the door of his cell and went away, coughing, and it took him some to cleanse his brain of all this rubbish.

Memories came back. He had been twenty-nine, at the height of his fame and fortune. Not far from his studio Minister Hashim Ufri, a rich industrialist and great lover of calligraphy, lived in one of the finest houses of the Souk Saruya quarter. He often ordered works of calligraphy both large and small from Hamid.

In 1949 Minister Ufri took King Farouk of Egypt a piece of Hamid Farsi's calligraphy when he was on a state visit. A month later the Egyptian ambassador came to Hamid's studio and told him, with great ceremony, that the king had never been so enthusiastic about a work of calligraphy as he was with that one – except, naturally, for some by the old Ottoman masters, but of course they were dead, and creating calligraphy for the Lord of all Lords.

"It may surprise you to hear that our king is a passionate calligrapher himself, like his father and his grandfather before him. He would like to buy the pens with which you conjured up that divine script."

All the colour drained from Hamid's face. He was pale with fury, but pulled himself together.

"If His Majesty is a calligrapher, then he knows that pens and knives are small but sacred objects and not for sale."

"There's nothing that is not for sale, certainly not to His Majesty. Don't make yourself and me unhappy," said the ambassador.

It suddenly struck Hamid that the King of Egypt was very close friends with the dictator Housni Hablan, who had been in power in Syria since March, and who in the last resort was a primitive illiterate who would not scruple to take the whole studio apart and ship it off to the King of Egypt to do him a favour.

Amazingly enough, the threat concealed under the ambassador's remarks did not look much better than the calligrapher's worst fears.

"They are not for sale, but I will give them to His Majesty as a present," said Hamid desperately, standing up and opening the cupboard behind him. There they lay. He wrapped them in a red felt cloth and gave them to the dark-haired little man with the big bald patch. The ambassador beamed all over his face. He marvelled at the inside knowledge of his friend in the Syrian Foreign Ministry, who had praised Hamid Farsi's extraordinary powers of reasoning.

"I will inform His Majesty personally of your generosity, because out of respect for you he has ordered me to bring these tools of the calligrapher's trade, which are indeed beyond price, to Cairo myself," said the ambassador.

Hamid Farsi did not mourn his loss for long. He spent two days cutting, splitting, and sharpening a new set of reed pens until he was satisfied with them.

A month later the ambassador came back to give Hamid a personal letter from the king. It contained one of the largest commissions ever entrusted to Hamid Farsi, and a question: "Why don't the pens write such beautiful script as yours?"

Hamid Farsi spent over three months working on the commission, which was more than well paid. It was for large scrolls of script for the palace walls. When he had finished, he wrote a letter to go with them.

"Your Majesty. As you and your ambassador, His Excellency Mahmoud Saadi, know, I sent you my best pens, but I could not and cannot send the hand that used them."

King Farouk was apparently more impressed by this letter than by the calligraphy, which he used to adorn his bedroom. He wrote in his diary that no one before had ever been able to tell, from a distance, what kind of pen he was using. Only this Syrian, who advised him never to write with the steel pens that had come over from Europe.

Hamid Farsi seldom wrote with a metal pen. He preferred reeds or bamboos, and cut his own reed pens for every script, however fine. There were certain strictly secret methods, decreeing the time when you harvested reeds, and how long you had to keep them buried in horse dung and other secret ingredients to end up with a good writing instrument. The best reeds came from Persia.

"Steel pens are dead metal ore. They write well, but in a coarse, cold way," Master Serani had always said. "Reed is both hard and flexible, like life."

The cutting and splitting of his pens was every calligrapher's best-kept secret. "A calligrapher who cuts badly can never write well," said Hamid. And when he cut his reeds he would never have anyone near him, not his journeymen and certainly not the errand boys. He withdrew to a small cubicle, closed the door after him, put on the light, and worked without stopping until his pens were cut, cleaned, and split.

He kept his knife hidden in the cupboard with the pens and notebooks containing his recipes for ink. No one was allowed to touch it even if it was left lying around.

11

Governor al-Azm liked the saying on the wall of Hamid's cell and wanted to own it. Hamid said he would like to keep this one piece of calligraphy, which his beloved teacher and master had given him. Instead, he said, he would write an equally beautiful new one for the governor. "Twice the size, if possible," said the governor, and smiled on his way back to his office because he could think of no better maxim to quote to his young mistress than, "God is beautiful and loves beauty." She was always asking, "Why do you love me of all people?" and he had found the answer here. Anyway, the calligraphy on Hamid's wall was dusty and torn at the edges, so he could make his point better with a brand-new one. Pleased, and proud of his craftiness, he entered his office.

Hamid, on the other hand, was deeply alarmed by the prison governor's wish. The idea of having to give away this particular work of calligraphy left him speechless, and only after a little while was he able to draft something new for the governor. He did not know the fear before a sheet of blank paper so often described by his colleagues. On the contrary, he felt full of power and courage. And that same feeling was the best moment of the work, the first touch of black ink on the featureless white surface. Experiencing the way black gave shape to white. It was not the ecstasy you could get from music and opium, when you felt airborne and dreaming, but ultimate enjoyment in a waking state. He sensed the beauty flowing from his hand to the paper, giving it life, form, and music. Only when he had finished writing the words did he feel exhausted. Then came the laborious routine work on the shading of the characters, the decorative line, the vowel sounds added below and above the characters to make easy reading possible, and finally the ornamentation of the surrounding surface. All that called for the craft that he had learnt and for patience.

He dipped his pen in the ink and wrote, all in one move at the top of the paper, the word "God." No word in one of his paintings might stand higher than the name of God.

When he had finished, two days later, he went over to the wall and caressed the old calligraphy. "Saved," he whispered.

"God is beautiful and loves beauty." Hamid read the saying, and pictures came before his mind's eye. His first wife Maha had been beautiful, but she was sick with stupidity. Had God loved her?

He remembered how it had all begun. Serani had recommended him, without circumlocution but very shyly, to take a wife, because Hamid's glance always became uneasy when he heard a woman's footsteps. Hamid did not think much of marriage at the time. He liked his independent life, he went to the brothel once a week, and often ate out in cafés. He had his clothes washed, ironed, and mended for a few piastres, so that he would have more time for his work.

A day after this remarkable conversation, and just as if misfortune had sent her, his Aunt Mayyada came to Damascus, in flight from the summer heat and the isolation of Saudi Arabia. She told him straight out that she knew a pearl among women, a girl who might have been made for him. Hamid wondered how a woman who spent nine months of the year in the Saudi Arabian desert could know what girl in Damascus would suit him, and he was even more surprised when she told him the woman's name: Maha, his master Serani's pretty daughter. Hamid didn't know her, but his aunt's enthusiasm infected him. Mayyada was fascinated by Maha's quiet beauty, and arranged the whole thing personally, since at this time his parents had already lost touch with the earthly side of life.

Maha was his master Serani's only daughter, and of course Hamid thought she would be a fortunate choice for him. His master, even though he had urged him to marry, expressed himself with some reserve, but that was his way. Hamid discovered, too late, that Serani did not know his own daughter. Otherwise he would have realized that she was far from loving him and his calligraphy, and indeed thought him a tyrant.

Was he really as bad as she painted him? All the stories Maha told of him, anyway, were horror stories.

"I'd have liked to be a reed," she once said, in tears, "because my father caressed and tended his reed pens every day, but he never once embraced me."

And as the similarity between her husband and her father became more and more obvious, she soon wanted nothing to do with Hamid either.

By now he was the leading calligrapher in his master's studio, and the first in a decade who had received his certificate from the hand of Serani himself. Now it was time to open a studio of his own. However, he dared not tell his master so, particularly when Serani – now that he was his father-in-law – spoke openly of the day when he would pass the studio on to him and retire. "When my hand begins to shake, say in twenty or thirty years' time," he added, with an ironic smile. There were indeed old master calligraphers who still wrote neatly and precisely at seventy-five.

So Hamid had to wait patiently for a good opportunity to give his master that bitter pill.

It was the time when he was searching for absolute black. Just after his wedding, he began experimenting in a little cubicle at the back of the workshop with all kinds of materials; he burnt them, dissolved the charred remains in water, and added various salts, powdered metals and resins, but he never achieved a darker black ink than the one they used already.

Serani had wasted ten years of his life searching for pure black. Hamid did not want to outdo his master, only to solve the secret of black and find its purest form. And in gratitude he planned to call the colour Serani Black. But hard as he toiled, putting questions to alchemists, druggists, spice dealers, pharmacists, and magicians, none of them was able to tell him the secret recipe.

Not until he was in prison could he assess how much strength he had squandered in the search for pure black. A whole chapter in his notebook was entitled "Ink," and under it he wrote later: "My ink is black, so order no rainbows from me."

"Black is the strongest colour. It extinguishes all other colours and kills the light. Black is bold as reason and cold as logic," he wrote confidently and with emotion when he had spent months reading all there was to know about the making of inks. Master Serani observed his passion with admiration, and not without amusement when Hamid went home with his face blackened.

He was looking for the dark hue of black velvet, and dreamed of the absolute black of the universe. Far away there, in the distance, the blackest of all shades is found. And suddenly he discovered his love for the night, and wondered why a desire for women always came over him in the darkness. When he told his master he thought that there was a connection between the night and Eros, Serani said he had better keep to his ink.

He began with well-known methods, let the pressed residue of grapes, logwood, oak-apples, bones, ivory, olive pits, the leaves of the sumac used by tanners, and aniline char in closed vessels, chopped them small, boiled them with salts of iron and copper or silver nitrates – but he did not find what he wanted.

He also tried to extract even more black hues with alcohol and vinegar. All this led to some slight improvements, but he never made the real breakthrough.

He found ancient recipes from Greece and Turkey. Charred beeswax, soot from lamps and petroleum could be used in making ink, mixed with ground resin, boiled, left to steep for a week, then sieved and thickened. Hamid meticulously followed every step, and in the end he had a deep black, but still not what he wanted.

One day, in a café near the studio, he came upon a Maghrebi alchemist. Hamid drank his tea and listened to what the alchemist was recommending his audience do to keep their sex drive going. The white-robed man had an intelligent face, and seemed to be tired of the men pestering him and buying his powders. Suddenly he fixed Hamid with a look that the latter could not forget even decades later. He had not avoided the man's gaze, but had given him a smile that spoke volumes, and the man had risen to his feet, picked up his glass of tea, and moved over to join him in the corner.

"The gentleman is concerned with other matters than the seduction or poisoning of women. Perhaps he is looking for the secret of making gold?"

Hamid had laughed. "I don't think we'll be doing business. I am not interested in either gold or women."

"But something dark and heavy oppresses your heart," said the man, undeterred.

"There you are right." The words had escaped Hamid. "I am looking for absolute black."

"Ah, then you are a calligrapher," said the stranger laconically. "The earth is restricted, why do you want the absolute? That exists only in heaven. But of all earthly colours, my black is the darkest," said the man.

Hamid had only smiled bitterly.

"I will give you a recipe, and if you are satisfied with the results you can send me, at an address in Beirut, a hundred small calligraphic works with sayings from the Quran or the Hadith of our Prophet. The pieces of paper must be no larger than the palm of your hand, and must all be in mirror script. Do you agree?"

"Why Beirut?" asked Hamid, amused.

"I must leave Damascus tomorrow. I am staying in Beirut for a month, and if you do not send me my fee I will curse you, and you will be plagued by misfortune. Write down what I am about to say," said the man gravely.

Hamid took out the little notebook that he always carried with him to write down ideas and record curiosities. He did it on the advice of his master Serani, who never left the house without a notebook and pencil.

The alchemist seemed to know the recipe by heart. He dictated, looking into the distance, the amounts of ingredients, the procedure, and the time it would all take, as if he were reading from an invisible book.

The recipe turned out to make not, perhaps, absolute black, but no one in Damascus could make the colour any darker yet. This ink was to bring Hamid fame and fortune later, but also sleepless nights, for he forgot the alchemist for a while, and when he did send the agreed fee to Beirut the taxi driver came straight back saying that the Maghrebi had already left the city.

Had the alchemist's curse caused his misfortune?

To make the ink he had taken the wool from the belly of a black sheep, singed it, ground it, mixed it with resins, gum Arabic, and tannic acids, dissolved the mixture in water, thickened it over a low flame, and kneaded the doughy result. Then he added metal oxide, dissolved it all, thickened it again, and had a paste that dried to a raven-black block as it cooled. A piece of it dissolved in water gave an extraordinarily black ink.

Soon word was going round of the high quality of his ink, and all calligraphers who valued their reputation ordered some. Master Serani did not like it. "We are turning into an ink factory," he muttered.

When Hamid had his own studio, he produced the fine black ink on a large scale.

Making it was expensive, but unlike the poisonous colours was harmless. Many calligraphers died very young, never guessing that they had poisoned themselves with the minerals from which they made their colours. Hamid thought of his colleague Radi, who had never taken any warnings seriously, and paid for it with his life.

When his first wife Maha was still alive, he often came home half-dead with exhaustion, stinking and with a soot-smeared face. His wife hated the stench that came into the house in his wake, and more and more often she looked for a reason not to have to go to bed with him.

Even when he set up independently, and a large commission from the Orthodox Church enabled him to buy the fine house of Ehud Malaki, a rich Jew, her temper did not improve. Maha did not give the house a single word of praise.

It was also partly for her sake that he had not opened his own studio in the calligraphers' quarter of al-Bahssa, but decided on the finest street in the Souk Saruya quarter, where only prosperous people lived. The Damascenes called this high-class district Little Istanbul, but Maha didn't even want to see the studio, and she never set foot in it.

For her sake, too, he stopped experimenting with colours, and came home in the evening just as he had set out in the morning, elegantly dressed and perfumed. But nothing did any good. His wife became ever gloomier and withdrew from the world more and more. For a year he put up with her wilful behaviour, but them, when she once again refused to do her duty in bed, he hit her.

About two years after the wedding she fell very ill, lost weight rapidly, and came out in a rash all over her body. The neighbours began whispering that Hamid's wife was sick because of the poison in the coloured inks that he kept in black boxes in the cellar.

Life in his house became hell. He was afraid that *she* would poison *him*, but she didn't want him dead. She did not envy the living. Her revenge, she whispered hoarsely on her deathbed, was to wish him a long life.

At first he had felt guilty, but then he began to relish his freedom and the absolute peace in his house.

Did he grieve for her? He was horrified when, lying now on his bed in the prison, he heard his own voice say, "Not for a moment."

From then on he lived alone in his fine house with no intention of marrying again. He was not interested in either women customers or lonely women neighbours, who were always finding some excuse to knock on his door. He knew exactly why they were knocking, and gave them a suitably ungracious reception.

And then, one day, along came one of his richest customers, Munir al-Azm. He had heard from his sister, he said, that the daughter of the scholar Rami Arabi, who was famous if not at all prosperous, was a marvel among women. She could read and write better than many men, she was very beautiful, and well brought up. He himself, he added, would have liked to make her his fifth wife, but her father declined his offer because his daughter wanted to be in sole possession of her husband's heart.

Hamid Farsi scarcely looked up from his work. "I'll have to wait a month for my aunt to come visiting from Saudi Arabia and take a look at her. Then we'll see," he said, joking.

"Why not come and visit us? I'll get my sister to bring the girl with her," offered the friendly man, but Hamid just shook his head. He had other things to do.

Soon after that Hamid caught a chill. He ran a high temperature, could hardly move, and wished for a helping hand. His household arrangements were going downhill, and he had to ask an elderly woman neighbour to do the essential cooking and laundry for him, and look after all the flowers.

By night he felt lonelier and lonelier, the empty house frightened him, and his loneliness was made worse by his own echoing footsteps. His desire for women forced him to seek satisfaction from a whore. But he felt revulsion on meeting the client who was just leaving her. A tall, dirty, vulgar man who, when he saw Hamid, turned to the whore and said, "Your garage can recuperate from my heavy truck with a little bicycle like that." When Hamid heard the drunken whore laughing, he walked out of the house.

And so he longed for his aunt's arrival. As for his aunt herself, she was very anxious to make up for her first unfortunate efforts to find him a wife. When he told her the young woman's name she quickly found, in the tangled maze of her relationships, a friend from her schooldays, Badia, who lived in the same street as the family of the girl in question. Badia too thought that Noura would be the perfect wife for Hamid.

Was she? He'd have given anything for that. She was a little too thin, but there was something irresistible about her face. And she talked too much for his liking. Outwardly she appeared to be well brought up, but she had not learnt to keep her mouth shut. Above all, when he wanted to tell her something she would pick up the thread of the conversation and join in. Sometimes he forgot what he had been going to say. She had somehow or other been brought up like a man, and thought she could talk about everything as men do. At first he thought that was amusing, but soon, as he saw it, she lost her feminine charms for him. He was not comfortable in bed, because she had very small breasts, and even after a month of marriage was getting her hair cut short like a boy's. But she had a pleasant body odour, and was elegant in all she did. Sometimes he saw that she was crying, but as his grandfather had told him one day, "Women are sea creatures. They have an endless supply of salt water." If he were to pay attention to his wife's tears he would never get anywhere.

He had hoped she would get pregnant. People had often told him that such women put on more flesh on their breasts, belly, and buttocks during pregnancy. He tried to sleep with her as often and talk to her as little as possible. And when she talked to him, he acted as if he hadn't heard her. But instead of getting either pregnant or more feminine, she turned wilful. Sometimes he had a feeling that her mind was unhinged. She would suddenly start laughing in the middle of love-play, and he could not shake off the idea that she was laughing at him.

Sometimes he came home tired and hungry, and realized that she hadn't cooked anything. She had spent all day reading and thinking, she said. Several times he came home unexpectedly, suspecting that she either had a lover or was spending time with the women neighbours, which he had forbidden her to do. But she assured him again and again that she never visited anyone, and no neighbours visited her, although she said it with a cold smile. The telephone often rang and, when he picked up the receiver, the caller hung up.

His suspicion that she was unhinged was confirmed when he saw her in the inner courtyard one day playing marbles. By herself! He was furious, and she only smiled. It was a shock for him, and at this point, if not before, he ought to have consulted a doctor. But he thought women understood the minds of other women better than any doctor. Next thing he knew, he told his Aunt Mayyada, Noura would be playing ball by herself.

And what did his damned Aunt Mayyada say to him? "Women only do that when they're left unsatisfied, so they despise their husbands. You must sleep with her more often and break her will. There are women who don't see reason and won't behave in a feminine way until then. Break her will, and your balls are the only ones she'll take in her hand to kiss them."

He slept with Noura every day now, and when, once, she laughed again, he hit her and then she wept for days on end and looked anxious. She didn't say much anymore, and she was getting paler and paler. Her father came to see him three times and told him to look after Noura; he had never see her so unhappy before, he said. Hamid must not immerse himself entirely in calligraphy, Rami Arabi told his son-in-law. Books and script were there to make human beings happy, but for him, Hamid, happiness, hospitality and marriage existed only as sacrifices on the altar of the book. He asked Hamid straight out when he had last entertained a guest in his house.

Hamid did not know what to say. He tried spoiling Noura, but she didn't want that anymore. She built a wall of housework and headaches against his attempts to take the fortress of her loneliness by storm.

One day her mother came to his studio and acted as if she herself had fallen in love with him. He went out to a nearby family café with her, because in the workshop Samad would have heard every word they said. In the café, Noura's mother confessed that she would willingly have come to his studio just to see him and for no other reason, but her husband had sent her. He wanted her to say that Hamid shouldn't work so much, and should take better care of his wife, but she herself knew that Noura was unable to judge men properly. She was immature, said her mother, for a mature woman would want a husband exactly like Hamid. Noura, her mother went on, had inherited many characteristics from her father, including her ready tongue. As Noura's mother, she was very sorry about that. But, she said, surreptitiously patting his hand, together they would teach the child to be a proper wife to him.

When they parted she kissed him ardently, and her body radiated a heat that he never felt in his wife.

He could make nothing of his father-in-law's advice, and his mother-in-law's warm affection alienated him from his wife. She came to see him more and more often to talk to him about Noura, and on her fourth or fifth visit to the studio he had to ask her not to come by herself anymore, because his assistants and the neighbours were beginning to whisper. That was a lie, but every time the woman touched him he felt a kind of frenzy. She was only three years older than him, and seemed to him younger and more erotic than her daughter.

When his Aunt Mayyada saw the mother with him once she said, smugly, that she could act as go-between here as well, exchanging the mother for the daughter.

"You bring bad luck," whispered Hamid, directing his gaze from the prison bed where he lay to the little photograph and assuming, from the right-hand half of it, that it showed Aunt Mayyada.

12

Hamid paced restlessly around his cell. He was wide awake, as if he had slept for ten hours. It was a long time since he had known such nights. Shortly before parting from his master he had been agitated in the same way. He slept no more than three hours a night then, and all the same, none of his preparations were any help. Weeks before he told his master his decision, Serani looked as old and sick, as sad and abandoned as if he could guess at the coming severance of the umbilical cord.

When they said goodbye Serani wished him success and good luck, but two days later he was calling the parting treachery. Even many years afterwards Hamid wondered why his master spoke of treachery when he himself had declined the large commission with which Hamid intended to finance the step he was taking into independence.

A month earlier, Serani had turned down work for the Catholic churches twice running. These were small but well-paid commissions, but Serani wasn't interested in the money. He refused to create calligraphic works for Christians on religious grounds. Both Arabic script and the Arabic language were sacred to him, closely bound as they were to the Quran, so he would never sell his calligraphy to unbelievers. Many of his colleagues held that against him, saying that Damascus had always been a city open to all, where Christian, Jewish, and Muslim architects and masons had often worked together on the renovation of mosques. Hamid had spent days trying to persuade Serani to change his mind, but in vain.

One day Alexandros III, Patriarch of the Damascene Orthodox Church and a great admirer of Arabic calligraphy, had sent an envoy to Master Serani with his request. He was asking him to adorn the newly renovated Church of St Mary with Arabic calligraphy and arabesques, and said he could name his own fee. Serani brusquely refused. He did not write in divine Arabic script for unbelievers, he said. All his life Serani believed that calligraphy makes the mosque a great religious book for the wise, while unbelievers turn their churches into picture books for simple souls.

Alexis Duhduh, the patriarch's envoy, stood there rooted to the spot, and for the first time Hamid felt ashamed on his master's behalf. He showed the elegant man out and told him, as they parted, to say nothing to his Excellency the Patriarch about Serani's abrupt refusal. He, Hamid, would visit him in his office within the next few days and discuss the whole thing with him again.

A week later, when Hamid had signed the contract with the Patriarch and received the first advance payment, he returned to the studio, took his few instruments, said a civil goodbye and indicated that he was setting up on his own. Serani, sitting hunched in his chair, murmured barely audible, "I know, I know. As your father-in-law I wish you luck, and as your master I give you God's blessing." Hamid felt like shedding tears of grief and embracing his master, but he turned away without a word and left.

So now he was independent, and doing the best-paid work in his life for the Orthodox Church. He designed the sayings as the architects and church elders wanted them, without doubting for a moment that Christians were stupid for believing in a God who sent his son to earth, had him tormented by a few emaciated Jews, and then executed by the Romans. What kind of God was that? In his place, Hamid would have pressed his thumb down on Palestine and made it the deepest point of an ocean.

The church elders were so grateful to him that they accepted his condition of putting in only three days a week working in the church himself, and then having the scripts, ornamentation, and arabesques he had pre-designed executed by his journeymen and apprentices in colour, marble, stone, and timber. On the other days he fitted out his new studio and looked for his first customers.

The work on the church took two years, and the governing body of St Mary's was generous. Hamid bought his house and furnished his studio with the money he earned. He was the only calligrapher in this rich neighbourhood, and he soon made sure, through his powerful customers, that no other calligrapher set up in the street to compete with him.

However, his master Serani boycotted him, and at the latest after his daughter Maha's death he kept out of his former protégé's way as far as he could. Many said the reason was that Hamid did not revere script as sacred, and not only worked for Christians and Jews but also adorned letters, death announcements, and even bathrooms with his calligraphy in return for pay. The whole city talked of the love poems he had written out on large tablets for the prime minister who, at the age of seventy, had married a wife of twenty who loved the poems of the learned Sufi master Ibn Arabi. The Damascenes called the poet, who was buried in their city, "the philosopher of love."

From now on Hamid was almost overwhelmed by commissions from parliament and the ministries. Some said that Master Serani thought him a genius but a man of poor character who would write calligraphy for anyone in return for his fee. But it was also said that Serani avoided Hamid because he secretly blamed him for his daughter's death.

Hamid did not discover the real reason until his master, now seriously ill, visited him in prison. Serani had cancer. He came to say goodbye and to persuade Hamid to stand down as Grand Master, leaving the way clear for a successor.

His master's visit had shaken him. Not only because Serani asked for the certificate conveying the post of Grand Master back, but because the old man frankly explained why he had not been able to get in touch with him earlier: his reason was fear.

Hamid had raced forward too fast, making too much noise about it, he said, and had impatiently brought the reform of Arabic script to public attention.

"And you had not only the conservatives against you but all the fanatics as well. That frightened me," his master admitted. "You can argue with conservatives or progressives, but the fanatics don't talk, they simply murder their opponents."

"You knew about criminals who had been set on me?" asked Hamid indignantly.

"No, I knew nothing. You never do until it's too late. There are four or five fanatically religious groups. They have more calligraphers and philosophers on their consciences than pimps. They go more carefully there."

"But those are just crazy…" Hamid began to dismiss what his master was saying. Serani looked at him despairingly. "They are not crazy," he said. "That's how it always was and always will be. That and that alone shames me, because I myself realized that our Society was on the wrong track. I ought not to have involved you in it, I should simply have burnt the documents and continued to encourage you as a fortunate and gifted master calligrapher. I drew you into it, and I ask you to forgive me."

"Oh," said Hamid, dismissing this, because he could not understand why his master felt guilty, "they are just a few crazed souls, and you'll see, we will…"

"Crazed, crazed, oh, stop that," his master interrupted him angrily. "They are everywhere, and lying in wait for us. They lie in wait for everyone who deviates a single step from the prescribed path, and suddenly he's found with a knife between his ribs, or dead drunk with a whore although he never touched a drop of alcohol. In Aleppo some twenty years ago they got a rent-boy into a great calligrapher's bed, and the boy swore to the Kadi that Master Mustafa had seduced him for money. All lies, but the judge found one of our best calligraphers guilty and sent him to prison for ten years. What more do you want by way of proof to open your eyes? Ibn Muqla built a world of philosophy, music, geometry, and architecture for the Arabic characters, for calligraphy. If the Prophet came into the world for the sake of morality, Ibn Muqla came as the prophet of script. He was the first to make it both an art and a science. To Arabic script he was what Leonardo da Vinci was for European painting. And was he rewarded? He ended worse than a mangy dog, with his hand hacked off and his tongue cut out. So we are all condemned to downfall.

"Look at the Ottomans, were they worse Muslims than us? Never! Their sultans revered calligraphers like saints. In times of war many a sultan hid his calligraphers like a state treasure, and it's a fact that when Sultan Salim I captured Tabriz he left its doctors, astronomers, and architects behind, but took all sixty calligraphers back with him to adorn Istanbul.

"Sultan Mustafa Khan held the inkwell for the famous calligrapher Hafiz Osmani, and asked the master to accept him as a pupil and initiate him into the mysteries of script. Have I ever told you what his last wish was?" asked Serani, smiling, as if to cheer his pupil with a story. Hamid shook his head.

"When Hafiz Osmani died in the year 1110 his pupils granted him his last wish. All his life he had collected and kept the shavings of wood that fell from his bamboo and reed pens as he cut them, ground them down and pointed them. There were ten large jute sacks full of them. His pupils were to boil up the shavings and use the water for the final washing of his body."

Serani looked sadly at his favourite pupil. "You know," he said, smiling, "when I was twenty I wanted to change the world and devise a new alphabet that everyone could use. When I was thirty I wanted only to save Damascus and carry out a radical reform of the Arabic alphabet. At the age of forty I would have been happy if I could have saved our street in the Old Town and brought about a few urgent reforms of Arabic script. I have given you all I could, as you know. When I was sixty, I still hoped that I could save my family."

Serani shed tears as they said goodbye in the visitors' room, asking his former pupil once again to forgive him, and Hamid assured him with emotion that he bore him no grudge at all, and his heart was full of nothing but gratitude to his master.

Stooping, and with dragging steps, the old master went out, escorted by the guard. He turned and waved, but Hamid could not summon up the strength to wave back.

He felt wretched, for he now knew that his master had not exaggerated. Some things that used to seem inexplicable or absurd to him were becoming clear.

But when exactly, he wondered, had the turning point come? He did not have to look for the answer long. The month before the opening of the School of Calligraphy had been full of activity. He had travelled widely, had written articles about the School for newspapers, and had been extremely cautious. Again and again he had indicated the necessity for reform, but always stressing, for the sake of reassurance, the fact that the Quran must remain inviolable. Only the correspondent of a small Lebanese newspaper, a great admirer of Hamid, gave away more than Hamid himself wanted. In an interview, he had asked directly about the necessity of reform. Hamid had replied that there were weak points in the alphabet, and it needed to be expanded to provide a more modern language for everyday use. As a second step – "and it need not be taken by our children and grandchildren for some fifty or a hundred years" – superfluous letters could be removed and the shape of the characters improved to the point where they would be less and less liable to be confused with each other. Without asking Hamid, the journalist cut the part about children and grandchildren and the long time-span, adding on his own initiative that the alphabet should be more like the Persian alphabet.

That laid Hamid open to abuse and three unpleasant phone calls, but then the situation calmed down again. Criticism from his own professional ranks was harder to take. Sunni calligraphers wanted nothing to do with Persia. He reassured them, knowing all the time that he was lying to them, because he was indeed planning to expand the alphabet and bring it closer to the Persian model.

Hamid smiled bitterly. As long as the idea of radical reform of Arabic script was merely a pipe dream discussed in the Society, all was harmony. But when it came out into the open, the entire organization split into groups and sub-groups. Suddenly he was no longer at the head of the Society, as the rules had prescribed hundreds of years ago. Instead, a many-headed hydra came into being. All this had come at the same time as the founding of the School, when he needed all the strength and solidarity he could get. Many of those who envied him thought it was just the right moment to get rid of him as Grand Master. Some thought his ideas of reform too tedious and watered down, others wanted to introduce a new alphabet at once when the School was opened, one that would do away instantly with all the weaknesses of Arabic script, a third group again suddenly wanted no change at all that had anything to do with Persia, but satisfied themselves with wailing about the inadequacy of the Arabic alphabet.

Hamid demanded discipline and obedience, and he had to throw his high reputation into the scale to achieve unity. Curiously enough, all the masters from the north of the country were behind him, but the two representatives of the city of Damascus left the Society.

Then there was a calm period. The opening of the School seemed to show that all the turmoil within the Society had been only a storm in a tea-glass. The elite of the country were delighted that this step had been taken.

However, soon Hamid realized that he had been mistaken. When the thugs wrecked and besmirched his school, the sheikh of the Umayyad Mosque gave them his backing, and in an interview deliberately misquoted Hamid. After that he was denounced as an apostate for the first time. And the democratic, allegedly civilized government banned his school, instead of declaring the Pure Ones enemies of the state.

His opponents in the Society of the Wise kept quiet, but only until he was in prison. Now the majority of masters in the south began insisting on a democratic election to choose a new Grand Master. The northern masters, led by Ali Barakeh, were solidly behind Grand Master Hamid, and asked him to choose his successor himself.

Yet it was not only in the ranks of the Society that Hamid had been rejected. From the day when he began taking steps publicly to make his ideas of radical reform known the religious patrons who commissioned his work shunned him. Two mosques instantly withdrew their commissions. Only now did it strike him that such incidents were always attended by dark hints.

And Serani's reasons for avoiding any contact with him were also clear to him now. Serani had feared for his own commissions and for his life.

13

Had he underestimated the Pure Ones because their bearded henchmen belonged to the most stupid stratum of humanity? Were the leaders of the Pure Ones perhaps clever enough to have planned all of it with cold calculation in order to destroy their enemies on several levels at once? Did they want more than the death of their adversaries?

Had the Pure Ones even infiltrated his Society of the Wise? He had noticed a certain sympathy for the Pure Ones in the views of many devout and conservative calligraphers in the Society of the Wise and even its Council, but could not speak to them openly on the subject, because the dividing line between religious conservatives and religious fanatics was blurred. Had they perhaps been involved in the resistance to him that broke out in the Society exactly when he needed the solidarity of all its members?

Had Noura maybe been abducted to dishonour him? Had the role of that goat Abbani been only to commission him to write letters that would read, to an outsider, as if he were pimping for his own wife?

Had he killed the wrong man?

Why had the café proprietor Karam given evidence against him? Had he perhaps been blackmailed by threats of statements incriminating him as a homosexual that might have landed him in prison? It had not been difficult for Abbani's brothers and lawyers to find out that Almaz, his fourth wife, had something to do with the murder. Abbani had only recently moved his hiding place to her house at the time.

But why had Karam set him on the track of Abbani? All because of that matronly figure his niece? It was hard to believe. Had the murder been planned as punishment for the lavish donations that Abbani had made to the School of Calligraphy. Or must Karam have wanted Abbani dead before he could tell Hamid the truth about the love letters?

Hadn't his neighbour Najib, a tight-fisted goldsmith who had never been to his studio before, suddenly visited him, indicating that distinguished personages had requested him to ask whether he, Hamid, would be prepared for an interview with Nasri and his business manager Tawfiq to clear the whole matter up? Hamid had thrown the man out in a fury, calling after him to go on steering clear of his studio, as in the past.

How could Karam have known of that attempt at mediation? He had given him advance warning of the goldsmith, describing him as an unbelieving Christian who had been cuckolded several times himself. Najib Rihan was almost sixty, and had married a young woman of twenty who was performing at the time as a third-class singer.

If Abbani had not been his own wife's lover, then why did he have to die?

Had he himself been made, by these events, an instrument to destroy the Society?

Hamid froze at the thought, and shook his head vigorously not in denial, but to rid himself of such a terrible idea.

He had no answer to any of these questions.

14

Hamid had been around twelve or thirteen when he first heard the lines of verse:

The rational suffer misery in heaven
And the ignorant take their heavenly ease in misery.

At the time he had thought it was just an acrobatic play on words.

But no, there was bitter truth in it. His knowledge of Arabic characters and the deficiencies of the Arabic language had brought him to hell, to a body of ignorant people who wallowed in their sins daily and the majority of whom were illiterate, who did not see script as an instrument of reason but as an inviolable shrine.

In Europe, the minister had said to him at the time, they would have put up a monument to him; here he had to fear for his life. His lips tightened at these thoughts, and he looked at his bare feet in a pair of shabby shoes that had once been elegant. Now, cut down at the back, they had to serve him as slippers.

What, he wondered, has become of my life?

15

For a long time Hamid Farsi thought the attacks on him had begun around the year 1956, at the time when the founding of the School of Calligraphy was announced.

However, one morning he found a remark in his secret diary that alarmed him. He must have overlooked it time and time again. It was just an inconspicuous little line: "An unpleasant phone call, an agitated man calling me an agent of unbelievers." It was dated 11 October 1953.

A page later he read: "Two large commissions for the renovation of the Umayyad Mosque cancelled." This was followed by an exclamation mark and the date of 22 November 1953.

Of course he had paid no attention to all this at the time because he had too many commissions anyway, and his assistants were working flat out.

How often had he overlooked this hint? Now, in his cell, he realized that his enemies had had him in their sights considerably earlier than he had previously thought.

That date was no coincidence.

Soon after his marriage to Noura, he and several other calligraphers had tried to convince liberal sheikhs, Islamic scholars, professors and conservative politicians of the necessity of a reform of Arabic script. They got nowhere.

His father-in-law Rami Arabi, regarded as one of the most radical champions of modernization in the country, was sure that corrections to the Arabic language and its script were needed. But he suspected that not a single Muslim would venture to make them, because so many thought, erroneously, that it would run counter to the Quran to do so. He too therefore withheld his support from Hamid.

When Hamid asked him why, as a highly regarded sheikh and scholar, he did not speak up for reform, particularly as his name reminded people of the highly esteemed poet and Sufi scholar Ibn Arabi, who was very popular in Damascus, he just laughed out loud. Hamid was naïve, he said; didn't he realize that he, Rami Arabi, had ended up in his little mosque because of many small differences of opinion with great sheikhs? A fanatic had come to the mosque recently with provocative questions about calligraphy and his son-in-law, and he had been afraid the young man might physically attack him as well, but God had been merciful. However, he added, even without a knife in his ribs his relegation to such a small mosque was bad enough. Sending a man of the Book to a congregation of ignorant illiterates was worse than the death penalty.

And had not Hamid understood yet, he asked, that the crucial question was not one of courage or cowardice, but of might and power in the state? Any radical alterations to the Arabic language and script had only ever been made by state decree. And the Arab state was never the result of the will or reasoning of the majority, but of the victory of one clan over another. So he did not have to win him, Rami Arabi, over to his cause; he needed the support of ten men of the strongest clans in the country. Then the Pure Ones would accept even a proposition for the Arabs to write their language in Chinese characters.

Hamid knew that his father-in-law was right, yet he was disappointed. He mustn't look like that, said his father-in-law as they parted, what was the sheikh of a mosque like him to do if he was finally dismissed from service? He couldn't beg, and he was too ugly for a singer. He patted Hamid affectionately on the shoulder and said maybe he could boil up ink for him and sweep the studio.

A week later Hamid had an even more sobering shock when he met Sheikh Muhammad Sabbak, considered a courageous reformer among Muslim scholars, and the author of daring and provocative works on the liberation of women and social justice. There was a joke in Damascus to the effect that the sheikh couldn't set foot in half of all Arab countries because of his ideas about women, nor in the other half because he was regarded as an undercover communist there.

However, he was highly thought of in Syria, particularly as he was the defence minister's father-in-law. In a private conversation between the two of them, Hamid told him his idea of the necessity for reforming script, and asked for his support. The stocky sheikh jumped up as if a scorpion had stung his buttocks. He looked at Hamid, wide-eyed. "Are you really crazy, or just putting on an act? I have a wife and children. Who's going to feed them if I die in disgrace as a godless unbeliever?"

At the end of 1952 Hamid had been told that the Islamic scholars of Aleppo were particularly courageous, but on a visit to them and to several professors in the metropolis of the north of Syria, he met with nothing but rejection.

When he told Serani about his setback in Aleppo, his master was unmoved, and showed not the slightest solidarity with him. Only as Hamid left did he say, "Don't try going so fast. People are very slow, and they will lose track of you if you're too far ahead."

At the time Hamid didn't understand that he was in the process of dissociating himself from his adherents because of the impatience always urging him on.

His meeting with the minister of culture also seemed to him at first a happy dispensation of providence. In fact it was a bad omen, as he now, in prison, recognized.

In the middle of April 1953 he received a letter from the Ministry of Culture, which distributed all school textbooks at the time. The new minister, working with authors, teachers, linguists, geographers, natural scientists, illustrators and calligraphers, wanted to bring the textbooks into line with the latest state of knowledge, giving them unity and above all elegance. That was all the invitation said.

Hamid was to give his expert opinion on all the scripts.

On the morning of the meeting, he rose at four in the morning with a premonition that this would be an important day. Once he arrived at the Ministry, Hamid found he knew no one but the famous old scholar Sati' al-Husri, who debated tirelessly in public and was highly respected by the nationalists. He regarded a nation's language as its most important foundation stone.

Hamid sat down on the nearest vacant chair and was surprised to see a card with a name that was strange to him. The man next to him explained that the minister had decided in advance who was to sit where. "It'll be a habit he learned from the French," added the man sarcastically. Hamid found his own place in between two taciturn printing press owners. Soon all the participants had arrived except for the minister, and it struck Hamid that there was not a single sheikh among this select company.

Then the minister entered the large room. They could all feel his aura of power right to the furthest seat at the large oval table. George Mansour was a highly educated young literary scholar who after studying in France had worked for a short time as a professor at Damascus University, until President Shishakli gave him the job of reorganizing the schools at the end of 1952.

Hamid could not understand how the president could have entrusted the education of children in a country with a majority of Muslims to a Christian. But after an hour he was so fascinated by the minister's charm and vision that he himself no longer understood why he had felt uneasy about it at first.

"I have not invited the religious teachers because we have to discuss reforms that do not affect religion," said the minister. "They are invited to a separate meeting tomorrow, at which not I but the learned Sheikh Sabbak will put the new guidelines on which our president has decided before them.

For today, however, I have invited the two best printers in Damascus so that they can advise us – and come to our rescue if we dream too much! As men acquainted with printers' ink, they know that it is sometimes impossible to pay for our dreams."

The minister knew exactly what he wanted. George Mansour was a gifted speaker, with a better command of Arabic than many Muslim scholars. He juggled quotations, lines of poetry, and anecdotes from Arabic literature with the hand of a master.

"Damascus has always been the heart of Arabia, and if the heart is sick how is the body to remain healthy?" he asked at the beginning of his speech

Like most of the men in the room, Hamid was hanging on the speaker's lips. He seemed to have prepared everything down to the last detail. He introduced his address by saying that the president had given the green light to a radical reform of the educational system, and that he intended to make open and generous scope for action available to them, the experts. Now it was up to them all to make the best of that for Syrian schoolchildren.

Hamid felt his heart beating fast, for he was beginning to see where the minister's path was taking them. He had not been wrong.

"The first radical reform concerns language," said the minister calmly, "for with language human beings design their thoughts. It is no secret that we have a beautiful language, but one that is also antiquated in many respects. It suffers from several weaknesses that I need not enumerate here. I would like to mention only one, so that you can see how delicate a matter it is to repair the ravages of time. Our language is overloaded with synonyms. No other language in the world shares this weakness, which shimmers as if it were a strength, and even fills many Arabs with pride. We must liberate Arabic from all its dead weight and make it leaner so that it becomes clear. Look at the French. They have reformed their language radically several times, until it became a language fit for modern life and set an example to other nations. Under the influence of Malherbe, the French began cleansing their language as early as 1605. A series of courageous reforms followed. All the steps taken seem to have been inspired by the maxim of the philosopher Descartes, making clarity the first commandment of language. Antoine Comte de Rivarol proclaimed boldly in 1784: *Ce qui n'est pas clair n'est pas français*, what is not clear is not French.

"What can we offer by comparison? A word that does not have over fifty synonyms is not Arabic?"

The men in the room laughed with some restraint.

"And in fact French is precise," the minister went on. "Every word has a meaning, but it can also be subject to poetic variation. However, the language is always undergoing renewal, and space is made for modern, living words that are necessary for the purposes of culture. Only this permanent process of rejuvenation drives a language forward and enables it to keep pace with civilization and even help to shape it.

"Our language is beautiful but diffuse, thus giving great scope to poets but causing confusion in the fields of philosophy and science. You know better than I do that we have over three hundred synonyms for the word 'lion' – according to Ibn Faris, as many as five hundred – two hundred for the bear, and an enormous number for wine, camel, and sword."

"But all these words are already recorded in dictionaries. Are we to throw them away?" asked a young linguist.

The minister smiled, as if he had known what was coming, Seventy-year-old Sati' al-Husri raised his hand. "Young man," he said in fatherly tones, "not throw them away but put them in the museum and produce new, fresh dictionaries. The Europeans have shown courage and buried the corpses of their words, words that no one uses anymore and only lead to confusion. Here the corpses are still walking around. A dictionary should be the house of living words, not the graveyard of dead ones. Who needs more than five words for a lion? Not I for one. Do you? Two or three for woman and wine are quite enough. Anything else will contaminate the language…"

"But the Quran – what do you want to do with the synonyms in the Quran?" a grey-haired man with a well-tended moustache interrupted him. He was the author of several books on education.

"Every word that occurs in the Quran will be in the new dictionaries; no one will touch it. But the Quran is too sublime to fill itself with synonyms for lions and other creatures," said old Husri impatiently.

"And it says nowhere in the Quran that we should lighten our language of so much ballast," the minister went on. "One example will suffice. It is estimated that about sixty thousand words are used in modern physics, a hundred thousand in chemistry, two hundred thousand in medicine. In zoology, there are over a million species of animals, and in botany over three hundred and fifty thousand plant species. I would be happy if we could take over all those species from their scientific Latin names and transliterate them into Arabic, but imagine the catastrophe of having to couple all those words with synonyms. So we should have the courage to unburden our language to allow us to accommodate all these new terms, which give us entry to civilization. Then the dictionaries will certainly be extensive, for they will also be full of life. That is why I am asking my honoured teacher Sati' al-Husri to chair a committee addressing this delicate matter in the next ten years." He turned to the old man. "I thank you for your courage."

Husri nodded, satisfied. "I will give you my committee's new dictionary within five years," he said proudly.

It is said that in the summer of 1968, fifteen years after this meeting, Sati' al-Husri looked back to this meeting on his deathbed. His boast was one of many for which life had punished him. At this time, in the fifties and sixties, he was regarded as the spiritual father of all Arab nationalists. Consequently his pupils, when they heard of his severe illness, came from all the Arab countries to take leave of their teacher and idol. They numbered twelve experienced men whose years in prison, taken together, amounted to more than a century, yet they had all now gained power in their countries – most of them through coups, but that did not disturb old Husri. Among the twelve were three prime ministers, two leaders of political parties, two ministers of defence, three heads of secret services, and two editors in chief of governmental newspapers.

They surrounded him that day like children around their dying father, thanked him for all he had done for them, and praised his life's work. Sati' al-Husri smiled bitterly at all these speeches. The reform committee under his chairmanship had failed, like all he had undertaken. He was unable to remove a single word from the Arabic dictionaries. Arabic, with all its deficiencies, remained exactly the same as it had been a thousand years ago. His idea of a unified Arab nation suffered a thousand and one defeats. The Arab countries were at odds as never before, and instead of uniting were going to great pains to increase by splitting. The greatest debacle that he and his ideas encountered, however, was in the summer of 1967 when Israel inflicted a major defeat on the Arabs. That was a year before his death, and the unctuous eulogies of his pupils were more than he could take. He raised his weary hand. "No more of this hypocrisy. You are boring me. I leave you as a failure of a man, and I am not alone. Wasn't the devastating defeat by Israel enough for you? And what did you do to prevent it? Instead of looking for mistakes, you found over seventy synonyms for the word 'defeat' in Arabic reference works, and invented more of them.

"Perhaps you are simply infantile and don't understand politics and the world order. Well, then tell me, dear children," he said in an artificially kindly tone, "what you call *this* in your countries." And raising his right buttock, he let out such a mighty fart that it roused his wife, who was sleeping in the next room.

"Well, what are your words for it?" asked the old man, smiling.

His pupils could not agree. Each of them gave several Arabic synonyms current in their countries for the word "fart."

"And you claim to be one nation?" Husri interrupted their quarrelling. "You can't even agree about a fart," he said, and laughed so hard that his aorta burst and he died then and there.

When his wife entered the room, the men had already left. It is said that her first remark was, "There's a bad smell in here."

But let us return to the meeting that Hamid attended, at which the minister of culture was not entirely convinced that his teacher would be able to produce the new dictionary within only five years, as he had boasted. He looked around at the company. The men were nodding thoughtfully.

"The way in which we learn is behind the times as well. We beat our children until they are parrots learning by rote. The principle of learning by heart makes sense and is useful in the desert, but here we now have books that hold knowledge better than any memory. Repetition parrot-fashion makes children submissive and stifles their questions. They pride themselves on being able to recite whole books at the age of ten, but without having understood a line of them. Our children should be able to learn to understand through asking questions, not just learn facts by heart. Enough of that. From the next school year I want to introduce a method that I have seen used in France: the alphabet will be taught to children by means of words that make sense. The children will learn from the way we speak. It is called the whole-word method." The minister paused, and looked searchingly at his guests. "About the alphabet. I am not of the opinion, like many would-be reformers, that the Arabic language will modernize itself if we deny our culture and write Arabic in the Roman alphabet, an approach forced on the Turks by Mustafa Kemal. Nor are such proposals either new or imaginative. The Arabs who had stayed on in Spain began writing Arabic in Roman letters out of fear and as camouflage after their final defeat in 1492 and their expulsion from the country. The script was called after them, like much in architecture that bears their name, *Mudéjar*.

"But in the past the French orientalist Massignon, the Iraqi Galabi, and the Egyptian Fahmi also allowed such tasteless mockery of the language to pass, and now along comes Said Akil of Lebanon acting as if he had split the atom with a pair of pliers. His suggestion, yet again, is to introduce roman letters, and then we will be civilized.

"No, roman letters won't solve a single one of the problems of our language, they will only create new ones," said the minister. "The house of the Arabic language is dignified and old. Someone must begin the work of renovation before it collapses. And do not let anyone intimidate you with the argument that the Arabic language does not change. Only dead languages never bear the impression of time.

"I think the honour of taking the first serious step toward reform should go to Damascus. From the next school year on, all Syrian schoolchildren should learn only twenty-eight letters of the alphabet. The penultimate character *LA* is not a letter. It is *a mistake over a thousand three hundred years old*. The Prophet Muhammad was a man, and only God never errs. So there is no need for us to force our children, at the young age when they learn the alphabet, to abjure logic and regard what is false as true. There are twenty-eight letters. That is only a small correction, but it is a step in the right direction."

A murmur ran through the assembled company. Hamid's heart could have taken off in flight with joy. Sati' al-Husri smiled a knowing smile. The minister gave his audience time. As if he had thought of everything, like a theatrical director in a well-thought-out play, as he finished speaking the door of the hall opened and servants of the Ministry brought in tea and biscuits.

All present knew what the minister was talking about. And the tea was just the thing to moisten their dry throats.

Many legends have accumulated around that letter *LA*. According to the best-known anecdote, a man who had been a companion of the

Prophet from the first asked how many letters God gave Adam, and the Prophet replied, "Twenty-nine." His scholarly friend courteously corrected him, saying that he himself had found only twenty-eight letters in the Arabic language. The Prophet repeated that the answer was twenty-nine, but his friend counted them again and said no, there were only twenty-eight. At that the Prophet, flushed with anger, told the man, "God gave Adam twenty-nine Arabic letters. Seventy thousand angels bore witness to it. And the twenty-ninth letter is *LA*."

All the Prophet's friends knew that he was wrong. *LA* is a word of two letters and means "no." But not only his friends: thousands of scholars and countless other people who could read kept quiet about it for one thousand three hundred years, teaching their children an alphabet containing a superfluous and therefore false letter that is really two letters combined.

"My aim," the minister went on, "is to educate Syrian children, and they need not learn anything that does not lead to truth. The Prophet himself was a fine example. 'Seek knowledge, even if it should be in China,' he rightly said."

He turned to Hamid. "I expect great things of you, my favourite calligrapher Hamid Farsi. Calligraphy creates something unique. It was invented to do honour to script, the characters of the language, on paper, and yet it destroys the language by making it impossible to read. The characters of script lose their function as signs conveying ideas and turn into purely decorative elements. I have no objection to that if the calligraphy is a frieze or arabesque to adorn walls, carpets or vases, but such flourishes are out of place in books. I particularly dislike Kufic script."

Hamid could have jumped for joy. He hated Kufic script himself. He was fascinated by the atmosphere that had been created among the experts, and moved when the minister beckoned to him during their break.

"I expect the utmost support from you. You must concern yourself with the books on the teaching of language. Calligraphers are the true masters of language, so devise or reform a script that will make reading easier instead of more difficult, like the scripts used by calligraphers until now."

Hamid had already developed several alternatives. He soon went to see the minister, who always seemed to have time for him, and drank tea with him while they compared styles together and read the samples in lettering of different sizes. After four meetings they had agreed on the kinds of script in which school textbooks should be printed.

The praise that Hamid won for his work was important to him as a lever with which he could set the stone of reform rolling, a reform that was to go further than the minister had told the assembled meeting.

For nights on end he slept poorly.

They often spoke openly to each other. When Hamid expressed his surprise that a Christian should pay such close attention to the Arabic language, which Muslims regarded as holy, the minister laughed.

"My dear Hamid," he said, "no language is holy. It was invented by men and women to alleviate their loneliness. So it reflects the many strata of human existence. With language you can speak of what is ugly and what is beautiful, express thoughts of murder and love, declare war and make peace. As a child I was anxious, and the slaps I got from the Arabic teacher because I insisted that there were and are only twenty-eight letters in the alphabet forced me to go looking for the facts of the matter. I wanted to defeat my teacher with my evidence, but by the time I was ready to do it, unfortunately he was dead."

"But we also need new letters," said Hamid, seizing this opportunity to realize his dream. "There are four missing, and we could throw out others to make room for them, so that in the end there will be a dynamic alphabet that can elegantly take in all the languages in the world."

The minister looked at him in surprise. "I don't entirely understand you. Do you want to change the alphabet?"

"Only to free it of dead weight and add four new letters," replied Hamid. "If our letters are lame, the language will limp and be unable to keep up with the rapid speed of civilization," Hamid pursued once more, adding, "I have been experimenting for years. I could derive P, O, W, and E from existing Arabic letters without much difficulty, and..."

"Oh no," cried the minister, outraged. "After all this, I find out what you've been thinking. My dear Hamid," he said, "I shall be glad if after next October I can put through my modest reform and retire without getting a knife in my ribs. Your suggestions may be brilliant, but they must win the approval of scholars first. With my proposition of doing away with *LA* and teaching reading by the whole-word method, I am already going as far as I can with the opportunities open to me."

He rose and gave Hamid his hand. "I think your idea is courageous, but it cannot be realized until the state and religion are separated. And that lies far in the future. I am in a hurry and want to change something now. But," said the minister, holding Hamid's hand firmly, "why not found one or two, three, ten schools of calligraphy all over the country? We shall need a great many for the new printing works and the stimulus that the press and the book trade will feel. And even more important, you must gain allies in the shape of the men you train, allies who will understand and defend your ideas. They will be more effective than ten ministries," added the minister. Finally, he told him in confidence to look after himself. Even here with him in the Ministry of Culture he should speak softly, because the place was full of members of the Muslim Brotherhood. Most of them were harmless, added the minister, but some among them formed secret underground societies calling themselves by such names as the Pure Ones, or Those of the World Beyond, fanatics who would not shrink from murder.

Hamid was not afraid.

When he left his mind was agitated. He felt like the fisherman he had once seen in a film, sitting in a tiny boat in the middle of the stormy ocean and riding so daringly over the crests of the waves and down into the depths that Hamid felt short of breath as he sat there in the cinema. The minister had cast him into total confusion by his rejection of the idea of new letters, followed by his encouragement. But he was right: schools of calligraphy must be founded as the basis for a small army of calligraphers who would fight against stupidity with their reed pens and their ink.

However, he could not be happy about the project, hard as he tried. The founding of schools of calligraphy meant that action was postponed again for years. On the way to his studio, however, he plucked up hope again. If he could convince a single influential Islamic scholar, he would surely be able to get the minister to support a second reforming step. In the studio he struck his assistants as absentminded, and indeed he felt no wish to work. He went for a long walk, and did not go home until nearly midnight. His wife asked if he had had an accident, he looked so pale and distracted. He merely shook his head and went straight to bed, but soon after midnight he woke again and went quietly into the kitchen, where he wrote down the names of several scholars who might agree with his ideas.

In the time that followed, Hamid tried to get each of those well-known Islamic scholars on his side, but they all reacted aggressively. One of them recommended that he go on pilgrimage to Mecca, to pray for healing there; another refused to shake hands when they parted. Three more refused to speak to him even before he told them what he wanted.

Could it be that one of them had given him away to those sinister circles?

Everything suggested that someone had, but he was not sure even now, after all these years.

The minister had been right, for as soon as his reform was made known at the end of September, even before the school year began, a wave of indignation ran through the mosques of the big cities, and fanatics denounced the minister of culture and his assistants as unbelievers. Many sheikhs called for the death of the apostates.

But the president acted with a firm hand, placed himself behind his minister of culture, and had the fanatical orators arrested and charged with stirring up popular unrest.

There were no more inflammatory speeches, but plenty of whispering. Some of it was aimed at him, and that was why his master Serani advised him at the time to attend the Umayyad Mosque and not only pray there, but dispel the prejudices about him by talking to the most respected men in the city.

Certain things became clear to him now, in prison. On 10 October 1953, a week after the introduction of the new alphabet of twenty-eight letters, a mosque and the central administration of the main graveyard had cancelled their commissions to him, giving no reason. He had entered the fact in his diary at the time, but did not even comment, because he was up to his ears in work. Only here in prison did he remember it.

That was the reason for his fears.

After the middle of 1953 at the latest, not only at the end of 1956 or the beginning of 1957, the fanatics had put him on their hit list. His name as a calligrapher was in every school textbook. The fact that they had not murdered him was a part of their malicious and subtly devised plan. They did not want him to die like a martyr. They ruined his reputation first, then they wanted to bury him alive, tormenting him daily until he longed for death.

"Not I," he said, in quite a loud voice. "You'll be surprised to see what I'm capable of yet."

نهاية قصة
وبداية إشاعة

The end of a story and
the beginning of a rumour

In the winter of 1957 joiners and their assistants in the large prison carpentry workshop began preparations for the creation of a great calligraphic painting. At the end of April the widely known calligrapher Ali Barakeh was to arrive from Aleppo to work on the great painting with Hamid.

Barakeh had already agreed to the arrangement. The gilding of the frame was to be begun, under Hamid's supervision, in May 1958 and to be finished by the middle of June.

Governor al-Azm was delighted, for this painting was to immortalize the name of his family as donors to a new mosque in Saudi Arabia. Although he was an atheist, his pride knew no bounds. As a lawyer, he was indifferent to all religions, but not to the name of his clan, and certainly not to the respect that all his relations would now owe him.

From now on he made sure that Hamid was treated particularly well. Beginning in January, the calligrapher had a hot meal brought in for him every day from the nearby Ashi restaurant, and Hamid slept more peacefully than ever before.

But not for long.

In February 1958 Syria over-hastily formed a union with Egypt. A dark phase of the country's history began. All political parties were dissolved overnight, all newspapers banned, and waves of arrests followed hard on each other's heels.

At the end of March 1958, al-Azm was dismissed as governor of the prison and soon afterwards arrested. He was accused of belonging to an organization supported by the CIA that had called for the overthrow of the new regime.

A new governor was to arrive soon.

Hamid felt the first step down to hell under his feet. He could scarcely move.

But Hamid was resilient, and the blow did not numb him for long. He overcame his shock and thought of making an offer to the new governor: he could inscribe a patriotic saying on the well-prepared wooden surface for the calligraphic painting, as a gift from the prisoners to their president. The time for Islamic sayings was over. The Saudis hated Nasser who, after a failed assassination attempt, had Islamists prosecuted, imprisoned, tortured, and killed.

He was waiting in suspense for the new governor. He felt it ungrateful of him to forget his protector al-Azm so quickly, but the Secret Society and his future came first. And he was happy with everything that would make it easier to hand over supervision of the work to the calligrapher Ali Barakeh.

However, the new prison governor was a bitter disappointment. He was an officer of peasant origin who could write his own name but no more. He always wore sunglasses, even in a closed room, as if to hide his eyes. His was a boorish nature, and he did not conceal his contempt for books and scholars. He regarded calligraphy as an underhand trick, executed at great expense, with the sole purpose of making reading more difficult. Only arrogant sadists could expect people to put up with it.

When Hamid heard about the new governor, he lay awake worrying for three nights, and not without reason. On the fifth day came the worst fall from grace of his life.

The prison governor roared with laughter at him and his idea. "Millions upon millions of patriots love our President Nasser, so why would he care whether a few rats in prison love him or not?" he cried, still splitting his sides. He had the great panel for the painting chopped up for firewood. But that was not the worst of it. As the new governor wanted the three cells for privileged prisoners for his own favourites among the inmates, he had their previous occupants taken down to the inferno of the ordinary cells. The governor had Hamid's calligraphic works hanging on the cell walls, along with his photographs, books, notebooks, and expensive calligraphic implements thrown away. It was forbidden to possess such things. As a convicted prisoner, his new guard told him cynically, he should be glad to be fed at the state's expense. Did he expect art in prison as well? "Where do you think we are? In Sweden?" asked the man, and did not wait for an answer. He didn't even know where Sweden was, but it was a saying current in Damascus. Many Arabs regarded Sweden and Switzerland as perfect examples of states full of happy people.

That day the garbage men's cart, still drawn by an ancient bony mule in those times, took away not only refuse from the kitchen, the workshops, and the prison office but also a treasure of calligraphic works beyond price to the garbage dump of oblivion.

No trace was ever found of Hamid's forty thousand lira. Apart from his clothes, he had nothing at all with him when he was taken to the communal cell.

At the end of April, after a tiring bus journey from Aleppo, a thin man asked civilly at the prison gates after Hamid Farsi and Governor al-Azm. He showed his written invitation. When the officer on duty saw the letter he sent the man brusquely away, saying he had better clear out before he lost patience. An old guard with two yellow teeth in the dark cavern of his mouth recommended the indignant stranger to make his getaway fast, because the former prison governor al-Azm had turned out to be a CIA agent spying for Israel, and Hamid Farsi was a serious offender.

Ali Barakeh, people said, had assured the man in tears that he knew nothing about al-Azm and the CIA, but he was sure that Hamid Farsi was a divinely gifted calligrapher who should be revered, not locked up in prison. He knew of several young calligraphers in Aleppo who would be ready to give their lives for him.

The guard shook his head over so much emotion. He pushed the thin and tearful man away. "Better for you not even to mention the names of those two. Now get out before I take you to join your friend."

Destitute and a broken man, Hamid arrived in the section of the prison housing the worst offenders, who had all been given life sentences, sometimes several to run concurrently.

This was hell on earth among rats and killers whose brains had been eaten away by the damp of the years. The walls sweated moisture, for the Citadel was near a small river. When the French occupied the country, a veterinary surgeon in the French army had said the ground floor of the building was unsuitable even as a stable for horses and mules.

None of this misery horrified Hamid Farsi more than the fact that a poor reputation had preceded him. His fourteen fellow inmates of this large dark cell treated him with contempt, and not one of them would believe his version of his story.

"But I killed him. I stabbed him twelve times with my knife," he said, trying to glean a little respect. He hadn't counted the stab wounds, but the Abbani family's lawyer had emphasized the number twelve.

"You're not just an idiot and a cuckold," said Faris, who was serving four life sentences, "you killed the wrong man. Nasri only fucked your wife, Governor al-Azm had her in his harem. Or do you really think he put you up there in the villa because you're so bloody good at writing?"

Hamid shouted and wept with rage, but to prisoners serving life that was only an admission of guilt.

Two months later the new prison governor, informed by the guards of cause for concern, had Hamid Farsi admitted to the Al-Asfouriyyeh psychiatric hospital north of Damascus.

He took a last look at the calligrapher, whose body was covered with bruises and filth. "I am a prophet of script and the great-grandson of Ibn Muqla. Why do these criminals torment me every night?" he cried. The other prisoners roared with laughter. "Give me a piece of paper and I'll show you how script flows from my fingers. No one can equal me," he whimpered.

"The same old fuss every day until we smash his face in, and then he howls like a woman," explained a heavily built prisoner with a scarred face and a tattoo on his chest.

"Get him hosed down and wash him twice with soap and spirit before the men from the hospital come," said the governor, revolted. "I don't want them speaking badly of us."

Hamid was sent to the hospital for several months, and from there, once he was a little better, to a closed psychiatric institution. After that his trail was lost. But his name lived on.

His sister Siham inherited all Hamid's property. She sold the house years later to a general. Even after ten years, however, the neighbours spoke of the property as "the crazy calligrapher's house." That was one of the reasons why the general sold the house again. The Finnish ambassador bought it. He had no objection to living in the crazy calligrapher's beautiful house. He didn't understand Arabic anyway.

The studio was sold, at a wickedly high price, to Samad, the senior member of Hamid's staff. Good businessman that he was, he kept the name *Studio Hamid Farsi* on the sign above the door, and on the stamps and all the official papers. He signed his name to his work in such small lettering that it was hard to decipher it. The reputation of the calligrapher Hamid Farsi had travelled as far as Morocco and Persia, and the studio got plenty of commissions from those quarters.

Samad was a good technician, but he never achieved his master's elegance, refinement, and perfection. Experts saw that at once, but for the majority of rich citizens, businessmen and company owners a calligraphic work was particularly valuable if it came from the Farsi studio. Samad was a modest but witty man, and if anyone asked him why his calligraphy was not as good as his master's, he would smile and reply, "So that I don't end up as he did."

But how did Hamid Farsi end up? That is a story with countless different conclusions. A rumour began circulating soon after he was transferred to the psychiatric hospital, and it persisted: Hamid, said the rumour, had escaped from the institution with the help of his supporters and was now living as a highly regarded calligrapher in Istanbul.

There were witnesses ready to support the story. Ten years later, a former guard in the Citadel told a newspaper that when Hamid was in the prison he had received three letters from Aleppo, which of course were inspected before they were passed on to him. They had been harmless letters with broad ornamental borders, written in beautiful script. He remembered very well that immediately after the arrival of the third letter, Hamid Farsi lost his wits, or that was how it seemed.

The psychiatric hospital declined to make any comment. Not that the flight of a madman would have interested anyone in Damascus, but his name was Hamid Farsi, and his sworn enemies, headed by the Abbani clan, suspected a cleverly planned escape behind everything.

Twenty years later, in a sensational report, a radio journalist revealed a scandal: Hamid, he said, had fled at the time, and the long-serving medical director of the psychiatric hospital had hushed it all up.

Hamid had never had any chance, said the reporter, of escaping from the Citadel, "and no wish to spend the rest of his life shut up with criminals, so by agreement with his friends in Aleppo he pretended to be out of his mind, and it obviously paid off. Here there was only a little garden fence for him to climb. And after a few presents to the medical director the fence was even lower," he said, interviewing passersby who assured listeners that anyone, even the least athletic, could easily get out from behind an unguarded wire netting fence. The broadcast caused great mirth in Damascus. Many jokes about swapping politicians for lunatics dated from that time.

However, the reporter's object was not to amuse listeners, but to settle accounts with the medical director of the hospital, who had held his position for forty years, and against whom he had a grudge. His broadcast ended with the statement that the medical director had been lying when he said that Hamid had died and was buried in the hospital cemetery. The calligrapher's sister said indignantly in front of the microphone that she would have known if her beloved brother had died. She added, in agitation, "The medical people at the hospital ought to show me and the press my brother Hamid Farsi's grave – if they can."

In spite of the scandal Dr Salam, medical director of the psychiatric hospital, had no cause to fear for his position. His youngest brother was a general in the air force. He kept his mouth shut. Not so the rich garage owner Hassan Barak. He gave the journalist an interview that created a sensation in the capital.

Hassan Barak spoke, straight out, about the decline of Arab culture. "Hamid Farsi was a prophet. And so you see," he said, hoarse with agitation, "a prophet in Damascus ends up as a rumour. We are a nation damned by God. We attack and persecute our prophets. They are banished, crucified, shot or sent to lunatic asylums, while other civilized countries revere them. Hamid Farsi is living in Istanbul to this day," he said solemnly. The man who, as a little errand boy over thirty years ago, had taken Hamid Farsi's advice to turn his back on calligraphy amd become a motor mechanic instead was now the best known and richest garage proprietor in Damascus. He was slow to calm down. He went on to tell the astonished radio listeners how, on holiday in Istanbul, he had by chance recognized a piece of calligraphy as the work of the master Hamid Farsi, and paid a high sum for that unique piece. The owner of the gallery where he bought it described the calligrapher precisely. But when he, Hassan Barak, asked if he could see his old master, the gallery owner dismissed the idea. The master calligrapher, he said, laughing as if it were a joke, would not see or speak to any Arab.

A little while later the radio journalist said that the garage owner had shown him, as well as other reporters and visitors, the calligraphic painting. Professor Bagdadi, an expert, had confirmed that it was certainly from the pen of the man who had signed it. He could also decipher the signature. It took the form of a rose of Damascus, and read: Hamid Farsi.

Three hundred and sixty kilometres from Damascus, a young married couple had moved into a little house in Arba'in Street in the April of 1957.

The street was in the old Christian quarter of Aleppo, the Syrian metropolis of the north. Soon the husband opened a small studio for calligraphy, opposite the Catholic Assyrian church. His name was Samir, and hardly anyone was interested in his surname of al-Haurani. He was particularly notable for his friendly nature and the way his ears stuck out. His talent was not above the average, but you could see the pleasure with which he went to work.

Mosques and Islamic printing presses rarely commissioned anything from him, but as he charged less than other calligraphers he got enough work in the way of signboards and posters from cinemas, restaurants, and Christian printers and publishers. Father Yousef Gamal commissioned him to design all the books for his recently founded publishing house. In return, Samir sold pictures of the saints in his studio as well as postcards, ink for calligraphers, and stationery. And at the priest's suggestion the calligrapher bought a small machine with which he could make the stamps for offices, schools, clubs, and associations.

However, that was only the way he earned his living. In every leisure moment he worked on his secret plan. He wanted to devise a new kind of calligraphy in Arabic script. Characters of a clarity that would make reading easier, show elegance, and above all breathe the spirit of modern times hovered before his eyes.

His wife Laila, as their women neighbours quickly discovered, was an excellent dressmaker and was the first in the street to own an electric Singer sewing machine. Soon she was better known throughout the Christian quarter than the young calligrapher, and after a year Samir was already known as "the dressmaker's husband."

Like the majority of Arab men, Samir wished for a son, but after several miscarriages Laila gave birth to his only child Sarah, a healthy little girl.

Later she became a famous calligrapher.